STRAITS OF MESSINA

STRAITS OF MESSINA

VICE ADMIRAL WILLIAM P. MACK

The Nautical & Aviation
Publishing Company
of America
1994

Library of Congress Catalog Card Number: 94-22931

ISBN: 1-877853-34-8

Printed in the United States of America

Library of Congress Cataloging-in-Publication Data

Mack, William P., 1915
    Straits of Messina: a novel / by William P. Mack.
        p.   cm.
    ISBN 1-877853-34-8
    1. World War, 1939-1945—Campaigns—Mediterranean Region—
Fiction.
    I. Title
PS3563.A3132S7 1994
813'.54—dc20   94-22931
                                                                          CIP

CHAPTER ONE

Captain Horace Phelps wedged himself deeper into the thickly padded, highly polished black leather chair secured to the deck of his cabin in his flagship, the 1,630-ton destroyer *Lawrence*. The new ship labored over the heavy Atlantic swells and slid down their backs into valleys of dark water.

Phelps was addressed as commodore by long naval custom because he was the commander of Destroyer Squadron Thirty-two. Only one other ship of his squadron, the *Grayston*, was in the group of eight destroyers forming the convoy screen on its voyage from Portsmouth, England to Oran in North Africa. The others were still being built or were training in the United States before joining the newly formed command.

Phelps had been called Horse since his Naval Academy days. At first he had resented the nickname, but then he began to realize that his face *was* long, and even horse-like, and he decided not to fight the truth. A firm jaw and a high forehead compensated for the length of his face and gave him an almost handsome appearance.

In a way Phelps was pleased with his nickname, because he liked horses, and was an adequate rider.

He and his second wife, Lady Claudia Staggers, had fourteen horses on her estate in Surrey, in southern England. Most were hunters and jumpers that were sometimes raced, but a few were comfortable nags brought out for visitors to ride.

Lady Claudia's first husband, Lord Staggers, was awarded his title in recognition of all the free beer he had supplied to the British armed forces. Lord Staggers met his end in 1941 when one of his breweries was bombed by the Germans. Phelps later met Lady Claudia (who was no longer legally entitled to be called Lady, although she never objected to its use) at a party at the U.S. Embassy.

Lady Claudia was slightly angular, but vivacious and entertaining, and Phelps was captivated. Two weeks before his assignment to the embassy as naval attaché had been scheduled to end, Phelps proposed. The wedding took place with a minimum of fanfare, as did most wartime affairs of that sort.

Just as the happy couple was about to start for Lady Claudia's estate for a honeymoon, Phelps received orders to join his squadron at Portsmouth. A rough crossing had damaged the two ships so much that they were granted two weeks in a Royal Navy yard to accomplish repairs. On the day repairs started, Commodore Phelps arrived in a Rolls Royce followed by a covered van loaded with unmarked boxes. A quiet conference with the captain of the *Lawrence* and the delivery of some of the boxes to shipyard officials resulted in a flurry of activity in and around the commodore's cabin. Some of the boxes had been unpacked in his cabin, and the remainder had been locked in a ship's storeroom in officer's country, reluctantly vacated by the wardroom mess treasurer. Phelps departed to resume his honeymoon, and returned to his flagship the day before it sailed.

Now at sea, he was hunkered down in his comfortable chair, facing Lieutenant Commander Adrian Cooper, his chief staff officer. Cooper was seated gingerly in a padded aluminum chair across from Phelps. Next to the chair was a large round table that Cooper grabbed at each time the ship rolled. Both chair and table were secured to the floor; otherwise Cooper would long since have ended on the deck.

Phelps watched Cooper's efforts to stay chair-borne with interest. "Yes, Cooper, I'm glad Lady Claudia insisted that I bring Lord Stagger's favorite chair with me. It's very comfortable."

Cooper nodded. "By the way, Commodore, what was in all those boxes we brought aboard from your covered van?"

Phelps gestured toward several rows of books in newly installed shelves. "Just some good reading from Lord Stagger's library. Help yourself anytime."

"But, sir, there were many more boxes."

"Oh, those, well, by George . . . er . . . I mean," Phelps stuttered. "Dammit, a man has to function. Most of those boxes contained cigars, and the rest a rather good brand of Scotch whiskey."

"And that's what bought, ah, produced, the bathtub in your head and all the other nice touches in here?"

"You might say it helped. I like to think British good-heartedness and appreciation of American assistance in the war effort did it."

"But sir, what about bringing alcohol aboard ship?"

" Must I remind you that I am strictly against drinking and gambling aboard ship? The liquor will be locked up until we reach port."

"Yes, sir, I agree about no gambling, aboard ship in particular."

Phelps suspected that, in reality, there would be an ongoing tournament of acey deucey at ten dollars a game in the chiefs' mess and a nightly crap game in one of the five-inch lower handling rooms, but decided to let young Cooper find out the facts of destroyer life for himself.

Cooper had come aboard in Norfolk, as had the rest of the newly assembled staff, and Phelps had only recently met him. Phelps liked Cooper's handsome appearance and knew from his file that he had served for three years in destroyers and one year as an admiral's aide and had entered the navy from the Princeton NROTC program. His six foot frame, topped with a reasonably regular face, would probably make him attractive to the ladies. Phelps, knowing Cooper was a bachelor, resolved to give him free rein ashore as long as he was available for the limited social functions the commodore hoped to host in the Mediterranean.

Phelps was about to ask Cooper a question when the buzzer next to his chair went off. At the same time the general alarm began sounding. Phelps picked up the sound-powered telephone next to the buzzer and listened intently for a few seconds. "Order the *Grayston* to attack and the *Lawrence* to assist her," he said. "Order Commander Destroyer Division Sixty to take charge of the screen. I'll be right up."

Cooper jumped up at the commodore's words and began assembling foul weather gear. Phelps had purchased a set of British sea boots and a heavy parka from a retiring British destroyer captain. Both were much warmer and drier than the American versions. Cooper started to help Phelps into his gear, but Phelps waved him away. "Thanks, I can manage. Get your own equipment and report to Combat Information Center. I'll be on the bridge. Send the staff duty officer up to brief me."

On the flagship's bridge, Commander Jackson Sperry took off his steel helmet and ran his hands nervously through his thinning red hair. He smoothed down his thin red mustache. Sperry was a capable commanding officer, but could never completely control his nerves in a crisis. He put his helmet on and jammed his hands in his pockets to conceal their trembling. He looked out the pilothouse door at the destroyer screen. The *Grayston*, next to them in the screen, was turning to approach her submarine contact. Sperry could hear on the bridge speaker the order going out over the TBS radio from the staff duty officer in CIC, and mentally calculated the course he would have to take to join the *Grayston*. His hands were now steady; he pulled them out and put on his heavy gloves.

Near him a stocky lieutenant named Brosnan, who had the watch as officer of the deck, stepped around the captain and headed for the chart desk. A green and white sheet of plotting paper, called a maneuvering board, was tacked to the chart desk.

The captain said, "Brosnan, keep the deck and give me a course to take position so we can circle the contact at a thousand yards. I have the conn."

Brosnan leaned over the chart desk and penciled in a few notations. In seconds he said in a slight mid-western accent, "Recommend course two six zero. Speed seventeen knots, our maximum search speed, Captain."

Sperry noted that the back of Brosnan's coat gapped at least two inches from his shirt collar. All his uniforms seemed to fit the same way. Brosnan told him once that thick pads of muscle had formed around his neck and upper shoulders after years of bridging on the wrestling mat at Iowa State University. The protruding backs of his uniform coats had earned Brosnan the nickname "Beetle."

The captain ordered, "Steer two six zero. All ahead standard. Make turns for seventeen knots." He turned to the bridge talker, Chief Yeoman Red Brill, who was following him around the bridge. "Let me know when general quarters is set and sonar is ready to attack."

Brill, who was barely four feet ten, stood on his toes to see the captain over the helmsman. "Aye, aye, sir."

Sperry saw Brosnan was listening intently to the sonar pings emitting from the bridge speaker. The pings were coming at regular intervals and trailing off into the sea without producing echoes.

The internal door to the pilothouse opened and Commodore Phelps appeared trailed by the staff duty officer. "Commodore on the bridge" shouted the messenger.

"Carry on," Phelps said. "Have we got the blighter yet? Er . . . I mean the bastard?" Phelps' two tours of duty in London had left him with a tendency to use British expressions when he was excited. He was trying to return to his New England origins.

Captain Sperry looked up. "No, sir, the *Grayston* is attacking, and we're going to circle until she's through. Then we'll attack if we have contact."

"Good. You seem to have the situation well in hand." He turned to Lieutenant Michael O'Grady, his staff operations officer. "How's the screen doing, O'Grady?"

"Fine, sir. ComDesDiv Sixty has filled the gaps forward and the convoy has changed course to clear the contact."

"Capital! I mean good! Let's go out on the wing and leave the skipper alone."

Phelps threw open the door to the port wing, and a blast of cold air made the members of the watch shiver. O'Grady, close behind him, closed the door quickly, then realized that he had forgotten his foul weather gear. The icy wind whipped through his thin shirt.

Phelps looked at him and laughed. "O'Grady, go down to CIC and make sure Cooper has all the information he needs. Then get your foul weather gear on the way back up here."

Through chattering teeth, O'Grady said, "Aye, aye, sir," and disappeared.

Phelps went to the starboard wing to watch the *Grayston* drop her depth charges. At intervals the K-guns fired arching charges that expanded the pattern to a potential carpet of death. The trick was to cover the maneuvering submarine and have the charges explode at the correct depth. The rapid interaction now going on in the *Grayston*'s steel belly was no mystery to Phelps.

The *Grayston* pulled away from the pattern of depth charges now pushing enormous geysers to the ocean's surface. Phelps could hear the rumbling explosions and feel the detonations though the deck. He resisted an impulse to go back into the pilothouse and look over the captain's shoulder.

The pilothouse door opened, and O'Grady came out, zipping his parka. "Sir, the *Lawrence* has sonar contact and is attacking. The Captain has directed the *Grayston* to circle at one thousand yards."

Phelps nodded. "Thank you."

The *Lawrence* headed for a position slightly east of the seething foam of the *Grayston*'s efforts. Phelps watched as the *Lawrence*'s plunging bow approached the foam, now mixing with the froth of the breaking wave tops. The long swells made keeping the ship on course difficult, and Phelps could imagine the helmsman in the pilothouse sweating to carry out the captain's rapidly changing orders. The *Lawrence*'s bow passed through the foam and then continued a few hundred yards beyond to compensate for the submarine's maneuvers. Again the depth charges rolled off the stern and the K-guns boomed. Soon Phelps could feel the explosions through the soles of his sea boots, much nearer this time. He searched the water aft, but other than the welter of foam, he saw nothing.

Phelps could no longer resist the impulse to get closer to the action. He turned and went in the pilothouse door, followed by O'Grady. This time O'Grady was even quicker to close the door, and Phelps noticed smiles of gratitude. "Captain, I'll just sit in my chair here and be quiet," Phelps promised.

Sperry nodded. "Thank you, sir. I think we'll get him next time. The last one was close. The next attack we'll try a deep pattern."

The *Grayston* attacked again with no visible results. Phelps squirmed in his chair, but said nothing.

Sperry brought the *Lawrence* around rapidly and headed for the contact. The range wound down. "Two hundred yards to drop point," came the report from sonar. Sperry could see that Brosnan was listening intently to the pings from the bridge speaker. Suddenly Brosnan straightened. "Captain, recommend coming twenty degrees left. Doppler is changing and I'm sure he's changed course to the left!"

Sperry looked at him strangely, but gave the order to come left with full rudder. The ship began to swing and steadied on a course to the left. Then sonar reported, "Doppler beginning to change. Submarine is changing course to the left. Fifty yards to drop."

Sperry gritted his teeth. "Now they tell me. Stand by to drop!" He looked at his stop watch. "We'll drop fifteen seconds early." The bridge fell quiet for a moment, then Sperry looked up and gave the order, "Drop!"

He turned to Brosnan. "Brosnan, either you are going to be a hero or a jackass."

Brosnan grinned, his small eyes almost disappearing in his full face. "I'll take a chance on that, Captain. It's just like a card game."

Phelps got up from his chair and led O'Grady, Sperry, Brosnan, and Chief Brill, the captain's talker, out to the wing of the bridge. The depth charges boiled up as they had done before, but they saw nothing else.

The captain turned to Brosnan and started to put his hands up to his ears in imitation of a jackass, but before he could do anything, the pilothouse door flew open. The junior officer of the watch shouted over the wind, "Captain, sonar reports they think the sub is damaged and is coming up."

Sperry brought down his hands and raised his binoculars. "There it is," he shouted.

Brosnan, looking aft, could see the bow of a U-boat begin to break the swirling surface.

The captain looked up at the gun director. The gunnery officer was looking back at him inquiringly. Sperry pointed his finger at the submarine and wiggled his thumb. That was all the gunnery officer needed, and in seconds the first salvo of five-inch projectiles roared out.

Concussions shook those standing on the open bridge. Dull yellow clouds of debris from the smokeless powder littered the bridge. They were so close to the surfacing submarine that even the forty-millimeter machine gun mounts joined in. Sperry could also hear the fire of the *Grayston*. Geysers of white and black foam rose around the center of the submarine, now fully surfaced and wallowing in the sea. A half dozen blossoms of red flashes showed where the five-inch shells were exploding against the thick steel pressure hull.

Phelps knew the submarine could not survive, and he watched as it began to sink stern first. At the last minute, a few men came up to the top of the conning tower, climbed down to the disappearing deck, and jumped over the side. The Sub was gone in a stream of foam and hissing water. The Germans flailed about in the water, trying to get away from the sinking ship.

Sperry sighed. "We'll go pick them up," he said to the commodore, and turned to go back into the pilothouse.

Phelps nodded. "Well, done, Captain. O'Grady, make up a message saying well done, to the *Lawrence* and *Grayston*, and start an action report for higher authority."

Phelps turned to Brosnan. "That 'well done' goes for you, too, Brosnan."

Brosnan grinned. "Luck of the draw, Commodore."

Phelps shook his head. "I don't think so. How did you know the Doppler was changing that soon? I couldn't tell it, and apparently the sonar operator couldn't either."

"I have perfect pitch discrimination, or so the priest who instructed our boy's choir told me."

"Catholic?"

"Yes, sir, but I haven't been to Mass since they kicked me out of the choir."

"You committed a sin?"

"No, sir. My voice changed."

CHAPTER TWO

Beetle Brosnan stood on the port wing of the bridge watching the massive Rock of Gibraltar emerge over the distant horizon. Two days of steady steaming had brought the convoy from the frigid Bay of Biscay to the more temperate climate of the western Mediterranean, and Brosnan and the rest of the crew were gradually shedding their cold weather clothing. Having corrected confidential publications in the stuffy radio room all morning, Brosnan was getting some fresh air before lunch.

The door of the pilothouse opened, and the short, wiry Executive Officer appeared. Lieutenant Commander Pete Fannon was deeply tanned, with black eyes, black crew-cut hair, and a gaunt face punctuated by a slight mustache. His stride was that of an athlete, but also revealed slightly bowed legs and a small limp. "Howdy, Beetle," he said with a faint Oklahoma accent. "I've been looking all over for you."

Brosnan cleared his throat. "I've been in the radio shack all morning with my nose buried in confidential publications and codes."

"Well, that's the one place I didn't look."

"How's the horse ranch?"

"Fine. I had a letter from my uncle who's running it."

"What do you raise on it?"

"Mostly quarter horses. We sell them to rich Texans. Can't afford to keep many ourselves."

"I thought you were married. Doesn't your wife live there?"

"Not any more. We're separated. She didn't like horses or the Navy."

"Brosnan shook his head. "That doesn't leave much. Where is she now?"

"She teaches art in San Francisco."

"She painted the pictures you have in your stateroom?"

"Yes. She's very good."

Brosnan shrugged. "I'm with her. I like art better than horses, too. Commander, I'm sure you didn't come up here to talk about horses and art. What's up?"

"Mostly the commodore's staff's tails. They're standing straight up. They're all in an uproar about how the ship's communicators won't cooperate with them."

Brosnan snorted angrily. "They don't want cooperation, they want surrender."

"Well, now, let's look at the corral fence, as we say in Oklahoma. After all, when a flag officer or unit commander takes over a flagship, his staff is supposed to run the communications for both the staff and the ship in his name. That means his chief signalman owns the signal bridge, his chief radioman owns the radio shack, and the Commodore just about owns you."

"Damn! I never thought of that."

"It means you work for two straw bosses: the chief staff officer, which is Adrian Cooper, and me."

Brosnan pounded his fist on the bulwark, "I don't mind working for you, but that ass-kissing bastard Cooper gets to me."

"Well, the commodore seems all right."

"He is. A friend of mine I met on leave in London said he's okay, just a little off the mark temporarily."

"What do you mean?"

"Well, my friend said the commodore was just like any other American naval officer when he arrived in London for his tour in the embassy. Then he found a rolled-up umbrella and a derby his predecessor had left behind in his office. In six months of wearing the derby and carrying the brolly he began to sound just like the Brits. By Jove this, and bloody that.''

Fannon laughed. ''I noticed that, but I think he's trying to get back to normal.''

''I guess so. He left the derby and brolly in the office for his relief, but he did bring a load of terrible cigars.''

''Has he smoked any?''

''Yes, he lit off one on the bridge wing yesterday when I had the watch.''

''It was bad?''

''Awful. The signal watch all went to the other side of the bridge. Even Chief Martin, the commodore's head signalman, said they looked like fat dog turds and smelled worse.''

Fannon shook his head. ''What else did you do in London?''

''Played a little bridge.''

''Did you meet some good players?''

''Fairly good. I stopped in at our Embassy and picked up a temporary membership in a military club. The first night I had dinner there and afterwards went into the billiard room. It was deserted except for me and a couple of brits. I practiced billiards for a while, then a British naval officer without a jacket came to the door and said, 'I say, any one for bridge?' The two brits looked at him and shook their heads. I decided to take a chance and raised my hand.

'' 'Well, come along, then,' the old guy said. I followed him into a card room where an American army general and a WAC were already seated, shuffling the cards.

''The old Brit said, 'My name is Cunningham.' The army general stood up and said, 'Please call me Ike. This is Kay.'''

''My God! Do you realize who they were?''

''No, but they weren't expert bridge players. Pretty good, though.''

"You were playing with Fleet Admiral Sir Andrew Cunningham, the commander of this whole naval spread in the Mediterranean, and General Ike Eisenhower, the army commander of the whole region."

Brosnan shrugged. "Who was the WAC, the Queen?"

"No, she was General Eisenhower's aide and driver, Kay Summersby. What were they doing back in the U.K.?"

"Something about a conference on the next Mediterranean operations. Sicily, I think. I didn't pay much attention. I was concentrating on bridge."

"How did the game go?"

"Cunningham and I smashed them. They weren't too much competition, although Ike had possibilities. He was too conservative a bidder."

"How do you know so much about bridge?"

"I worked my way through college playing bridge. I was the duplicate bridge tournament champion of Iowa for four years. I've always had a knack for cards."

"Poker, too?"

"Nah, it's too easy, and too much luck's involved."

In a few minutes the signalman of the watch, who had his telescope trained on the convoy commodore, shouted, "The convoy is wheeling to course zero nine zero!"

Fannon said, "That makes sense. We're now due west of the Strait of Gibraltar."

Now the signal watch, led by Signalman First Class Roscoe Barley, were scurrying around the flag bags, getting ready for hoisting the signals they knew were coming. Barley, the ship's leading signalman, was about five feet ten, slim and wiry and very intense, with short brown hair and snapping brown eyes. His New England heritage had provided him with a strong work ethic, although his puritan forebears would have cringed at his freewheeling sexual activities ashore.

Chief Martin, the staff senior signalman, stuck his pinched face around the back of the pilothouse and said in an overbearing and irritating voice, "Both sides, hoist zero nine second repeater turn! Barley, get a move on!"

By the flag bag on each side, a signalman began snapping on to the hoisting halyards the appropriate signal flags. Seconds later, a back-up man pulled the groups of flags out of their holders and two identical hoists flew up to the yardarms, the metal blocks screeching in protest.

Chief Martin yelled, "This signal will be paralleled by TBS. I'll give you the execute from inside! Be ready and don't foul it up, Barley!"

Brosnan could hear Barley mutter, "We're always ready, and we don't foul things up, and why don't you stuff the damned hoists!"

Two minutes later the signalmen manning telescopes reported, "Signal answered and ready." Soon Chief Martin stuck his head out the pilothouse door and yelled, "Execute!"

Barley repeated the order, and the two hoists came down together rapidly. The signalmen took the hoists apart and stowed the colored flags.

Fannon looked at the other ships in the screen. "Looks like everybody got the word." All the destroyers in the circular screen were turning together.

Brosnan looked at the convoy. "The convoy commodore must be a little unhappy about now. A couple of the columns are dropping astern."

Fannon nodded. "I don't think it matters. The course change wasn't much. The heavy British air patrols around Gibraltar keep these waters safe. We shouldn't have any trouble between here and Oran."

Brosnan did a little mental calculation. "One day to Oran. Maybe I ought to go below and square away the radio gang. Looks like the signalmen are learning to live together."

Fannon laughed. "They'll be okay. You're the one I worry about."

Barley watched Lieutenant Brosnan go below. He turned
to the third class signalman standing next to him. Acton
was the exact opposite of Barley. Where Barley was
thin, nervous, and dark, Acton was a typical Californian:
plump, happy-go-lucky, and very blond. Despite their
differences, the two were good friends. Barley said, "If
Mister Brosnan doesn't get these staff types off our backs
soon, we're going to be in a helluva mess."

Acton laughed. "Don't let Chief Martin hear you say
that. I don't want the signal gang to lose their liberty
when we get to Oran."

"I'll be careful. If I don't get ashore there, I'll pop my
gourd."

"Didn't you go ashore in Portsmouth?"

"No. Chief Martin had me busy every day."

"I've never been to Oran. How is it?"

"Full of all kinds of people. Mostly Arabs. I hear a lot
of the Arab women and some of the men have the clap
or something worse. They both wear long gowns."

"Jesus! How can you tell the men from the women?"

"Easy. Although they both wear long gowns, the
women cover their faces."

"Why?"

"The Moslem religion requires it. They're very sensi-
tive about it."

"I heard all Arab men wear mustaches."

"Yes," Barley laughed. "So do some of the women,
only smaller ones."

Acton shook his head. "Are there any other women
we might have a chance with?"

"Most of the others are French and Spanish. They're
pretty snooty."

Acton sighed. "You've ruined my whole day."

"Don't let that happen. Go ashore anyway. Just carry
a lot of condoms and don't drink anything that doesn't
come from a sealed bottle."

Brosnan stood on the wing of the bridge watching the
ships of the convoy. The waters of the Mediterranean

seemed bluer than the blue-green rollers of the Atlantic, and they certainly were calmer. The deck of the *Lawrence* was very steady. Brosnan sighed. Life was good. But then he sensed an evil presence. He turned around and Cooper was standing there.

Brosnan frowned. "I thought you were somewhere near."

Cooper smiled. "I'll always be around until your communication gangs get better. Barley is just too slow." Cooper turned on his heel and went below.

Brosnan watched him disappear, and then turned to watch the Mediterranean again. Somehow the water was not as blue and the seas were not as calm as they had been a few minutes ago. "Damn!" he muttered. "That bastard is going to be trouble."

CHAPTER THREE

In the early morning light of another beautiful Mediterranean day, Brosnan stood on the wing of the *Lawrence*'s bridge watching Oran grow in the distance. He knew the detail for entering port would be called away soon, and since he was officer of the deck for entering and leaving port, as well as for general quarters, he wanted to get a look at Oran before he was too busy.

Fannon came out of the pilothouse, stretching and yawning, and joined him. Brosnan saluted and said, "Good morning, Commander. You seem to be having some trouble waking up. Will you be ready to go ashore?"

Fannon shook his head. "Nah, too much to do. Maybe later, but you can go if you don't have the duty. You've taken a lot of horse shit from the staff lately, and I think you've helped some. I only get about one complaint a day now."

Brosnan laughed. "From Cooper, no doubt."

"Sure. That's his job."

Brosnan asked, "Have you ever been ashore here?"

"Yeah. The people aren't much, but the sightseeing is good. This is a beautiful old city with many well-preserved buildings. At least you ought to take in the Kasbah."

"I thought the Kasbah was in Tangiers?"

20/

"It is. There's a Kasbah in every African Mediterranean port. Kasbah doesn't mean what most tourists think it means. They only hear about the flea-bitten, stinking hole in Tangiers. Kasbah means fortress. Every old seaport along the African coast had a stone-walled fortress in the original old city that was built to keep pirates at bay. When the United States did away with the worst of the pirates, the old fortresses weren't needed anymore and became tourist attractions. There are also some attractive modern hotels with sidewalk cafes."

"That's more my speed."

Brosnan looked at the growing panorama of Oran spreading before him. He raised his binoculars and scanned the rising terraces behind the harbor.

"What do you see, Beetle?" Fannon asked.

"That's the damnedest collection of architecture I've ever seen."

"It should be. The Spanish, Arabs, Turks, and finally the French have all owned the place at one time or the other. Each culture put its stamp on the whole, but never completely erased the preceding cultures. They built cathedrals on top of mosques and forts over everything."

"What's that pile of stone high on the hill in back of the city?"

"The old Kasbah, or castle, that we were talking about earlier."

"It all looks beautiful from here."

"When we get closer you'll see a lot of damage from our invasion."

"If you still feel it's okay for me to go ashore, I'd like to see more of it."

"Just go before the commodore or Cooper send for you. I can't do anything about them."

In a few minutes the word came out over the loudspeaker to man all stations for entering port, and Brosnan went into the pilothouse to relieve the officer of the deck. The commodore came up from below, closely followed by his chief staff officer. The Boatswain's mate of the watch called out, "Commodore on the bridge," and Phelps waved his hand. "Carry on."

Brosnan, who hadn't as yet even come to attention, slumped visibly. Cooper looked at him quizzically, but didn't say anything.

The captain, already on the bridge, followed the commodore out to the wing, and Cooper stayed behind. "Didn't you hear the boatswain's mate of the watch call out attention on deck?" he said to Brosnan.

Brosnan grinned. "Oh, sure, but I'm not as fast at that stuff as you are."

Cooper rolled his eyes and went out on the wing of the bridge to join the commodore.

The destroyers formed an entry screen to guard the convoy from submarine attack as it entered the harbor. Brosnan was kept busy plotting the screening stations and patrolling the *Lawrence*'s station. He was pleasantly surprised at the rapid passage of time before the commodore hoisted a flag signal to the screening destroyers to enter port.

Cooper poked his head in the pilot house. "The *Lawrence* is to lead the screen in and moor at the forward inner berth at the long mole."

Brosnan looked up from the chart, "Got it."

Cooper looked at him patiently.

Brosnan grinned and said, "Aye aye, sir."

In half an hour the captain took the conn and headed the ship in, his hands thrust deep in his pockets. Brosnan, standing beside him on the wing of the bridge, noticed that his small red mustache was quivering slightly, but his strong face seemed calm. Brosnan said. "Should be a piece of cake, Captain. No wind, no current, and a straight shot at the mole."

Sperry nodded, and the encouragement seemed to be all he needed. He straightened, pulled his hands out of his pockets, and made a perfect landing.

The executive officer snugged the ship to the pier with the anchor windlass and doubled up the mooring lines. Sperry said, "Good job, Fannon. Start liberty right away. It expires at midnight."

Brosnan went below to the cramped quarters he shared with Doctor Taylor. The arrival of the staff had required that the captain move up to his sea cabin permanently. He was reasonably comfortable, after joining in on the commodore's ploy to have some extra construction done in Portsmouth. The bottles of Scotch had produced an inside commode and a minute shower in the Captain's sea cabin and a few more lockers for his clothes. Even a tiny desk had been fitted in.

The ship's officers were not as fortunate. Cooper had insisted on a room of his own, which meant everyone except the executive officer had to share a room with at least one other officer. The other members of the staff moved in with ship's officers who were already doubled up, and the net result was that some of the ensigns were now in triple-bunked rooms.

Brosnan was only doubled up, but the volume of the books and manuals associated with the communications officer's job crowded him. Doctor Taylor also had a large assortment of medical manuals stuck in odd corners. Brosnan threw several of these on Taylor's bunk and started looking for some non-classified manuals he knew he had to correct, but before he could find them in the clutter, a messenger knocked on his door. "Sir, Mister Cooper would like to see you in his room."

Brosnan groaned. "I'll be right there."

At Cooper's door he knocked. "Come in," Cooper said.

Brosnan opened the door. "You sent for me?"

"Yes. Come in and sit down. Move that overnight bag off the chair."

Brosnan picked up the bag and moved it to the adjacent bunk. It was heavy, and he heard a definite clink of glass from inside it.

Brosnan grinned. "I hope I didn't break anything."

"Oh, no. They're well padded with underwear. Are you going ashore?"

"Yes. The Exec gave me permission to go. I hope to do a little sightseeing."

Cooper said, "I think we ought to get better acquainted. After all, we should be working closely together. I'd like to take you ashore with me." Cooper grinned and looked toward the overnight bag. "I can offer you something better than just sightseeing. I've got three bottles of the commodore's best Scotch in that bag. One for us and the other two to buy the two best girls in the city. That stuff is worth its weight in gold here. Also some cartons of cigarettes."

Brosnan raised his eyebrows, knowing he would hate himself later for having sold his soul for three bottles of Scotch and some cigarettes. "What time do we leave?"

An hour later Brosnan and Cooper were sitting at a table on the terrace of a fashionable hotel. Cooper waved his hand. "Look at that. And we've got our choice."

Brosnan looked at the women passing by on the sidewalk. "I don't see what you see, I guess. Half of them are wearing veils and the other half should be. Where are the Europeans I've heard about?"

"Don't be so plebeian. Where's your romance? This is the place to try something different."

Brosnan shook his head. "Probably the same venereal diseases all along the coast. That isn't very romantic to me."

Cooper shrugged. "I assume you're carrying condoms."

Brosnan renewed his search of the passing crowds, but none of the women seemed attractive to him. Then Cooper grabbed his arm and pointed at a girl just getting up from a nearby table. She was dark and beautiful with pale brown skin. "Look at that! She's been eyeing me for several minutes. I think that's for me, but there's only one of her. You mind if I go after her?"

Brosnan nodded his head rapidly. "Be my guest. I'll be all right. See you back at the ship."

Cooper grabbed the bag, its contents clinking loudly. As he walked away, he opened it, rummaged around in the bottom, and threw a carton of cigarettes to Brosnan. Brosnan bent over sideways to catch the carton and put his foot back behind him to keep his balance. It came down on a soft object.

"Oooh, that hurts!" a soft feminine voice said with French accent.

Brosnan stood up and looked down at the source of the voice. All he could see was the top of her head, bent over two feet in black pumps, one being massaged by her hand. "Mademoiselle, I'm sorry. I didn't know you were there."

The girl raised her head. "No matter. I'm not hurt too much. These tables are too close together."

Brosnan lost his ability to speak for a moment. The girl was beautiful. Below the shoulder-length brown hair, held back by a silver barrette, were two full eyebrows, shielding two large brown eyes. When he recovered, he said, "I'm sorry. Can I do anything to help?"

"I don't think so." She looked up at him with what he hoped was interest. "Please sit down."

Brosnan pulled his chair around to her table. "I'm Lieutenant Robert Brosnan, United States Navy."

"Oui. I can see that. You come from those destroyers at the mole?"

"Yes. The *Lawrence*. We just got in."

"Are you sightseeing?"

"Not yet. I was about to have lunch. Will you join me?"

"I would like that. What are you having?"

"I'd like to have some local dish, but I've never been here before."

"Let me help." She beckoned to a waiter. "We'd like two orders of *L'Hamrack*, please."

"What's that?"

"Algiers' most famous dish. Beef soup."

Brosnan liked the soup, and he liked the girl even better. Her name was Annette Duchamp. After dessert and French coffee laced with Cognac, he said, "Will you take me sightseeing?"

She shrugged. "Well, I have the rest of the day off. If you'll go shopping with me first for an hour, I'll take you to the places I know best."

"That would be nice. If we're going to get to know each other better, you'll find out soon enough that my nick-name is Beetle."

She laughed. "Beetle. I like that. You can call me Ann if you like."

"I prefer Annette. Have you lived here long?"

"Not too long. My home is in Paris. I am the executive secretary to a French importer. He has offices in each large North African port."

"And you live here?"

"I have an apartment here, and smaller company-owned ones in each of the other ports. I go where my boss goes."

The rest of the afternoon passed in a daze for Brosnan while they talked of many things. At dinner time he found himself in her apartment.

"Take off your jacket, tie, and shoes," she said. "It's the North African custom."

She went to a back room and returned in a long Caftan with her hair cast loose from its barrette. She lit a set of candles. "I'll fix a supper of scrambled eggs if you'll open that bottle of wine," she said.

While Annette was busy cooking, Brosnan sat back on the cushions and watched her moving around in the tiny kitchen. He knew he liked her. He began to analyze the little bit he knew about her. His French teacher had been a Parisian, and he was able to recognize a Parisian accent when he heard one. Usually that meant upper class. Annette was definitely not a Parisian. Probably her accent was that of the area of France she lived in. Was she what she seemed? A middle class girl from central France? She had mentioned she had studied at the Sorbonne. A botany major, she had said. That seemed reasonable since she also said she had been raised in a vineyard, and jokingly that she had not learned anything about wine-making at the Sorbonne. "They knew more back at home," she had said.

She stopped moving about the kitchen and asked him, "How do you like your eggs scrambled?"

Brosnan came back to the present. "Soft, please."

The eggs reminded him of his early life in a small town in Ohio. His family was definitely middle class. His father had been the owner of been a small business, unable to send Brosnan to an expensive university. Brosnan had taken care of the matter by winning an athletic scholarship in wrestling to Ohio State University. Once there, he had paid for the rest of his expenses by joining the Naval Reserve Officer Training program and by his winnings at bridge. Now, as a commissioned officer, he was financially independent, but he would have to make sure Annette was not too far above him in the social and financial ladder. He knew she must be financially independent and capable in the business world, but there was something strange about her also. She had avoided some of his questions. Still, he trusted his instincts, and they were positive. He knew he wanted to see more of her.

Supper was simple but good. Scrambled eggs and sauteed mushrooms were followed by sliced fruit, dates, and nuts. They sat on pillows and thick carpets. When they had finished coffee, Brosnan said, "Can I see you again?"

"Any time you like, Beetle." She wrote a telephone number on a piece of paper. "This is my office number. They will know where to find me, either here or in another city."

"I have to be back by midnight tonight, but I'll call you as soon as I can. I've had a wonderful time."

He kissed her gently, and went out to find a taxi, wondering why he was such a damned fool not to press her further even if the time had been so short.

The next day Brosnan raced through a mound of corrections, hoping to be free to leave early. Just as he was finishing, a messenger knocked on his door. "Sir, the captain wants to see you."

Brosnan threw the last publication on his desk and went to see the captain in his sea cabin. He knocked on the door, and the captain said, "Come in."

Brosnan pushed open the door. The captain was seated at his small desk. "Ah, Brosnan, I wanted to see you. The commodore wants to play bridge tonight after dinner. He has Cooper for a partner, and I want you to play with me."

"But, Captain—"

"I know, Brosnan, but this is a command performance. You can go ashore tomorrow."

The evening was a nightmare for Brosnan. He was so upset, he tried to concentrate on winning instead of thinking about Annette. The commodore finally called a halt to the one-sided performance. The Captain and Brosnan were far ahead.

At breakfast, the captain said, "Brosnan, you overdid it last night. Now the commodore is insisting on a rematch. We'll have to play again tonight. This time, let's lose gracefully."

Brosnan pushed back his partially eaten eggs and said, "Aye, aye, sir. It won't happen again."

It didn't. Brosnan did everything he could to lose but drop the cards, and the commodore and Cooper won handily. As they finished, the commodore slapped his thigh and said, "Well, Cooper, I guess we showed them. Now we can all go ashore tomorrow."

Brosnan began to think about the delights of meeting Annette again, but then he remembered he had the day's duty. The next morning it was too late to get anyone to trade duties. He spent the day and the evening in brooding silence, and the next day the *Lawrence* was ordered to get under way to join a convoy bound for Malta.

CHAPTER FOUR

Brosnan was still mad at Cooper and the commodore as the *Lawrence*, closely followed by the *Grayston*, left Oran Harbor and set course to intercept the convoy passing fifty miles to the north. He had the first watch, so after the special sea detail was secured, he moved out to the bridge wing and watched the terraces of Oran recede into the distance. Somewhere over there was Annette, still expecting his phone call. He banged his fist on the bridge rail in frustration.

The ship's medical officer walked out the pilothouse door and came over to Brosnan. Lieutenant Junior Grade Braxton Taylor was tall and thin, and under his uniform cap his high forehead rose into a sparse growth of brown hair that was rapidly receding. Sometimes he complained that his medical abilities were suffering from lack of patients. Every time a case became complicated enough to be interesting, the patient was transferred ashore or to a tender. "Hi, Beetle," he said in a strong New England accent. "I hope you were careful ashore."

"Careful! I never even got up to bat."

"Well, then, I don't have to worry about you."

"You might check Adrian Cooper. He was headed for trouble when he left me."

"I think he's all right. I'll know soon. By the way, do you know where we're heading?"

"We join the screen of an important British convoy and help get it to Malta."

"Good God! The British convoys are catching hell near Malta."

Brosnan nodded. "So will we."

Back near the signal bags, Signalman First Class Barley was nursing a lukewarm cup of coffee. Acton, standing near him, had the first watch. Acton looked at Brosnan for a few minutes and then said to Barley, "What's the matter with the Beetle? He looks like someone stepped on him."

"Don't know. Some female trouble, I guess."

"Too much or too little?"

"Since the doctor is talking to him, maybe too much."

Acton shook his head. "I don't think so. He's too smart for that. I take it you got your ashes hauled."

"Finally. I had to wait until Chief Martin left the ship. But I made up for it. Found a hell of a nice French girl, and had a great night."

"What did she sell?"

"Souvenirs."

"Oh, oh, I hope you didn't get the wrong kind."

Barley bridled. "Of course not. She was a nice girl."

Acton laughed. "I've heard that before."

"Where?"

"In the sick call line."

Chief Yeoman Red Brill was locked in his office below decks working on entries for service records. He had two extra cushions in his chair to bring his hands up to the normal typewriter level. A mug of coffee was perched near his elbow.

There was a loud knock on his door. Brill stopped typing. "Who is it?"

"Martin."

Brill gritted his teeth. He didn't like Martin, but he had to remember that a guy only four feet ten had to be friends with everybody. "Come in," he said, and got up and unlocked the door.

Martin came in, a mug of coffee in his hand. "Better lock that again," he said with a sly grin.

Brill turned the lock lever and looked at Martin. There was a bulge under his foul weather jacket. "What the hell is that?" Brill asked.

Martin grinned and pulled a bottle of Scotch whiskey from under his jacket. "Thought you might like this. We could christen it with a little dollop in our coffee."

Brill looked at the label on the bottle. "My God! That stuff is a hundred dollars a bottle. Where'd you get it?"

"I liberated a few bottles from the commodore's stock when we moved it aboard. I'll leave the rest of this bottle with you."

Martin sat down without being invited and poured a generous measure into each coffee mug. Then he pulled a small package from under the other side of his jacket and unwrapped it.

"What's that?" Brill asked.

"Two cinnamon buns I bummed from the commodore's steward, Stevenson."

Brill pursed his lips. "He's a funny guy. From his service record I see he's a third class, but he's only been in the Navy for a few months. Shortest service record I've ever seen."

Martin laughed. "He told me how it happened. Stevenson is from Bermuda. He was a footman in the British Embassy when he met the commodore. The commodore liked him and wanted him for his personal steward. Stevenson said okay because he figured a tour in the U.S. Navy would give him American citizenship."

Brill took a swallow of his enhanced coffee, sniffed the rest of the contents of the mug, and sighed. "Greatest Scotch I've ever tasted. Go on. What happened then?"

Martin lowered the level of his mug by a full two inches and went on. "Stevenson says he's not sure how it happened, but he knew the Commodore had a big pull with the American and British Embassies. He said one day he was sworn in, given a uniform, and told to report to the Commodore."

Brill laughed. "That's why he didn't even know he was supposed to salute the colors and the officer of the deck when he came aboard."

"Yeah, I had to teach him a lot in a hurry."

Brill took the last bite of his cinnamon bun and licked his fingers. "You didn't teach him how to make these."

After lunch the commodore called the Captain, Cooper, Fannon, Ensign Anderson, who was the sonar officer, and Lieutenant Kuberski the gunnery officer, down to his cabin. When they had all assembled and had been served coffee by Stevenson, Phelps lit a cigar. Every one in the room looked for the nearest ventilator outlet except Kuberski. Kuberski had been a chief fire controlman when the war started, then suddenly found himself made an ensign and a year later a full lieutenant. He had never completely made the transition from the chiefs' quarters to the wardroom, but he was trying. One of the habits he had brought with him was cigar smoking, but the captain would not allow it in the wardroom. Kuberski had to go topside when he wanted to smoke. Now the wafting aroma from the Commodore's stogie filled his nostrils, and he looked expectantly at Phelps. The Commodore could read the signal from a fellow indulger and said, "Kuberski, would you join me in a cigar?"

Kuberski beamed. "Why certainly, sir."

After Kuberski had brought the proffered cigar to a glow, the commodore looked around the cabin and said, "I brought you all together to advise me. I know the commodore of the British destroyers we will join is senior to me, and I'll have no role in the command of the screen unless he gives it to me. Just the same, I need to pick your brains so I'll be ready."

The captain said, "We know very little about the task. The orders to get underway were quite sudden."

The commodore deposited some cigar ash in his ash tray. "I know all there is to know about our assignment. We meet a convoy taking aviation spares and aviation gasoline to Malta. They need both badly. The convoy now has a screen of six British destroyers, and apparently they asked for American help. All we could spare were the two of us."

Sperry nodded. "With their ships there'll be enough for a circular screen. I take it the greatest threat is German and Italian aircraft from Sicily, Italy, and the small island of Pantelleria."

"That's right. I have a chart on the table. If you'll all gather around, you'll see that we have three days steaming at twelve knots to the vicinity of Cape Bon on the northern tip of Tunisia. Unfortunately, the British and Americans are still mopping up the Axis forces in Tunisia and have not as yet built any air bases there."

"So we're on our own."

"Yes. Except for the RAF fighters on Malta. Malta is about twenty-four hours steaming from Cape Bon. Pantelleria lies right in the middle of that last leg. There is no way we can make all of the last stretch in darkness. I think the convoy commodore will try to approach Pantelleria just before dusk and arrive at Malta just after dawn."

Sperry picked up a pair of dividers and did some measuring. Kuberski leaned over his shoulder, but Sperry coughed pointedly, and Kuberski moved back with his cigar. Sperry said, "You're right, Commodore. We'll just have to steam ahead at the convoy's speed and take it."

Phelps turned to Ensign Anderson, the sonar officer, who was standing well back. "Come closer to the chart, son. What do you know about sonar conditions around this last stretch?"

Anderson, young and inexperienced, cleared his throat nervously, coughing as a cloud of cigar smoke wafted by him on its way to the ventilator. This was Anderson's first sea assignment and the first time he had been in the same room with a commodore. "Sir," he said nervously, it should be very good. Also there haven't been many "Axis submarines reported in the lower Mediterranean lately."

Kuberski let out a huge puff, carefully directing it away from the Captain. "That means we can pull in the screen to give the convoy more antiaircraft protection from all those Heinkels and Focke-Wulfs the Krauts will throw at us. I hear the Limey radar fire control isn't as good as ours, so I suspect the screen commander will put us on the side nearest the direction the threat will probably come from."

Phelps rubbed his long cheeks. "That's funny. They invented the bloody . . . er . . . damned stuff. Their radar should be better than ours."

Sperry said, "I agree it should be better. But it isn't. Maybe it would be best to split the American forces and put the *Grayston* on the other side of the screen."

Phelps nodded. "Good idea. I'll suggest it to the screen commander."

Cooper cleared his throat. "Commodore, I suggest you don't tell him why. He might not take it so well."

Phelps grinned. "Always thinking diplomatically, Cooper. I like that. Let's call it a day and get on with finding the convoy."

Late that night the two American ships joined the plodding convoy and were assigned stations next to each other in a circular screen. As they approached, a light flashed from the Screen commander's flagship. Chief Martin read it word by word to the Ccmmodore. "It says, 'Is that you, Horse?'"

The Commodore laughed. "Send back, 'Affirmative. With whom do I have the pleasure of serving?' "

In a few minutes a reply came back. Chief Martin read off, "Captain D. Alexander Moresby. We served together in London. I wanted to impress Lady Claudia but lost to you. Good luck to you and best regards to your wife when you write."

Phelps grinned nervously. "I don't think he'll hold it against me. He was a good sport."

Two days later Phelps leaned over the bridge chart watching Fannon, who was the navigator as well as the Executive Officer, plot the position of the convoy. Fannon pointed to his latest fix. "Cape Bon is fifty miles ahead. About time for the kraut aircraft to appear."

Phelps wrote a dispatch and handed it to Chief Martin. "I'm suggesting that the *Grayston* be put on the other side of the screen," he said to Fannon.

Fannon nodded. "Good idea. The weather is clear now, but when darkness approaches the clouds tend to drop down, and we'll be dependent on our fire control radar."

The captain, dozing in his chair, woke up when Chief Martin handed him a copy of the dispatch the commodore had just sent. He looked over at the *Grayston*, now underway for her new station. "Good," he said.

An hour before dark the air search radar reported bogies approaching from the north.

"Here they come," Phelps said.

Sperry climbed down from his chair and thrust his hands in his pockets. "Sound general quarters," he said to the officer of the deck. "I'll take the conn."

Two minutes later Beetle Brosnan had taken over as officer of the deck and was able to report to the captain that the crew was at battle stations in record time. Above the bridge, the five-inch director began to train to the north, its hydraulic motors growling with the effort of moving the heavy director box. Brosnan could hear the motors of five-inch mounts fifty one and fifty two below the bridge whining in their own peculiar fashion, a much higher note than the sound of the director motors. The five-inch mounts trained to the north and matched the director. Brosnan looked aft and could see five-inch mounts fifty three and fifty four paralleled with the director. Above he could hear Kuberski's stentorian yell, "Switch to automatic." The mounts jittered slightly and then began to be controlled automatically by the director.

Up in the director, Brosnan knew that the five-inch fire control radar was engaged in seeking the target designated to them by CIC from the air search radar high on the foremast. Then he heard Kuberski shout, "Got it" and the director began to move smoothly as it followed the progress of the incoming aircraft.

The commodore, the Captain, and Brosnan all had their binoculars trained in the direction the director was pointed trying to pierce the murky atmosphere. Brosnan was the first to see the incoming aircraft. "Jesus!" He said. "There's fifty of the bastards at least."

Then the captain sighted them. He turned to his talker, Chief Brill. "Gun control, do you have a solution, and are they in range?"

Chief Brill relayed the message, and Kuberski's voice was so loud all those on the bridge could hear his reply before Chief Brill could repeat it. Kuberski said, "We have a solution. One minute to in-range. Request permission to open fire when in-range."

"Permission granted," the captain shouted.

One minute later Kuberski yelled, "Commence firing," and the guns crashed as one, sending flashless powder residue and pale yellow smoke swirling around the bridge. The concussion of the two forward guns pushed the air out of Brosnan's chest and hurt his ear drums.

A second and third salvo were fired before Brosnan could see bursts near the incoming aircraft. Suddenly the leading element of nine aircraft that Brosnan recognized as Heinkel medium bombers, apparently surprised that the *Lawrence* could shoot accurately that far, peeled off to their left. The second element of nine changed course to their right. Brosnan guessed that the Heinkels were armed with torpedoes and were taking position for a simultaneous torpedo attack. Then one Heinkel, a little late turning, burst into flames and spiraled down to the sea.

The remaining flights came over the formation. Brosnan recognized them as Ju88 medium bombers.

Sperry said, "The main flight is going to make a horizontal bombing attack."

Phelps laughed. "Good! The British convoy commander will make them miss."

The high flight came on, undeterred by the growing screen of black explosions as the *Grayston* screen and the British destroyers opened fire. Two Ju88s joined their comrade in the sea and others turned back, trailing smoke. Still twenty bore on, braving the dense clouds of fire. Just as they were about to reach their drop point, the convoy commodore ordered a turn to the north, and the ponderous ships wheeled like overweight ballet dancers, spurred on by the knowledge that their continued existence depended on the speed with which they turned.

The bombs started down, glistening in the last rays of the sun. Those on the bridge watched breathlessly, even as they felt the continuing blasts from the five-inch guns. Three more Ju88s burst into fire, but all eyes were fastened on the scurrying behemoths of the convoy. Geysers of white and black water began to rise around the large ships. When they fell back into the water, Brosnan could see only one ship in trouble from a near miss, and she kept up her speed.

Now the main threat was from the circling Heinkels, flying low and waiting to coordinate their torpedo attacks with the bombers. The convoy commodore was an experienced hand, and he turned immediately to bring the nearest Heinkel formation on his bow. The destroyers now shifted their fire to the Heinkels and one by one, as the first formation came closer, the lowflying aircraft exploded or cartwheeled into the sea, out of control. Only one survived the heavy barrage of fire, and his torpedo was dropped from too high an altitude to function properly. The explosive caromed harmlessly into the sea.

The second flight of the eight remaining Heinkels was now inbound, and the Convoy commodore labored to turn in time to bring it on his bow. Brosnan tried to help with body English, but there was not enough time to bring them head on. Still, fire from the screen was so heavy that only two aircraft were able to get close enough to drop. One torpedo hit a freighter with an explosion that lit up the increasing darkness.

Sperry said, "I hope that wasn't a tanker."

Phelps, looking through his binoculars, said, "No. It was a freighter of some kind."

The bridge group and the gunnery department had been so preoccupied with watching the low level attackers from the starboard wing, that they had neglected to keep a watch upward or to port. The first indication of disaster was a shout from one of the lookouts: "Two aircraft diving from the port beam!"

Phelps, Sperry, and Brosnan spun around and looked upward. Two Focke-Wulf fighters were in shallow dives heading right for the *Lawrence*. Sperry reacted instantly. "Left full rudder! All ahead emergency."

Brosnan looked at the belly of the German fighters. Each was carrying two small bombs. Black Swastikas on the bottom of their wings stood out against the silver paint. The director swung around and pointed the five-inch guns at the rapidly descending aircraft. Salvos began to blast out, forming a curtain in front of the diving fighters. Then the forty-millimeter machine guns began to chatter, and even the twenty-millimeters joined in. For a moment Brosnan thought the aircraft would break off in the face of the overwhelming fire, but they kept on, boring right for the *Lawrence*. Then one burst into flame and the other, realizing the danger of holding his dive much longer, dropped his bombs a little early. They were headed right for the bridge. Brosnan watched in horror, fully expecting that they both would hit their target. At the last moment the maneuvers that the captain had started a few seconds earlier paid off, and the bombs began to move over the bridge, narrowly missing the top of the mast. Those on the bridge watched as they fell into the sea and exploded with a roar.

Brosnan let out his breath. Then from behind him a third explosion knocked him across the bridge into the bulwark. Phelps, the captain, and the signal gang all landed on top of him. Sperry was the first to recover. "What the hell happened?" he yelled.

Chief Martin, who had been behind the pilothouse and had escaped the force of the explosion on the deserted port wing of the bridge, said, "Sir, one of the bombs from the aircraft we shot down kept on coming and hit us."

Sperry reached down and picked up Phelps. "Are you all right, sir?"

Phelps felt his legs and then his body. "Seem to be except for a knee in the kidneys. That was a hell of a surprise."

Brosnan, still on the deck, said patiently. "I'd like to get up if all you big shots would let me. I still have the deck and I think we're still turning in circles."

Sperry looked ahead, "Damned if we aren't!"

He shouted in the pilothouse. "All ahead standard! Rudder amidships."

Sperry went over to the port side. The whole wing of the bridge was a shambles. The pelorus was gone and the bulwark was flattened. "My God," he said. "I'm glad we were all on the other side of the bridge."

The two Focke-Wulfs were the last aircraft to attack before dark. At dawn the next morning, thirty miles from the haven at Malta, the convoy was met by a combat air patrol of British Spitfires based at Malta.

As they soared over, Sperry said to Phelps, "That's a welcome sight."

Phelps nodded. "Yes. If we come this way again, I think the British will have taken Pantelleria and will also have an air defense organization set up on Cape Bon."

Sperry grimaced. "We still have to get out of Malta after we fuel."

"That shouldn't be too tough. We go back with only the *Grayston* and we'll make all the speed we can. I think I'll go below. I don't feel so well. Ask the doctor to come down to my cabin, would you?"

Sperry watched the harbor entrance at Malta as they approached. It looked very small. Brosnan, standing next to him, said, "No problem, Captain; big hole, there."

Sperry shook his head. "Maybe, but the navigator says there's a nasty cross current."

"Sir, I'd like to take her in."

Sperry laughed. "Okay, Beetle. She's yours."

The convoy screen broke up, and the *Lawrence* and *Grayston*, who were to fuel first and leave that night, entered the harbor first. Brosnan sterred the *Lawrence* toward the narrow entrance. At first he was quite confident, but as they got closer, he noticed the bow kept moving to the left. He tried to compensate with one degree changes, and then two degrees, but in the end he had to head ten degrees to the right of the channel course. He began to sweat, even in the cool of the morning, and he wished he had kept his big mouth shut. Sperry, watching carefully from the wing, suppressed a smile but did not interfere.

Brosnan grabbed the bulwark in front of him, trying to will the ship to starboard, but the current continued to pull at the hull. Brosnan increased speed, and the sudden thrust of the propellers did the trick. The *Lawrence* slid through the narrow opening with plenty of room to spare, and Brosnan let out his breath. The captain breathed easier, also. "Good job, Beetle. Now slow down before you ram the pier, and then get us alongside."

Fannon came out of the pilothouse and pointed out the fueling jetty to which they were to go, and Brosnan headed the *Lawrence* toward it. After the task of getting through the entrance, the smooth waters of the harbor were no trouble, and in a few minutes Brosnan brought the ship alongside the fueling jetty. A crew of Maltese workmen waited stolidly to bring the fueling hoses aboard.

Sperry looked at Brosnan and grinned. "Good job, but you were sweating a bit at the entrance."

Brosnan sighed with relief. "Thank you, Captain. Next time I'll keep my mouth shut."

The captain laughed. "That won't do you any good. Now you can take her out this evening. Secure the special sea detail. I'm going below to see how the commodore is feeling."

Sperry knocked on the commodore's door. The doctor opened it, his stethoscope hanging around his neck and a concerned look on his face. Sperry said, "May I come in?"

Doctor Taylor said, "Sure. I've finished my examination and taken some blood."

Sperry looked over at the commodore, who was lying lethargically on his bunk. "Was his kidney injured?"

"Oh, no. They're all right. This is something unrelated to the explosion on the bridge. Appendicitis, I think. I'm going to take this blood sample over to the local laboratory. We may have to transfer the commodore ashore to the hospital."

Phelps tried to sit up, but his gut hurt him and he laid back down. "Oh, no you don't. The hospital over there is full of casualties from the daily bombings. I'm staying aboard."

Sperry looked inquiringly at the doctor.

Taylor sighed. "I can operate at sea if I have to, but I don't like to do it. We're pretty primitive compared with a shore-based hospital. Wardroom table and all that stuff. How long will it be before we get back to Oran?"

Sperry rubbed his chin. "We'll leave just before dark. At twenty-five knots we'll make it by dawn of the second day. If necessary we can divert a few hours earlier to Algiers."

Taylor shuddered. "Nothing but a field hospital there so far. I'll know more when I come back from the laboratory with his white blood count. If it isn't too bad, I'll take a chance."

"Damn right," the commodore said.

"Go ahead ashore," the Sperry said. "I'll stay with him."

"Don't need a nurse maid," the commodore said. "If you stay, I'll light up a cigar."

Sperry laughed. "All right. I'll go. If you need anything, send Stevenson after me."

Two hours later the doctor was back and went right to Phelps' cabin. "The count is marginal," he said to Sperry following him. "I'll take a chance. If I don't the old boy might split a gut."

Sperry nodded. "I think you're right. Let me know if he gets worse, and we'll crank on some more speed."

The *Lawrence* got underway just before dusk, Brosnan at the conn. This time as the bow slid out the entrance Brosnan rang up flank speed, and the ship shot out of the entrance like an arrow from a taut bow.

Sperry laughed. "The British destroyer captains like to make fast entrances and exits from port. I watched them come in last night. You'll make us a legend here."

CHAPTER FIVE

As soon as the *Lawrence* was clear of the harbor of Malta, the captain, now in command of the two ships with the commodore on the sick list, directed the *Grayston* to take position two thousand yards on the starboard beam of the *Lawrence*. The formation speed was set at twenty-five knots, and the two ships sped on through the gathering dusk.

When Brosnan had been relieved by Kuberski as officer of the deck, he went over the to chart desk in the pilothouse and looked over Fannon's shoulder at the track he was laying down. Fannon noticed him and said, "We'll pass Pantelleria Island about twenty miles abeam about midnight. Then we'll change course to the right a little to pass Cape Bon. After that we'll follow the coast to Oran, arriving about 0800 the day after tomorrow."

Brosnan looked at the Tunisian coast behind Cape Bon. "Do we have any late dope on what the British and American armies are doing over there?"

"Some, although the situation is hazy. They're cleaning up pockets of Italian and German troops still roaming around the countryside."

Brosnan yawned. "Well, I hope it's quiet tonight. I have the midwatch. I think I'll go down and get a little sleep."

Brosnan's sleep was short. At 2200 the general alarm sounded, and Brosnan was soon on the bridge, taking the conn from

Ensign Tubby Raymond. Raymond said, "Sorry to get you up, but there's a large flight of aircraft headed this way from Pantelleria."

Brosnan nodded. "I see we've slowed to ten knots."

"Yeah. The Captain thought our wake would be less noticeable from the air at slow speeds."

"I've got it, Tubby. Go to your station."

Brosnan pushed back his steel helmet so he could get his eyes as close as possible to his binoculars and searched the skies to the north. There was nothing but blackness in the overcast. No moon. No stars. No aircraft engine exhaust. He went over to the other wing to talk to the captain and executive officer. After a brief conference, Sperry sent Brosnan back to the other wing. "We don't want to concentrate too much on one side again," he said.

Brosnan was careful to stay away from the piece of line Barley had used to make temporary lifelines across the wrecked portion of the port wing of the bridge. He raised his binoculars again. Then he was aware that someone was standing behind him, and a familiar snarling voice said, "Well, are you going to open fire, or just piddle along at ten knots and take it?"

Brosnan lowered his binoculars slowly. "Ah, the master tactician again."

"Don't try to be funny."

Brosnan sighed patiently. "Kuberski is locked on and ready to fire. Those aircraft don't have any radar up there. And they don't know we're down here. If we fire at them, our gun flashes will give them a good target. They'll split up and attack, and we won't be able to keep them all under fire, not even with the *Grayston*'s help."

"So you agree with doing nothing?

"Certainly."

"Well, it's a stupid idea."

"Maybe you ought to give the captain your advice."

"I think I will." Cooper said, and he started to walk away.

Brosnan savored the moment, imagining what the Captain would say. Then he realized that not even Cooper should have to suffer that much, and he said, "Wait a minute, Cooper, I just heard the captain talking with the Executive Officer about this, and he said, 'No one in his right mind would open fire now.' ''

Brosnan was able to get back to sleep by 2230, but at 2330 the messenger shone a light in Brosnan's sleepy eyes. "Sir, it's 2330. You have the next watch."

Brosnan groaned. "You woke me up just when I was about to see my new girl friend."

The messenger laughed. "Sorry, sir, but there's a war on."

Brosnan stopped in the wardroom to fix a cup of coffee and eat a sandwich left there for the midwatch, but the sandwich was so soggy and the coffee so stale he left them in the wardroom and went up to the bridge. After he had taken over the watch, he went out to the open bridge, remembering again not to go near the gaping hole roped off on the port side. The night was now clear, and the moon and a host of stars were visible. The sea was slight, and he leaned on the bulwark thinking about Annette.

He was rudely disturbed by the talker who poked his head out of the pilothouse and said, "Mister Brosnan, Combat Information Center reports two surface contacts bearing two zero zero, headed north, speed forty knots."

Brosnan said, "Aye, aye. Tell CIC to track them and give me the closest point of approach." Then he said, "Messenger, call the captain and tell him about the contact."

Sperry was out on the bridge in seconds and headed for the PPI, a square box with a round top on which the surface search radar picture was displayed. "Beetle, what do you make of this?"

Brosnan was bent over the chart plotting the contact on it. "Sir, I think the contacts are headed for Pantelleria Island. From their speed, I'd say they were Italian E boats, or what we call PT boats, full of escaping troops."

Sperry came over to the chart. "I agree. Sound general quarters."

Just then the talker reported, "CIC says the contacts will pass across our bow at four thousand yards in ten minutes."

Sperry picked up the TBS radio transmitter. "Sandstone, this is Fantastic," he said, using the codes for the *Grayston* and the *Lawrence*. "Do you have the contacts on our port bow?"

"Affirmative. Believe they are PT-type boats, probably Italian E boats."

"Roger. Concur. I will turn to starboard to unmask my after guns and fire a starshell spread when they are ten degrees on my port bow. I feel we must identify them before opening fire. They might be friendly. We have PT boats along the coast. Follow my motions and be ready to take them under fire."

Phelps came to the bridge, holding his side. He said to Sperry, "I heard what you said, and I concur. Go ahead with your plan."

Sperry said, "Sir, I relieved you in accordance with Doctor Taylor's advice. You shouldn't be up here."

"I know, but this isn't getting any worse, and I can't miss the show. I know you're in command, and I'll keep my mouth shut. I'll just sit in my chair."

Sperry grinned in the dark. "I understand. I'd feel the same way."

The sleepy men manned their stations, and soon all stations reported ready. Kuberski leaned over the side of his director. "Beetle, what the hell is going on?"

Brosnan looked up. Even over the wind generated by the ship's motion he could hear Kuberski plainly, but he had to crank up his own voice to be heard. "Two contacts on the port bow. Probably Italian E boats. Be ready to fire a starshell spread for identification and then shift to destructive fire if they're enemy."

Kuberski shouted. "Got it. I'll get the details from CIC."

Brosnan went inside the pilothouse and peered over the captain's shoulder at the two small dots of light moving rapidly across the PPI's darkly glowing screen. The captain said, "Fast little devils. They're PT-types all right. I just hope they aren't ours."

Brosnan did some quick mental calculations. "We should know in about three minutes."

Chief Brill, the talker, reported. "Gun control reports on target and ready to fire starshell spread."

The Captain acknowledged the report and said to Brosnan, "I have the conn."

Brosnan continued to watch the PPI, and Sperry went out on the bridge, ready to spot the contacts as soon as the starshells went off. Brosnan went to the door and shouted, "Contacts ten degrees on the port bow, sir."

Sperry turned to him in the darkness. "Very well. Tell gun control to fire starshell spread. Right standard rudder. Come to course three two zero."

As the ship began to swing, all four guns crashed out, the after guns able to fire forward because they were all elevated for starshell firing. Soon all guns were clear for surface firing. Brosnan waited impatiently for the starshells to burst. The time of flight was only seconds, but it seemed minutes. Then all four shells burst and balloons of green light filled the sky, falling slowly. The star-like points of light below their parachutes began to descend. As soon as the shells had burst, Sperry and Brosnan had glued their eyes to their binoculars, searching the horizon below the curtain of bright light.

The captain said, "There they are to port! Italian E boats all right, and their topsides are full of men. Maybe a hundred on each one!"

Brosnan said, "Italian troops trying to escape to Pantelleria."

Sperry said to Chief Brill, now standing next to him "Gun control, put a shot across their bow."

Mount fifty-two crashed out, filling the air with a sudden flash of light added to the glares from the descending starshells. Brosnan, following the flight of the projectile, saw it land in front of the leading E boat. The boat suddenly veered to starboard toward the destroyers, and stopped. The second boat followed. Brosnan said, "Look out, Captain, They may be turning toward us for a torpedo attack."

Sperry laughed. "I don't think so. There are soldiers draped all over their torpedo tubes."

Then Brosnan could see men on the decks frantically waving white flags of some sort. He laughed, "Looks like they're airing bedding."

Sperry came into the pilothouse and picked up the TBS transmitter. "Sandstone, this is Fantastic. I'm going to come alongside the leading PT to take off her load. Circle at a thousand yards and cover me. If they try anything funny, sink them both. I'll let you take the men off of the second PT while I circle you."

Phelps grinned in the eerie light. "I love this! Good work. It makes my gut feel better."

The *Grayston* acknowledged the order, and Sperry started for the lead E boat, now wallowing in the calm waters. He turned to Brosnan. "Brosnan, go down to the forecastle. Secure the crew of mount fifty-one and arm them with guns from the landing force locker. Release the cargo nets on the life lines, and I'll bring the ship alongside the E boat so they can climb up to the forecastle. Herd the bastards back to the quarterdeck and keep them under guard."

Brosnan left the bridge, leaving Fannon to assist the captain. Down on the forecastle he shouted instructions to the captain of mount fifty-one, Gunner's Mate Third Class Bronski, and soon the forecastle was full of activity as the crew of the mount hurriedly buckled belts of ammunition around their waists and slung rifles over their shoulders.

Behind them the signalmen turned the signal searchlights on the stopped E boats as the captain brought the *Lawrence* alongside the lead boat. On the decks of the E boat, laughing Italian soldiers waved and shouted in Italian and broken English.

Phelps said, "I'm glad you didn't have to kill the poor bastards. They haven't been very happy under Mussolini."

After the E boat was secured alongside, the soldiers and then the boat crew clambered up the cargo nets and were herded aft. The first ones up embraced Brosnan, but the smell of their dirty uniforms and bodies was so intense he moved back behind the armed men to avoid the compliment from the next men.

Bronski, standing wheel watches on the bridge, laughed and said, "What's the matter, Mister Brosnan? They're just trying to say how grateful they are."

Brosnan shuddered. "They smell worse than the commodore's cigars."

In a few minutes the last of the Italians had been taken aft and put under a guard organized by Bronski, and Brosnan went back to the bridge. Sperry said, "We're going to leave the E boat here, withdraw a little and sink it. Then the *Grayston* can do its thing with the other boat."

Brosnan nodded. "Shall I tell Kuberski what to do?"

"No. I've already told him." Sperry picked up the TBS transmitter. "Sandstone, this is Fantastic. Your turn. I'm going to sink the empty E boat."

The *Lawrence* began to vibrate as the captain moved her away from the empty boat, and in a few seconds the after guns and the forty-millimeters opened up. Two salvos later the gas tanks of the wallowing hulk erupted with a heavy roar, and the boat went down rapidly.

Sperry said, "Brosnan, take the conn and circle the *Grayston*. I've told Kuberski to keep a careful eye on the second E boat."

Ten minutes later the Captain of the *Grayston* reported that all men were off the second boat. Then he added, "Fantastic, I'd like to try to tow this one in. She'd make a contribution to our intelligence."

Sperry thought for a moment. Then he answered, "I'll check with the commodore. I've got to go on to Oran at high speed with a patient. Take the boat under tow to Bizerte. Then rejoin at Oran."

The commodore said, "Your call, but I agree."

The captain turned to Brosnan. "Let's go. Make twenty-eight knots to make up for our delay."

Then he said to Fannon, "Do you think there was some other reason why the *Grayston* wanted to take that E boat in?"

Fannon laughed. "Maybe he thinks he can claim prize money."

"I don't think it's possible. Maybe he's read too many Horatio Hornblower books."

Brosnan was quietly figuring on the margin of the chart. Then he said, "If we can assume that the E boat is worth three hundred thousand dollars, each man would get one thousand dollars."

Sperry shook his head. "Don't worry. It won't happen. The Navy's legal eagles would find some way to deny the claim."

Phelps said quietly, "From my time with the Royal Navy, I'm sure you're right. I'm going below. Thanks for the show."

The *Lawrence* steamed at high speed through the Mediterranean night. Below deck the commodore held his side and regretted his earlier trip to the bridge.

Early the next morning the executive officer stood near the back of the bridge watching the Italian prisoners below. They were guarded by a dozen armed sailors, who kept carefully to windward to avoid the smell of the prisoners. Next to Fannon stood the senior officer of the prisoners, an Italian army major, who spoke fairly good English. "Sir," he said to Fannon, "I apologize for the condition of my men. We only had a little water to drink and none for anything else. They haven't been able to bathe or shave for two weeks. You can see that they've been lined up at your drinking fountain ever since they've been aboard."

Fannon said, "I see what you mean. As soon as they fill themselves with water, they go back to the end of the line." Fannon leaned over the rail so that he could see the deck below better. He laughed. "I think this will break up the line." Two mess cooks brought out wooden crates of apples and oranges and put them down on deck. They tried to open them, but the laughing Italian soldiers pushed them aside and tore the wooden crates apart with their hands. In seconds the fruit was gone, and the mess cooks went below for more. Additional crates soon appeared and were quickly destroyed. Then tubs of baloney sandwiches followed, and pitchers of black coffee. As fast as thick white mugs were filled, they were emptied.

The Italian officer standing next to Fannon began to get restless. Fannon laughed. "You'd better get down there to supervise them. If you don't you'll miss breakfast."

All morning long the Italian soldiers ate and drank and by noon were stretched out on the deck asleep.

After lunch, the Captain gave Brosnan a message to encode and send to the commanding officer of the newly formed naval operating base at Oran. Brosnan read it carefully. It gave their time of arrival and requested an ambulance and four trucks to be at the pier to meet them. He encoded it and had it sent off. Then he sat down in his room and thought about Annette, wondering if she were still in Oran. He went up to the bridge where the executive officer was plotting his noon sights. "Commander, I have a heavy need to go ashore tomorrow afternoon and, if possible, to stay overnight."

Fannon looked up from his plot. "Well, Beetle, liberty ends at midnight, but if you promise to stay off the streets after that I'm willing to take a chance." Then he laughed. "There shouldn't be any bridge games to keep you aboard, and the captain and I appreciate how you gave your all for your country on our last visit."

Brosnan grinned. "Sir, I can promise you I won't be on the streets after midnight."

The next morning the *Lawrence* slid quietly into Oran Harbor, but the scene on the pier was far from quiet. An ambulance was drawn up to the section of the mole where they were directed to moor, and four covered Army trucks, with twenty armed troops, were parked nearby. The navy cptain in charge of the new operating base paced up and down the pier edge.

"Good God!" Sperry said when he saw the entourage. "What have we done!"

Fannon shook his head. "They must have gotten word about the *Grayston* bringing in that E boat in addition to our arrival dispatch."

When the last lines were secured and the brow moved aboard, the Commander of the Naval Operating Base rushed aboard. He went through the formalities of arriving and then said to Sperry, "What have you done to Horse? Is he badly wounded?"

Sperry winced. "The commodore? Oh, he isn't wounded. He has acute appendicitis. We'll bring him out on a stretcher in a few minutes." Captain Sperry nodded toward the prisoners, gathered on the main deck aft of the quarterdeck. "As soon as the Commodore leaves, we'd like to turn these men over to the Army."

The Italians, noticing that they were bring talked about, smiled and waved.

The commodore emerged from the door to the quarterdeck, walking slightly bent and surreptitiously clutching his right side. Doctor Taylor trailed after him, obviously worried. Phelps muttered, "No damned stretcher! I'll walk off."

The Doctor said, "But, sir!"

Then Phelps saw the commander of the NOB standing on the quarterdeck. He smiled and straightened up. "Ah, Greaseball, what are you doing here?"

The four-striper smiled, gritting his teeth politely. "Hello, Horse, I came down to see if you needed help. But I see you don't. How the hell are you?"

"A little under the weather, but I think I can walk out to the ambulance. Sorry I don't have time to receive you properly and smoke a cigar for old time's sake."

The captain rolled his eyes. "Horse, I know all about your cigars. Let's get you to the hospital."

Phelps walked carefully over the brow and insisted on getting in the front seat of the ambulance. The doctor resignedly clambered in the back and the ambulance drove off at a stately pace.

Sperry watched the ambulance drive off and then looked back at the group of prisoners. "Let's get these stinkers off the ship, and then hose down the area." He looked down at the apple cores and orange peelings at the feet of the smiling Italians. "We'll never get the smell off the ship."

Brosnan didn't notice the smell. He was headed for his room to get ready for his day ashore. He spent half an hour in the shower, shaved carefully, and then rubbed his face with after shave. He carefully loaded his watch pocket with condoms, just in case the evening went well, but he didn't really expect to use them. After all, he had barely kissed the girl.

At 1300, when liberty for the crew started, Brosnan was close behind. He headed for the nearest French-style telephone box. He fumbled with the French coins he had saved from his first visit, put the required amount in the slots, and dialed the number Annette had given him. He waited tensely for several rings, and was about to give up when the ringing stopped. "Halloo," a feminine voice said.

Brosnan recognized her voice. "Annette?"

"Ah, Beetle! Where have you been? You promised to call me."

"A long story. Can you meet me at the hotel where we met last time?"

"Oui. In about an hour. I'll take the afternoon off."

"Wonderful!" Brosnan said, and he left the booth in a daze. The sky had never been brighter and the gentle breeze cooled his warming cheeks. "Yahoo!" he shouted. Two passing Arabs looked at him strangely, but he paid no attention to their stares as he headed for the hotel.

CHAPTER SIX

Brosnan sat at the same table he had occupied when he had first met Annette. He looked around the crowded terrace. There were people of all nationalities around the tables, but Annette wasn't there. He called a waiter over and ordered a beer. He had hardly touched it when he saw Annette coming through the crowd on the sidewalk. Her shining hair was pulled back with the usual silver barette, and she wore a summery suit, severely tailored, but with a full skirt that swung gracefully as she walked, accentuating her slim, shapely legs. Brosnan sighed. She was just what he had always wanted.

He stood up as she approached and gestured to her. She smiled, knowing just where to look for him. As she came closer, Brosnan wondered whether he should kiss her, not knowing what the local custom was. She solved the problem by rising on her toes and kissing him on the cheek. "Thank you," he said. "I'd heard that the Arabs didn't like public displays of affection, so I didn't know what to do."

She laughed. "Forget them. This is still a French town, and you know what we think about kissing."

"Yeah. I like it to."

"Beetle, why didn't you call?"

"You may not believe this, but my boss made me stay aboard and play bridge."

She raised her eyebrows. He saw her questioning mood and went on. "Well, it was worse than that. I wasn't playing for fun. My captain was forced to play, too, with our commodore. Then on the last day in port, when I had permission to come ashore, we were suddenly ordered out to sea."

Annette did not appear to be completely satisfied with his explanation, but she soon forgot it, and they chatted for an hour over a light lunch. They talked of many things. He found out that her company had sent her south from Paris just after the war started in Europe, and she had been in Oran or other ports of North Africa ever since. Then she offered to take him sightseeing, and they went to see the buildings they had missed on his last trip to Oran.

About five o'clock, Annette said, "Would you like to have dinner with me again?"

Brosnan beamed. "I thought you'd never ask. Let's go. I'm starved."

They stopped at several native markets, buying cheese, wine, fruit, vegetables, and a piece of lamb. Annette bargained at each store, and Brosnan followed the exchange as well as his limited French would permit. As they went in the front door of Annette's small apartment, Brosnan said, "I have the whole night off."

Annette didn't say anything, but she squeezed his hand and started to the bedroom area. "Beetle, get comfortable. I'll be out in a minute."

She appeared in a few minutes, this time in a bright caftan that buttoned all the way down the front. Brosnan noticed her swelling breasts under the swaying garment. He felt for the package of condoms in his watch pocket. It was gone. "Damn!" he said under his breath.

"What did you say, Beetle?" she asked.

"Ah, nothing." He rummaged around under the cushions he had been sitting on, and then his hand touched the packet. He quickly pulled it out and put it back in his pocket, this time making sure it was secure.

"You found something?" she asked.

"Ah, just a little piece of trash, or something. I'll get rid of it later."

Brosnan helped her get dinner, and afterward they leaned back on the cushions enjoying the last of the cheese, wine, and strong French coffee.

Annette said, "Tell me what took you to sea so quickly on your last trip."

Brosnan described the trip, ending with the commodore's walking out to the ambulance.

Annette said, "I like your commodore, even if he did keep you aboard for something unimportant."

Brosnan hesitated. "Well, I wouldn't call him likable. More like interesting. He's a little more, ah, sophisticated than I am."

"Ah, Beetle, that's what I like about you. You're so uncomplicated and cute."

Brosnan colored. "I may be uncomplicated, but I know what I like." He moved closer to her on the cushions and took her in his arms. She returned his embrace, and in a few moments was responding to his deepening kisses. He ran his hands through her soft hair and caressed her neck. Then he moved to the top button of her caftan. She didn't resist, and he moved down, button by button. Her breasts were as firm and pointed as they had seemed to be under the caftan, and she helped with the next buttons. Then she slipped completely out of the caftan and helped Brosnan undress. At the last minute he rescued the condoms from his trouser pocket.

Annette laughed. "So that's what you were looking for. You're a bad boy!"

She was obviously somewhat more experienced than Brosnan so that he found it easy to make love to her. The evening passed in a blur, as they moved around on the cushions, seeking to enjoy new experiences. By dawn they were exhausted, and as the Moslem muezzin's calls to morning prayer came through the open window, they dropped off to sleep in each other's arms.

The strong Mediterranean sun woke Brosnan, and he looked at his watch. It was almost ten o'clock. He awakened Annette with a kiss. "Annette, I have to be back at the ship by noon. Could we get some breakfast?"

She smiled sleepily and rubbed her eyes. "Ah, Beetle, all you think about is eating."

"Oh, no it isn't." He took her in his arms and made love to her one more time. But in half an hour his stomach was sending him strong messages, and he got up to look for something to eat while Annette dozed in the sun. She heard him and said, "Beetle, put the water on for coffee and I'll get the rest in a minute."

While he was dressing, she disappeared into the back room and came out in a new caftan, brushing her long brown hair. He noticed how closely the color of her hair matched the color of her eyes, and the strong and beautiful lines of her face. Only her nose marred the perfection of her beauty. It was slightly Roman, but Brosnan thought it gave her beauty character and tradition. She knew he was looking at her appraisingly and she didn't seem to care. She smiled and said, "You can have the bathroom, Beetle, while I get breakfast ready."

In ten minutes she called him and they went out on the balcony to eat a breakfast of fruit, coffee, and toast. It was the best breakfast Brosnan had ever had, and he lingered until he knew he would have to run all the way back to the ship if he couldn't find a taxi.

As he left, he said, "This time I promise to call you tomorrow."

He was able to call her the next day, but only to tell her the ship was about to leave for an emergency assignment.

She sounded disappointed. "But, Beetle, you told me you had a big piece of your ship missing and it would take several days for it to be fixed."

His voice was full of dispair. "Yes, I did, but the repair ship came over and took measurements and is making the replacement sections. Now we're needed for some damn fool job, and we'll come back in a week and the repair ship will weld on the parts they will have been making."

"Oh, Beetle, I don't understand this Navy stuff, but I trust you. Call me when you come in."

The *Lawrence* and Grayston left Oran Harbor at 1300, bound for a rendezvous off Mers-el-Kebir, a harbor a few miles to the east of Oran Harbor. Their orders called for them to join Destroyer Squadron Sixteen and patrol the coast of North Africa looking for Axis submarines.

Brosnan looked at the chart as they turned northeast, then he walked over to where Sperry sat in his bridge chair. "Captain, can you tell me what this is all about?"

"Yes. The Allies are getting ready to invade Sicily in a month or so. There are a lot of convoys of new landing craft and transports crossing the Atlantic and entering the Mediterranean. They'll go to the bigger ports on the north coast of Africa: Oran, Algiers, and Bizerte, mainly. Then they'll refit, train, and get ready for the invasion."

"Will we be part of it?"

"Of course, but we won't know what force we'll be a part of for a while. The planners are working on that now. In the meantime, our job is to protect these convoys from the German and Italian submarines lying in wait along the coast and from long-range aircraft that will be hunting for them."

"And today?"

"We join the search group commanded by the Commander Destroyer Squadron Sixteen and conduct an anti-submarine sweep along the coast."

At 1400 the CIC reported several surface radar contacts ahead, and soon Barley, temporarily freed of the presence of Chief Martin, reported seeing destroyer masts in the distance. Chief Martin, with the commodore absent, had chosen to stay below and Barley was in heaven, running the signal gang just the way he wanted to. His black eyes crinkled with pleasure as he shouted orders. Acton laughed, his slightly pudgy body jiggling, "Cool it, Barley, you'll bust a gasket."

The captain picked up the TBS transmitter. "Fairhaven, this is Fantastic. Reporting for duty with Sandstone."

In seconds the answer came back for the two ships to take stations at the northern end of the search line. Brosnan, who had the watch, used a recommendation from CIC and took off at twenty-five knots. Before they reached their station, however, a new set of orders came over the TBS. Each ship was assigned a sector of an arc around Oran Harbor, and two Royal Air Force antisubmarine search aircraft were assigned to search the same circle from the air.

The *Lawrence* was assigned a sector between the *Grayston* and the destroyer *Nields*. Brosnan plotted a search pattern in the sector and showed it to the Captain. Sperry looked at it carefully and nodded his approval. "Good. Let's get started. There are a lot of important ships approaching this harbor, and we don't want to lose any. We'll need them all."

Bronski, the mount captain of mount fifty-one, had the wheel watch. As Brosnan went by on his way out to the bridge wing to look at the adjacent ships, Bronski nudged the messenger, a seaman first class named Swenson, who was a pointer in his gun mount. Bronski said in a low voice, "Look at the Beetle. He's skittering around like he owned the world."

Swenson smiled. "Yeah, I saw him come back aboard this morning. I guess he had special permission from the exec to stay ashore overnight."

"And something to stay for. I saw him sitting on a hotel terrace with a spiffy French girl yesterday."

"Nice?"

"That and a lot more. Classy, I'd say, and old Beetle was really living it up."

The boatswain's mate of the watch, a hairy-chested first class named Reagan, cleared his throat. "All right, you hams. Keep quiet and do your jobs. This ain't no theater."

Just before the watch was due to be relieved, the *Nields* reported that one of the RAF search aircraft had spotted a periscope off her bow. The squadron commander promptly designated the *Lawrence* to assist. The captain, sitting in his chair, said, "Brosnan, sound general quarters. I'll take the conn."

The *Nields* reported sonar contact and then said she was attacking. Sperry stood up, cramming his hands deep in his pockets. He felt the familiar rush of anxiety as he went out to the wing of the bridge, but he breathed deeply, his thin red mustache vibrating as he took in the extra air. Soon the adrenalin began to flow, and he steadied down. His hands stopped shaking, and he took them out of his pockets. He headed the *Lawrence* in a circle around the *Nields*, waiting for his own ship to man its battle stations.

In two minutes Brosnan reported ready, and Sperry could hear the slightly excited voice of the sonar officer, young Ensign Anderson, report, "Sonar contact. Bearing two six five! Range one five double oh." The *Lawrence* had quickly gained the contact the *Nields* was attacking. Sperry, now calm and even eager to close with the submarine, grabbed the bridge bulwark and steadied himself as the ship rolled slowly across the slight seas.

Sperry could see the K-guns on the *Nields* fire and the depth charges and their attached arbors fly up and out from the sides in lazy arcs. Soon the pattern of depth charges erupted in a black and white carpet of rising foam. The RAF aircraft droned across the depth charge pattern, and then resumed its circling. Sperry headed for the contact and had the word passed that the *Lawrence* was commencing an attack.

As they steamed toward the wide field of rapidly subsiding foam, Sperry could not see any debris, and he judged the *Nields'* attack had missed. The RAF aircraft reported negative results. Anderson, his voice rising in pitch as the range decreased, continued to give the ranges and bearings of the submarine as the *Lawrence* closed. Sperry made a mental note to remind Anderson to keep his voice at a lower pitch and not to let himself sound excited. He remembered that he had sounded just like that only a few years ago.

Then Anderson reported, "Lost contact due to short range! Recommend drop on time!"

Sperry took the stop watch off of its storage bracket. When the second hand reached the proper point to allow for the ship's forward progress after the contact was lost, he shouted, "Drop depth charges!"

Chief Brill, the talker, his finger glued to the button on his transmitter, immediately repeated the order. Sperry gave orders to the helm to bring the ship around to a circle again, and the *Nields* started back in for another run.

Sperry raised his glasses and searched the depth charge pattern. He thought he could see oil and maybe even some debris floating on the water, but the foam obscured his view. The RAF aircraft reported no debris in sight.

The *Nields* bored in for another attack, Sperry and Brosnan watching anxiously. The now familiar sounds of the depth charge explosions rumbled across the water. Sperry realized that he could feel the vibration of hundreds of pounds of explosives through the deck. On the first runs he had been so preoccupied he hadn't noticed the phenomenon, but now it was readily apparent.

As the *Nields* pulled away, a giant burble of oil came to the surface, and pieces of wreckage were plainly visible. Anderson said excitedly, "We hear breaking up noises. I'm sure the *Nields* got the sub."

The RAF aircraft flew over the spreading pattern of petroleum and reported large quantities of oil and debris on the surface.

There was a mixture of disappointment and satisfaction in Sperry's voice as he said to Brosnan next to him. "I'm glad the bastard sank, but I wish we'd gotten in the last blow."

Anderson, his voice now steadied, reported there was no other sonar contact, and Sperry ordered, "Secure from general quarters, set condition III."

For a week the group of destroyers swept back and forth north of Oran, watching the seemingly endless convoys of new classes of amphibious ships called LSTs and LCIs plodding along the coast at ten knots. The LSTs had smaller landing craft called LCTs on their decks, and some had ungainly sections of giant steel causeways rigged to their sides. Brosnan looked at them through his binoculars. "How do they get the things off?" he asked Fannon, standing next to him. Both were carefully avoiding stepping off the jagged end of the missing bridge wing.

Fannon said, "The causeway sections are resting on brackets welded to the sides, and are held fast by large pieces of chain. When they reach the landing area, the chains are released, and the sections fall sideways into the sea."

Brosnan nodded. "I can follow that, but how about those big bug-like LCTs sitting on deck?"

Fannon rubbed his chin reflectively. "I've never seen them put over the side, but a friend told me they're on rollers. The LSTs are designed to be able to shift ballast very easily so that they can raise their bow area for grounding on the beaches. They flood one side of these ballast tanks and produce a healthy list. Then the LCTs are released and slide on the rollers right over the side."

"They must make a helluva splash."

Fannon laughed. "My friend says they do, but it works, and they're very valuable for getting heavy equipment over shallow beaches."

At the end of a week, as their fuel began running low, the *Lawrence* and *Grayston* were released to return to Oran. This time the *Lawrence* was ordered alongside a repair ship moored at a small mole near the larger mole. Even before the lines were doubled up, a huge section of the new port wing of the bridge was lowered over the side of the repair ship and positioned for welding to the remains of the existing structure.

Brosnan noticed Chief Martin watching the brow being put over from the repair ship. "What's the matter, Chief," he said, "no commodore in sight?"

Chief Martin sighed. "I guess he's still in the hospital."

Brosnan grinned. "I doubt it. He'll be the first one over the brow."

Phelps was smiling and apparently fit, although Brosnan noted a slight stoop and a hesitancy as he stepped down off the brow onto the *Lawrence*'s deck.

Chief Martin, now visibly encouraged, said, "Sir, now we'll get back to normal."

Brosnan said quietly, "Yeah, all fouled up."

Martin said, "What was that, sir?"

Brosnan gritted his teeth. "I said, Yeah, I hope so."

Brosnan had the duty the first day and spent most of it watching the workmen reassemble the bridge structure.

By night they had the outlines finished, but needed at least four more days to complete the installation of a new pelorus and all the necessary wiring that had been carried away.

At noon the next day, Brosnan was on the quarterdeck ready for leave. Again he had permission from the executive officer to stay overnight, and he watched nervously for any approaching messengers who might bear bad tidings from the captain or the commodore. As the ship's bell sounded 1300, Brosnan bounded up the brow to the door in the side of the repair ship. As he was disappearing inside the huge hull, he heard a plaintive call from a messenger running up the deck. Brosnan ignored the summons and barreled through the men blocking the passageways of the repair ship. In seconds he was on deck of the repair ship. He reported to the officer of the deck that he had permission to leave the ship, saluted the colors, and bounded down the brow. He was free. Even then he looked surreptitiously over his shoulder to make sure the messenger wasn't following him.

At the first telephone call box he stopped and called Annette. She answered promptly, and Brosnan was off on another trip to paradise.

The next day at noon he walked down the brow from the repair ship and reported his return aboard. Kuberski, who had the day's duty, met him. "Beetle, the exec wants to see you right away. What the hell have you done?"

Brosnan shrugged. "Nothing that I know of, except go ashore and enjoy life."

A few minutes later he knocked on the Fannon's door. "You wanted to see me?"

Fannon squinted in his direction. "Ah, yes, the messenger yesterday reported that you are a good broken field runner with a poor sense of hearing."

68/

Brosnan raised his eyebrows. "I don't understand."

Fannon said impatiently, "Come off it, Beetle, you know damned well the messenger was after you."

Brosnan said, "Did I miss something? Another bridge game perhaps?"

"You know damned well you did. I had to take your place."

Brosnan said innocently, "You won, of course."

Fannon shook his head. "The captain and I might have, but those damned cigars broke my concentration. We lost badly."

Brosnan grinned. "Good. The Captain will want you as a partner again."

"No he won't. He wants you tonight."

"Why?"

"He's decided to change strategy. He figures that if the commodore loses badly enough, he'll lose interest."

Brosnan brightened. "I think I can handle that."

That night the combination of Brosnan and Sperry triumphed by a large margin. At the end of the last rubber, Phelps threw down his cards. "Enough of this game. Brosnan, do you play Acey-deucey?"

Brosnan thought for a few seconds, wondering how to reply. He decided to try the reluctant dragon ploy. "Sir, I'm not very good."

The decision was a mistake. Phelps slapped his thigh. "Good! I'll see you after dinner tomorrow. Maybe I can get back on the winning side."

It took two evenings for Brosnan to convince the Commodore that Acey-deucey was not his game either. When he finally got ashore to call Annette, her office informed him that she had gone to Algiers for a month.

CHAPTER SEVEN

A week later the repairs to the *Lawrence*'s bridge were completed. The new piece fit perfectly, and replacing the wiring below it brought all the equipment on the bridge back into commission. Barley, Acton, and even Chief Martin labored overnight to put an initial coat of red lead primer and a first coat of gray over the new metal.

Commodore Phelps went to the APA *Samuel Chase*, flagship of Rear Admiral Hall, to report the availability of his three ships, including the newest ship of his squadron, the *Hanly*, which had just arrived from the States.

When he returned to the *Lawrence*, he called a conference of the three commanding officers and his staff. When all were assembled in his cabin, he directed Lieutenant Commander Cooper to spread charts of the Mediterranean for the area between Oran, Malta, and Sicily on his table. He lit one of his cigars and began to use it as a pointer, waving it expansively over the whole Mediterranean Sea. "Gentlemen," he said, "this is all top secret. The Allied forces are now planning for the invasion of Sicily."

Sperry whistled thoughtfully, looking at the chart. "Will we have any air cover?"

Phelps said, "Very little, and we will suffer for it until we establish air fields here and here." He waved his cigar over the chart. The cigar suddenly stopped over Sicily, scattering ashes over the island's southern beaches. Phelps scraped the ash off the chart and ran his finger along a stretch of shore of Southern Sicily between the small villages of Licata and Scoglitti. "Here's where our forces will land, on this forty-mile stretch of beach." Then Phelps moved his cigar east around the southern point of the island. "Around here, on the southeastern coast of Sicily, the British forces will land at the same time."

Captain Sperry traced the long stretch of beach on the chart with his finger and said, "Our area covers a lot of beach. Will it be divided between our forces?"

Phelps nodded. "Oh, yes, into three parts; from left to right, called JOSS, DIME, and CENT. We'll be part of the central, or DIME Force."

Phelps turned to Cooper, who was standing behind him. "Put the large chart of Sicily on top."

Cooper took a chart off a large pile on an adjacent chair and spread it on top of the other charts on the table. Phelps bent over it and temporarily put his cigar behind his back. The assembled officers moved carefully to the other side of the table to avoid the curling smoke. Phelps cleared his throat, blowing a cloud of retained blue smoke indirectly into Sperry's face. "Here's Geta, where we land. We don't need to go into further details yet, and as a matter of fact, we can't. We don't have the full operation order yet. Let's go back to the larger chart."

As Cooper took the chart of Sicily off the pile on the crowded table and returned it to the stack on the chair, Sperry seized the opportunity to move away from Phelps, leaving the other two commanding officers near the rising smoke. Phelps puffed on his cigar several times and put it in an ashtray near Sperry's new position. Sperry sighed and moved again.

Phelps tapped the city of Algiers on the coast of North Africa with his finger. "We move to Algiers tomorrow in company with the *Samuel Chase* and the other ships of the force under Admiral Hall's command."

Sperry said, "How big will the command be?"

"Two cruisers, the *Boise* and *Savannah*, the *Samuel Chase*, his flagship, eight APAs, two LSIs, thirty-four smaller but seagoing landing craft of various kinds, eight mine sweeping vessels, and several assorted support ships. Then there will be about fourteen destroyers."

"Do we know how long we'll be in Algiers?" Cooper asked.

Phelps nodded. "Yes. We know we'll be there until just after July fourth. We'll sail east close along the coast of North Africa, rendezvous off the island of Malta, and turn north toward our landing beaches about July ninth, arriving there in time for a D-day of July tenth."

Phelps picked up his cigar again, and the senior officers retreated, leaving the staff to bear the brunt of the smoke. The commodore accidentally tapped the long ash from his cigar onto the carpeting, looked at it, shrugged, and said, "This is all we need to go over now. We'll get detailed information later. When we get to Algiers, we'll make final repairs, top off on ammunition, food, and supplies. Above all we should remember security. Not a word to anyone. That's all." He waved his cigar, now a stub, and the assembled officers gratefully left for the open air, leaving Cooper to brush the ashes off the charts and fold them.

The next morning the *Lawrence* got under way together with the seven destroyers of Destroyer Squadron Seven, the four destroyers of Destroyer Division Thirty-four, and the ships of her own squadron. The fourteen ships formed a departure screen in a long arc around the entrance of Oran Harbor as the rest of the force filed out within its protection. When the larger ships had taken station in a rectangular formation, the destroyers formed a circular screen around the big ships. The commander of Destroyer Squadron Seven was senior to Phelps, so the commodore had little to do. He settled back in his chair and watched the destroyers scurrying to their assigned stations, occasionally commenting on their maneuvering.

Brosnan watched Oran recede as they steamed east. Algiers was only two hundred miles east, and he hoped to find Annette there. If all went well, he would have at least a week before the DIME Force had to leave for Sicily, or Annette had to return to Oran. The weather was clear, the sky was blue, the sea was calm, and Brosnan felt all was right with the world. Even the commodore seemed resigned to his passive role, and Brosnan hoped he could escape the bridge games he knew the commodore must be planning for the evenings in Algiers.

On the newly repaired wing of the bridge, Barley leaned on the bulwark talking to Acton. Both were drinking coffee from cracked white mugs. "Barley, that wooden board across the front of the signal bag looks great. Did you varnish it?" Acton asked.

"Sure. I did a great job."

Barley walked over to the signal bag, and ran his hand over the surface of the wooden board. "Damn!" he said. "It's still sticky. I should have painted it sooner."

Acton shrugged. "It'll dry soon."

Chief Martin strolled out of the pilothouse, carrying a monogrammed mug. "Good morning, men," he said, his face breaking into a tentative smile.

"Good morning, Chief," the two signalmen answered without much enthusiasm.

Chief Martin walked over to the signal flag bag and leaned against the varnished board. Acton opened his mouth to warn him, but Barley muttered, "Let the bastard find out the hard way."

Martin sensed that something was wrong, and tried to stand up. His trousers stuck to the board. "Damn! What the hell is this?'' He put his hand behind him and pulled his trousers away from the board. He looked at Barley. ''Why didn't you tell me about the wet paint, and why did you paint it just before getting underway?''

Barley looked at Acton. ''Acton, did you paint it?''

Acton shrugged. ''Not me.''

Barley grinned slyly. ''Sorry, Chief. I'll see what I can find out.''

Martin frowned, testing the stickiness on the back of his trousers. ''The bastard that did it ought to stay aboard in Algiers.'' He stalked off, spilling coffee from his mug.

Barley grinned with pleasure, looking at the spreading brown spots on the back of Martin's trousers, and turned to Acton. ''I wasn't going ashore in Algiers anyway. It was worth it.''

Early the next morning the force arrived off Algiers. Merle Bronski had just been relieved of the wheel watch. His assistant, Larry Swenson, a seaman in Bronski's gun mount, had also been relieved of the messenger watch.

Bronski paused for a moment on the bridge wing to look at the looming coast of Algiers. Swenson came up behind him. ''Pretty, ain't it?''

Bronski nodded. ''Yeah, it's beautiful. Nothin' like it in the States. Look at those white terraces rising behind the water front. The green hills behind the terraces look like a picture in a frame.''

''Are you going ashore?''

Bronski laughed. ''Of course, if there's any liberty.'' He caught the sound of Brosnan's voice behind him and glanced in his direction. Brosnan sounds pretty chipper. I thought he'd be down in the dumps, having to leave his French chick in Oran.''

Swenson shook his head. ''Nope. I heard him tell the exec that she's here. He asked permission to go ashore.''

"Did he get it?"

"Yeah."

"Then I guess there'll be liberty. Let's you and me go below and get our mount squared away. We don't want Lieutenant Kuberski to be ornery about letting us go ashore."

"What's with you Polacks?"

"Don't know what you mean. Lieutenant Kuberski is the best gunnery officer in destroyers and I'm the best mount captain. That speaks pretty well for Polacks. Let's go. To hell with this sightseeing."

Brosnan walked out on the bridge wing in time to see Bronski and Swenson disappear down the ladder. He looked at the rising white terraces of Algiers and wondered where Annette's apartment was located. He swept the nearing shore with his binoculars, but all the houses looked the same. He felt in his pocket to make sure he still had the piece of paper with her telephone number. It was there, carefully folded.

The screen commander signaled for the destroyers to form an entrance screen, and Brosnan bolted for the pilothouse to compute the course and speed to their station. Before he could finish, CIC gave him the data, and he got permission from the captain, now lolling in his chair, to take station. The wake boiled behind the *Lawrence* as Brosnan put on speed, watching the other destroyers carefully to make sure none of their courses would intersect. When CIC informed him that they were on station, Brosnan slowed and reported the information to the captain.

The captain yawned and said, "Well done, Brosnan. I suppose you want to go ashore tonight."

"Yes, sir. I hope the commodore doesn't want to play bridge."

Sperry grinned. "I think you're safe in Algiers. The commodore has a lot of friends in the force, and he said he expects to be ashore every night with them. He said to tell you he hopes you won't be disappointed about the bridge. I told him we could get a replacement for him from the wardroom.''

Brosnan looked carefully at the captain, who was rubbing his red mustache and trying to conceal a smile. ''Aw, Captain, you're pulling my leg.''

Sperry laughed. ''Yes, but I've had my fun. You can go ashore all you want, provided you ask the executive officer for permission.''

The commodore came to the bridge and looked at the ships entering Algiers Bay. ''It'll be our turn soon,'' he said. ''Do we have a berth assigned?''

Sperry said, ''Yes, sir. We're to nest in the location on the chart.''

Phelps nodded. ''Fine. When we're released to enter port, anchor as assigned and I'll tell Cooper to send a message to the other two ships to come alongside you to port. I'll need the gig right away.''

Brosnan heard him and decided to go whole hog. ''Commodore, may I ride in with you?''

Phelps smiled. ''Of course. I'm sure the captain has told you how disappointed I am not to be able to get in some bridge sessions here.''

Brosnan kept a straight face. ''Yes, sir. I'm sure we'll make it up later.''

The commodore nodded. ''You can bet on it. In the meantime, we can discuss a little bridge game strategy on the way in on the boat.''

CHAPTER EIGHT

Just before 1300 Brosnan was on the quarterdeck waiting for the commodore. Promptly at 1300 he appeared, grinning. "Let's go, Brosnan, there's not a minute to waste."

Brosnan ran down the small accommodation ladder and got in the rear compartment of the gig. The engine burbled smoothly. Brosnan hopped down into the cockpit as the boat engineer steadied the boat alongside. "Take it easy, Mister Brosnan, she'll wait."

Brosnan looked up in surprise, "My God! Does the whole crew know about her?"

The boat engineer grinned. "Just about."

Brosnan started to say something to the engineer, but he could see the legs of the commodore at the bottom of the ladder, and he pulled back. The commodore got into the boat and sat down, rubbing his hands eagerly. "Cigar, Brosnan? I know we can't smoke in the boat, but you might like to take one ashore."

Brosnan shook his head. "No, thanks, sir, I don't think my date would like it."

"Ah, Brosnan, sometime you've got to learn to like cigars. Most of my friends that I'm having dinner with tonight will be smoking them."

"Commodore, is there some connection between smoking cigars and attaining higher rank?"

Phelps pursed his lips. "Not really. Just coincidence. Admiral Hall doesn't smoke at all."

As they neared the landing, Phelps got up and poked his head out the port compartment door. "Look at those big stone buildings," he said. "They used to be forts for holding off the pirates that sailed at will off the North African coast."

Brosnan got up and stuck his head out the other door. "Yes, sir, I see them. They look like tourist traps now."

"They are. So is a lot of the rest of the waterfront. The only trouble is that there aren't many tourists right now. You'll notice that there is a broad drive all along the waterfront about fifty feet above the water. The buildings in back of it are beautiful, and the view from the terraces in front of them and on top of them is great."

Phelps turned and looked back toward the harbor entrance. "See those islands out there? The city and the bay were named after them."

"The Algiers Islands?"

"No. Originally they were named Al Jazair. That became corrupted over time to Algiers."

"You've been here before?" Brosnan asked. "You seem to know a lot about it."

"Yes. A long time ago on a midshipman cruise. Doesn't look like much has changed, though. The strip of land along the coast about fifty miles deep is called a Tell. Almost all of the life of Algiers is located along it. Behind that slim belt of habitation is mostly desert where the Berbers live. Also some wandering Bedouin tribes move about in it. Most of the population is Berber, with a sprinkling of Arabs, Bedouins, Turks, Greeks, Spanish, and a lot of French, who still run the country. An interesting place. Are you sure you wouldn't like to join my group for dinner? We're a lot of old fossils, but you'll learn something."

"No, thank you, sir. I have plans."

The commodore's eyebrows shot up. "My God! You haven't even been here and you have plans. Brosnan, there's a depth in you I never suspected."

Brosnan colored. "Sir, you give me too much credit. I'm meeting a girl I first met in Oran. She's visiting here on business."

Phelps grinned. "That's even better. A new version of the old saw about a girl in every port. You have the *same* girl in every port."

The gig cruised into the landing at the mole and came alongside a flight of stone steps. The commodore climbed out and took his departure with an airy wave of his hand and shouted, "Good luck." Brosnan headed for the nearest telephone booth. With his limited French, he had a hard time with the voice on the other end of the number Annette had given him, but she finally came to the phone. He cleared his throat nervously. "Annette, this is Bittle . . . er . . . Beetle."

Her voice was warm and eager. "Beetle! Where are you?"

"I'm down at the mole landing. I just got in."

"I hoped so. I saw all those American ships come in, and I hoped one of them was yours."

"Can I see you?"

"Of course. I can't tell you how to get to my apartment. The streets are too, how you say it? Winding. I'll meet you on the terrace of the Café Bad Azoun. All taxi drivers will know it. Fifteen minutes."

Brosnan was there early, eagerly scanning the crowd walking along the broad sidewalk. Arabs and Berbers in long gowns and colored headdresses walked by rapidly on obviously important missions. Women in black chaidors and veils mixed with American soldiers and Europeans in white suits.

Suddenly Annette appeared and Brosnan rose to take her in his arms. She was just as responsive as when he had last seen her, and he sighed with relief. They sat down and Brosnan ordered drinks.

"Beetle, I know you can't tell me what you've been doing, but I hope you haven't been in more trouble."

Brosnan laughed. "Nothing I can't handle. The most trouble I expected was getting ashore, but a miracle happened. My commodore not only didn't keep me aboard, but he brought me ashore in his gig."

"Gig? What's that?"

"His boat."

"Oh. I learn more English every day. Would you like to see some of the city?"

"Yes. I saw it coming in, and the white terraces are nice. Do you live there?"

"Yes, or at least my company apartment is there. We'll see it soon. Let's call a taxi."

For two hours they drove to the most interesting sights in town, and then Brosnan could stand it no longer. "Can we see your apartment?"

Annette grinned. "You haven't been to sea long enough. I thought you'd ask sooner."

This time they made love just inside the door. By seven o'clock they were relaxed enough to get dressed and go out to shop for supper. Annette made several simple dishes, and they finished with fruit and dates. Brosnan pushed back on the inevitable pillows and stretched his arms. "Annette, I've been thinking about making this arrangement permanent. Would you consider marrying me?"

"Oh, yes, Beetle, I've already considered it, but I'd like to wait until the war is over. Then ask me again."

"But I'm not in much danger."

"That's what my first husband said before the Nazis marched in to France. He didn't last long."

Brosnan face clouded. "I'm sorry. I didn't know. Is that why you work now?"

"No. I'm well off. I work to help the war effort."

"But how could importing help France?"

"We import lots of things that I can't talk about, just like you can't talk about what you do. I'll tell you some day. Now let's enjoy the moment. By the way, I may not be in North Africa next time you call.''

Brosnan's heart sunk. ''Where will you be?''

''Wherever my company sends me. Probably London.''

''That's a strange company.''

''Yes, it is, and I can't tell you any more. Call the same number when you come in to port, and they will tell you how to find me.''

Brosnan enjoyed the rest of the week. When it was over he was exhausted, but surer than ever that he wanted to marry Annette. On their last day in Algiers, the orders for the Sicily operation arrived, and Captain Sperry called a conference in the Wardroom.

When all the officers were assembled, he began. ''You all know we're going to assault Sicily. The only unknowns are exactly where and when. You should know that the Allies have begun an elaborate deception trying to make the Axis powers think we're going to invade Greece.''

Sperry went over to the large chart of the Mediterranean taped to the bulkhead. ''As you can see, we are to get underway tomorrow. The other two American attack groups and the British force will leave Oran and Bizerte in such a fashion as to follow these courses.''

Sperry pointed to a penciled course along the coast of North Africa. It was so faint the officers had to strain to see it. ''If you have difficulty seeing it, it follows closely the shore line to Cape Bon and then goes directly to the Island of Gozo, a small island near Malta. Then we turn north, and each force heads directly for is own unloading area.''

Fannon said, ''Pardon me, Captain, but your plot shows us arriving about midnight and landing in the dark. All of the American landings up to this time in the Pacific theater have been in daylight after several days of shore bombardment.''

Sperry shook his head and scratched his red hair. ''This astounds me, too. Apparently the high command thinks we can mislead the Axis forces into staying put in their defensive positions until we get ashore. Then we can bombard them as they move against us after we have established ourselves ashore.''

''What about air support?'' Kuberski asked.

Sperry shook his head sadly. ''There isn't any.''

Kuberski was shocked. ''No carriers? No Army Air Force?''

''No. The big carriers are all needed in the Pacific. The CVEs are all in the Atlantic fighting the German submarines. The Army Air Force thinks it can prevent air attacks on us by destroying the Axis aircraft on their home fields and then cratering the runways so that reinforcements can't be flown in.''

Kuberski groaned. ''We've heard that crap before. Can't any one get to them? We'll get murdered.''

Brosnan said, ''Well, at least your five-inch gun battery will get a good workout.''

''I'm not worried about us. I'm concerned about protecting the big, slow ships in the force. I just hope most of the troops get ashore before they're sunk.''

Sperry cleared his throat. ''Let's stick to how we get there first. We'll worry about surviving later.''

Fannon, who would be doing the navigation, stood up and looked closely at the chart. ''The shore doesn't have many distinctive features that we can get radar fixes on. I'll have to study it in detail.''

Sperry laughed. ''Don't worry. You'll have a lot of assistance from the navigators of the large ships. Also, there will be a beacon submarine in place. Individual submarines will go in submerged to each area in daylight and locate themselves accurately in the positions marked here. As the force approaches, a destroyer will be detached from each force to steam ahead and locate the beacon submarines. The destroyer will anchor near the submarine and the rest of us will use it for a navigational marker.''

Fannon rubbed his chin. ''Should work, but I don't like depending on other people's navigation.''

Sperry nodded. ''Neither do I, but we don't have any other choice.''

''What do we do when we get there?''

''Our initial assignment is as a member of the antisubmarine and anti-PT boat screen.''

''PT boats?''

''Yes. Italy is lousy with them. You know, those E boats. I don't really think we'll see many of them until we land on the mainland some months from now. Their bases in Italy are too far away from southern Sicily. Now we aren't going to talk any more about the landing itself at this time. I want each of you to read the operation order in the next two days and be prepared to discuss it just before we turn north toward Gozo. I won't be able to come down to the wardroom then, but the executive officer will conduct the discussion. Right now we know enough to get us to Malta. We start a long cruise tomorrow and at the end of it will be long days of danger and little rest. Turn in and get as much sleep as you can now.''

CHAPTER NINE

The next morning the destroyers got underway with a great deal of whistle and siren testing that shook up the pigeons nesting ashore. The churning wakes scattered debris on the surface of the harbor. The *Lawrence* was the last out of the channel and took her position in the departure screen without any trouble. Brosnan had the conn under the captain's watchful eye.

For an hour the screening destroyers wheeled and searched, stirring up the blue Mediterranean into foam. Gulls dipped into their wakes, searching for floating pieces of garbage or unwary fish.

Then the large transports began to sortie, backing away from the piers where for the last week they had been loading the elements of the first Army Division. While this task had been going on, two Dutch transports with large landing craft had joined the force. Two American civilian transports not equipped with landing craft had also joined and loaded reserve elements of the first Army Division. This floating reserve would accompany the APAs but would not be landed unless needed. If their troops were required, the APA's boats would be used to unload them. The two cruisers came out the wide channel and took lead positions in the rectangular cruising formation. The lesser seagoing landing craft had sortied at dawn and were in a separate formation shepherded by the eight mine sweeping vessels. They could still be seen to the east as they tried to gain distance ahead of the formation and to the north of the bigger ships' track.

Captain Sperry, nervously pacing the bridge, said, "Brosnan, take a look at the operation order and tell me again what the other forces are doing."

Brosnan turned to the movement annex of the operation order lying on the chart desk. "Captain, a group of LCIs is at the front of the long column. Then comes a Canadian convoy that will join the British Force. Our DIME Force is next. Then the CENT Force from Oran under Admiral Kirk will follow us, and after we are all clear of the port of Bizerte east of here, JOSS Force under Admiral Conolly will sortie from there and bring up the rear. That completes the sortie.

"We stay in one gigantic column from then on, passing through the Tunisian minefield channel. After we're abreast of Cape Bon, the British head south and we follow them south about fifty miles until it is time to head directly east for Malta. We turn east and when we are sure we know where we are off Malta, we head north. There will be a formation of our LCTs slightly north of us and a formation of our LSTs south of us. That way we won't run over them if they're delayed."

"Thank you. Do we have a late weather report? There's a feel of bad weather in the air, and I don't like the way the barometer is dropping."

Brosnan searched a pile of dispatches on the chart desk. "Yes, sir. Here it is. Good weather until the eighth. After that, they don't know. The weather in this part of the Mediterranean is hard to predict."

"I don't feel right about it."

The commodore, sitting in the opposite chair, said, "Local storms have been blowing up around here since the time of the ancient Greeks. Many a Greek sailor went to the bottom because of sudden changes of weather."

"You must have read a lot of Greek history," Brosnan said.

Phelps laughed. "Yes, I did. My father liked classic Italian poetry, and he even named me after Horace, an Italian poet who lived just before Christ. I hated the stuff. All Horace cared about in his poetry was meter. The substance of the poetry was secondary. I started reading the ancient Greek poets, and I had a hell of a row with the old man. Learned a lot about weather in these parts, though. The Greek poets described it very accurately."

Brosnan nodded. "You mean it can't be described very accurately because it doesn't follow any set pattern?"

"That's right, and unless I miss my guess, we're going to see an example of it soon."

Sperry hunched his shoulders. "I don't feel right."

At sunset on July eighth the DIME Force passed Cape Bonn and headed south for the fifty mile leg before their turn to the east toward Malta.

The weather looked ominous. The sky around the sun was blood-red. Phelps watched it. "Just like the ancient Greeks described it. We're in for trouble."

At dawn the sea was calm and there wasn't much wind, but the sky was dark and overcast. Without warning, a steady wind began to blow from the north. Phelps said, "This is a mistral, just like Menelaus suffered through in old times."

Sperry turned to the officer of the deck. "Send word to the first lieutenant to batten down everything and check lashings on the boats and liferafts." Then he grinned and added, "If you see Menelaus down there, tell him to turn to and help."

As the day wore on, the wind increased to fifty knots and piled up steep but short seas from the north on the port beams of the ships of the formation. The *Lawrence* began to roll deeply. Sperry said, "If we're rolling this badly, the small LCTs must be in terrible shape." He raised his binoculars and looked at the nearest LCTs in the formation on their port beam. The LCTs had slowed and were wallowing heavily in the beam seas and slowly straggling out of formation. Solid water burst over their low decks and shot high above their battered sides and small superstructures. The LCT formation began to fall behind slowly. Sperry shook his head. "What a hell of a way to go to sea."

Then the squawkbox erupted. "The lead LCT reports a man overboard."

Phelps moaned. "Poor blighter . . . er . . . I mean bastard."

The screen commander on the TBS transmitted, "Barracuda, this is Abacus. Send a small boy to look for the man."

Barracuda was the Commodore's call, and he moved rapidly out of his chair and looked at the surface search radar PPI over Sperry's shoulder. "You're the closest, Captain. Go after him."

Phelps turned to Cooper, barely visible in the subdued red lighting of the bridge instruments. "Cooper, tell Abacus what I've done."

Cooper picked up the TBS transmitter. "Abacus, this is Barracuda. Sandstone is on the way."

Sperry pushed the handle down on the squawkbox transmitter. "CIC, give me a course and speed to the man."

In seconds the information came back, and Sperry changed course to the north at fifteen knots.

"Commodore, this is all the speed I can make in this sea."

"I agree. Do the best you can."

Kuberski, who had the deck, hunched over the PPI to make sure there were no surface ships along the *Lawrence*'s course. "Course is clear, Captain."

Sperry nodded in the dark. "Thank you. Keep me informed."

The *Lawrence* pounded into the heavy seas for almost five minutes with solid water crashing against the bridge structure. Phelps flinched as the last sea struck. "Good thing we aren't in the Atlantic. These seas would be twice as bad. Sicily is so near these haven't had a chance to build up."

Sperry said, "These are short and nasty, but I think we'll be all right."

Then the squawkbox came alive again. "An LCT to the rear of the column reports they have recovered the man."

Almost instantly the TBS followed with a transmission, "Sandstone, this is Abacus. Return to station."

This time Kuberski picked up the TBS transmitter. "Abacus, this is Sandstone. Wilco."

Sperry said, "Kuberski, get me a course to rejoin at fifteen knots."

Before Kuberski could ask CIC, the answer came up over the overworked squawkbox, "Recommend course one five zero. Ten minutes to station."

Sperry said, "Pass the word to stand by for heavy roll. All hands hold on. I'll come across the seas as fast as I can. Right full rudder."

Kuberski nodded to the boatswain's mate of the watch who passed the word to stand by for a heavy roll.

The ship began to swing and the seas shifted from the starboard to the port bow. One boomed across the forecastle, but the succeeding rollers began to hit the beam and rolled the ship forty degrees. Phelps, wedged in his chair, said, "Uncomfortable, but not dangerous."

After the *Lawrence* was safely on station, Sperry said. "Fannon, how far to Gozo Island, the small island just to the west of Malta?"

Fannon looked at his chart, using a red flashlight. "About twenty miles, Captain. Our surface radar should pick it up any minute."

Over the squawkbox came the report, "The LCT formation has changed course to the north early to try to make up for lost distance, but has had to slow to three knots."

"Damn!" Sperry said. "That means the mine sweeping vessels escorting them won't get there in time to sweep the transport and screen areas for mines before we arrive."

Kuberski snorted. "Hell, Captain, what else is new? We aren't going to have any air support either."

The commodore cleared his throat. "Not only that, maybe the landing craft can't operate either in these seas."

Sperry said, "Surely Admiral Hewitt will delay the landing."

"You don't know Admiral Hewitt. At the landings at Casablanca he had a similar set of problems and he went right ahead."

"Did he succeed?" Sperry asked.

"Sure did. Lost a few landing craft, but he made the landing on time."

"But isn't this a little different?"

"As a matter of fact, it's an even tougher decision. The high command has decided they have to have surprise. If we turn around or slow, the enemy will find us in the daylight tomorrow. Then we'll really be at their mercy when we land. No, I think he'll go ahead with D-day as scheduled."

The squawkbox came alive. "Gozo Island on radar. Twenty minutes to time to turn north. We're on schedule."

Sperry muttered, "Yes, but the mine sweepers aren't."

In twenty minutes the force commander ordered a course change to north, and the force was off on the last leg, at a speed designed to bring them into the unloading area at midnight. Fannon turned to the captain. "Sir, you wanted some of us to have a last minute conference while we were on this leg and before we get to our destination.

I think there won't be any navigational problems for several hours. May I go below and start the conference?"

"Please do. I'll call you if I need you."

Kuberski, who had been relieved of the watch, Brosnan, Cooper, and Lieutenant Michael Farraday, the torpedo officer and assistant communication officer, were waiting for Fannon in the wardroom. Fannon was able to get into a chair without losing his balance. Now that the course had been changed the seas were coming from ahead, and the roll had changed to a sickening pitch, with the bow plunging into the oncoming seas and then rising rapidly, only to plunge again into the succeeding trough.

Fannon said, "Stinking weather, but it seems to be easing. The barometer is going up, and I think Admiral Hewitt may luck out again."

Kuberski shook his head. "I hope so. My feet are dead from four hours of standing on that rolling desk. Can we get on with this?"

Fannon laughed. "I've been up there longer than you have. Let's get at it. The captain wants us to be sure we're ready to get into proper position tomorrow and will be ready to render fire support if called upon."

Brosnan said, "As of now we're just part of the circular ASW screen. Our assigned station will be to one of the northern stations in the screen."

Kuberski nodded. "Yes, but that's the direction the boats will come from about the second night we're there."

Fannon said, "I agree, but the captain thinks we'll only be called upon the first day to assist the fire support group."

Kuberski scratched his burly chest. "We're ready. CIC has the bombardment chart on the DRT, and Beetle has told us what communication circuit we'll use. We can't test it yet because of radio silence, but we will as soon as we arrive and radio silence is lifted.''

Brosnan nodded in agreement. "We should be okay. We also have a spare receiver we could put on the landing force command circuit. I think the commodore and captain will want to know what's going on over on the beach.''

Fannon said, "I agree. Get it ready. I'll recommend that Farraday relieve you as officer of the deck for general quarters and that you put on a headset on the bridge and keep all of us informed.''

Farraday cleared his throat nervously. Fannon knew he was an ex-chief torpedoman commissioned about a year ago. With torpedoes, he was superb, but the assistant communications part of his job and the deck watches still seemed to make him nervous. "Er . . . Commander, I don't know if I'm ready for that responsibility. I just qualified as officer of the deck a few months ago.''

Fannon looked at Farraday's bald head, pale face, and anxious eyes. He grinned. "Farraday, you'll have no trouble. Between the commodore, the captain, me, and Brosnan, you won't be allowed to do anything but carry out simple orders. If you're in doubt, ask any one of us. And you'll have the best seat in the house. If I'm right, this is going to be one of the most fouled-up operations since Gallipoli in World War I.''

Kuberski laughed loudly. "I'll buy that. No air cover, no mine-sweeping, and no boating. We'll just be sitting there waiting for the ME 109s to arrive for target practice.''

Brosnan shook his head. "I don't think so. Surprise will help. All the unloading will be done before dawn. The German aircraft can't get at us at night. We may make out all right.''

Kuberski said, "How can we unload if it's too rough for the landing craft to be launched?''

Brosnan said, "Maybe you haven't noticed, but the seas have been easing a lot. Just since we've been sitting here I've noticed a change.''

Fannon put his hand on the table tentatively. ''Yes, you're right. The table isn't vibrating any more when we pitch, and we aren't pitching as much.''

Kuberski said, ''I hope you guys are right. If you aren't, this may be our last peaceful night.''

Fannon stood up. ''Let's all get an hour or two of sleep. Tomorrow will be a hell of a day no matter what happens.''

CHAPTER TEN

Brosnan tossed in his bunk. He could not find a comfortable position to compensate for the short pitches of the ship against the steep, short rollers coming from the north. In the lower bunk, Doctor Braxton Taylor alternately moaned and got up to retch in the wash basin. Brosnan was senior to him and ordinarily would have occupied the lower bunk, but the first night with Taylor in a rough sea convinced him that be was safer and out of the line of fire in the upper bunk, giving Taylor a clear and easy path to the wash basin.

Brosnan looked at his watch. It was 2300. He stretched, yawned, grabbed the angle iron above him, and heaved himself out of his bunk to the uncertain deck below. Just as he was testing his balance, there was a loud knock on the door. "Yes?" Brosnan said.

"Sir, it's the messenger. General quarters at 2345. When I came through they were serving breakfast in the wardroom."

Brosnan rubbed his tired shoulders. "Thanks. I'll tell the doctor." Brosnan looked at Taylor, now in a deep sleep as the pitching motion eased. He shook his head. "No use calling him," he muttered. "He can't eat, and he'll hear the general quarters alarm."

Brosnan dressed quickly, adding his pistol and webbed belt to his khakis. He picked up his life jacket and steel helmet, then went to the nearby wardroom.

Kuberski looked up from an enormous plate of hot-cakes as Brosnan entered the wardroom. "Ah, Beetle, I thought I was going to have to finish all the hotcakes myself."

Brosnan looked at the mess attendant standing attentively back of Kuberski, although there were six other officers at the table he was supposed to serve. Most were nervously toying with their breakfasts, and Jason sensed where his business would be heaviest. Brosnan said, "Jason, if there are any hotcakes left, I'd like a stack."

Jason grinned. "I'll look. Last time I was in the pantry Stevenson was leaving for the commodore's cabin with a dozen or so."

Kuberski said, "I'm pretty full. If there aren't any left, I'll share this last stack with you."

Brosnan sat down and searched for his ringed napkin in a pile in the center of the table. By the time he had it spread on his lap and had yawned and stretched a couple of times, Jason was back with a plate of hotcakes and a steaming cup of strong, black coffee. Brosnan downed the entire cup without bothering to put anything in it and handed it to Jason for a refill.

Kuberski looked at him slyly. "You didn't sleep last night?"

Brosnan groaned. "You wouldn't either if you had to listen to Doc Taylor all night. I hope we don't need him too soon or too much today."

The Executive Officer, at the head of the table, was pushing around some scrambled eggs. "Beetle, when you've finished that lot, let's go up to CIC. The commodore and the captain want to have a last minute meeting before general quarters."

Brosnan looked at the clock on the wardroom bulkhead. "Aye, aye, sir. Aren't we due to arrive in the transport area about 2400?"

"Yes, and we're on time. Admiral Hall didn't wait for the mine sweepers. We picked up the destroyer by radar that was marking the point five miles south of the transport area. She reported that she had the American beacon submarine in the transport area on her radar. We know we'll be on time now and will have an accurate navigational position.''

Brosnan shuddered and drank a deep draft of his second cup of black coffee. ''Jesus! We might be on the way to meet our maker any minute.''

Fannon nodded. ''We're in mineable waters now.''

One of the ensigns looked up in alarm.

Brosnan shoved back his chair. ''In that case, I'm ready to go to CIC now.''

Kuberski laughed loudly. ''Sounds like a good idea. The higher you are in the ship the better chance you'll have when the first mine goes off.''

Three of the junior officers looked at each other, got up quietly, and followed Fannon and Brosnan out the door. Kuberski beamed. ''That thinned out the competition. Jason, bring on some more hotcakes.''

Fannon and Brosnan opened the door into CIC. The subdued red lighting and the hum from the cabinets of electronic equipment was a soothing change from the wardroom's white light, the booming voice of Kuberski, and the chatter of the nervous junior officers. Brosnan looked around. The regular members of the watch were bent over plots and radar repeaters, telephone headsets firmly clamped on their heads. There was a low murmur of voices as data was transmitted and plotted on charts or status boards. Louder voices came from a group bent over a chart taped to the glass top of the Dead Reckoning Tracer.

Brosnan could see the commodore and the captain pointing to features on the chart and Lieutenant Commander Cooper nodding knowingly. Fannon and Brosnan leaned over a vacant side of the DRT and looked at the chart.

Phelps said, "Here's the transport area, a rectangle about five miles by two miles located six miles off the beach in front of the town of Gela. Gela is a little place up on the bluff back here." Phelps tapped the village with his finger. "The rangers will have to fight their way up the bluff. There's a long steel pier sticking out into the open water just here. The other parts of the landing force will land on these beaches about two miles to the right of Gela pier. There's no protection at all from the seas for any of the beaches."

Sperry rubbed his recently shaven jaw. "Yes, sir, but the weather is easing. Maybe it'll be all right for boating by H-hour at 0245."

Phelps nodded. "I hope so, but the transports have to begin putting their boats in the water at 2400."

Sperry looked at his watch. "That's about now." He pulled down the squawkbox transmitter handle. "Bridge, this is the Captain in CIC. Sound general quarters."

In seconds the strident tones of the general alarm could be heard through the bulkhead. Then the word was passed to man all battle stations, and feet began to pound on the deck outside. Fannon said, "Captain, I've authorized Farraday to relieve Brosnan as officer of the deck, and Brosnan will man a radio headset with one ear tuned to the fire support circuit and the other to the landing force commander's circuit. Hopefully he'll be able to keep track of what's going on ashore."

Phelps laughed. "Brosnan, if you can make any sense out of all the stuff that will be coming over both those circuits, you'll deserve a medal."

Cooper sniffed. "That won't be so hard."

Phelps looked at Cooper patiently. "If you think it isn't, you can relieve Brosnan every two hours."

Brosnan looked at the ceiling, but said nothing.

Cooper glared at Brosnan and then looked back at the commodore and smiled. "Aye, aye, sir."

Phelps went back to the chart. "We all know that the other two American forces are on either side of us and the British force is around the southern tip of Sicily to the north. We'll all be the target of the Italian and German air forces and eventually some E boats, and there won't be a damned thing to stop them for the first two days until the British establish some Spitfire fighter squadrons ashore. All of us will suffer."

Sperry gritted his teeth. "And the damned Army Air Force will go its stubborn, independent way, trying to stop the enemy by bombing their airfields and putting a few potholes in their roads."

"Let's not be too hard on them. General Eisenhower could have put a stop to this silliness."

"Maybe he will when he sees what happens. At least for the next operation."

Fannon, thumbing through the operation order, said, "And that's not all the Army Air Force has done. They've got a large parachute drop scheduled for tonight in an area very close to the beach."

"Good God!" Phelps said, "I'd forgotten about that. Well, we've got more immediate problems to solve. Let's go up on the bridge and see what this looks like."

The commodore led the way to the bridge and out onto the open wing. Brosnan put on the radio headset he found hanging on a hook on the bridge. He couldn't tell whether it was on the proper frequencies or not because radio silence was still being observed. Sperry said to the commodore, "I've ordered the officer of the deck to take our screening station. The executive officer will oversee Farraday, and I don't see any trouble. It's a simple maneuver, and he'll have lots of help."

Phelps said, "I concur." He turned to Brosnan. "Anything yet?"

"Brosnan said, "Nothing but static, sir."

Phelps and Sperry looked at the transports through their binoculars. Sperry said, "I see boats being hoisted out and some in the water. Even though it's getting calmer, the boats are really bouncing around."

Phelps said, "I can see them. There'll be a lot of seasick soldiers."

Cooper, standing nearby, said, "They're all rangers. They'll be tough."

Phelps laughed. "There's one thing the Army can't teach them. How to control their stomachs. They'll be as sick as anyone else."

Brosnan said quietly to Cooper, "Maybe you ought to ease up. That's two you've lost tonight."

Cooper growled and moved away.

Brosnan lifted his own binoculars and searched the beach. It was too dark to make out the features of it, but he could see the long pier jutting out from the smooth shore line and the high bluff jutting up behind the low beach. A few lights shone in the windows of the small houses in the village of Gela high on the bluff.

Fannon came up behind Brosnan. "Poor bastards are sleeping peacefully. In a few minutes all hell will break loose."

CHAPTER ELEVEN

Brosnan moved aft from the pilothouse to the signal bridge and bummed a cup of coffee from Barley. Even in the darkness he could tell Barley just from his New England accent. "How do you like your coffee, Mister Brosnan?" he asked.

"Black, just like the night."

"That's easy. I don't have to see to put anything in it. But watch it, it's hot."

Brosnan gingerly took the mug, held it in his hands for a few minutes to enjoy its warmth, and then downed half its contents. "Good stuff," he said. "How's it going with you and Chief Martin?"

"Not too good, and its getting worse. I think I'll have to request a transfer."

Brosnan laughed. "Take me with you."

Chief Martin's unpleasant voice came out of the darkness. "Barley, where the hell are you? Have someone keep a sharp lookout toward the shore."

Barley groaned. "See what I mean? Who does he think will signal us from ashore? Looking ashore is what the lookouts are for, not the signalmen." Then he said through clenched teeth, "Right away, Chief."

Brosnan put his coffee cup down in the signalmen's shelter and went back to the wing of the bridge, trailing the long wire of his headset behind him.

At 0145, right on schedule, the first boats headed for the distant beach, their white wakes easily visible behind them. The commodore said, "We may not be doing it well, but we're doing it on time."

Just as the first boats hit the beach, a searchlight beam stabbed out into the darkness. It missed most of the ships, but settled on a single transport. Brosnan said, "Now they know we're here."

Sperry cleared his throat and looked at Brosnan. "Has the admiral authorized gunfire support yet?"

Brosnan answered, "No, sir, nothing yet."

Machine guns started to chatter on the beach, firing wildly, and Sperry began to pace nervously. "Damn!" he said. "Our fire support ships ought to be firing. There's a cruiser and destroyer close in on each side."

Brosnan listened carefully to his ear pieces and said, "No orders yet." But the *Shubrick*, a destroyer in the left-hand fire support group, wasn't waiting any longer, and a full salvo from her five-inch battery blasted the darkness ashore. "That's better!" Sperry shouted.

Two more salvos followed, exploding near the base of the searchlight, and the light sputtered briefly and then went out. "Got the bloody bastard!" Phelps yelled.

Then a huge explosion tore the middle out of the steel pier. When the geyser of water subsided, a long gap appeared in the middle of it, visible against the glowing curtain of increasing firing ashore. "They made sure the landing craft won't be using that any more," Fannon said dolefully.

The circuits Brosnan were listening to came to life, and he began to relay the information to Phelps and Sperry. "The Rangers are all ashore and are in close contact with the enemy. Three LCIs have grounded on a false beach about three hundred yards short of the shore and are having trouble getting their men through the deep water between the false beach and the shore. Shore batteries are beginning to fire on our troops and boats. The task force commander has ordered the fire support ships to begin their bombardment."

Fannon said, "The bastards are all awake now. It'll be tough from now on."

Brosnan broke in again. "The fire support ships are doing well against the shore batteries."

Phelps, following the action ashore with his binoculars, said, "I can see from the gun flashes that the fire from ashore is diminishing and ours is increasing."

Farraday came out to the wing and found the captain. "Sir, we've just been ordered on TBS to join the *Savannah* and *Shubrick* in the left hand fire support group as soon as possible."

"I'll take the conn. Tell CIC to give us a course and speed to our station." By the time Sperry, Farraday, and Brosnan were inside the pilothouse, CIC had recommended course and speed, and Sperry headed the *Lawrence* for the area just to the left of the transports.

Brosnan said, "We've just been assigned a shore battery as target."

The telephone talker spoke up. "Captain, CIC has the coordinates of the target and is giving Lieutenant Kuberski the range and target direction."

Sperry said, "Good! We've got a present for these clowns. Let me know when we're in range."

In three short minutes CIC sent the word up that they were in range, and Sperry ordered, "Commence firing!"

Only the forward two mounts would bear for the first salvo, and the flashes from the so-called flashless powder in the half-light blinded all those on the bridge who hadn't shut their eyes at the salvo buzzer.

The Captain turned the ship to starboard enough to clear the after guns, and the next salvo was even more blinding as all four guns boomed.

Now Phelps could see the flashes coming from the gun battery ashore that was their target. He watched anxiously as more salvos followed. Then there was an explosion in the vicinity of the gun battery. Sperry, also watching, said, "I think we got them. We'll keep firing until we're sure."

Three more salvos produced another explosion, and the naval gunfire officer ashore reported the target destroyed. Brosnan relayed the information to the captain. "Cease firing,"Sperry ordered.

Brosnan noticed that the landscape was becoming visible, and he looked at the clock on the bridge bulkhead. It read 0400. It was dawn, and sunrise was due in less than half an hour. He shook his head. The night that had at first seemed to last forever had suddenly speeded up. He felt his stomach growling and wished he had eaten more of the pancakes he had left on the wardroom table. It would be a long time before he ate again, even sandwiches.

Twice more the *Lawrence* fired on shore batteries, but by 0430 the regular fire support ships had the situation in hand. The *Lawrence* was sent back to its screening station.

On the way back, CIC reported incoming aircraft. Kuberski swung his guns around to cover all sectors. Just before 0500 a huge flash lit the gray sky to the south.

The commodore said, "Good God! What was that?" CIC almost immediately reported, "The destroyer *Maddox* has been hit by a German dive bomber."

A second explosion from the same area reddened the entire sky. Sperry shook his head. "That had to be her magazines. She's gone."

Brosnan reported, "There are a lot of attacks on the ships to the south off Scoglitti. We may get some more here."

But by 0900 there had not been any more attacks, and the situation ashore eased. Sperry ordered the executive officer to feed the crew sandwiches and coffee. Brosnan waited patiently, his stomach growling, until a large pan of sandwiches arrived on the bridge. When Cooper had eaten two, Brosnan edged over to him and said, ''Now's the time to relieve me so I can eat and go to the head.''

Cooper looked up at him. ''Oh, yeah,'' he said through a mouthful of ham sandwich. ''I believe the commodore did say something like that. But hurry back. I'm a busy man.''

''Bull shit. You haven't done anything all morning.''

Cooper choked on his sandwich, but before he could say anything, Brosnan handed him the headset and walked off.

By 1000 the crew had been fed and Brosnan was back to his radio headset. Cooper stalked off to find the commodore.

The first report Brosnan heard from the landing force commander was that several columns of tanks were advancing down the roads toward Gela. He moved over to the commodore, who had returned to the bridge after a hasty breakfast below. ''Sir, there are enemy tanks approaching Gela. I think we'll be needed soon; maybe the *Grayston* also.''

By the time Brosnan had made the same report to the captain, the TBS began to squawk, ordering the *Lawrence* to reinforce the fire support ships. This time Sperry let Farraday take the ship to her new station, and Farraday responded well, quickly conning the ship to her new position. Brosnan grinned and poked Fannon in the arm. ''I may be out of a job.''

Fannon laughed. ''I don't think so, but it's good to see you have a relief when you're needed elsewhere.''

Just after they reached station, Brosnan reported, ''We've been assigned to fire at a column of five tanks approaching on the coastal road to Gela.''

Almost before the telephone talker finished reporting that CIC had plotted the target and the gunnery officer had the necessary information, Kuberski asked permission to open fire. Sperry shouted back, "Permission granted!"

In the daylight the effect on the eyes of the four-gun salvo was not as bad, and Brosnan could follow the flight of the projectiles toward the tank column, barely visible over the crest of the bluff. They were speeding along the road, apparently oblivious of the certain death approaching them from the sea.

Before the first salvo landed, another boomed out, and Brosnan lifted his glasses and fixed them on the tank column. He counted the seconds as the first four projectiles arched toward the target, and just at the time they should have arrived, a huge column of smoke, dirt, and tank parts blossomed on the road around the leading tank. "Got them!" he heard Sperry yell exultantly.

The second salvo landed in the same vicinity before Kuberski could shift fire, but he shifted the third salvo to the second tank. Two more salvos blew it apart, and the rest of the tanks slowed, stopped, or headed off the road for cover. Kuberski got two more salvos in flight, leaving huge columns of black smoke to mark their ends. The last tank fled back up the road, zigzagging as Kuberski's salvos chased its retreating form. When it was out of range, Sperry reluctantly ordered, "Cease firing. Brill, tell gun control that was a good job!"

Brosnan brushed the flashless powder residue off of his life jacket and opened his jaw to ease the temporary loss of hearing from the firing. Phelps, still following the action ashore with his binoculars, said, "All the tanks ashore have retreated, except for a few that got all the way into Gela. From the smoke, I'd say the rangers took care of them with antitank weapons. I hope the army appreciates what the navy has done."

Brosnan, listening on the fire control circuit, laughed and said, "Commodore, the army general in command ashore must have been listening to you. He just told Admiral Hall that's the finest display of supporting gunfire he's ever seen, his own artillery included."

The TBS came alive, ordering the *Lawrence* back to ASW station and concluding with a "well done."

The captain decided to feed the crew sandwiches again about 1400. This time Cooper showed up to relieve Brosnan on time. Just as Brosnan returned, CIC reported a large flight of aircraft approaching from the north.

Kuberski swung his battery north and Sperry increased speed to give himself maneuvering capability.

Brosnan searched the overcast to the north, but it was too thick to see through. The flight got closer and closer and then broke out into the clear. The lookouts spotted them and reported, "About thirty aircraft approaching. Bearing three three zero. Altitude five thousand. Look like ME109s."

They were ME109s, the large German swastikas standing out on their lower wing surfaces against the silver background. Three broke off and began to dive on the *Lawrence*. Sperry shouted, "All ahead flank!"

Kuberski began to fire the five-inch battery immediately, and the machine gun battery trained on the diving aircraft, waiting for them to come within their range. When Sperry thought the oncoming aircraft had committed themselves to an attack course, he ordered, "Right full rudder!"

Brosnan watched the black bursts blooming around the menacing aircraft in their shallow dives. One suddenly burst into bright red flame, scattering debris in the air, but the other two kept coming. He was sure their bombs would hit the ship, but he could feel the increasing vibration as the *Lawrence* increased speed and as the rudder thrust her stern over. At the last minute, just before Brosnan hit the deck, one of the two remaining aircraft exploded, and the other, whose pilot apparently lost his nerve, pulled up with his bomb still under his wings. The machine guns were now in range, and Brosnan could see small holes beginning to appear in the last ME109's wings. Kuberski kept firing at the retreating aircraft, but its violent escape maneuvers made it a difficult target, and it disappeared to the north, trailing smoke.

As the rest of the long afternoon wore on, there were increasing signs of heavy fighting ashore. Brosnan relayed the reports of the landing force commander. Twice the captain took the headset himself for short periods. The last time he took it off, he shook his head. "Sounds tough over there. I'm glad I'm out here."

Brosnan did a few deep knee bends and stood up on his toes to ease the fatigue in his legs and feet. He and the rest of the crew had been standing up at general quarters since midnight, and the strain was beginning to show. Talkers stuttered when passing the word over telephones, and general efficiency decreased. Even Chief Martin stumbled coming out of the pilothouse, causing Barley to snicker, "See that, Mister Brosnan, he's human after all. He's getting tired, but he won't admit it."

But Chief Martin was alert enough to see four low-flying aircraft coming in down the coast that were too low to be picked up by radar. As soon as he reported them, Kuberski swung his battery around and began to fire. Their change of deflection was so rapid the five-inch director couldn't obtain a satisfactory solution, and the projectiles that went out burst harmlessly behind them. The machine gun battery had the same difficulty, the gunners swinging their mounts as rapidly as they could.

The aircraft passed so close that Brosnan could easily identify them as ME109s and could see the German swastikas on their sides and the numbers on their tails. He pounded the bridge bulwark in frustration as he watched them get through the *Lawrence*'s curtain of fire and then pierce the heavier screen put up by the nearby *Savannah*. As they approached the transports they dropped even lower and split into two groups of two. One pair skip-bombed one of the transports and the other an LST on the beach.

Brosnan watched, first with satisfaction as the bombs fell well short of the transport, but then in horror as the other two aircraft put their loads squarely against the side of the LST. The LST was still filled with gasoline-laden vehicles, and they soon cooked off. Huge flames rose five hundred feet above the stricken LST.

"Jesus!" Brosnan said sadly. "Those poor bastards."

Sperry said to the commodore, "Can we help?"

Phelps shook his head. "The LST on the beach next to them is retracting and going alongside. That's the best that can be done. We'd just be in the way."

The LST burned until darkness descended, and for hours afterward a red glow lit up the area. Sperry took advantage of the darkness to set condition III so the crew could eat a hurried meal and go to the head. Most men laid down on deck near their battle stations. Three times before midnight Sperry sounded general quarters when CIC reported approaching aircraft, but no aircraft was able to make a successful attack. Some of the aircraft turned out to be friendly transports, trying to leave the area after dropping paratroopers.

After midnight, The Landing Force Commander reported that, although the situation ashore at the time of the tank attack had been touch and go, the navy fire support had decided the day, and the landing force was now digging in for the night. The captain gratefully ordered condition III set again, and Brosnan led a parade of weary officers and men below for a few hours of sleep. It had been a tough day, and the beginning of the next day was only a few short hours away.

CHAPTER TWELVE

Brosnan could hear the sound of metal banging on metal somewhere in his subconscious, but he was so exhausted he tried to block it out. It kept on, and he began to realize he would have to come back to reality and deal with it. He took a deep breath. "What the hell is it?" he moaned.

A voice outside his room said. "The messenger of the watch, Mister Brosnan. Wake up. It's 0300 and general quarters is at 0345."

Brosnan stretched and groaned. "Thanks. I'm awake."

He grabbed the steel beam overhead and swung out of his bunk. He spread his legs, gripped the cold steel deck with his toes, and tested his balance. This time the deck was steady, and he leaned over and shook the lanky form in the lower bunk. "Get up, Doc, you need to eat. You're getting too skinny."

Taylor rolled over, stretched his arms, and yawned. "I feel better. This damned thing has stopped behaving like a runaway horse."

Brosnan laughed. "It's calm as a mill pond out there. Get up and eat. I think your services will be needed before the day's over." Brosnan grabbed a towel and headed for the shower. Then he stopped and said over his shoulder, "I suggest you follow me to the shower. You've been in that bunk for most of the time for the last three days. You're beginning to show mold."

In fifteen minutes Brosnan and Doctor Taylor were both in the wardroom, clean and hungry. This time the junior officers, now ancient veterans of one day, were laughing and joking. Brosnan took a seat next to Fannon and pulled his napkin out of its ring. "Sounds a little more cheerful down here than it did yesterday," he said, looking around the table.

Fannon nodded at the young officers at the other end of the table and wiped some clinging egg off his wispy mustache. "They think this is easy now that they've had a few hours sleep. I just hope today doesn't knock the ginger out of them."

"You sound pessimistic."

"I am a little. The Germans have had time to react a little more strongly, and I expect a lot of tanks to show up ashore. Also a lot more air attacks. It could be tough, both ashore and out here."

Brosnan ordered hotcakes again and this time finished them all. He watched Taylor wolf down a huge breakfast and grinned. "Doc, there will be more. Take it easy."

Taylor laughed. "I'm making up for three days of eating nothing at all. I need this."

Brosnan ran his eyes up the part of Taylor's thin torso above the table and then his angular face, topped with a shock of black hair and set off with heavy glasses. "Didn't they feed you anything at Harvard Medical School?"

Taylor grinned. "It was a hell of a tough grind. I was too busy to eat. That's where I first got thin. I weighed two hundred pounds in high school, enough to play in the line on the football team."

Brosnan shook his head. "There isn't enough left of you to play receiver now."

Just as Kuberski was finishing the last of the hotcakes, the general alarm went off. Brosnan pushed back his chair and headed for the bridge.

On the bridge the first glimmer of light was showing in the east. Brosnan realized the captain had deliberately delayed general quarters a few minutes to allow the crew to get some more rest, and he was grateful. He thought about how much he admired Sperry's concern for his men, and he stored the message away in his mind for possible use some day if he ever got a command.

Brosnan put on his radio headset. This time there was a lot of chatter on both radio nets. The Captain walked over. "Anything new?"

Brosnan said, "Nothing yet. The big shots aren't awake yet. Their radio operators are just shooting the breeze."

As the sky lightened, Brosnan went over to the big twenty-power signal bridge telescope and swept it along the beach. Fannon came up behind him. "What do you see over there?" he asked.

Brosnan stepped back from the telescope and said, "Sir, do you want to look through it?"

"No thanks, I won't have time. Just tell me what you see and keep looking."

"There's still a lot of fighting back about ten miles from the beach where the front lines are. I can see gun flashes and smoke and dust. The landing force commander just gave the coordinates of the front lines, and I'm sure CIC is plotting them if the commodore and captain want to see them."

"I'll remind them. What can you actually see?"

"Not too much back in the hills. The scene of the fighting is too far away for us to shoot that far. The British monitor *Abercrombie*, which has fifteen-inch guns, is on the way from Scoglitti. With its range, it can reach back into the hills. The *Boise* and *Savannah*, with their six-inch guns, can still reach the front in its present location."

Fannon pursed his lips. "I still think the German army will counterattack today, and we'll be needed in a hurry. How's the beach look?"

Brosnan swung his telescope across the beach and whistled softly. "Jesus! What a mess. There's stuff piled six feet high all over it."

"What seems to be the trouble?"

"I think the sand must be too soft for the bigger wheeled vehicles to move across. A lot of them are stuck and just spinning their wheels. Some are moving over narrow roads made of steel matting, but there isn't enough of it to go around."

"What about the LST ramps?"

"There's one in use that I can see. The others were either destroyed by German air attacks or were broached sideways in the heavy surf yesterday and are still lying broadside to the beach. I can see a lot of engineers working on them to get them free of the beach and straightened, but there isn't much progress yet. They're very heavy."

Fannon sighed. "I hope the tanks that couldn't land yesterday get there today. They'll be needed."

From the nearby cruiser *Savannah*, the cough of aircraft engines being started and warmed up came across the still air. Brosnan swung his telescope. "She's warming up her SOC observation aircraft," he said. "Looks like she's about to catapult at least two of them."

Fannon shook his head. "The guys who designed those crates should be here flying them today. The cruisers lost two apiece with their crews yesterday to German fighters. Now they have only two left on each ship."

Brosnan looked at the sturdy but awkward scout planes sitting on their catapults. "They look pretty good to me."

Fannon laughed. "They look even better to an ME109 pilot. They're so slow the ME109 has trouble not overrunning them on an attack, but yesterday the German pilots were able to shoot them down on the first pass."

One of the SOCs ran its engine up to full speed, and in a few seconds the pop of the catapult shot came across the water. The heavy scout aircraft shot forward, dipped alarmingly, and then struggled into the air. Fannon said, "He's got a full load of gas."

Then the second aircraft followed, and a few miles away to the south Brosnan could hear the similar but fainter sounds as the *Boise* launched her two aircraft.

Fannon shook his head. "They're off for a long day of fun, and I've got to go inside and help Benson plot a good navigational fix before we move in closer."

For over an hour the sun struggled to break through the overcast, but never quite made it. Brosnan stretched his still tired muscles and paced up and down, listening to the terse reports from the Landing Force Commander. All seemed to be going well ashore, but about 0700 the reports became more urgent, and Brosnan could detect more and more tension in the voice of the radio talker. Then a deep voice took over the transmitter ashore, and there was no mistaking the urgency of the messages or who was sending them. It was the commanding general himself. "Many tanks coming south on all roads," he said. "I don't think we can hold them all. We need a lot of naval gunfire support urgently, and I mean now!"

Brosnan moved into the pilot house where the commodore and captain were stretched out in their chairs and relayed the messages. Both the commodore and the captain came out to the open bridge with Brosnan following, dragging his long cord. They raised their binoculars.

Phelps said, "I see the cruisers are moving in closer to the beach."

Sperry nodded. "And the British monitor *Abercrombie* is changing her ballast aft so she can elevate her guns more and get more range."

Soon the two cruisers and the monitor began firing full salvos, and large explosions could be seen far to the north as the *Abercrombie*'s heavy salvos landed there.

"What's going on?" Phelps asked.

Brosnan said, "The landing force commander says the naval gunfire support is helping, but there are too many approaching tanks for them to handle them all. He predicts some will break through and get close to Gela. He ordered all the men on the beach to pick up their rifles and portable antitank weapons and go to the top of the bluff."

The captain opened and closed his hands nervously, and then put them in his pockets as he realized what he was doing. "That sounds serious. I think they'll need us again. We'll have to be ready," he said.

The commodore nodded. "I'm sure you will be, but this time I'm going to take the *Grayston* in with us. I think we'll need all we've got."

The columns of heavy smoke drew steadily nearer, and by 1000 Brosnan, looking through the big telescope, could plainly see the advancing columns of German tanks. Some were being destroyed by naval gunfire and army artillery, but there were too many to stop them all. The tank columns looked like long steel caterpillars, slow but relentless.

At 1100 the task group commander ordered the commodore to move additional ships into the fire support area, and Phelps promptly dispatched both the *Lawrence* and *Grayston*. This time Sperry had only to nod, and Farraday confidently brought the *Lawrence* to a skidding halt in her new position. Brosnan grinned and looked at Farraday. "Nice job," he said.

Farraday grinned back. "Thanks, Beetle. I'm beginning to like this."

In about five minutes the tanks were within five-inch gun range, and Sperry gave Kuberski the order to commence firing. This time the five-inch director could see the tanks, and opened fire with its own data. Brosnan watched anxiously through the signal bridge telescope. The second salvo stopped the first tank in the group assigned to the *Lawrence* and it burst into heavy flames. The second tank slowed to try to pass the burning hulk of the lead tank. Brosnan grinned. "Kuberski got the interference. Now for the guys with the ball!"

Kuberski picked the second tank off promptly and shifted fire to the third tank. Brosnan said, "The rest of the column is trying to turn around. The whole damned team is headed back to the bench!"

Soon the entire column of nine tanks was either burning or disabled. Brosnan said, "I can see the crews bailing out and running for cover. The place looks like a used car lot. It's a long way back to Berlin."

The *Grayston* soon dispatched her group of tanks, and the cruisers took care of those at greater ranges. Columns of black smoke from burning tanks, fuel, and exploding ammunition reached up through the overcast and spread for miles into dirty clouds.

For the first time Brosnan lifted his surveillance high enough above the battlefield to see the *Savannah*'s two SOCs lazily circling above the carnage and relaying spots to the cruiser. Then one SOC banked and headed for the previous front lines. As Brosnan watched it go, he saw a streaking ME109 come across the mountains and head for the oblivious and plodding SOC. The German was like a falcon, intent on its prey. "Watch out!" Brosnan muttered. The SOC never had a chance. There was a blinking of machine gun fire from the German's wings, and the ME109 sped past the falling SOC and headed for the second one, now circling over the tank columns. The second SOC pilot dove and then headed for the ocean and the support of the ships.

Kuberski saw it coming and began to fire at the ME109, but it was too late. The German fighter splattered the SOC with a long burst, and smoke began to stream from its engine. Kuberski managed to shoot down the ME109 as it tried to escape, but it was too late for the SOC. It lost altitude steadily and headed for the *Lawrence*. Two hundred yards away it plopped into the water, bounced twice heavily, and stopped nose down, floating like a top-heavy pelican.

Sperry shouted, "Tell gun control to secure the crew of mount fifty-one and stand by to pick up the crew of the aircraft!"

Brosnan could hear Kuberski giving the orders, and as he looked down at the forecastle, he could see the men of mount fifty-one spilling out of the mount doors.

In Mount fifty-one Larry Swenson, wearing the telephones to gun control, heard the orders from Lieutenant

Kuberski and turned to repeat them to the mount captain, Merle Bronski. Nothing happened for a few seconds, and then Swenson shouted, "Bronski, get off your ass and do something. There are a couple of guys out there who need help!"

Bronski shouted back, "Don't get in a sweat. We're going out."

Bronski climbed down from his seat, opened the mount door and jumped to the deck of the forecastle. "Follow me," he shouted. The rest of the crew of the mount were right behind him.

When Bronski looked over the side, he could see the fuselage of the SOC, nose down, apparently sinking slowly. One of the wing pontoons and the end of the wing were missing, and there were many holes in the fuselage. The pilot was slowly hoisting himself out of his front open cockpit with one arm, but the observer was slumped over in his after cockpit.

Bronski could feel the deck vibrate as the *Lawrence* moved back, then the vibration ceased and the forecastle slid up abeam of the SOC about fifty feet away. The captain, using a megaphone, shouted, "That's all the closer we can get until the man in the after cockpit is free. If we bang against the aircraft, it might sink. You'll have to go after him."

Bronski raised his hand to acknowledge the order, and looked around for Swenson. "You and me," he said. "Let's go."

Bronski climbed over the lifelines, closely followed by the grinning but apprehensive Swenson. Both hesitated for a few seconds to get their bearings, and then Bronski jumped in the water. Swenson hesitated for a few more seconds and then followed him. Bronski came up, cleared the water from his eyes, and began to swim strongly toward the aircraft. Swenson came up slowly, gasped, and began to flounder.

Up on the bridge Brosnan was leaning over the rail watching what was happening on the forecastle, and he could see Swenson in the water. "Jesus!" Brosnan said. "I don't think he can swim very well." The men on the forecastle were watching Bronski's rapid progress, and no one was watching Swenson.

Brosnan took off his radio set, hurled it at Cooper, and ran down to the forecastle. He put a hand on one of the lifeline stanchions and vaulted over the lifelines, landing in the water near the floundering Swenson. As he got near him, he took off his life jacket and thrust it at Swenson. "Here, hold on to this until I come back."

Brosnan made sure Swenson was able to keep himself afloat and then he struck out for the SOC.

On the bobbing SOC, Bronski climbed up on the wing root and then to the forward cockpit. He tried to find a purchase for his feet so that he could pull the observer off of the seat harness buckle, but he didn't have the strength to do it from that awkward angle. He cursed loudly and pulled again, but he couldn't move the dead weight of the unconscious observer. The pilot was barely conscious, and Bronski could see that one of his arms was broken. He had all he could do to hold on to the aircraft. Bronski shouted, "Swenson, where are you?"

There was a thrashing in the water, and Brosnan grabbed the edge of the wing and climbed up on it. "Jesus!" Bronski said. "Where's Swenson?"

"He's all right. Move over so I can get above the man. When I heave up, you lean in and undo the buckle."

Brosnan put both feet on the forward edge of the forward cockpit and heaved the unconscious man upwards. Only his thick wrestler's neck and shoulder muscles could have made the lift. Bronski leaned in and unlocked the buckle. The man slid forward, and Brosnan pulled him clear and dropped him in the water. Bronski jumped in behind him and held him up while Brosnan helped the dazed pilot into the water that was now up to the front of the after cockpit.

Bronski spit out some salt water and said, "Thanks. I thought we were all going down together. I don't know how you did that."

Brosnan was treading water, supporting the pilot, but he managed to say, "A hundred neck bridges every day."

Brosnan was able to pull the toggles on the rubber life jacket on both the pilot and the observer. Soon the two men were pulled over to the cargo net rigged over the side, and willing hands helped hoist them up to the forecastle. Swenson had been retrieved and was stretched out on the forecastle, heaving up sea water under Doctor Taylor's watchful eye.

When they were up on deck and he had regained his breath, Brosnan said to Bronski, "Why the hell did you take Swenson with you when he couldn't swim?"

Bronski shrugged. "I didn't know he couldn't swim. He always said he could, and he jumped over on his own."

Brosnan went over to Swenson, who was now sitting up and looking around. He kneeled next to him. "Swenson, why did you jump over the side when you knew you couldn't swim very well?"

Swenson looked up at Brosnan's wet face and shrugged. "I can swim a little, but jumping off the side threw me. I couldn't get the water out of my mouth when I came up. And then things got worse and worse. Besides, Bronski told me to follow him, and I didn't want to let him down."

Brosnan grinned. "I think there'll be a shot of medicinal brandy waiting for you as soon as Doctor Taylor examines the rest of his patients."

Brosnan went below to change into dry clothes and then went to the wardroom to see about the rescued men.

Doctor Taylor was bent over the form of the observer on the wardroom table examining his back. Brosnan didn't want to interrupt him, so he went over to where the chief pharmacist's mate who was putting a soft cast on the pilot's arm. "How is your observer?" he asked the pilot.

The pilot was still pale, but alert. "He has a bullet in his back. He can move, so I don't think he's paralyzed."

Taylor heard the conversation and looked up. "No, he isn't, but he needs to be x-rayed soon and operated on to remove the bullet. I can't do it here."

Brosnan said, "I'm going to the bridge now. I'll tell the captain."

On the bridge, Captain Sperry saw Brosnan approaching and grinned. "Well done, Beetle. I thought you'd gone off your rocker for a few minutes until I saw Swenson. He was hidden by the flare of the forecastle."

"Yes, sir. I was standing at the side of the bridge, and I could see him better. Nobody else was watching him."

The commodore came over. "Brosnan, I think I'll recommend you for an award. That was magnificent."

Brosnan shook his head. "Sir, I didn't do anything I didn't think I could do. If anyone deserves an award, it's Swenson. He didn't hesitate to follow his leader, no matter what the consequences. That's my definition of courage."

The commodore nodded. "Mine, too. I think we can include both him and Bronski. In a few more seconds you'd all have gone down with that aircraft."

Brosnan said, "Captain, there's something more urgent. Doctor Taylor says the observer has a bullet in his back near the spine, and he needs more medical assistance than we have here. I recommend that both of the men be transferred to the *Savannah* by boat as soon as possible."

Sperry nodded. "I agree." He turned to Barley. "Barley, give me a message pad." The captain quickly wrote out a message and handed it to Barley. "Get this out as soon as possible, and Farraday, head for the *Savannah*."

By the time the message had been answered, the two aviators were in stretchers and loaded in the whale boat. Farraday neatly brought the *Lawrence* to a stop near the *Savannah*, the boat was lowered, and the patients were soon delivered to the waiting cruiser.

The boat returned and was hoisted aboard. Farraday asked, "Sir, request permission to return to station?"

"Granted," Sperry said, and he turned to Brosnan. "See, Beetle, we don't even miss you." Then he grinned. "That's not true. You do a great job, and I appreciate it."

The calm of the late afternoon allowed the crew to enjoy a full meal while the *Lawrence* patrolled her sector. On the second leg, just as she was about to turn toward shore, a lookout shouted, "Life raft two points on the port bow. Distance four miles. Looks like some men aboard."

Kuberski, who had the deck, reported the sighting to the Captain, who was napping in his chair. "Let's see what it is," Sperry ordered.

As they neared the raft, Kuberski could see six men, four of them paddling slowly toward the shore. As the *Lawrence* approached, the exhausted men stopped paddling and waved. Kuberski, looking through his binoculars, said, "Looks like American soldiers."

Sperry looked at them carefully and confirmed his report. "Yes, they're American all right. I'd guess they're paratroopers who were aboard some of the transport aircraft shot down around here last night."

Kuberski brought the ship alongside the raft, and Bronski again led his men out of the mount. This time he pointed at Swenson. "You stay aboard." Bronski and two men climbed down the cargo net and helped the exhausted soldiers up the side. When they reached the deck, the soldiers flopped down and asked for water.

The executive officer came down to the forecastle and ordered water brought to the men as the doctor quickly examined them.

In a few minutes he announced, "I don't find any wounds or injuries. They're just dehydrated."

Fannon said, "Can I question them?"

"Yes, sir."

Fannon picked a corporal who seemed to be senior and was in good shape. "Corporal, can you tell us what happened?"

The corporal shrugged. "Damned if I know, sir. We were all ready to go out the door when the loadmaster said to sit down. It was dark outside, and we couldn't see anything. The aircraft banked and jerked around, and we could hear antiaircraft fire outside. We fastened our seat belts again and held on. Then something hit the port wing, and I felt us going down. The back part of the aircraft broke off, and we spiraled down by ourselves. It wasn't far to go. About a hundred feet, I guess. We hit the water with a helluva splash, but we all survived. I guess the others in the front of the aircraft didn't make it. At dawn we found a raft floating and the six of us who had been in the rear section climbed on it. We've been paddling ever since."

Fannon said, "I think we'll take you back to North Africa, probably Oran, when we leave."

The Corporal beamed. "That's great. We hear the navy feeds pretty well."

Fannon turned to the doctor. "If you're through with them, let them sample our chow."

The doctor looked glum. "What's the matter?" Fannon asked.

Taylor shook his head. "I've had a total of eight patients, and I haven't treated a one of them. You sent the first two back to the cruiser, and these guys are so healthy it hurts."

The corporal grinned and said, "Don't worry, Doctor. We won't be in this kinda shape after a night in Oran. We'll give you plenty of business."

The *Lawrence* went back to station, and Brosnan prayed for a quiet afternoon and night. The captain secured from general quarters long enough for an evening meal, and by dark it was quiet enough to set condition III. Brosnan hurried below and threw himself in his bunk fully dressed.

Doctor Taylor said, "What's the matter, are you sick?"

Brosnan mumbled through his pillow, "No, dammit, I've got the midwatch in three hours. If you say one word more I'll barf all over you."

CHAPTER THIRTEEN

In his deep sleep Brosnan thought he was being thrown by a wrestling opponent, but then he realized he was on his stomach instead of his back. He tried to say something, but his mouth was blocked by something softer than an opponent's arm muscles. Gradually he realized his pillow was still over his head and that someone was shaking him.

"Jeez, Mister Brosnan, get with it. First I banged on your door, and now I've been shaking you for over a minute," a voice said.

Brosnan pushed the pillow off of his face and tried to focus his eyes. "Huh?"

"Sir, you've got to wake up. I can't waste any more time on you. I've got a lot of other calls to make. You're supposed to relieve the midwatch at 1145."

Brosnan drew in a deep breath, and the cobwebs began to dissipate. "All right, I'm awake," he mumbled.

"You don't sound like it," the messenger said patiently. "I'll give you another check in five minutes."

Brosnan heaved himself out of his upper bunk, walked unsteadily over to the wash basin, and splashed water on his face. He looked back at Doctor Taylor snoring peacefully in the lower bunk and threw a handful of cold water in his face. The doctor hardly flinched, and only stopped snoring for one or two snorts. Brosnan mumbled, "Some guys can sleep through just about anything, and one of them had to be my roommate.''

After he had shaved hurriedly and washed his face, Brosnan went to the wardroom for a cup of coffee and a sandwich, traditionally prepared for the officer having the midwatch as officer of the deck, and never touched by any of the other officers no matter how hungry they might be. He found one small, thin sandwich, tastefully prepared by Jason, with the crust cut off. He gulped it in four bites, washed it down with stale coffee, and went out to the pantry to find more substantial fare. He remembered he would be relieved at 0345, just in time for general quarters, and wouldn't be able to eat breakfast. Whatever he could find now would have to hold him at least until noon, and probably longer. In the refrigerator he found a lone withered apple and stuffed it in his pocket. Then he cut an inch thick piece of cheese and put it and three slices of bologna between two large pieces of bread. He smeared butter copiously on all the parts of the sandwich to hold it together, wrapped it in a piece of paper labeled ''Plan of the Day,'' and added the sandwich to the apple in his pocket. He picked up his cap and life jacket and headed for the bridge.

As he trudged slowly up the ladder, he could feel the fatigue that started with his head, ran down his back, and extended clear down through his calves to his feet. Two men were ahead of him, climbing slowly up the steep ladder, going to the bridge to relieve the watch. One said, ''Damn, I can hardly walk. I haven't had a total of three hours sleep in three days.''

Brosnan tried to add up the hours he had slept, but his brain rebelled at even this simple task, and he shook his head and plodded on.

One of the two men above him said, ''This is the worst kind of war I've ever seen.''

''Whaddaya mean?''

''Usually we just fight one thing at a time. Now we got both kraut and Italian submarines, E boats, surface ships, airplanes, radio-guided bombs, tanks, artillery, and even British fighters.''

"Spitfires? They're on our side.''

"Yeah, but how the hell do we sort'em out of all those damned Stukas, Heinkels, ME109s, and Focke-Wulfs? It's a helluva mess up there in the air, and I'm so damned pooped I can hardly see which is which.''

Brosnan tried to grin, but his facial muscles were too tired. When he reached the open bridge, he looked up. He could see that an overcast sky cut out all moonlight and starlight. The horizon was also almost completely black except for a few smoldering fires that broke the inky curtain. When he went into the pilothouse, subdued red lights lit the navigational instruments and reflected from the tired faces of the men who bent over them. The surface search radar repeater, known as a PPI, gave off a green glow as the lighted cursor swung around the circular screen making small dots of light appear as it painted each surface contact.

Brosnan went to the chart desk to familiarize himself with the ship's position and patrol area. When he was ready, he went over to Ensign Jerry Raymond, the first lieutenant who had the deck. Raymond, called Tubby, looked fat, but was actually quite fast on his feet and the best dancer in the wardroom. His dark red hair matched the red glow of the magnetic compass he was leaning over, checking its reading with the gyro compass. Brosnan punched Raymond playfully in the kidney and said, "Ready to relieve you, Tubby.''

Raymond turned to Brosnan. "Jesus, I'm glad to see you. I don't know how I've stayed awake the last four hours. They're the worst I've ever spent.''

Raymond gave Brosnan all the necessary data and Brosnan said, "I relieve you. Get below, and don't fall down the ladder.''

For four hours Brosnan paced the deck outside the pilothouse, occasionally beating his face with his hands to stay awake. Just before 0330, the Captain came on deck from his sea cabin. "How's it going, Brosnan?'' he asked.

"Very quiet, sir, but I think business will pick up after dawn."

Sperry nodded. "We go to battle stations at 0345. I'm afraid you'll miss breakfast."

Brosnan grinned in the darkness. "No, sir, I've got it in my pocket."

Sperry said, "In that case, I'll take the deck for fifteen minutes while you eat."

Brosnan went out on the bridge wing, leaned against the flag bag, and pulled out his sandwich. Butter was beginning to seep through the plain paper. Barley came over to see what he was doing. Brosnan opened his mouth wide and bit off a huge chunk of the thick sandwich.

Barley, still not able to see much in the darkness, said, "That sounds like a cement mixer starting up but it smells like a cheap delicatessen."

Through a mouthful of food Brosnan said, "Just an Iowa sandwich. Wait until you hear the apple."

"How about a cup of good old signal bridge coffee to wash it down?"

"Great. Just black, like the night."

Brosnan rustled the paper around the sandwich with his fingers as he took another huge bite. Barley said, "Jesus, Mister Brosnan, you ain't eating the paper, too?"

"Sure. It's better than the bologna and it has fewer calories."

Barley shrugged. "You officers will eat anything."

In the pilothouse Captain Sperry looked at the chart and reread the operation order. As he was finishing, Sperry heard the commodore's distinctive British leather heels and turned to him. "Good morning, sir. Ready for another day?"

Phelps was tired. "My butt's dragging, but I know I have it easier than these young watch-standers. Does that order say anything about when we might be released?"

"It says we're to be released when we are no longer needed for fire support or screening."

Phelps brightened. "That might mean today. The front lines are too far away for us to render fire support, and the mine vessels have finished laying friendly mines around the transport area. At noon we'll be able to stop screening against submarines and let the Jerry and Italian submarines worry about where the new minefields are."

The captain looked at the small sliver of light appearing in the east under the overcast. "Time for general quarters. Boatswain's mate of the watch, sound battle stations."

The general alarm sounded and feet began to pound on the decks below. Brosnan walked into the pilothouse and said, "Sir, shall I take the deck again?"

Sperry shook his head. "No, go ahead and man your radio headset. Farraday will be here soon."

Sperry walked out on the open bridge and sniffed the air. There was a mixture of moisture, powder smoke, diesel fumes, and burning wood in the air. Still, he liked the morning freshness of it, and he continued to breathe heavily. The deep breathing helped to still the nervousness he always felt rising when something different was about to happen. Even the strident sound of the general alarm made his hands begin to shake and his palms perspire. He put them in his pocket and continued to breathe deeply. Soon he could feel his hands come back to normal, and he started to pace up and down the wing. He thought about his wife and two children back in Washington, DC, and he wondered if he would ever see them again. The commanding officer of the destroyer *Maddox*, sunk the first day, had not been found, and would never see his family again. Sperry thought that even if he got back to his own family safely in a year or so, his small children would hardly recognize him. He stopped pacing and searched the shore with his binoculars, now held in his steady hands. Whatever happened, he would have to be ready for it. The safety of the ship and all the men in her depended on him and his reactions. Tired as he was, he would have to call on his deepest reserves, and he was determined to be ready. That was what a captain had to do.

Up in the bulky five-inch gun director, Lieutenant Kuberski rolled an unlit cigar around in his mouth and chewed it gently. He could still taste the large breakfast he had just put away, and the cigar, even though unlit, made him relax. He eased the tight telephone headset, and stood up in the director so that his upper torso stuck out the port in the top of the director. He stretched his arms and made a mental note that he was beginning to put on weight and would have to cut down on the chow. Maybe he could eat hotcakes without syrup and butter. He shuddered. They'd taste like cardboard. There had to be something else to cut out, and he enjoyed for a few minutes going over in his mind the roster of rich and fattening foods with which Jason would tempt him.

He looked down on the platform below where Tubby Raymond was pacing up and down, dragging a telephone cord behind him. Raymond commanded the machine gun battery at general quarters. Some gunnery officers preferred to take their station on the platform with the machine gun officer and control the five-inch director by telephone, but Kuberski felt the five-inch director was where the big action was, and he wanted to be in the middle of it. He watched Tubby, noting his graceful walk in spite of the extra pounds he was carrying. Maybe he should ask Tubby to teach him to dance when they were ashore next time. Maybe weight reducing wasn't even necessary. Kuberski sighed. Dancing was only one of the social accomplishments he had missed out on over the years. After high school he had enlisted in the navy and had been sent to fire control school. His natural intelligence had placed him at the top of his class, and rapid promotions had followed. The beginning of the war had brought him a commission, and he had progressed steadily up the ladder of promotions in the last few years. He knew he was well-qualified professionally, but he also knew he had missed the fine points of a college education. He felt uncomfortable in the wardroom amongst all the college graduates when they began to talk about subjects he had never heard of, and ashore he used every conceivable excuse to avoid social occasions.

He shook his head. He knew he would have to change his attitude, and he wanted to improve. One of the first steps would be to learn to dance. He rolled the cigar in his mouth and then pulled it out and looked at it. On an impulse he threw it far over the side. He grinned. Maybe that was the first step in the social rehabilitation of Stanley Kuberski, and dancing would be the next. After that, what the hell, it couldn't be too bad.

As Kuberski finished watching the cigar arcing over the side, he turned and surveyed the coastal plain. Small clouds of dust were rising along the bluff as trucks carried supplies to the front lines. Suddenly, low over the bluff, a column of three aircraft cleared the top of the bluff, just feet above it, and bored straight at the *Lawrence*. "Air action port!" Kuberski shouted. The director trainer swing the director rapidly to port and picked up the leading aircraft. Down below Kuberski could hear the hydraulic motors of the five-inch mounts whining as their trainers followed the director. "Shift to automatic!" Kuberski roared, and the gun mounts quivered as the system locked them into alignment with the director.

"Solution!" the director pointer yelled.

Without waiting for an order from the bridge, Kuberski yelled, "Commence firing."

Kuberski quickly looked at Raymond on the platform below. Raymond was shouting over his telephones, and a rapid glance aft assured Kuberski that the machine guns would be ready when the aircraft came within range. The first five-inch salvo crashed out, and Kuberski watched the faint white tracers arrow toward the approaching aircraft. He was fairly sure the first aircraft was an ME109, but the next two were hidden by the first. In a few seconds the three aircraft were so close to the *Laweance* that the machine guns aft began to chatter. Then the projectiles of the first salvo burst, slightly ahead of the leading aircraft. It jerked slightly, but kept coming. Kuberski could still feel the taste of the cigar on his tongue, and he decided he would give them up. He gritted his teeth and cursed the slowness of the second salvo. Finally it went out, and he watched without breathing as the tracers converged on the lead aircraft. There was a large explosion as at least two of the projectiles burst almost on the nose of the first aircraft. The aircraft dissolved in a cloud of projectile fragments, pieces of its own bombs, and burning fuel.

In seconds the second aircraft burst through the smoke and debris of the first aircraft, still headed at low altitude for the *Lawrence*. Just as Kuberski was about to order the director to shift to the second aircraft, he noticed winking flashes from the wings of the third aircraft. The wing of the second aircraft was beginning to crumble, then the whole wing separated, and the crippled aircraft dove into the sea, cartwheeling in violent sprays of salt water. Kuberski's gut tightened. Something was not right.

The third aircraft pulled straight up at maximum speed, and before it disappeared into the overcast above, Kuberski could see the British insignia on the bottom of its wings. ''Cease firing!'' he bellowed, and he could hear Raymond down below yelling the same thing. ''Jesus!'' Kuberski said. ''It's a Spitfire. The Brits are here!''

The director pointer laughed. ''And where the hell is the Army Air Force?''

Kuberski shook his head. ''I don't know, but that guy sure looked good. We'll have to be more careful from now on before we open fire.''

The morning passed quietly except for a few air alerts that were apparently taken care of by the newly stationed British fighters. None got close to the *Lawrence*.

Brosnan paced the open bridge, his feet feeling like two bags of lead. Now and then Barley showed up with a steaming cup of coffee that revived him for a few minutes, then the old leaden feeling returned. About noon the captain set condition III and Brosnan went below to eat lunch. He could barely keep awake at the table, and only about half of the officers showed up at all. Doctor Taylor was there, obviously feeling fit and rested. Brosnan moaned when he saw him walk in. "Doc, just don't try to be cheerful."

Kuberski said, "Yeah, if you do, Doc, it's gonna be soup in the lap time."

Just after the soup was served the general alarm began clanging, and all the officers raced for their stations.

Brosnan got to the bridge without falling over his tired feet and strapped on his radio headset. Sperry looked at him and said, "Brosnan, there isn't anything coming over those circuits of interest to us any more. You can secure that job. Right now we've got an air alert, but I can't see anything up there through the overcast."

Brosnan took off the headset and rolled up the cord. Just as he was hanging up the set, he heard Kuberski roar, "Air action starboard! Commence firing!"

Brosnan dashed out to the starboard wing of the bridge and looked up. An ME109 was right on top of them, diving out of the low overcast. It was coming so straight at them that he had to fight the impulse to hit the deck. He kept watching the black Swastikas on its wings getting larger, and he was almost paralyzed. A bomb was nestled under each wing, and the whirling propeller seemed to be boring holes in the heavy atmosphere.

It was too late for the five-inch battery to be able to fire effectively, but the forty-and twenty-millimeter guns aft began to chatter. A few tracers passed close to the diving aircraft, but none seemed to hit. Brosnan watched as the plane released its bombs. It pulled up wildly and banked to port. The bombs came down, and Brosnan knew they couldn't miss. Sperry was trying his best to avoid them by using full rudder, but he was too late. The bombs bore down relentlessly. Brosnan thought they might hit the bridge, and he was sure he wouldn't survive. At the last second, the radical maneuvers of the *Lawrence* caused the bombs to drift aft, and then Brosnan knew he would live. The bombs disappeared behind the forward stack, and there was a tremendous explosion on the torpedo deck. The concussion knocked Brosnan to the deck. When he got his breath back, he got up and looked around. The other members of the bridge crew were struggling to their feet also, and Brosnan ran over to help the captain up.

Sperry shook him off. "I'm all right, Beetle. Go aft and see what happened. I'll send the repair crews to help you."

Brosnan went down the ladders to the torpedo deck and ran aft. Both repair crews pounded down the main deck and climbed up the nearest ladder. Dr. Taylor and two corpsmen climbed up from the main deck.

Brosnan looked at the torpedo mount. It was a bloody shambles. The bombs had apparently hit the breech end of the heavy mount. It was so solid some of the bomb blast had dissipated in the air, riddling the outer casings of both stacks. Two of the torpedoes had been blown forward through their tubes and were hanging out on deck.

Brosnan went over to the side of the torpedo deck so he could see the bridge. He pointed at Farraday, who was standing next to the captain, and wiggled his finger, signaling him to come aft. Sperry said something to Farraday, and Farraday nodded and came running down to the torpedo deck.

When he arrived, Brosnan said, "Farraday, look at these fish. Do you think the war heads are dangerous?"

Farraday nosed around the wreckage and then stood up. "They're safe. The exploders weren't in the war heads, and the explosive is very stable without them. Looks like the oxygen flasks are leaking, and there's some alcohol leaking on deck, but the wind will evaporate it. All we have to do is keep clear for an hour or so, and then we can dispose of the two damaged fish over the side. Looks like the other three torpedoes are damaged, but we can keep them aboard because they aren't leaking anything. The whole mount will have to be replaced. These mounts are pretty tough, otherwise the bombs would have done more damage down below them."

Dr. Taylor was looking around the mount. "Oh, Jesus!" he moaned. "There isn't anything left of the two torpedomen except blood."

Brosnan felt his stomach rebelling, but he breathed deeply and tried to keep the nausea from rising any farther. He struggled to control his voice as he said, "Let's get the hell out of here until the alcohol evaporates."

Back on the bridge, Brosnan and Farraday reported the damage to the captain. Sperry said to the commodore, "We'll have to report this to the task force commander."

Phelps nodded. "Do it. I think we'll be sent back to Oran with a convoy leaving tonight."

He was right. The *Lawrence* and the other two ships of the squadron were ordered to screen a group of unloaded transports leaving at dusk.

When they were clear of the Gela area, the damaged torpedoes were jettisoned over the side and the blood was hosed off the torpedo deck. Brosnan watched the operation, and then went below and dropped into his bunk fully clothed. The Gela operation was over, and he didn't care if he ever saw Sicily again.

CHAPTER FOURTEEN

On the second day after the *Lawrence* left Sicily the crew assembled on the main deck for a memorial service for the two torpedomen who had been killed by the German bombs. The weather was mild, and the men standing in ranks were solemn. Some of them occasionally glanced at the damaged torpedo mount.

Captain Sperry read burial service passages from the Navy Hymnal, and Ensign Farraday, the torpedo officer, gave a short eulogy for the two men. Dr. Taylor led the crew in the singing of the navy hymn, Eternal Father, and then Lieutenant Commander Fannon dismissed the solemn crew.

Two days later the familiar hills behind Oran rose over the horizon, and soon the harbor entrance appeared. After the transports had entered the harbor and moored to the mole, the three ships of Commodore Phelps' small squadron entered the large bay and moored to a navy repair ship.

As soon as the brow was over to the repair ship, the officer in charge of repairs came aboard the *Lawrence* and headed for the torpedo mount. He examined it carefully, attended by the captain, the executive officer, and an anxious Farraday. The repair officer peered into the two empty and twisted tubes and tried to get a look at the fronts of the remaining torpedoes, then straightened and shook his head. "The whole thing has to go," he said. "I don't even want to try to unload the remaining torpedoes here. We'll lift the whole mount off, put it on a barge, and take it out to sea. We'll try to take the remaining torpedoes out of the tubes there. If we can't get them far enough out of the tubes to get the war heads off safely, we'll push the whole thing over the side in deep water."

Farraday looked concerned. "Do you have a replacement mount aboard?"

The repair officer shook his head. "No. We'll have to order one from the States. We'll have it sent to the Royal Naval Yard at Portsmouth. You'll be able to have it installed when you go back there for upkeep."

The captain grinned. "The commodore will like that and so will most of the crew."

The repair officer next examined the shrapnel holes in the sides of the stacks. "We'll patch these temporarily," he said. "You'll look kind of funny, but Portsmouth can make permanent repairs. Everything else is small potatoes. You'll be ready to go in a few days."

While the examination was being conducted by the repair officer, the commodore called on Admiral Hall, the task force commander. When he came back, he sent for Captain Sperry and Adrian Cooper, who was his chief staff officer. Sperry knocked at his door and came in when the commodore said, "Enter."

Sperry said good morning to Cooper and said to the commodore, "Anything new and exciting, sir?"

The commodore, engaged in lighting one of his cigars, said, ''Not even this cigar. Somehow cigars have lost their charm for me. Please sit down.''

Sperry sat down, hoping that the commodore might consider giving up cigars.

Phelps said, ''We'll be here for several days while your repairs are being done. We'll also load ammunition, stores, and food. You can start liberty immediately. Cooper, please get the word to the other two ships. I have found that we may be needed to reinforce the destroyers that are being sent to Palermo Bay on northern Sicily. The army expects to capture it soon, and they'll need naval gunfire support. The Italians are making a major effort to defend it. After we take it, our Seventh Army will push on east toward Messina.''

''How about the straits between Sicily and the Italian mainland?''

''You mean the Straits of Messina?''

''Yes, sir. Won't there be an effort to prevent the German and Italian Armies from retreating across the straits to the mainland of Italy?''

''I hope so, but I think the British, whose responsibility it will be, think it would be suicide to put ships in the narrow straits against all the shore artillery the Germans could bring against them both from Sicily and the mainland.''

''Hmm,'' Cooper said. ''I know what that means. Some great strategist will decide to put destroyers in there.''

Phelps shook his head. ''I don't think anybody would do that. More likely torpedo boats at night.''

''We're supposed to have a lot of them up there.''

Phelps nodded. ''Admiral Hall says a lot more are being sent forward.''

Sperry frowned. ''That means we'll have to do some instruction to assure that our lookouts and gunners know the difference between ours and theirs.''

Phelps turned to Cooper. ''Make sure the other ships get that information and direct that they start a good identification program.''

Brosnan went to Fannon's stateroom as soon as he could and asked for permission to go ashore.

The executive officer looked up from his paperwork and grinned. "Beetle, you're going to wear yourself out with paperwork. Get off of the ship before the commodore or Cooper think of something useless for you to do."

Brosnan took a quick shower and then came back to his room to shave. Doctor Taylor was sitting at his desk filling in some forms. He looked up as Brosnan lathered his face. "Beetle, you've lost ten pounds. There isn't an ounce of fat on your upper body any more."

"Do you think there's something wrong with me?"

Taylor laughed. "Sure. The same thing that's wrong with everybody."

"Except you?"

"Well, I guess you're right. I get my sleep, but everybody else is suffering from chronic fatigue and poor diet. I can't treat that."

Brosnan looked at his face in the mirror. "My face is thin, too. I can see all the angles in it. Even the pads of fat around my eyes are gone now."

Taylor nodded. "You look a lot better. Your girl friend must like it."

Brosnan shrugged and began to shave. "I don't know what she sees in me, but I know I'm happy about it."

Brosnan dressed quickly and went over the brow into the large door in the tender's side. All the way over he kept expecting to hear someone calling him back. Once inside the tender, he dashed up the ladders to the quarterdeck and then down the long brow to the pier. Halfway up the pier he found a telephone booth. He dialed Annette's number and waited anxiously for her voice. A man answered. Brosnan hesitated, and then said, "May I speak to Annette Duchamp, please?"

The man hesitated for a few moments, obviously talking to someone else. Then he said in a pronounced French accent, "Who is this calling, please?"

"Lieutenant Robert Brosnan, of the American navy. She knows me."

There was another pause. Then the voice said, "Lieutenant Brosnan, I think we should talk. Come to the French Export Company on the main boulevard at Printemps Street. Ask for Emile Piccard. I'll be waiting."

Brosnan said, "I'll be there in ten minutes."

When Brosnan walked through the doors of the French Export Company, the offices looked almost deserted, but there was a receptionist partially hidden behind a row of empty desks. Brosnan walked over and said, "Monsieur Piccard, *sil vous plaîs.*"

The receptionist looked up and said, "Ah, Lieutenant Brosnan. Monsieur Piccard is expecting you. Third door on the left."

Brosnan found the door and knocked. A voice said, "*Entre,*" and Brosnan pushed the door open. A middle-aged man got up from behind a desk and came forward with his hand extended. "Ah, *oui,* Lieutenant Brosnan, Annette has told me much about you. Please sit down."

Brosnan took the chair he was offered and said, "Has anything happened to Annette?"

Piccard said, "Yes and no. She is in good health, but she is not here. How much has she told you about what she does for our . . . er . . . Company?"

Brosnan said, "I understand she works for your company and that it deals in exports, but I don't know what she does. She told me she's a secretary and that she travels with you."

Piccard nodded. "She couldn't tell you much. Perhaps you can guess that our export business is very small and only a cover. Now that the Allies have occupied all of North Africa, we are going out of business."

Brosnan said, "I'm beginning to see the light. This isn't an exporting business. It has something to do with the French government."

"Ah, yes, it does, but we did a little of the exporting for cover. Not many things, you understand, but lots of intelligence. But we aren't needed here any more. So we are moving to London. That's where Annette has gone. She has joined the group there. I don't have to tell you that there will soon be need for intelligence from France."

"Is Annette an expert in intelligence?"

"No. Not before the war. When the war started she was married to a rich Frenchman who lived on a large estate near Tours. The vineyards he owned were extensive. When the Germans invaded France, he sent Annette to England and stayed on the estate. He was part of the underground until the Germans killed him. Annette thought working for us was the best way she had to avenge him. She has been very good."

"From what you said about her large estate, I take it Annette is rather wealthy?"

Piccard shrugged. "Maybe not in terms of money. Who is any more? But she has what's left of a magnificent chateau, and a large amount of land, including many hectares of vineyards. I don't think the Germans can destroy it all. No, she is not rich now, but she will be when the war is over."

Brosnan shook his head. "I'm afraid she was just putting me on."

Piccard frowned. "What is this 'putting me on?'"

Brosnan shrugged. "I mean she didn't really like me."

Piccard smiled. *Au contraire, Monsieur* Brosnan, she likes you very much."

"Do you think I should try to see her again?"

"She would be disappointed if you didn't make every effort to do so. I think you are a very lucky man."

Piccard reached in a drawer and brought out a memo pad. He wrote several words on it, tore off the sheet, and handed it to Brosnan. Here is a telephone number in London. Please memorize it and then destroy it. The person who will answer will put you in touch with Annette. She will be very unhappy if you do not try to find her.''

Brosnan brightened and stood up, ''*Merci, Monsieur* Piccard. I will do it.''

Piccard walked out with him and shook hands at the door. ''Oh, *Monsieur* Brosnan, if I were you, I'd start studying the French language and French wine-making seriously. Your French is worse than my English.''

Brosnan walked in a personal fog all the way back to the harbor, up the brow to the tender, and across to the *Lawrence*. As he was walking aft on the forecastle, a familiar and unpleasant voice pierced the fog. ''Brosnan, where the hell have you been and why didn't you ask my permission to go ashore?''

Brosnan looked up. Cooper stood in front of him, his face a mask of unpleasantness. ''Brosnan, I asked where you've been. I've been looking all over for you.''

Brosnan took a deep breath and tried to control his temper. ''Cooper, I've been ashore with the permission of the executive officer. Any objections?''

''Damn right. You seem to forget that the communications officer of a flagship is ex officio a member of the squadron commander's staff, and as such works for me as his chief of staff.''

Brosnan sighed. ''Cooper, you're full of it. I may work for the commodore, but I don't think that means I have to get permission from you to go ashore.''

Cooper's face clouded. ''Well, we'll see about that. The Commodore might even be persuaded to dispense with you altogether. You'd make a fine commanding officer of one of those old slow LSTs.

''Cooper, you can't even get that right. They're not old, they're right out of the shipyards. And if the alternative is putting up with your crap all the time, I might prefer the change.''

"I hope you're not thinking of going ashore any time soon. If you are I'll stop you.''

Brosnan shook his head disgustedly. "As a matter of fact, I'll probably be staying aboard for the rest of our time in Oran.''

"Good. You're due for bridge with the commodore at 1900.''

Up on the signal bridge, overlooking the forecastle, Barley and Acton leaned on the bridge rail and watched Brosnan and Cooper below. Most of the conversation was loud enough for the eavesdroppers to hear the essentials.

Acton turned to Barley. "Jesus, did you hear that? They're really getting into it.''

Barley shook his head and rubbed his thin nostrils. "Nah, you ain't heard nothing yet. Wait until Mister Brosnan lets him have a full salvo. There wasn't a single cuss word used.''

Acton was obviously disturbed. "Well, that's just the way them officers talk. What I could hear was pretty warm. Do you think we'll lose Mister Brosnan?''

"Not unless he falls over the side some night. He likes destroyers too much. He'll even put up with that bastard Cooper if he has to.''

There was a clearing of a throat behind the two signal-men. A familiar and unpleasant voice said, "I heard that. I ought to tell Mister Cooper what you said.''

Barley turned around, looked at Chief Martin, and shrugged. "Life on an LST wouldn't be too bad if Mister Brosnan was the skipper. Go ahead.''

Chief Martin sneered. "Not on your life. You're not getting off that easy. I've got lots of surprises planned for both of you guys. And Acton, this isn't some Southern

California beach. Put your surfboard away, stop working on your tan, put your cap on, and get to work.''

Acton whistled softly as Martin stalked off. ''You were pretty close to the edge then.''

''Nah. The old briar patch ploy worked just fine. He knows I'm the best signalman in destroyers. If I left, he might have to go to work.''

Brosnan went down to the executive officer's stateroom to report his return. Fannon looked up in surprise. ''What the hell happened, Beetle? Trouble in paradise?''

''Not exactly, sir.'' Brosnan told Fannon what had happened at the French Export Office.

Fannon pursed his lips when Brosnan had finished and sat back in his swivel chair. ''Sounds interesting, but I don't think you should say anything about what you learned to anybody else. I don't think it would hurt, since intelligence operations are all over down here, but you might get in trouble anyway. These spooks are funny.''

Brosnan nodded. ''I don't intend to say anything, sir, but I thought you should know. There's something else I'd like to talk about if you have a few minutes.''

''Shoot.''

''I've had about all I can take of Adrian Cooper. He seems to think he owns me.''

Fannon laughed. ''Well, he does, sort of. I don't think you realize how patient the commodore has been. He listens to Cooper's complaints about you, nods wisely, and says he'll take it up with me.''

''Does he?''

''Sure, but he says he does it just to warn me that it's going on. He doesn't want me to do anything about it. But he may have to take action if you get too bad. My advice is to cool it a little.''

''I guess I can, but if he gets much worse I'd like to be able to request a transfer.''

Fannon laughed. "I know all about that LST Cooper keeps threatening you with. As a matter of fact, you'd make a good skipper of one."

Brosnan blanched. "Oh, no!"

Fannon said, tongue in cheek, "Why not? You'd be your own boss."

"At nine knots? I couldn't stand it after a destroyer. All I've ever wanted is to get to be the executive officer and then the commanding officer of a destroyer." Brosnan paused and looked around the stateroom. "Just like this one."

"Then you'll have to be patient."

Brosnan scratched his head thoughtfully. "I'll give it a try."

"That's a wise decision. You can start tonight after dinner. We're scheduled to be partners in the commodore's bridge game."

Brosnan said, "Thank you, sir, I knew about that, and I've already told Cooper I'm staying aboard the rest of the time in Oran."

"Good. Take some day's duties for your shipmates. That way you'll be free to go on leave for a couple of weeks when we get to Portsmouth."

Brosnan broke into a huge smile. "Portsmouth? Do you really mean that?"

Fannon laughed. "Certainly, but not before we do a little chore in Palermo."

That night in the commodore's cabin, Brosnan sat down opposite Fannon at the bridge table. The commodore looked at him slyly and said, "Brosnan, you and Cooper have been getting along so well lately that I think you should be partners tonight. Move over to that other chair."

Cooper, already shuffling the cards, lost his grip on the deck and the cards spurted out on the table.

Phelps looked at him with a straight face. "What's the matter, Adrian, did I touch a nerve?"

Cooper labored to produce a smile. "Oh, no, sir. We'll do fine."

Brosnan looked at Fannon and silently mouthed the words, "Ass-kisser."

Fannon frowned, and looked at the commodore, who was busily setting up the score pad. Phelps said, "Did you say something, Brosnan?"

Brosnan paled. "Oh, no, sir. I think we'll have a close game."

CHAPTER FIFTEEN

On the seventeenth of July the commodore was summoned to the flagship. Upon his return he told the captain that the squadron would get under way at dawn on the twentieth and proceed at high speed to Palermo. Sperry passed the word to the officers to complete all replenishment by the twentieth, and the officers and men bustled about on important last minute errands. Brosnan cast a few mournful glances toward the hill where Annette's apartment had been, but most of the time Cooper kept him busy correcting the commodore's confidential publications and doing menial tasks. Brosnan didn't object; it kept his mind off Annette, and he hoped it lulled Cooper into a false sense of security. Brosnan vowed to strike when he was ready.

On the morning of the twentieth, as the formation cleared Oran Harbor, Bronski and Swenson sat in mount fifty-one, idly looking out the mount door at the men on the forecastle who were securing the anchor for sea. They were waiting for the setting of condition III, and knew mount fifty-one had the first watch.

150/

Suddenly Swenson laughed. "Look at Ensign Raymond. If he hadn't been warned by the chief boatswain's mate, he'd a come a cropper then. Almost fell over the chain."

"Don't be so sure," Bronski said. "He may not know much about seamanship yet, but he's pretty light on his feet. I saw him and Lieutenant Kuberski over in a night club last night."

"Good dancer?"

"Yeah, but the gun boss was terrible. I think he's just learning."

"Didja have a good time last night?"

"Naw. I ain't seen a good looking Arab girl yet. All the Frenchies have gone back to France."

Swenson yawned. "I'm glad I didn't go over to the beach. Reveille was too early this morning."

Bronski looked inquiringly at Swenson. "You don't go over to the beach much. Ain't you got any girl friends?"

Swenson shrugged. "Not many. Never did have."

"How about back home?"

"Never had a home. I was raised in a Catholic orphanage in Minnesota by nuns. When I finished high school, I joined the navy. I guess you're the best friend I've got."

Bronski laughed, his square face radiating strength. "If I'm the best friend you've got, you're in trouble. But if you need company on your next liberty, I'll go along."

"I'd like that."

Bronski rubbed his tough beard. "You may have to bring me back to the ship. I get kinda wild sometimes."

"You didn't have any friends back in Detroit either?"

"Hell, yes, too many. I had to join the navy to get away from them. Otherwise, I'da been doin' time."

Over the loud speaker came the message, "Secure ship for high speed. Condition III will be set in ten minutes."

Swenson brightened. "Good. I always did like to steam at high speed. It's something only destroyers can do."

Bronski nodded. "Yeah, that and roll around and get you seasick. But I like it in good weather, too. I think we must be needed up at Sicily again. Maybe Old Montgomery ran into Patton and they're fighting each other."

The boatswain's pipe sounded again, and the word came out of the loud speakers. "Set Condition III."

Bronski and Swenson got up and headed for their positions in the mount. "Here we go again," Bronski said, as he climbed up to his position in the top of the mount.

The deck of the mount began to vibrate as the *Lawrence* picked up speed.

In the wardroom, Fannon, Kuberski, and a few others were trying to finish a quick breakfast before the watch was set. When the word was passed, Kuberski reluctantly pushed back his chair, got up, and stuffed two pieces of toast and an orange in his pocket.

Doctor Taylor eyed the disappearing food. "Do you have a friend somewhere, Ski?"

"No. Gotta go. Got the first watch. Don't want to get too weak to get to the bridge."

"I hear you were pretty strong on the local dance floor last night."

Kuberski laughed. "Yeah, I've got to learn more about the rules of the road on the dance floor. I really clobbered some Frog broad last night. Thought I'd have to fight a duel."

"You didn't have to?"

"No. Tubby Raymond got me out of it. He's a helluva good diplomat. Before we left the joint, the Frog broad was trying to teach me the tango."

Taylor grinned and turned to Fannon. "Ski is making real progress. Now if Tubby can teach him how to bow and Beetle can teach him how to play bridge, he'll be almost civilized."

"Maybe. But it takes more than that to make a gentleman, although I think at heart Kuberski is one. You might help by calling him by his first name, instead of Ski."

152/

Taylor almost choked. "Stanley? If I called him that he'd kill me!"

Fannon got up to leave for the bridge. "He doesn't say anything to me when I call him that. Maybe he just has to get used to it."

On the bridge, Brosnan had the deck for getting underway. He watched the flag hoist calling for twenty-five knots flutter up to the yardarm under Chief Martin's critical eye. When the commodore ordered it executed, Sperry turned to Brosnan and nodded.

Brosnan acknowledged the captain's order and turned to the man on the engine order telegraph. "All ahead flank. Turns for twenty-five knots."

The breeze from the ship's movement was pleasant and moderated what might later turn put to be a hot summer day. The Mediterranean was a deep blue, and the sun, still low in the east, sparkled on the tops of the small waves.

Brosnan thought about the heavy weather on their way to Sicily for the invasion. He hoped they would have good weather all the way to Palermo, some seventeen hundred miles away.

He walked over to the chart desk and looked over the shoulder of the chief quartermaster, Jack Benson. "What's our estimated time of arrival, Chief?"

Benson pointed to some figures on the chart. "Our ETA's about 1200 on the twenty-first. By the way, Mister Brosnan, the executive officer says I'm to check you out on a day's work in navigation. When's a good time for you?"

"Why does he want to do that?"

Benson shrugged. "Search me. You know executive officers better than I do."

Brosnan frowned. "I think I'll wait to do it on our trip back to Portsmouth."

"Okay with me, but the horizons in the Med are nice and sharp. The Bay of Biscay can be a bastard."

Chief Brill was sitting in the chief petty officer's mess playing acey-deucey with Chief Marusak. Brill's mind was so quick that he often got bored waiting for Marusak to move. He watched a cockroach march across the deck, and when it got close enough, he stepped on it. Still Marusak studied the board, clicking the counters in his hand.

Brill thought about the pleasant evenings when he had been alone in his office with the door locked and his feet up on his desk. The Scotch in his evening coffee had been wonderful, but the bottle was almost empty. Martin had begun to make a habit of sharing the bottle. Soon his evening hour of pleasure was going to disappear down Martin's throat.

Brill sighed. "As long as we're not doing much, how about some help with a social problem?"

Marusak put down his markers. "Sure. I think you got me here. I give up. What do you want to know?"

"What do you do when you're sitting in a bar with a full bottle in front of you, you want to be alone, and some moocher comes along and sits down?"

"I guess you have to offer him a drink."

"Sure. Then another and another, and the bottle runs dry. What else can you do?"

"Well, you can give him the old Shanghai shuffle. Frenchy Bennaret, who used to be in the Asiatic Fleet, told me about it."

Brill looked across the board eagerly. "Tell me about it."

"Well, when you go in the bar, you buy a full bottle of booze and ask the bartender to give you an empty bottle."

Brill looked bewildered. "So?"

"You sit down, make yourself a drink, pour an inch or so in the empty bottle, leave it on the table, and put the nearly full bottle under the table."

"And when the moocher comes along?"

"Ask him to sit down and offer him a drink from the last of the booze in the bottle on the table."

"So he takes it."

"Sure, and he feels so bad about taking your last drink, that he orders a round for you."

Brill looked puzzled. "And after six of these moochers come along, you've given away six drinks and gotten six drinks for free. Is that good?"

"Sure. You haven't lost anything, and you've created a lot of good will. You can mooch something back later."

Brill shook his head. "And that's the Shanghai Shuffle?"

Marusak nodded. "According to that master moocher, Frenchy Bennaret."

Brill pushed his chair back. "Thanks for the advice and the game. I've got to go to work."

In the early afternoon of the next day, Destroyer Squadron Thirty-two rounded Cape Gallo and began its approach to Salerno Harbor. Other American destroyers were visible off the entrance, and the signal bridge soon identified them as Destroyer Squadron Eight.

Orders came to Phelps to have his ships patrol off the entrance in case Italian surface ships should approach. Phelps had Cooper set up a patrol about ten miles north of the harbor with a ship in each station. When they were in position, Phelps sat down in his bridge chair and began to read through the morning's dispatches. When he was halfway through, he exploded with laughter. "Listen to this, Jack, the Brits will love this. It's just their style."

Sperry came over to the commodore's chair and began to read over his shoulder. "Oh, you mean the Americans did something that would please the Brits?"

"Right. Listen to this. It happened at Port Empedocle, around the corner in southwest Sicily. It seems that a good-sized force composed of the monitor *Abercrombie*, our British friend from Gela, and the American light cruisers *Savannah*, *Philadelphia*, and *Birmingham*, and several destroyers, had been pounding Port Empedocle for several days. On the sixteenth Admiral Davidson thought they had had enough ashore so he had the *Philadelphia* launch two SOC scout planes. One carried his chief of staff, Captain Davis. As soon as they landed in the harbor, both flew white flags. Then they taxied into a jetty hoping to induce the local government to surrender."

The commodore exploded again. When he could stop laughing, Sperry said, "What then? They surrendered?"

Phelps wiped his eyes. "No. The chief of staff was met by some American army rangers, who had entered the city several hours before and had taken over the city all by themselves. The rangers gave the captain a big welcome and said they had two problems: they couldn't take care of all their Italian prisoners, and they didn't have much to eat."

"What happened then?"

"The chief of staff said they'd have to take care of the prisoners themselves, and he flew back in the SOC to the *Philadelphia*."

"What about the food?"

"Oh, the *Philadelphia* sent in two whaleboats loaded with food. Two days later Port Empedocle was being used to land shiploads of supplies with Italian labor."

"Anything else in those dispatches? I haven't had time to read them yet."

Phelps said. "I'm only halfway through."

Brosnan, standing near, said, "Sir, I read them last night. The big news is that General Montgomery is stalled south of the Catania Plain around Mount Etna. He won't use British naval gunfire along the coast or go via routes where he can use his armor. General Patton is mad as hell at him and says the American army will reach the Straits of Messina first. He has told General Truscott to take Palermo by tomorrow. Truscott's army has Palermo surrounded and will enter tomorrow, the twenty-third.''

Phelps nodded. ''I guess we're just in time.''

Brosnan said, ''Yes, sir. Some of the other ships left southern Sicily last night for some much needed upkeep. The ships around here will be doing most of the work for the movement east along the coast of Sicily toward Messina.''

''Then we'd better get a good night's sleep. The Italian Navy is going to be here soon.''

The next morning Phelps moved his ships in closer to the port of Palermo. ''We've got to see this,'' he said. When the patrol had been established two miles off the harbor entrance, Phelps swept the harbor with the big signal bridge telescope. Sperry stood next to him using his binoculars. The commodore gave a running commentary of what he was seeing through the twenty-power lens. ''It must have been a beautiful harbor. Now most of it is in ruins, although I can see a few undamaged buildings.''

Sperry said, ''The area back of the harbor is still beautiful. Mostly dark green orange groves, I think. What is that big church-like structure?''

Phelps swung his telescope to the building. ''That's the Cathedral of Monreale. It's very old. All the buildings in the city date back for centuries. This port has changed hands a hundred times over the years. Now Americans are about to occupy it for the first time.''

''Can you see any troops moving about?''

Phelps swept the port area carefully and then said, ''Don't even see any Italian troops. I think they've all left.''

Brosnan came to the bridge clutching some dispatches. "Commodore, I think you'll be interested in these."

Phelps took one of the dispatches, read it, and laughed. "This is from General Patton and it tells General Truscott not to occupy the town until he, Patton, gets there."

Brosnan handed the commodore a second dispatch. "This is the answer from General Truscott."

Phelps read it and shook his head. "History won't wait sometimes," he said. "General Truscott says he's waiting on the outskirts of the town, but the people of the town are coming out to his troops and surrendering anyway."

All that day the commodore watched the movement of people ashore, and in the late afternoon he shouted. "Here he comes. This looks like a circus."

Sperry, also watching, said, "That figure standing in the jeep must be General Patton."

Phelps nodded without taking his eye off of the telescope eyepiece. "It sure in hell isn't General Truscott. Patton would fire him."

"When do you think we can enter the harbor?"

Phelps shrugged. "A group of PT boats will enter the harbor at dawn tomorrow. I'll request permission to go inside in a couple of days to fuel."

For the next two days the ships of Destroyer Squadron Thirty-two patrolled off the entrance to Palermo. On the third day a tanker arrived, entered the harbor, and anchored. Phelps requested permission from the senior destroyer squadron commander to send his ships, one at a time, into the harbor to fuel. When permission was granted, he ordered the *Lawrence* in. The captain conned the ship in carefully, avoiding several sunken hulks in the harbor. When the ship was secured, Phelps and Sperry looked around. The commodore said, "There must be a thousand Italian workmen clearing wreckage over there."

"They've got a lot of the debris cleaned up and many of the pier berths are cleared."

"Yes. The plans called for using Palermo for a major staging point for the push east."

About fifteen minutes after the pumping had started, the executive officer came to the bridge and said to the captain, "Sir, the tanker had a draft of one officer and two men for us. When would you like to meet them?"

Sperry scratched his jaw. "Let's wait until we're back on patrol. Where did they come from?"

"From a four-stack destroyer named the *O'Leary*. She's from the Asiatic Fleet."

"Didn't you do a tour out there?"

"Yes, sir, just before the war started. I remember the *O'Leary* well. She had quite a time escaping from the Japanese down to Java."

The ship had stayed at condition III even while alongside the tanker. Just as the fuel hoses were being returned, CIC reported several planes were approaching the *Lawrence* from the east.

Sperry yelled, "Bear a hand with those lines. Standby to get underway in an emergency!"

On deck the crew took the lines in as fast as they could. When Fannon reported all lines were in, Sperry ordered, "All back full! Sound general quarters!"

Water boiled up between the two ships and pushed the stern away from the tanker. As soon as the *Lawrence* was clear of the tanker, Sperry ordered, "Port ahead full! Right full rudder!"

The ship shuddered and slowed, but began to twist rapidly. As soon as Sperry was satisfied that she was headed out on a safe course between the wrecked ships, he ordered, "All ahead flank!"

A gigantic boil of white water built up astern as the ship gathered way, and in minutes she was up to twenty-five knots and outside the harbor.

"Keep going," Phelps shouted over the wind blowing across the bridge. "Martin, hoist a signal to our other two ships to maneuver independently."

Chief Martin shouted out the flags for the hoist, and on the signal bridge there was a flurry of activity as the appropriate flags fluttered out of the flag bag and up to the yardarm, the halyard blocks squealing in protest as Acton and Barley put all their weight on the down hauls.

By now the ship was at general quarters, and Kuberski had the five-inch battery trained in the direction of the approaching aircraft. CIC reported, "The raid is separating. Most are headed for the harbor. A small raid is headed for us, and another small raid is headed for a group of ships approaching the harbor from the east."

Kuberski reported, "We're locked on the raid approaching us. Request permission to open fire when they're in range." Chief Brill relayed the message and waited expectantly for an answer.

Sperry hesitated and looked at the commodore. "They might be friendly."

Phelps shook his head. "There hasn't been a friendly aircraft around here for days. I think the pilots are all polishing their brightwork in an officer's club somewhere. Shoot the bastards."

Sperry grinned and turned to Chief Brill. "Permission granted to open fire."

Sperry watched the guns as they slowly followed the unseen aircraft, their hydraulic motors muttering and groaning. Then a lookout shouted, "Four aircraft bearing zero two zero relative. Altitude ten thousand. Position angle two zero."

Sperry said, "They won't bother us up that high."

Phelps looked at them through his binoculars and said, "They look like Stukas. If they are, they're dive bombers, and they'll try to get up in the sun and then dive."

Sperry turned to Chief Brill. "Ask the gunnery officer if he can identify the targets."

Back came the answer: "They're Stukas, and Mister Kuberski says he's ready for them."

Sperry turned the ship so that it was headed into the sun, and watched the circling Stukas take position high overhead. In minutes the first aircraft began its dive, and the others followed in a loose column. The five-inch battery began to fire, and Kuberski went to continuous fire, each gun firing as it was loaded. The loud crashes of the guns became an almost continuous explosion. Sperry strained his eyes trying to follow the dive of the oncoming aircraft through the powder smoke blowing across the bridge and the jarring concussions of the guns. When he thought they had reached a position where they had to commit themselves to dropping their bombs, he yelled, "Right full rudder!"

The helmsman shouted back, "Right full rudder, sir," and the wheel became a blur of shining spokes as he twisted it with all his strength. The ship swung rapidly, the sudden heel throwing those on the bridge off balance, but now Sperry could see a little more clearly in the bright sun. He saw a burst blow the wing off the leading Stuka. The others flew through the debris and bored on. Then smoke poured from the engine of the second, and it tried to pull up. The smoke became flame, and it spiraled downward out of control.

Sperry could see two more Stukas still coming, but the fate of their comrades apparently induced them to drop their bombs early. The bombs bore down, and for a moment Sperry thought he had miscalculated. As he opened and closed his fingers, trying to will the bombs to miss, they slowly passed over the ship and plunged into the blue ocean at the position the *Lawrence* would have been in if she had not changed course. The bombers pulled up as fast as they could, but now they were in range of the machine guns, and they opened up with a staccato roar. One Stuka burst into flames and crashed into the water, sending up a geyser of white water. The other fled low over the water, trailing a thin wisp of smoke.

Sperry ordered, almost with regret, "Cease firing!" His palms were wet from apprehension, and he remembered how his hands had shaken when the Stukas had started down. Now he was almost exultant, and he hoped more aircraft would come at them. He shook his head angrily. If only he could get over his initial reaction to stress. Then he shrugged. What the hell, he thought. The payoff was on what you did when the situation got hot, not at the start. He grinned and turned to see what the other ships had done. Phelps was doing the same thing. Phelps said, "You seem to draw Germans like flies. The other two ships weren't even attacked."

Sperry nodded happily and turned to a grinning Chief Brill. "Tell Mister Kuberski congratulations."

Phelps said, "And add mine. That was magnificent, and a helluva good maneuver, too, Captain." He turned to Chief Martin, who was looking in the bridge door. "Hoist the signal to resume station."

CHAPTER SIXTEEN

The next morning, as the *Lawrence* cut lazy circles in her patrol station off Palermo, Brosnan brought the night's radio traffic up to Captain Sperry on the bridge. Sperry had just finished an early morning breakfast of his favorite shirred eggs and grits and was feeling good, remembering their triumph over the attacking German Stukas the day before.

Brosnan said, "Captain, I've got the night's traffic. Would you like to go over it now?"

"Sure, Brosnan, let's see what the score is now."

Brosnan grinned. "First, we've been given credit for three German aircraft destroyed yesterday."

Sperry nodded. "I'll bet the fourth never got home, but I guess nobody saw it go down. What damage did the other aircraft do?"

"The other small flight sank the *Mayrant*. She had just gotten there yesterday."

"Jesus! Short cruise. I'm sorry. I knew her skipper. Was he saved?"

"Don't know yet. The larger part of the flight attacked ships and shore facilities in Palermo. They did some damage ashore, but most of it was repairable. Those poor Italians have gotten it from both sides. First we bombed them, and now the Germans are doing it, too. One minesweeper was destroyed."

Sperry beat his fist on the arm of his chair. "Damn! Where was our air force?"

Brosnan shrugged. "I don't think they'll ever show up unless General Eisenhower gets madder at them. He says there'll be some fighters there tomorrow, or the Air Force will be disbanded."

"Anything else?"

"Intelligence predicts Italian boat attacks the next few nights, and maybe a raid by Italian cruisers on Palermo."

"I guess we'll bear the brunt of that."

"Help is on the way. A group called Task Force 88 has been formed to take care of all the naval tasks along the coast of northern Sicily."

"Good. When do they get here?"

Brosnan laughed. "They're here now. They're us. Headed by Admiral Davidson."

"What! You mean the cruisers *Philadelphia, Savannah,* and the two destroyer squadrons here? That's it?"

"Well, we could do worse. Those light cruisers can really pump shells out of their fifteen six-inch guns, and the destroyers are all experienced, even the *Hanly* over there."

"Anything else?"

"Not from me. The executive officer wants to bring our new ensign up to see you."

"Good. When you go below tell him to come up at his convenience."

An hour later the executive officer came to the bridge followed by an ensign in new khakis and shining shoulder boards.

"Captain, this is Ensign Aronson. He just reported aboard. He came to us on the tanker together with two petty officers. I'll bring them to you later. This is his first commissioned duty, and he's fresh from gunnery school."

The new officer saluted and said, ''Sir, I'm glad to meet you and to be aboard. This ship has a fine reputation.''

Sperry grinned. ''Well, you started off right. Tell me a little about yourself.''

''I went to high school in San Diego and then to the University of California. In my freshman year the war started. I was a seaman in the naval reserve, so I asked to be called up right away.''

Sperry interrupted him. ''Why the hell did you do that? You could have finished college and then been commissioned.''

''Yes, sir, I guess that would have happened, but I wanted to fight the war right away. I was sent to fire control school as soon as I got out of boot camp. Then to a five-inch gunned destroyer. She was sunk soon, and I was sent to a 4-inch gun ship when I'd been to all those five-inch schools. I guess the Bureau of Personnel finally figured out their mistake because I got orders to leave the *O'Leary* and go to advanced fire control school. While I was there, I was commissioned ensign and for some reason sent to sonar school. When I finished that, I was sent here.''

Sperry looked at Fannon. ''My God! What can we do with him to use all his qualifications?''

Fannon looked at Aronson, noting his upright posture, young face, and intelligent expression. ''I think we should ask him what he wants to do.''

Sperry nodded. ''Good idea. Aronson, I can put you in the lineup as assistant gunnery officer in charge of the machine gun batteries or I can make you sonar officer. Which appeals to you?''

Aronson thought for a moment, obviously pulled two ways. Then he said, ''Sir, I've always wanted to be the gunnery officer of a ship like this, but I understand Lieutenant Kuberski and Ensign Raymond are very good and it might be a long time before I could get anywhere in the gunnery department. Could I be the sonar officer and still keep my hand in with the gunnery department?''

Sperry beamed. "Damned right! You're now the sonar officer. We haven't had one since Ensign Anderson was sent over to the *Grayston*. The first class sonarman has been doing a good job, but he needs help." Sperry turned to the Fannon. "In the meantime, Pete, tell Kuberski to give him a watch in the director."

Sperry turned back to Aronson. "How was your tour on the *O'Leary*?"

Aronson seemed to shiver. "Cold. We spent a lot of time chasing submarine wolfpacks in the North Atlantic. I haven't been warm since. Other than that, the officers and crew were great. I hated to leave them."

Fannon grinned. "Were there a lot of Asiatic Fleet sailors left aboard?"

Aronson laughed knowingly. "A few, and they were really something. The chief engineer had been there for years, except when he was ashore . . . ah . . . exploring. But he was a fine man. I miss him."

An hour later the commodore came to the bridge, stretching and yawning. Sperry grinned. "You had a good night?"

"Yes, I always sleep well after we've knocked off a few Nazis. I see by the dispatches we're now part of Task Force 88."

Sperry laughed. "For what that gets us."

"Don't knock it. For one thing it gets us a fine task force commander. Admiral Davidson won't take anything off anybody. Not even General Patton, for whom our task force will be working."

"What do you think we'll be doing?"

"By the instructions in the operation order, we're supposed to defend Palermo, give gunfire support to the Seventh Army as it advances along the coast of Sicily toward Messina, and guard the amphibious forces as they ferry

heavy army equipment along the coast and make amphibious landings behind the enemy lines.''

"Sounds like a large order.''

"Not too bad, but what has me worried is the intelligence dispatch about the Italian navy. We may have some
business any night.''

Brosnan had the watch that evening, and the night was
very dark before the moon came up. Barley, prowling
the signal bridge, brought him a cup of coffee. "Mister
Brosnan, do you think we're in for it tonight?''

Brosnan nodded in the dark, and then realized Barley
couldn't see him. "Yes, if I were to guess about it, I'd
say we'll see Italian E boats before the moon comes up at
2300. They won't hang around much after that.''

There was anxiety in Barley's voice. "I don't like those
bastards. I'll have my signalmen keep a sharp lookout in
case the lookouts and radar miss them.''

At 2000 the *Plunkett*, a destroyer on patrol to the east,
reported that she had picked up four unidentified surface
targets approaching at high speed. Brosnan immediately
called the commodore and captain, sounded the general
alarm, and headed for the contacts at high speed. He
listened as the crew rushed to their stations.

Barley strained his eyes trying to see the contacts, but
they were too far away to see even their white wakes.
Then the *Gleaves*, next to the *Plunkett*, illuminated the
E boats with her searchlight and opened fire. The *Lawrence*, now within range, opened fire, and Brosnan could
see tracers arcing toward the speeding boats. One caught
fire from the *Lawrence*'s projectiles, exploded, and disappeared in a column of fire and smoke. The *Gleaves* got a
second boat. The others continued toward the onrushing
destroyers for a few minutes and then turned and fled.

Sperry, now on the bridge, laughed. "It didn't take long for the crews of those boats to convince their skippers to bug out. Let's go back to station."

Brosnan reluctantly turned the ship and slowed, and the *Lawrence* went back to her boring patrol.

The next morning, about 0900, the radar reported a large formation of aircraft approaching. Kuberski, who had the deck, sounded general quarters, and left for the director as soon as Brosnan arrived to relieve him. "Gotta new boy up there with me this morning. I'm gonna break him in right."

The formation came in at high altitude. Phelps, again watching the approaching aircraft, said eagerly, "More of those damned Stukas."

With ample warning, the destroyers of the screen were able to put up a solid barrage of fire, but the Stukas came down anyway, and chose the destroyer *Shubrick* as their main target. At least six bombs closed in around her as she maneuvered at high speed, and some hit. Steam and smoke rose from amidships.

Brosnan shuddered. "That might have been us yesterday, if the old man hadn't been on the ball," he said to Benson, standing beside him.

Benson nodded. "He knows what he's doing, all right."

Two Stukas broke off and headed for the *Grayston*, next to the *Lawrence*. Above, in the director, Brosnan could hear a new voice, not as loud as Kuberski's, but just as confident. Kuberski, true to his word, was breaking in Aronson. The Stukas came down intent on dropping their lethal bombs, plainly visible beneath the Swastika wings, on the *Grayston*. The *Grayston* fired back at the diving aircraft, and several projectiles burst near them. Now the *Lawrence* was also putting up a fight, and it was clearly one of the *Lawrence*'s projectiles that bagged the lead bomber. The bridge crew cheered as it burst into flame, but it kept coming, the pilot apparently dead. The *Grayston* got the second Stuka, and it exploded into small pieces. The first Stuka kept diving relentlessly. From the bridge of the *Lawrence*, it looked as if the *Grayston*'s radical maneuvers would make the first Stuka miss, but it dove into the *Grayston*'s stern.

The commodore winced. "Damn!" he said. "I hope those depth charges don't go off."

The men on the bridge of the *Lawrence* waited tensely for several minutes while they watched the men on the *Grayston* running aft. Hoses could be seen playing on the stern area. Phelps picked up the TBS transmitter and said, "Dolphin, this is Barracuda. Do you need help?"

The TBS was silent for several seconds, then a slightly shaky voice said, "Barracuda, this is Dolphin. Negative. The fire will be out soon. Two men slightly burned. All depth charges jettisoned and the depth charge rack is out of commission. After deck house riddled with shrapnel."

Brosnan could hear the commodore let out his breath. Phelps said, "A small price to pay."

Sperry called down to the CIC on the squawkbox. "CIC, any bogies on the screen?" CIC replied in the negative and Sperry gave the order to set condition III.

Just as it was reported set, CIC reported, "A large flight of friendly fighters approaching from the east."

Sperry laughed. "Maybe we ought to go to general quarters. They might attack us by mistake."

Phelps shook his head. "I don't think they're quite that bad, but I don't know why they're so late."

Brosnan said, "I know. They won't accept orders from anyone else but another Air Force type. The air defense center ashore, run by the navy, warned them of the approaching raid thirty minutes before it arrived. The air force waited until the message had been relayed clear to Malta to their headquarters and then back again. That took thirty minutes, and here they are, thirty minutes late."

Phelps shook his head. "I still think General Eisenhower will drop the bricks on them."

Sperry said quietly, "That won't do the men on the *Shubrick* and the *Grayston* any good."

As the director crew secured from general quarters, Kuberski came down to the bridge, followed by a grinning Ensign Aronson. "Captain," Kuberski boomed, "Ensign Aronson is no longer a virgin. He was running the director crew when we shot down that damned Stuka."

Aronson, standing behind Kuberski, blushed.

Sperry grinned. "Congratulations. Now see if you can get us a submarine."

General Eisenhower fixed the problem with the air force as well as he could. The next afternoon a flight of two aircraft approached Palermo. The army air force fighters arrived just in time to intercept the pair and chased the Germans off to the north. Then, as the Air Force fighters ran low on fuel and reported they were returning to base, the usual large flight of German aircraft showed up and bombed the port unopposed. The crew of the *Lawrence* watched the formation eagerly, hoping for more targets, but the Stukas had been replaced by twin engine Ju88s that did not relish tangling with the ships and stayed away from them. Still the crew knew life around Palermo would never be easy. The Italian and German air and naval bases were much too close.

CHAPTER SEVENTEEN

About midnight the next night, Lieutenant Junior Grade O'Grady, the commodore's operations officer who had the staff duty in CIC, came to the bridge to see the commodore. Phelps could not sleep, and was sitting in his bridge chair talking to Brosnan, who had the watch. "Sir," O'Grady said, "you have orders to proceed north to intercept two Italian light cruisers headed this way from Naples. They should arrive at Palermo about dawn unless we stop them."

Phelps jumped down out of his chair and headed for the chart desk. "By Jove! What the hell are three destroyers going to do to stop two light cruisers?"

O'Grady, suddenly aware of the seriousness of what he had said, was speechless.

"Well?" Phelps said.

O'Grady found his tongue. "Sir, our cruisers and the other squadron of destroyers are well down the coast rendering fire support to General Patton's troops and can't get here in time to help us. We're all that's available."

Phelps shrugged. "Well, so be it." He bent over the chart, chose a course, and said to Brosnan, "Come to course zero one zero at twenty-five knots. O'Grady, go down to CIC and tell the other two ships to fall in astern."

Brosnan gave the necessary orders and told the messenger to inform the captain, who was in his sea cabin. In seconds Sperry was out on the bridge, rubbing the sleep out of his eyes. "What's up, Brosnan?"

Phelps answered, "We've been sent to intercept two Italian cruisers headed this way." Phelps bent over the squawkbox. "CIC, give me your best estimate of when we will meet the cruisers and what intelligence we have of the area."

In a few minutes O'Grady was back on the bridge. "Commodore, I thought it would be easier to show you on the chart what we know." In the darkness, under a red flashlight, O'Grady, Brosnan, Phelps, and Sperry bent over the chart. O'Grady began, "Naples is about two hundred miles almost due north of our present position. Here's the latest reported position of the Italian cruisers. Assuming they are also making twenty-five knots, we should meet them approximately here." He penciled in a position on the chart about thirty miles north of the *Lawrence*'s present position. "Over here, about twenty miles to the west of the course line, is the small island of Ustica. Our forces captured it a few days ago. There's a small American convoy headed toward it, and we may run into it. We don't know what's in the convoy, but we should try to get to it before the Italians discover it."

Phelps studied the chart and then shook his head and said to Sperry, "All we have between the three of us is twelve five-inch guns and ten torpedoes, with yours out of commission. I think we'll do best if we form a line of bearing so that all of our ships can fire forward."

Sperry said, "That makes sense. I'm sorry we don't have any torpedoes. We carried the damned things around for months and now that we have a chance to use them they're gone."

Phelps turned to O'Grady. "Thanks for the information. Go back to CIC and send signals out by TBS to form a line of bearing to starboard, distance between ships one thousand yards. Also tell all ships we expect to meet the enemy in about an hour and that if possible we'll launch torpedoes first before we open fire with our guns. Remind the other ships that the Italian cruisers do not have surface radar, but they do have torpedoes."

Brosnan said, "Sir, they have two torpedo mounts apiece, but they'll have to change course at least twenty degrees to either side to be able to train their mounts out and fire their torpedoes."

"Thank you, I'll remember that."

Sperry turned to Brosnan. "Let's go to battle stations now. I don't want these bastards to sneak up on us."

Brosnan gave the necessary orders to the boatswain's mate of the watch, and the general alarm began to clang stridently. Brosnan could hear the pounding of feet below, and men began to stream up to the bridge to take over their positions. Brosnan went out to the open bridge wing while the new men on watch settled down. Since he would keep the deck for general quarters, he would have a few minutes to himself while the members of the watch exchanged information. He raised his binoculars and scanned the horizon. The night was so black he could see nothing except the stars and the phosphorescence of the wave tops breaking back from the *Lawrence*'s speeding bow. The other destroyers were faintly visible. There was little wind on the bridge except from the movement of the ship. It was a perfect night for anything but battle. At least they would have an advantage with their surface radar. The Italians would be blind in the darkness. They would not know whether cruisers or destroyers were speeding at them.

When the watch had settled down, Brosnan went back into the pilothouse and watched the cursor of the surface search PPI lazily circling the round face. Now he could see the Island of Ustica to the northwest, but otherwise the scope was clear. He walked around the pilothouse, checking the alertness of the men at their stations.

In a few minutes CIC reported, "Two small contacts slightly off the port bow."

Phelps looked at the PPI briefly and said, "Must be the small convoy going to Ustica."

Sperry said, "If the Italians get to the convoy before we do, the convoy won't know what hit it."

Brosnan called down to CIC, "Any more information on the convoy?"

CIC replied, "On course three zero zero. Speed five knots. Apparently heading for Ustica. One contact out in front is about the size of a sub chaser and the other is slightly larger." There was the urgent sound of voices in the background, and then CIC reported, "Two faint contacts bearing zero one zero. Forty thousand yards. We are tracking."

Sperry paced nervously up and down, waiting for an amplifying report. Brosnan looked at the PPI and said, "I think I have that contact on the PPI."

Sperry and Phelps looked over Brosnan's shoulder. Sperry said, "They're still way out there and headed almost directly for the convoy."

Then CIC reported. "The two contacts are on course one nine zero at twenty- five knots. Range thirty thousand."

Phelps looked at the chart. "The convoy is in their gun range."

Sperry said, "Yes, but they can't see it yet in the dark without radar."

Then there was a faint flash ahead, and the lookouts reported, "Gunfire ahead."

Phelps said, "I'll be damned! It must be coming from the convoy."

As the *Lawrence* got closer, the flashes and thunder of gunfire became louder, and return fire began to come from the Italian cruisers. The single rounds being fired from the convoy appeared to be no match for the salvos of the six-inch projectiles repeatedly blasting the black night with monstrous flames of orange fire.

Sperry said, "They certainly don't have flashless powder."

"My God!" Phelps exclaimed. "Our guys don't have a chance. We can't get there in time."

Then the firing ceased, and Phelps shook his head. "We'll at least be able to get a little revenge."

Brosnan lifted his head from the PPI. "Our ships are still there, at least on radar."

CIC broke in. "The enemy contacts have reversed course and are heading north."

Phelps lifted his head from the PPI. "I'll be damned. Cooper, make the signal on TBS to increase speed to thirty knots."

Cooper hesitated. "Sir, the Italian cruisers can make thirty-five knots."

"All right, increase speed to thirty-four knots. That's all we can make."

Soon they passed the small convoy abeam to port. Phelps picked up the TBS transmitter. "Unknown ship on my port beam, this is Barracuda. Say your call."

Back came the cheerful transmission, "Barracuda, this is Peabody five three zero. Welcome."

Phelps turned to Brosnan, but he was already looking up the call sign. "She's the SC 530," Brosnan said. "One three-inch gun and two machine guns."

"Jesus wept!" the commodore said. He picked up the TBS again. "Who is with you?" he asked.

Back came the answer. "A water barge."

The commodore said, "Peabody, this is Barracuda. What did you do to those cruisers?"

On the SC the radio operator apparently forgot that his key was down, and on the bridge of the *Lawrence* they could hear the conversation on the bridge of the SC. "Cruisers!" an excited voice said. "I thought they were E boats."

The shaken radio operator answered, "Barracuda, this is Peabody. We just shot at them and they turned around and ran."

Phelps shook his head. "Nobody will ever believe this."

"The Italians must have thought they were cruisers," Sperry said.

Brosnan said, "We're gaining slowly on the cruisers and they don't know we're here. Maybe we can catch them."

Sperry asked CIC for the speed of the cruisers. Back came the answer, "Speed thirty knots. Range seventeen thousand and closing slowly."

Phelps rubbed his hands with satisfaction, and Sperry put his shaking hands in his pocket. Sperry said, "We'll be in gun range soon."

Down in mount fifty-one Bronski fidgeted, waiting for something to happen. He called out to Swenson, who was at his pointer's station. "Swede, can you see anything through your scope?"

Swenson said, "Naw. Too dark. We're in automatic, so I'm just along for the ride, but the sights indicate about seventeen thousand yards to the target. The range is decreasing slowly. Should be firing in about five minutes."

Ten minutes later the order came to load the forward guns, and Bronski watched tensely as the shellman and powderman threw their loads into the breech and the rammer pushed them forward. The breech closed with a metallic clang, and Bronski reported, "Mount fifty-one loaded and ready."

On the bridge Brosnan waited tensely as the range closed. He stole a glance at the captain. Sperry still had his hands in his pockets, but in the light of the PPI Brosnan could see a fierce glare in his eyes. Brosnan smiled. Maybe the captain was like an eagle about ready to pounce on its prey. Then he had other thoughts. The enemy was a hell of a big quarry. It might turn and pounce on them instead.

As the range decreased to sixteen thousand yards, Phelps said, "Captain, you may fire your guns when ready. We're never going to get within torpedo range unless these guys turn around and head for us, and they aren't likely to do that."

Sperry nodded in the dark. "If they do, the other destroyers will still have their torpedoes." Sperry turned to Chief Brill, waiting patiently beside him. "Tell gun control to commence firing."

Above the bridge Kuberski's voice boomed out, and the salvo buzzer sounded. All those on the bridge closed their eyes to preserve their night vision as the forward guns crashed. The yellowish glare of flashless powder lit the night briefly, and then the residue floated back over the bridge. Brosnan could feel it settling on his shoulders and getting in his nostrils, and he brushed it off his uniform and tried to snort it out of his nose.

The other two ships followed the *Lawrence*'s lead, and soon four more projectiles were on their way. Two more salvos boomed out, and then Kuberski checked fire to see if a correction was needed. Brosnan could hear Kuberski above in the director talking to his radar operator, who was watching the fall of shot on his radar. "No change," Brosnan could hear the radar operator yell out, and the firing resumed.

Two small blooms of sparks followed by explosions lit the black night ahead. "Got him!" Phelps yelled. "Right in the tail!"

But the Italians were not entirely asleep. Four large orange flashes loomed ahead as the second cruiser fired her twin six-inch mounts.

Brosnan drew a deep breath as the projectiles came toward them. Four large geysers of white water rose off the starboard bow. They were much larger than the American destroyers' five-inch explosions. Barley, standing next to Brosnan on the wing, said, "Jesus! look at that! One salvo could take us out."

Brosnan tried to keep a confident voice. "Don't worry. They can only see our gun flashes. They don't have any means of finding our range."

"Well, let's hope they don't get lucky."

CIC reported, "The cruisers have speeded up to thirty-five knots."

Phelps shook his head. "That does it. We can't keep up with them. We'll keep firing for a few minutes. Maybe we'll get a lucky hit."

CIC said excitedly, "They're turning twenty degrees to port."

Sperry said, "That means they're about to fire torpedoes."

"Right you are," Phelps said. "And we're about to call it a night."

"But if we can hang on we might catch them if they get low on fuel or have a casualty."

Phelps nodded in the dark. "I've already thought of that. But we'll also be in a hell of a mess at dawn. We'll be so close to the Italian mainland that every aircraft for a hundred miles will be using us for target practice."

CIC reported, "The cruisers are steady on their new course. I think they may be firing torpedoes."

Phelps said, "That's that. Bug out time." He turned to Cooper standing at his side. "Cooper, send over the TBS, immediate execute, turn one eight."

Cooper ran inside the pilothouse, and Brosnan could hear the signal going out over the bridge speaker. Brosnan turned toward the other two ships of the division and raised his binoculars.

Cooper said, "Dammit, Brosnan, that signal was immediate execute, and you aren't doing anything."

Brosnan said calmly, "Yes, I am. I'm watching the other two ships."

"To hell with them. You're supposed to turn right now."

Brosnan continued to watch the other two ships. "Now they're turning. I can see their wake knuckles. Cooper, get the hell out of the way."

Brosnan pushed Cooper aside and yelled into the pilot-house, "Right standard rudder!"

The helmsman answered the order, and Brosnan could feel the ship heel over to port as it swung to starboard at high speed toward the *Grayston* on the beam. Cooper would not let it alone. "Brosnan, you deliberately failed to obey that order."

Phelps, standing nearby, said, "Forget it, Cooper, he was doing the right thing. He wanted to make sure the *Grayston* was turning in the right direction. If she had mistakenly turned toward us at a thousand yards and thirty-four knots, we'd have had a garden party on the quarterdeck. Use a little common sense."

Cooper turned and stalked off. Brosnan shrugged. "Sorry, Commodore, I didn't mean to upset him."

Phelps laughed. "He needs a little polishing. You were just the sandpaper he needed. Well done."

Brosnan steadied on course, and after they had passed out of possible torpedo range, the commodore slowed to twenty knots. After the run at thirty-four knots, the ship seemed to Brosnan to be crawling.

Sperry sat down in his chair. "Brosnan, set condition III. Well done." He turned to the chief quartermaster, bent over the chart desk. "Benson, what's our ETA at Palermo at this speed?"

Benson said, "1000."

"Good. We'll need some fuel and we'll have a chance to see what damage the Germans have done to Palermo."

CHAPTER EIGHTEEN

At 1000 the next morning the three ships of Destroyer Squadron Thirty-two steamed into the wreck-infested harbor of Palermo and went alongside a pier. Sperry, carefully conning the *Lawrence*, said, "The army has done a good job of putting the Italians to work. This fuel pier is working again, and a lot of the wrecks have been cleared out."

After the mooring lines were over, an army sergeant came aboard with the news that mail was arriving regularly. The mail orderly dashed over to a repaired building housing the army post office and came back with twelve bulging sacks of mail. The officers and crew lounged about talking as the mail orderly, assisted by several volunteers, sorted his haul.

On the signal bridge, Barley and Acton leaned on the bridge rail watching the action on the well deck below. Acton said, "Do you think we'll get any of that mail?"

Barley laughed. "I've never seen you write any letters to those dollies you claim you used to date in Southern California, and I know all I'll get is some complaints from my ex-wife about the alimony check not showing up."

Acton nodded. "Why don't you make her out an allotment? Then it would always get to her on time."

Barley snorted. "To hell with that. Let her work for the money just like I do. That's the way she always treated me."

Acton was listening carefully to Barley's voice. "Maybe she just couldn't stand your Yankee voice. Where was she from?"

"South Carolina."

Acton laughed. "That explains it."

Barley shrugged. "When she used to start talkin', I never got a word in. When I talked she never listened."

Acton laughed. "I can see why. You sound like a wood saw going through a piece of tin."

"All us Yanks talk like that."

"No wonder there was a war between you. None of those Rebs could stand you, and your wife musta been leadin' the pack. After listenin' to you, I don't think I'll ever get married."

Barley hesitated. "Kid, don't listen to me. There must be a lot of fine broads back there for you. I just never found any. Where's your home town?"

"Before I moved to Southern California it was Newsome, Iowa, home of the tall corn."

"Well, you seem to carry a lot of it with you. There should be a lot of farm girls waiting for you if you'd stay away from them broads on the beach."

"My high school sweetheart is still unmarried. I think I'll write to her."

The mail orderly finished sorting the last bulging bag, and the petty officer of the watch passed the word, "All division mail petty officers lay to the quarterdeck and draw mail." Acton roused himself from his reverie. "That's me. I'll be right back."

By the time he was back, all the bridge crew was gathered at the top of the ladder. "Stand back and give him room," Chief Martin boomed. The knot of sailors gave a little, but still crowded Acton. Acton began to read off names, and the happy recipients came forward. When he was through he looked at Barley. "Sorry, Barley, nothing for you or me."

Barley said, "To hell with it. This ship is my home now. I don't need no mail."

Acton frowned. "Mine, too, but I'm going below and write some letters."

"As he stepped on the top rung of the ladder, a familiar voice rang out. "Where the hell are you going, Acton? It's still turn-to time. Grab a bucket and get this deck cleaned," Chief Martin snarled.

Barley gritted his teeth and walked away. Acton reluctantly picked up a bucket.

On the small deck outside the commodore's cabin, Phelps stood with Cooper looking out at the town back of the harbor of Palermo. Phelps said, "The Italians have done a lot to put the town back together."

Cooper nodded. "But the German air attacks just seem to knock it down again every day."

"I think they're making progress. There hasn't been a raid in three days. Either they're running out of bombs or the Army Air Force is getting better."

Cooper cocked an eye toward the sky over head. Two friendly fighters were circling lazily above. "Must be the Army Air Force is getting better. At least they're here."

Lieutenant O'Grady came up to the small deck, carrying a decoded dispatch. "Sir, here we go again. As soon as we fuel, we're supposed to go east along the coast to intercept a German convoy of two MFP lighters escorted by PT boats."

"Where are the cruisers?"

"They're coming back here to fuel. Admiral Davidson seems to think we can handle these guys. The cruisers didn't give us any trouble."

Phelps snorted. "These are German forces, not Italian." He turned to Cooper. "Just what are MFPs?"

Cooper frowned. "They're real porcupines. They're called self-propelled armed motor barges, and they make about eight knots. They have a lot of heavy steel armor. Also good armament. Three seventy five-millimeter guns and six twenty-millimeter machine guns. We'll have to stay well away from them."

Phelps nodded. "I agree. Pass the word to the three skippers that we'll get underway as soon as fueling is completed."

In an hour Destroyer Squadron Thirty-two was in column, steaming at twenty-five knots east along the coast of Sicily. Phelps swept the land with his binoculars. "Looks like a desert, except for the green irrigated sections around the towns."

Sperry said, "Not much rain in the summer. Everything dries up, and the tanks and trucks raise a curtain of dust."

"Yes, I can see it along the coastal highway."

"One of the Army guys who came aboard in Palermo said the dust is a mixture of cattle and horse dung and fine sand from the roads. It chokes everybody and also the carburetors of the tanks and trucks."

Phelps pulled down his binoculars. "That's one reason why I always liked the navy. Never could stand mud, dust, snow, or a lot of dung."

Sperry looked at him inquiringly. Phelps swallowed and said, "Well, horse dung is all right in its place."

Phelps and Sperry went into the pilothouse to study the chart. Chief Benson had the approximate position of the MFP convoy plotted. "Sir, they're headed for this little port, here, near Cape Colava. We should be able to intercept them about 2200."

The commodore said, "Good. I need a nap. Jack, I'll see you up here about 2000."

Sperry went over to his chair, sat down, and pulled out a packet of letters from his wife. He read them again and again, smiling as he finished each one. He wondered if he would ever see his wife and children again, and if his young children would recognize him if they saw him. He sighed, put the letters in his pocket, and went to his sea cabin for a brief rest.

At 2000 the captain came on the bridge and told Raymond, who had the deck, to sound general quarters. As the men thundered up the ladders to the bridge, Sperry looked at the sweeping cursor of the PPI and then went over to the chart to compare the PPI picture with the chart. Benson was bending over the chart, penciling in a notation below his latest radar fix. Sperry said, "I take it that point is Cape Colava."

Benson said, "Yes, sir. We're right on track and right on time. We should pick up the convoy in the next hour."

Phelps came on the bridge and went over to the chart desk. "Jack, I've got a battle plan here. I'll read it to you. 'Battle Plan. Form ninety degree line of bearing to starboard at 2030 without signal. Battle speed twenty-five knots. Do not expect to use torpedoes. Follow flagship in opening fire at about ten thousand yards. *Hanly* assigned E boats. *Lawrence* left hand MFP. *Grayston* right hand MFP.'"

Sperry said, "It's plain and simple, just like it should be. I like it."

Phelps turned to Chief Martin, who had followed him into the pilothouse. "Chief, get this dispatch out by blinker gun right away."

Martin left, and soon Sperry could see Barley hunched over the blinker gun. He pointed it carefully at the *Grayston* and started transmitting.

Above the bridge, Sperry could hear the director slew around as Kuberski tested it, and below the five-inch mounts' hydraulic systems whined as they too were tested.

Sperry paced the wing of the bridge, hands deep in his pockets. His throat was dry and he was breathing faster than usual, but he was looking forward to the forthcoming battle. If only he could get through the first few minutes. He swallowed and thought about searching ahead with his binoculars, but decided not to because of the tremor in his hands. Instead he said to Brosnan, "Can you see anything ahead?"

Brosnan, already searching, said, "Nothing yet." Then the squawkbox sounded, and Sperry and Brosnan went into the pilothouse. CIC reported, "Surface contacts bearing zero nine five. Range twelve miles."

Brosnan looked at the PPI. "I see them, but they're very faint."

Sperry pulled down the transmitter handle to the squawkbox. "CIC, this is the captain. Do we have any friendly forces in the area?"

Back came the answer. "Negative, sir."

In a few minutes the contacts became stronger, and CIC reported, "Five ships in the formation. Three ships in a screen and two in column. The two in column are slightly larger. Range ten miles. Speed zero eight. Course two six zero."

Sperry acknowledged the transmission and turned to the commodore. "That's our target."

"Agreed. We'll open fire at ten thousand yards. A little far, but we don't need any fire from those seventy-five-millimeter guns or torpedoes from the E boats."

Sperry said, "A very good decision." He turned to the bridge talker, Chief Brill. "Tell gun control to open fire without further orders at ten thousand yards."

Brill repeated the order and then said, "Gun control reports they have a solution and both forward guns are loaded."

Sperry felt his hands steadying, and he took them out of his pockets. There was saliva in his mouth again. He was ready.

The range ground down rapidly. At ten thousand yards, Sperry could hear Kuberski bellow, "Commence firing." The salvo buzzer sounded. Sperry closed his eyes, and the familiar concussion of the five-inch guns pressed on his chest and rang in his ears. He opened his eyes and looked at the two tracers arcing ahead. The other two ships began firing. Sperry closed his eyes as a second salvo from the *Lawrence* followed the first out into the black night. The first landed, and Kuberski bellowed a corrective spot. The third salvo, bearing the correction, left the guns, and Sperry waited tensely. Kuberski kept the salvos going out. Then a dull red glow appeared ahead on the rapidly closing target, and Kuberski yelled, "Hit! No change! No change! Rapid fire."

The salvo interval decreased and a steady stream of projectiles flew toward the target, now at eight thousand yards. Fire was beginning to come back toward the on-rushing destroyers, but it was erratic.

Phelps, watching the enemy projectiles land ahead, said to Sperry, "They don't know our range, but they can aim at our gun flashes."

Sperry said, "I have a counter to that. Request permission to weave."

Phelps answered, "By all means."

Sperry took the conn from Brosnan and made a turn to port toward the last projectile explosion. When the enemy projectiles began to land in the area the *Lawrence* would have been in had she steered a straight course, Sperry turned back to starboard, and the enemy projectiles missed again, this time to port.

Sperry stole a few seconds to see how the other ships were doing. The MFP assigned as a target to the *Grayston* was burning furiously, and its fire illuminated the *Lawrence*'s target. Most of the hits from the *Lawrence* seemed to be hitting the MFP's armor. The *Hanly* had hit one PT that was stopped and burning. As Sperry watched, a second E boats exploded with a blinding flash.

Kuberski was still hammering away at the left hand MFP without visible results, although they were scoring occasional hits. Then, in one brief terrible moment, the MFP became a column of flame a thousand feet high. A dull roar rumbled over the water and rolled toward them. In a few seconds, the concussion battered the chests and ears of those standing on the open bridge.

When he recovered, Phelps said, "She must have been full of ammunition."

Now the second PT boat appeared to be sinking, and the third fled to the east at high speed. All that was left was a towering column of smoke and flame from the MFP still afloat and burning furiously.

Phelps said, "That's that. We'll run through the area and look for survivors." He turned to Cooper, "Tell the other ships to proceed independently and pick up survivors."

Cooper sent the message by TBS, and Sperry, who still had the conn, headed the *Lawrence* for the last position of the MFPs. Brosnan sent word down to mount fifty-one to secure and standby to pick up survivors. Soon Sperry could see men piling out of the mount and rigging a cargo net over the side. Bronski's stentorian voice was everywhere, and men scurried to carry out his orders. Life jackets and helmets reflected the dancing flames from the burning MFP as the *Lawrence* slowed and approached the wreckage.

There was nothing but small pieces of debris to mark where the MFP that had exploded had sunk, but several men could be seen swimming around the burning MFP. Both the *Lawrence* and the *Grayston* closed in. Sperry stopped the *Lawrence* near a small group of men in the oily water.

Down on the forecastle, the chief boatswain and Bronski put men over the side on the cargo net to assist the exhausted survivors. Soon four men in German army uniforms were sprawled on deck. One who had a sergeant's insignia on his arm insisted on standing up. He was wobbly, but still managed to stand. Sperry could see him salute the chief boatswain and talk to Bronski. Bronski turned to Swenson, still wearing the telephones, and said something. Chief Brill listened carefully and said, "The mount captain of mount fifty-one says the German NCO is speaking German and seems to be upset about something. They can't understand him."

The executive officer pulled down the squawkbox transmitter. "Send Ensign Aronson to the forecastle."

Sperry said, "What can he do?"

"According to his record he speaks German. We'll soon find out if he does."

While Ensign Aronson was on his way, Doctor Taylor and his pharmacist's mates had the survivors carried below. In a few minutes Sperry could see Aronson running up the forecastle. The chief boatswain beckoned him over to where the German NCO was now leaning weakly on the railing. The NCO talked to Aronson for a few minutes, and then Aronson led him down below.

The captain said to Chief Brill, "What was that all about?"

Chief Brill listened intently for a few seconds and then said, "Swenson on the telephones says the German NCO just wanted to be sure his men were going to be taken care of. They were all wounded."

The executive officer headed below and said over his shoulder, "I'll go to the wardroom and look into this."

Sperry raised his binoculars and searched the area. "I don't see any other survivors."

Phelps picked up the TBS transmitter and asked the other two ships if they had picked up all the survivors they could find. The *Grayston* reported ten survivors from the second MFP and none from the first. The *Hanly* reported eight survivors from the two PT boats that had been sunk. Phelps turned to Cooper. "Let's start back to Palermo. Form us up in a column at fifteen knots."

In the wardroom Fannon found Doctor Taylor and his men busily patching up the four German survivors. Fannon looked over Taylor's shoulder. "What's the score?"

Taylor said happily, "Not bad. A lot of small stuff, but some big wounds, too. Fortunately I can take care of all of them without x-rays. I haven't had this much fun since I was an intern in a trauma center."

Fannon said, "How's the NCO?"

"Oh, him. Nothing physically wrong except for swallowing some salt water."

Fannon went over to the corner of the wardroom where Aronson was giving the NCO a hot cup of coffee. The sergeant tried to struggle to his feet and salute, but Aronson said something to him, and he sat down again. Fannon sat down across from the NCO and said to Aronson, "Ask him if he knows what the two MFP were carrying."

Aronson said a few words in German, and the NCO's eyes got very wide. Fannon heard him say *"Minen."*

"Mines?" Fannon asked.

The NCO grabbed the arms of his chair and said, "*Ja! Jawohl! Minen! Viele!*"

Aronson talked to him for a few minutes. Then he turned to Fannon. "He says his MFP carried artillery pieces and the other MFP carried all the ammunition for the guns and a lot of land mines. Enough to mine the entire road system all the way to Messina."

"Jesus!" Fannon said. "We've saved hundreds of GIs."

Aronson nodded. "But at the cost of over a hundred German lives."

Fannon was sober, but he soon brightened. "They asked for it. They could have gotten rid of Hitler."

Aronson said, "By the way, the Allied news broadcast said Mussolini was deposed on the twenty-sixth. We're just now getting the news."

"Who's taking his place?"

"Some old army guy named Badoglio."

Fannon groaned.

"What's the matter?"

"He won't be any improvement. The Italians don't like him either."

"Is that why they don't fight so well?"

"I guess so. You'd think descendants of the Romans would be able to fight like they did in the old days. These guys sure don't. There's some reason, and that may be it. Tell the NCO we'll feed his men as soon as they're fixed up, and they'll be ashore in Palermo in a few days."

Aronson relayed the message, and the sergeant bristled and spewed forth a torrent of German.

Fannon laughed. "What now? Does he expect beer and sausages?"

"No. He says they don't want to be put in any prison camp with the Italians."

Fannon shrugged. "Tell him I'll relay his request to the American army."

On the bridge Phelps and Sperry settled in their chairs for what they hoped would be a peaceful return to Palermo.

O'Grady appeared on the bridge, obviously searching in the dark for the Commodore. Phelps groaned when he saw him and said, "Over here." O'Grady pulled out a red flash light and a dispatch form. Phelps said, "Just tell me what's in it."

O'Grady cleared his throat. "It's from Admiral Davidson. You're to head for the coast of Sicily near Saint Stefano. There's a large bridge there behind the town. A lot of vehicles are crossing it heading east. We're supposed to destroy it if we can or at least to deny it to the German and Italian forces using it.''

Phelps and Sperry got up and trudged over to the chart desk. Sperry yawned and said, ''Seems like we've been here before.''

Benson, listening to the conversation, had already marked the position of the bridge on the chart. ''Here it is,'' he said. ''At twenty knots we'll arrive at dawn. Course one two eight.''

Phelps said to O'Grady, ''That's it. Go down to CIC and put us on that course and speed. Draft a dispatch telling the three ships what we're going to do and when we're going to do it.''

Sperry took off his helmet and rubbed his head vigorously. ''I think we've made it a lot easier for the GIs chasing those bastards.''

Phelps looked at him. ''How so?''

''They won't have to dig out all those mines we destroyed.''

''I see your point, but tomorrow will be a hell of a day just the same.'' He looked at the clock on the bulkhead. ''And tomorrow is almost here.''

CHAPTER NINETEEN

At dawn the three ships of Destroyer Squadron Thirty-two steamed west at ten knots along the coast of Sicily, a little to the east of Saint Stefano. Phelps and Sperry, after an early breakfast, stood on the open bridge scanning the area ahead. Phelps said, "There it is! A helluva big bridge."

Sperry said, "I see it."

Sperry went into the pilothouse to check the chart. Benson said, "Here we are. All good water ahead, and I'm sure we have a good fix."

"Thanks," Sperry said. "Where's that dispatch giving the battle plan the commodore sent out last night?"

Benson shoved a flimsy dispatch form in front of the captain. "Here it is, sir."

Sperry read it again slowly in the dim light of dawn. "I see we're assigned to knock out the near end of the bridge. The *Grayston* gets to pop the vehicles on the road, and the *Hanly* rides shotgun, searching for shore batteries that might be there and might fire on us."

Benson nodded. "I'm glad the commodore thought of that. I'll feel safer."

Sperry laughed. "No one is safe in a destroyer. It's all relative. A lucky shot could blow us all up." He went back out on the wing of the bridge, and said to Chief Brill, "Ask gun control if they understand our orders."

The talker relayed the question and in a few minutes he said. "Mister Kuberski said he stopped in CIC before general quarters and looked at the bombardment chart and the battle plan. He's all squared away, and he can see the near end of the bridge now through the director optics. He says it looks like a swarm of men is working on the supports under the end of it nearest to us."

Phelps heard the report and said to Sperry, "My guess is they're mining the supports so they can blow the bridge after they no longer have use for it."

"Good," Sperry said. "We'll help them along, but before they can all get across it."

Now they were approaching their chosen firing position, and there was almost full daylight. Brosnan, also looking through his binoculars, said, "I can see a column of vehicles five miles long to the west of the bridge. The lead vehicles are about to enter the bridge."

Phelps said, "We'll collect a toll. Jack, if you're ready, commence firing."

Sperry gave the order to commence firing, and in seconds Kuberski let fly the first salvo of four guns. He waited for the projectiles to land before sending off the next salvo. Following the *Lawrence*'s lead the *Grayston* began to fire.

On the *Lawrence*'s bridge Sperry and those watching waited tensely for the first rounds to land. Then four geysers of the familiar brown dust of sand mixed with dung rose at the base of the east end of the bridge. Barley, unable to resist the urge, shouted, "Dung Ho!"

Sperry frowned, but the commodore laughed, and Sperry decided not to say anything to Barley.

In the director Kuberski shouted "No change! Rapid fire!" and the next salvo arced out. It was a little low, and Sperry could hear Kuberski making adjustments. The subsequent salvos walked up the bridge support, each shot spraying pieces of concrete and steel from the support.

Sperry said, "The guys mining that bridge sure left in a hurry. I can see them running down into the river bed."

Brosnan, who had been watching the *Grayston* fire, said, "The *Grayston* is playing hell with that column of tanks and trucks. I can see a half dozen vehicles burning, and most of the others are heading off the highway toward the orange groves. Also many men are abandoning their intact vehicles, running to the side of the road and jumping into the ditches."

Kuberski began to walk the salvos back down the main support and a salvo from the *Lawrence* landed directly at the base of the eastern bridge support. Almost immediately there was a huge explosion. Dirt and smoke rose around the end of the bridge for several hundred feet, and then the end of the bridge slowly toppled into the river bed. Up above, Sperry could hear Kuberski shout, "Got the bastard!"

Kuberski shifted fire to the few remnants of the vehicle column, but there weren't many targets left.

The *Hanly*, riding comfortably and silently on the *Grayston*'s engaged quarter, had been silent during the firing, and Phelps said, "I'm sorry she didn't get to fire."

Suddenly her guns opened up. Sperry could see splashes around her, and he searched the shore. Smoke was rising from a concrete bunker that had been nearly invisible before the guns in it began firing. More projectiles burst around the *Hanly*.

Sperry said, "She got to fire after all."

Phelps said, "Let's get the hell out of here! We've done our job."

Sperry leaned into the pilothouse. "Right full rudder! All ahead flank!"

The *Lawrence* shuddered as her propellers bit into the blue Mediterranean, pushing foam behind her, and the ship heeled from the rudder action. Above the bridge, Kuberski shifted fire to the shore battery, and the *Grayston* followed his lead. A screen of bursting projectiles surrounded the shore battery, and it stopped firing, but not before it had put a round in the *Hanly*. Smoke and steam began to billow out of her deck amidships. Both the other ships were now following the movements of the *Lawrence*, and Phelps said, "I hope to hell the *Hanly* can keep up."

Phelps paced the bridge wing impatiently, looking back at her. The flow of smoke and steam began to diminish, and in a few minutes the TBS crackled. "Barracuda, this is Lion. Took a shot in my after fire room. It has been evacuated without serious personnel casualty. Able to make twenty-five knots on two boilers."

Phelps sighed. "Thank God. I thought she would have a lot of steam burns."

He walked over to the chart desk where Sperry was watching Chief Benson plot a fix. "Give me a course for Palermo and tell me what our ETA will be at twenty knots."

Benson swung his dividers across the chart and made a quick calculation. "Initial course two seven five. ETA 1300."

Phelps turned to Sperry. "Make it so, skipper, and let the crew go to breakfast. They've done a full day's work, and it isn't even eight o'clock."

Back on the signal bridge Acton and Barley heard the word passed to set condition III and that chow was down, and both grinned and started below.

"Wait a minute!" Martin yelled. "What about all this powder debris up here?"

Barley didn't even pause. "After breakfast, Chief, unless you want to sweep down yourself."

In the wardroom Kuberski sat down at the table, rubbing his hands. "Tough day at the office, Jason. Bring on the hotcakes." Then he thought better of it. "But leave off the syrup and butter." He sighed. "No, to hell with it. I'm celebrating. Bring on the works."

Jason said, "It'll be a few minutes, sir. The cook has to warm up the grill."

Kuberski beamed. "Tell him to take his time. I'll have a bigger appetite."

Doctor Taylor, just sitting down, said, "Stanley, how do you do it? You've been on a diet for only two weeks and you've lost ten pounds."

Kuberski glowered. "What's this Stanley stuff? Only my mother calls me that."

Taylor shrugged and said patiently, "That's what the exec said to call you."

Kuberski scowled and then grinned. "If he says so, do it. I'll answer up to anything." Then he turned to Ensign Aronson, who had just come in. "Kid, if this shooting keeps up, you may never find out where the sonar is located."

Taylor said, "Why should he? We haven't run across a submarine for weeks."

Aronson laughed. "I'll find it, and I could get down to sonar in seconds if I were needed. I appreciate all you've done for me, sir. I think I could even be a gunnery officer some day."

"Don't be so modest, Aronson, you are one now. You just don't know it."

The chief engineer came in and sat down. Kuberski said, "How's it going down there, Chief?"

Kelly sighed. "If we don't get some time to clean the firesides of our boilers soon, we won't be able to steam any more."

"Why not?"

"The engineering regulations say we can't."

Kuberski guffawed. "I'd like to be around when you tell that to the captain."

Taylor said, "We're going to Palermo next. Maybe you can do it there."

The chief engineer shook his head. "Not with all those German aircraft around. We'll have to wait until we get to Oran."

Kuberski's hotcakes came and he lifted a huge forkful. "Well, that's all right with me. I'm sure your engineers don't want to wrestle with all that gunk in the boilers in Palermo."

Taylor stared pensively through his large glasses. "I don't think any of us will have much time in port. There's a lot of unfinished business back along the way toward Messina, and a lot of it will fall to us."

CHAPTER TWENTY

By 1300 the ships of Destroyer Squadron Thirty-two were in Palermo alongside the fuel pier. Chief Machinist Marusak was standing with a foot on the hatch to the forward engine room talking to Frenchy Bennaret, his former shipmate from the old Asiatic Fleet four-stacker, the *Parrot*. He looked forward toward the bow and saw the chief engineer striding aft. He took his foot off the hatch, stood up reasonably straight, and saluted. "Good morning, sir. I didn't see you down below when we came into port. Was anything wrong?"

Bennaret didn't salute because he wasn't wearing a hat, but he smiled crookedly to cover up two missing teeth and said, "Good morning, sir."

Kelly acknowledged Marusak's salute and nodded toward Bennaret. "Couldn't make it. Had a lot of paper work. These damned boilers need cleaning, and I wanted to be sure their logs were up-to-date in case anything happened to them."

Chief Marusak raised his eyebrows. "Boilers one and two are close, but we have a good many hours left on the other two."

"If we have many more hours steaming on all four boilers at high speeds we'll soon be over the limit on all of them and well over on two of them."

Bennaret shrugged. ''In the Asiatic Fleet we used to go over the hours all the time. Sometimes it was too damned hot to clean them, and we just waited until it got cooler. Nothing ever happened to any of them.''

Marusak could see the color rising in Lieutenant Kelly's neck, and he tried to divert attention from Bennaret. ''Sir, I—.''

Kelly would have none of it. ''Dammit, that Asiatic Fleet was full of rejects.''

Now Marusak began to color, and he rose to his full height of five feet six inches and his meaty hands clenched at his sides. ''Sir, The men in those ships were outstanding. When the war started they proved there were none better. While the rest of the Pacific Fleet was either caught asleep at Pearl Harbor or was steaming around trying to get away from the Japs, we went after them. Sunk a lot, too.''

Kelly began to calm down, and he took a deep breath. ''Sorry. I know you all did a lot, but I'm worried about our boilers. I know how they're designed and what can happen if some of the tubes burn up because they're too dirty.''

Marusak's ample chest muscles rippled as he tried to maintain control. ''But, sir, those boilers were also designed to take a lot of punishment.''

Kelly's brow wrinkled. ''I hear what you're saying, but I think I'll go see the captain to see if we can put two boilers out of commission today and get started.''

Marusak frowned. ''Sir, I don't think that's a very good idea. We can wait until we get to Oran. Nobody is going to question us, no matter what the regulations say. After all, you're the acting squadron material officer.''

''That's just it. I have to set a good example.''

Marusak shook his head. ''Maybe so, but I don't think the captain is going to like it.''

Kelly started for the bridge, and the two petty officers watched him go. Bennaret said, ''I'd like to be up there to see this.''

Marusak shook his head. "No, you wouldn't. It won't be pretty. The old man will clobber him."

On the bridge Sperry was reading a letter from his wife that had just been delivered. He hardly noticed Kelly standing beside him. Kelly cleared his throat. Sperry stopped reading and looked up. "Yes, Chief?"

"Sir, I'd like to put boilers one and two out of commission for two days and clean their firesides. They're overdue."

Sperry laughed. "Where have you been the last two weeks? There are a lot of targets up the line waiting for us, and the task force commander likes the speed with which we get there and the way we do whatever has to be done when we arrive."

"Sir, I don't understand."

"We've used four boilers on short notice several times, and I expect to keep on doing it for at least two weeks. You'll get time to clean them in Oran."

"But, sir, the manual says—."

Sperry shook his head. "The guy who wrote the manual isn't here and probably never saw a shot fired. We'll have to wait. Now let me get back to this mail, and I hope you got some, too."

On the quarterdeck Lieutenant Commander Fannon, assisted by Ensign Aronson and Doctor Taylor, was supervising the landing of the German prisoners. All of them except the sergeant were in stretchers. The doctor took a last look at his patients and gave last minute instructions to the of Army MPs and medical personnel who had come to pick them up. The prisoners collected by the other ships were already being brought across the *Lawrence*'s quarterdeck and loaded into waiting trucks.

Taylor straightened and looked at the departing prisoners sadly. "Here we go again. I have interesting patients for two days, and then they leave. I don't think I'm needed on this ship very much."

Fannon said, "I'd be thankful if I were you. Sometime soon you may have to do more than you'd like."

Aronson exchanged a few last minute words in German with the sergeant, and then the sergeant straightened and saluted Fannon. "*Danke shon*," he said.

Fannon grinned and returned his salute. "That bastard certainly doesn't look defeated," he said to Aronson.

"Nice guy," Aronson said. "He wants to come to the States after the war and open a garage."

By 1600 they were fueled and underway for patrol stations off the entrance to Palermo Harbor. Just after they took their stations, Lieutenant O'Grady came to the bridge, trailing the inevitable dispatch forms. Phelps was sitting in his chair, and when he saw O'Grady he groaned. "O'Grady, you always seem to bring me bad news. What now?"

O'Grady grinned. "We have to keep you in shape, sir. No sense getting too much sleep."

"I'm too tired to read those damned things," Phelps said. "What do they say?"

"The first dispatch is a long one. It sets up an amphibious operation loading army troops into two LSTs, seven LCTs, and an LCI at San Stefano Beach. After loading, they'll take a short trip up the coast and land at Santa Agata beach behind the German lines on the eighth of August. Task Force eighty-eight is to cover the operation, providing protection against submarines, E boats, and aircraft, and giving fire support as necessary."

"But not tonight?"

"No, you get to sleep tonight. The second dispatch says you are to bring your ships to join Task Force eighty-eight off San Stefano tomorrow afternoon. We'll form an antisubmarine and antiaircraft screen while the troops are loaded."

"Who else will show up? So far we've done most of the work for the task force."

O'Grady grinned. "This time the big boys will be there, the light cruisers *Savannah* and the *Philadelphia*. Also six other destroyers."

Phelps stretched and yawned, and ran his fingers through his thinning gray hair, his long face showing fatigue. "I'll be in my cabin. Call me at dawn."

Sperry, who had been listening, said to the officer of the deck, "That sounds good to me. Call me at 0400 unless you need me sooner."

At dawn the commodore issued orders to head for San Stefano, and at 1600 they were in a screen with six other destroyers arced around the beach of San Stefano.

At 1700 the amphibious ships arrived and beached on the sloping sands. Immediately long columns of Army troops came down out of the trees and began filing aboard the LCI. Others boarded the LST and the LCTs, backing their vehicles and artillery pieces up the ramps.

Brosnan, who was the officer of the deck, occasionally looked at the loading activities ashore through his binoculars as he conned the *Lawrence* around her patrol station. Suddenly he was aware of someone standing behind him. A voice said, "Does that look good to you? I can get you a command of any of those."

Brosnan grinned weakly, but kept his binoculars pointed at the beach.

Cooper said, "Just keep fouling up and coming between me and the commodore, and I'll get him to give

you an engraved invitation to join the amphibious navy."
Cooper turned away and left before Brosnan could think
of a good answer.

The loading operation continued past dark. Brosnan
could see flashlights waving around on the decks of the
ships as men directed the movement of the vehicles. At
about 2000 the landing force commander announced on
the TBS that the loading was complete and that the landing craft were retracting. Soon the slow clumsy vessels
were underway in some semblance of a formation, and
four of the destroyers screened them. Commodore
Phelps' ships and two other destroyers formed a screen
around the two cruisers seaward of the slow landing ship
formation.

At 0200 they turned south toward the beach at Santa
Agata, and at 0300 all the landing craft reported beaching.
Although the *Lawrence* was too far away to see the operation, reports of its success filtered up to the bridge from
CIC where they were listening to the landing force radio
circuit. By 0400 all troops and vehicles had gone ashore
without meeting opposition. The landing ships retracted
and proceeded west with one destroyer escorting them.

Admiral Davidson received a dispatch at midnight
warning him that two Italian cruisers were heading south
toward Palermo. For two hours Phelps fidgeted, walking
up and down the bridge wing, expecting orders to proceed north with the cruisers. At 0200 the message came
over the TBS, and Phelps' ships were ordered to form a
column on the cruisers' bow at five thousand yards to act
as an advance attack force. The *Bristol* and *Ludlow* formed
a screen in front of the cruisers, and the formation
steamed off at twenty-five knots.

Phelps said to Sperry, "I hate to have to remind the
Admiral that you don't have any torpedoes."

Sperry shrugged. "The other ships have enough. We probably won't get close enough to use them anyway."

Barley put down his signalman's telescope, hitched up his trousers, and headed for the signal bridge coffee locker. He was troubled, although in his usually simplistic world of signal flags, liberty, beer, and girls, there wasn't usually much trouble unless he was taken off the liberty list, caught a venereal disease, or came back late.

He poured a mug full of coffee, added an extra spoonful of sugar, and headed for the after corner of the signal bridge. A steady breeze threatened to blow off his hat. He put the coffee mug down on the deck, jammed his hat firmly on his head, and picked up the mug. He leaned back against the flag bag and watched Chief Martin talking to Lieutenant Commander Cooper near the forward bulwark. Martin's face was wreathed in a sycophantic smile. Barley guessed he was recounting some alleged failure of Lieutenant Brosnan or the signal bridge crew.

Barley growled and swished the coffee around in his mug angrily. "Ass-kisser," he muttered. He turned away and looked out across the advancing wave tops. There was a regularity and orderliness about them that he liked, and watching them calmed his resentfulness. He tried to put Chief Martin out of his mind, but the wind brought back to him the sound of Martin's voice, although he could not make out the words. Barley ground his teeth and swallowed the mouthful of coffee he had been swishing around in his mouth. There was pain somewhere in his mouth. At first he thought it came from his resentment of Martin, but then he knew it was an aching tooth. "Damn!" he muttered. "Now I'll have to see a dentist next time we're in port. That'll be worse than listening to that bastard Martin."

About an hour later Chief Benson came out to the wing of the bridge and stood next to the commodore, who was sniffing the wind in the moonlight, his long nose and face sagging with the effort. Benson said, "Something wrong, Commodore?"

Phelps stopped sniffing. "What was the latest humidity reading?"

"Fifty percent, sir."

"I thought so. The atmosphere smells just like London, only better."

"I've never been there," Benson said.

"You will be, in about a month."

"Do you think there's fog ahead?"

"Can't see it yet, but it's there. The air is getting heavier and heavier."

About 0300 the lookouts reported, "Fog bank ahead."

Sperry put down his early breakfast tray and walked over to the PPI. "All clear ahead on the radar," he said.

The squawkbox came alive. "Bridge this is CIC. We are hearing transmissions in German on a medium frequency circuit the Germans use for controlling aircraft."

Sperry went to the squawkbox and pressed down the transmitter handle. "Is Ensign Aronson down there?"

"Yes, sir. He's listening to the conversation."

Sperry went to his chair and sat down to finish his breakfast, but before he got to the toast the squawkbox sounded again. "Sir, this is Aronson. The aircraft just reported to the Italian cruisers that there was a fog bank ahead of them and that they thought they saw the wakes of several ships on our side of the fog bank in the moonlight before we entered the fog. The aircraft must be pretty high."

"Do you have the aircraft on radar?"

"No, sir. But our cruisers just reported that they have him. Their radar antennas are higher than ours."

"Thank you. Report the aircraft conversation to Admiral Davidson on the CIC circuit."

"Aye, aye, sir."

Phelps came to the bridge, having eaten an early break-fast below. Sperry said, ''It's all over. The Italians won't go into this fog without radar.''

Phelps shrugged. ''I wouldn't either.''

Before Sperry could finish his toast in the dark, CIC reported that the cruisers had told the German aircraft they were returning to port.

Admiral Davidson ordered a reversal of course. Phelps said, ''That's a little dangerous. Those ships in his group have never steamed at high speed in formation at night in a fog before. I think I'll do the maneuver in two steps. Cooper, send on Screen common circuit, ''Corpen Nine.''

Cooper sent the signal, and Farraday, who had the deck, ordered, ''Right standard rudder.'' The ship began to heel in the high speed turn, and Farraday steadied on the new course, ninety degrees to the right. As soon as Phelps could see the other two ships steadying astern, he said, ''Cooper, another 'Corpen Nine.' ''

The previous maneuver was duplicated, and when they were steady on a reverse course, Phelps said. ''We only lost fifteen seconds, but we were a lot safer.''

Sperry was watching the maneuvers of the cruiser for-mation and their screen on the PPI. He laughed. ''The destroyers in the screen are giving the cruisers a wide berth.''

Phelps nodded. ''They should. A course reversal in the fog at night at twenty-five knots with no practice is no joke. Admiral Davidson is a hell of a fighter, but he was in too much of a hurry. One mistake would have done more damage than the Italians could have done all night.''

''Maybe he wants to get back to the landing operation as soon as possible.''

''I'm sure he does, but I'd rather get there a few mi-nutes later with all my ships.''

Phelps watched his ships on the PPI as they settled down in their stations, then he walked over to his chair and sat down. It had been a long night, and he was more tired than he wanted to admit. He was not a young man anymore, and the long hours on his feet tired him. The chair eased his tightened muscles, and he leaned back and took several deep breaths. His tension eased, and he began to think of the past. The smell of the fog earlier had brought back memories of London and the time he had courted Lady Claudia there. Then he thought about her estate and the wonderful days they had shared on it. He hoped there would be more, but who could tell. A single stray bullet or a mountainous mine explosion could end his days in a second.

More days would be nice, but if they were not to be, he had lived enough. He looked around the flagship's bridge at the young officers and enlisted men. If he couldn't make it, he hoped they would.

At dawn the ships under Admiral Davidson were off the beach at Santa Agata and firing support for the troops ashore, using a shore fire control party and an artillery spotter airborne in a small aircraft. There were not enough targets for all the destroyers, so Phelps kept most of his ships offshore in screening stations, looking not only for submarines but also for aircraft.

Shortly after 0900 a flight of Heinkels came in low, and the cruisers broke off their fire support and maneuvered to avoid the attacks of the Germans. The *Lawrence* immediately increased speed to thirty knots and steamed out to sea trying to protect the cruisers from the oncoming Heinkels, which had been circling ominously just out of range. In the director, Brosnan could hear Kuberski giving orders to the director crew to keep on the nearest aircraft, and the machine guns were eagerly tracking the circling targets.

Then, as if on signal, the aircraft began low-level approaches on the cruisers. The cruisers began to fire as the aircraft came within range. Sperry maneuvered radically to keep the maximum number of guns bearing on the most dangerous targets. The cruisers fired rapidly, their twin five-inch mounts looking like machine guns. A Heinkel burst into flame and plowed into the water. A second began to trail smoke and turned away. Several others pressed their attacks in spite of the curtain of fire in front of them. One fell to Tubby Raymond's machine guns, and Brosnan could hear a cheer aft as the gunners realized they had downed an aircraft. Others began to plow into the water, but one came on steadily, wiggling its wings to avoid the cruiser's fire. A bomb from it fell close to the *Philadelphia*, raising a huge geyser of water. Two other aircraft escaped, and Brosnan watched as Army Air Force aircraft, which had wisely waited outside the formation, pursued them and eventually shot them down.

Sperry swore. "Damn! We almost got one of our own. I'm not used to seeing friendlies around."

Phelps said. "They came right in close to pick up those Heinkels. A lot of guts."

By 1000 the ships were back on fire support stations, but not for long. A flight of six Heinkels flew in low over the water, but this time the army air force fighters drove the planes off before they could attack the cruisers.

Kuberski watched them go. Brosnan heard him say, "Dammit, those guys are taking our targets away. This is no fun."

Brosnan laughed, "Some people are never satisfied."

Phelps said, "No, but I'll take the help. This ship has already shot down more than its share."

For two hours the communicators tried to reestablish communications with the landing force ashore, but without it and with no direction, the ships were unable to fire. Admiral Davidson apparently lost his patience with the situation and ordered the ships to return to Palermo.

By dusk the now familiar port of Palermo loomed ahead, and before dark all the ships of Destroyer Squadron Thirty-two were moored at the fuel pier.

Commodore Phelps was invited to dinner by Admiral Davidson, and walked over to the *Philadelphia* at the next fuel pier.

The captain anxiously awaited his return, but when Phelps came back, he waved his hand wearily and said, "I'll tell you what I know at breakfast, but we aren't going back to Oran for another ten days."

Sperry said, "That means we'll be busy."

Phelps nodded. "But not for a few days."

Sperry was tired, and as the commodore disappeared toward his cabin, Sperry trudged wearily up the ladder to his sea cabin behind the bridge. His dinner lay heavily on his stomach, and although he knew he needed sleep, it would be an hour or so before his stomach would relax enough so he could doze off.

He decided to write to his wife, and he sat down at his small desk and picked up his fountain pen. He had purchased the pen at the ship's store, and it had never worked very well. He pulled a piece of stationery out and looked at the blank sheet of paper. He missed his wife and children, and he wanted to write to them, but he didn't know what he could say without violating censorship. He couldn't tell them where he was, what he was doing, or even describe the scenery ashore.

He shifted his position at the cramped desk, trying to find a position to ease his tired muscles. As he moved, the fountain pen disgorged a blob of black ink all over the top of the his letter, covering the only words he had been able to produce, "Dear Sarah." He swore and threw the fountain pen in the miniature waste basket next to his desk. "Damn!" he muttered. "Why can't someone invent a pen that won't leak."

He picked up a government issue wooden pen holder with a steel nib and dipped it in a bottle of ink. It scratched when he wrote again the words "Dear Sarah," but at least it didn't leak.

He tried to describe the daily routine, but found himself producing uninteresting banalities in order to stay within the rules of censorship. He balled up the page and tossed it onto the growing pile in the waste basket.

As he pulled a new piece of stationery into place, he noticed that his hands were trembling. Not as much as when they were going into battle, but more than he liked. He grinned, remembering how his wife had noticed the trembling on their wedding day. She had laughed, not a derisive laugh, but an affectionate, understanding laugh, and later she had said, "A little tension is a good thing. It shows that you really care, and I like it."

Their married life had proved it. It had been a good life, and he hoped it would not end for him on the bottom of the Mediterranean as it had for the skipper of the *Maddox*.

He sighed. He was not in the mood to write, and he threw the government issue pen into the waste basket on top of the fountain pen. Tomorrow he would try again when he was rested. He climbed into his bunk, fully clothed, stretched his tired muscles, and took a deep breath. Before drifting off to sleep, he thought about Kelly and his boilers. Perhaps he had been too short with him. What if a boiler did burn out? Some bun-faced minion back in the Washington hierarchy might try to blame it on him and succeed. His post-war career would go down the drain when competition for promotion in peacetime might turn on such small issues.

He sighed deeply. "To hell with it," he muttered, and he fell into a deep sleep.

CHAPTER TWENTY-ONE

The ships of the squadron had arrived in port late in the day, and the next day the commodore declared a holiday. Cooper said, "But Commodore, tomorrow is Tuesday, and a working day. I don't know of any holiday in August."

Phelps looked slightly pained. "Just do it, Cooper. The men haven't had a day off for two months. Call it Saint Horace's day if you have to have an excuse. We wouldn't want to offend the Italians."

Brosnan, standing nearby on the bridge, looked at Cooper and mumbled, "Damned thick-headed jackass!"

Phelps turned to him. "You had some comment, Brosnan?"

Brosnan grinned. "Not really, sir. I think it's a great idea. Saint Horace is one of my heroes."

Phelps also grinned. "I know him pretty well, too, and he's no saint."

The next morning reveille was held late, and breakfast was served at 0900 in all messes. Almost all of the officers missed it, but Brosnan joined the captain and the executive officer in the wardroom. Fannon, engrossed in reading a dispatch, didn't notice Brosnan sit down. When he finished reading and saw him, he said, "Brosnan, why aren't you sleeping in?"

Brosnan put down a forkful of hotcakes. "I have to get here when Kuberski isn't eating to make sure I can get some of these hotcakes."

Kuberski came into the wardroom, stretching and yawning. "I thought I smelled hotcakes cooking. Jason, bring me two stacks."

Brosnan groaned. "I thought you were on a diet."

"Oh, yes, thanks. Jason, make that one stack and I'll leave off the butter and syrup, or at least some of it." Kuberski sat down, rubbing his hands and smiling. "I've already lost five pounds and my muscles are showing again."

"Why are you so happy this early in the morning?" Fannon asked through a mouthful of eggs.

Kuberski grinned. "Today is the day I paint some more German aircraft symbols on the bridge. We've got quite a collection of German and Italian aircraft, E boats, MFPs, and even half a submarine."

Brosnan said, "With all this time today, let's you and me try a little bridge. Your lessons are coming along, and it's time for you to solo."

Kuberski's big, florid face clouded. "I don't know about this gentleman stuff. The dancing was okay, but this playing cards is something else."

Fannon said, "I don't know why you're so afraid to play bridge. You're smart enough to learn the rules and procedures. There must be something else."

Kuberski dropped his eyes. "Well . . . er . . . as long as I'm among friends, it's that damned shuffling of the cards. My hands are just too big. Every time I try it I squirt them all over the table."

Brosnan guffawed. Kuberski frowned and said, "See, I knew you'd laugh."

Brosnan sobered and wiped his eyes. "Stanley, I'm sorry. Right after breakfast we'll have a shuffling lesson. Now eat your hotcakes before I deal myself some of your stack."

At 1000 the commodore left to call on Admiral Davidson. Just after lunch had begun, he popped into the wardroom. All the officers stood up except Brosnan and Doctor Taylor, who had their backs to the door and were deep in conversation. Cooper yelled, "Attention on deck." Brosnan and Taylor stopped talking and looked at Cooper. Cooper scowled and nodded toward the commodore. Brosnan and Taylor looked toward the door and immediately stood up.

Phelps waved his hand and said, "Carry on, please, gentlemen." He looked toward the captain, "Jack. I haven't had lunch down here in the wardroom in some time. If you'd be so kind as to invite me, I'd like to join you and tell you about the forthcoming operation."

Sperry beamed. "Of, course, Commodore, I'd be delighted. Please join me at the head of the table."

The executive officer scurried to move his place down to make room for the commodore, but Phelps said, "Please don't move. Just set a place on the corner of the table."

As Jason and the commodore's steward, Stevenson, were making the changes, Cooper leaned over to Brosnan and said in a low voice, "Brosnan, I thought I told you to move faster when I give the order to come to attention."

Brosnan raised his heavy dark eyebrows and said innocently, "Sorry, I didn't see anybody. I thought you were just practicing."

Cooper's face and neck got red, but before he could say anything the commodore said, "What was that, Brosnan?"

Brosnan looked toward the commodore and said innocently, "Nothing much, sir. I was just complimenting Mister Cooper on his strong military voice."

Sperry interrupted the conversation. "Commodore, we're ready for you. Please sit here."

The commodore sat down and dug into the curry and rice served to him. When he had eaten a plateful he said, "That hits the spot. Now while we have our coffee and desert I'll fill you in." When his coffee was fixed to his liking he began. "We get underway early tomorrow and proceed to a small town named Caronia, near Santa Agata. We'll cover the same amphibious ships we operated with before. When they're loaded they'll get underway and move to a place called Brolo somewhat nearer the eastern tip of Sicily."

Sperry interrupted. "Another short jump behind the German lines?"

"Yes. This is the second such movement in three days, and I hope the Germans aren't anticipating it."

"Will we have any friendly aircraft protecting us, sir?" Kuberski asked.

"Yes. Some Army Air Force night fighters. Also some day fighters after dawn. The landing will take place at night at about 0300. I think that's all. Now let's all of us get a good nap in honor of Saint Horace. Sorry no one can go ashore here."

As the commodore left, Kuberski said, "What's this Saint Horace stuff? I've been going to Mass for twenty years, and I've never heard of him."

Brosnan said patiently. "The commodore's first name is Horace. He's just putting us on. Now let's get on with this lesson on how to shuffle. If you learn well, I'll show you some extra stuff, such as how to make sure that the bottom card is always an ace. It helps your honor count."

"Honor count? Oh, yeah, I remember that."

Brosnan said, "But you can't use it playing with us."

"Why not?"

"You just can't. Another lesson in how to get on in the social scene."

The next day the ships of Destroyer Squadron Thirty-two arrived at Caronia late in the afternoon under an overcast sky and watched the amphibious craft loading on the beach. Just before dusk CIC reported incoming aircraft, and the ships of the screen speeded up and changed course to clear their batteries. The aircraft could not be sighted in the low overcast, but the destroyers opened fire using their radar for guidance. A small group of Stukas suddenly burst through the overcast, taking the ships by surprise. One of the LSTs took a bomb and burst into flames. The Stukas stayed low after dropping their bombs and escaped, much to Kuberski's disgust.

The fire on the LST was brought under control, but the commander of the landing force reported that she could not continue her mission. Her load had to be crowded aboard the other ships. Because of the delay, Admiral Davidson announced that the landing would be postponed for twenty-four hours, and the escorting vessels ushered the amphibious ships out to sea where they would have more maneuvering room in case of additional air attacks.

The next night the task force approached the Brolo beaches in moonlight. Two Army Air Force fighters droned overhead. As the task force approached the landing area, Benson pointed to a pip on the radar. "Big rock there, near the beach. We have a good navigational fix using it."

The amphibious ships beached off Brolo about 0300, and by 0400 all troops and vehicles were ashore and the amphibious ships were on their way back to Palermo.

The *Savannah* was suddenly sent off on another mission near the Straits of Messina. The three ships under Commodore Phelps and the *Bristol* and *Ludlow* took position close in to the beach to be ready to render fire support. About 0530 the *Philadelphia* commenced supporting fire on gun batteries ashore, but the destroyers were not needed.

Then CIC reported a flight of aircraft approaching. The Army Air Force fighters missed an interception, and it was soon apparent why. The aircraft turned out to be four Italian torpedo bombers flying in just over the water. Kuberski opened fire at long range, and the aircraft turned away at high speed.

Sperry shook his head. "Lucky for us. The Luftwaffe wouldn't have done that."

At 0930 Admiral Davidson decided the landing was going so well that the ships were no longer needed for gunfire support. They were formed into a long column and a course was set for Palermo.

Just as the crews were relaxing at their noon meal, the TBS crackled, and the *Philadelphia* suddenly turned around and speeded up to thirty-one knots. The admiral ordered the destroyers to form a circular antiaircraft screen, and they raced to take stations around the speeding cruiser. Sperry, when the movement was reported to him, rushed out on the bridge, still trailing his napkin. "What's happening?" he asked the officer of the deck, who was Tubby Raymond.

"Don't know yet, sir. CIC is listening on the landing force circuit."

In a few seconds CIC reported, "There's been a counterattack on our troops near Brolo, and we're urgently needed to help the troops ashore."

By 1400 the ships had reached Brolo. The *Philadelphia* began to fire full salvos of fifteen six-inch guns as she approached and continued firing for forty-five minutes.

The *Lawrence* fired at several targets designated by the shore fire control parties, but by 1500 communication with the shore fire control parties was lost. After an hour of lying to, Admiral Davidson departed again with his ships. This time they were only an hour away when another urgent message turned them around again.

Phelps, now pacing the bridge impatiently, said, "I'd like to get this thing settled. We're burning up too much fuel going back and forth at thirty-one knots."

Sperry laughed, remembering Kelly's plaintive request to clean boilers. "I think my chief engineer must be about ready to jump over the side."

This time, while all ships were firing, another air raid came in. When the approaching aircraft could be seen, Sperry said, "Damn! This won't be as easy as before. These are German FockeWulf 190s."

Phelps nodded. "Yes. They're very fast and maneuverable."

Several Army Air Force fighters roared down from above and made passes at the approaching fighters. Kuberski held his fire, afraid to hit friendly aircraft, but when the Germans got close he had to fire in self defense. Brosnan could hear him roar, "Commence firing!"

The five-inch battery began to fire rapidly at a low angle, and even the machine gun battery was soon in range. One German dove into the water from a low altitude, and Brosnan could see at least two others shot down by the friendly fighters.

From the *Philadelphia* came a deep rumble as all of her double five-inch mounts and machine guns opened up. Two Focke-Wulfs managed to drop bombs near her before exploding into balls of fire at short range, and two others went down on their way out. Now all ships were turning at high speeds to avoid the attacks, and Brosnan had to keep a sharp eye out to help the captain avoid hitting nearby ships. Whenever he saw danger, he grabbed the captain's arm and pointed to it. The steady firing of all the five-inch guns and the machine guns was too loud to shout over.

Then the last lone aircraft flew off low over the water, pursued by angry fighters. There was a sudden silence.

Brosnan let out his breath. "Jesus!" he said. "What a mess that was."

Brosnan noticed the gleam in the captain's eye. "I hate to say it," Sperry said, "but that was fun."

The destroyers headed for the beach while the cruiser remained off shore in case of other attacks. As the *Lawrence* neared the beach, Brosnan said, "I see several DUKW landing craft headed this way."

Sperry looked though his binoculars. "They're waving at us. Take the conn and close them. They must need help."

Brosnan took the conn and maneuvered alongside the first DUKW. Two others also came alongside. Fannon went down to the forecastle to see what they wanted. In a few minutes he came back, and below on the forecastle Brosnan could see the men in the DUKWs climbing up the cargo net.

Fannon puffed up to the bridge and went over to the commodore and captain. "They say they were chased off the beach by German troops, and that all of our troops are somewhere inland. We don't control the beach any more. They want to come aboard and have us sink their DUKWs."

Sperry shrugged and looked at the commodore.

Phelps nodded. "If that's what they want, do it. I'll notify Admiral Davidson." Phelps went into the pilothouse and reported the to Admiral Davidson over TBS.

Back came the answer, "I'm departing. Join me after you sink the DUKWs."

Sperry laughed. "The admiral must have an urgent appointment in Palermo."

Fifteen minutes later the DUKWs were empty, and Sperry directed Brosnan to pull off a hundred yards away so Raymond's machine guns could sink them.

They went down quickly, and the *Lawrence* set off at thirty-four knots to catch the speeding *Philadelphia* and the other destroyers.

Down in the forward engine room at main engine control, Lieutenant Kelly paced furiously across the bright steel gratings, muttering quietly to himself. From time to time he looked at the RPM indicator. "Thirty-four knots again!" he said to Chief Marusak. "The Admiral must be mad."

Marusak watched Kelly, turning his head to keep up with him, but occasionally looking at the dials and gauges on the control panel. When he was satisfied the engineering plant had settled down at the latest speed, he said, "Sir, don't worry so much. The captain has full responsibility for what's happening. You've told him our problem. Now you should let him carry the load. That's what captains are for."

An hour after the *Lawrence* had picked up the crews of the DUKWs, Fannon came to the bridge to report to the captain and the commodore. A second Lieutenant in battle dress followed him. Fannon introduced him to Phelps and Sperry. Phelps said, "How are your men?"

The second lieutenant said, "They're basically in good shape. A little hungry, but they've just eaten some of your good chow. My crews weren't fired on very much, but the troops ashore are in trouble. They have some air support and their own artillery, but there's a big fight going on. The landing wasn't as easy as the one at Santa Agata. I think the Germans were expecting us."

"What happened on the beach?"

"The Germans waited until our troops were well inland and then took over the beach from the flanks. We had to go out to sea to escape them."

"Shouldn't we do something about it?"

The young officer shook his head. "No, sir, more of our troops are coming from the east. They're only a few hours away. When they get here the Germans will leave. They're only fighting delaying actions anyway."

"We'll have to take you to Palermo."

The second lieutenant broke into a huge smile. "Can I tell my men that?"

"Certainly. I think we're all due for a rest."

CHAPTER TWENTY-TWO

The next morning the commodore sent Cooper scurrying off to the *Philadelphia*, moored across the fueling pier, to arrange a call for himself and his three commanding officers on Admiral Davidson. "We should have done this before, but just as I got ready to arrange it, we shoved off for somewhere at high speed," he said to Cooper.

Cooper came back soon with the word that Admiral Davidson was on his way over to the army headquarters at Palermo to inquire about the status of the campaign on Sicily and to find out how the Navy could help. His flag lieutenant scheduled the call for 1300. Phelps said. "Good. Get the word to all of my skippers. We'll meet here first."

At 1250 the three commanding officers were chatting on the *Lawrence*'s quarterdeck. At 1255 the commodore appeared and gave them a cheerful greeting. After he had returned their salutes, he led the way over the brow, across the pier, and up the brow of the flagship. The boatswain shrilled his pipe, and Brosnan, who had the day's duty, could see side boys standing at rigid attention on the flagship's quarterdeck. "Jesus!" he said to Cooper, who had come to see the commodore off. "I couldn't stand all that formal stuff."

Cooper sneered. "Don't worry. Nobody will ever visit you on your LSST, except maybe a German Focke-Wulf with a bomb like the one that clobbered the LST on the beach a few days ago.''

Brosnan groaned. ''Cooper, stop pulling that old saw. I'm not that bad.''

Cooper grinned evilly, his handsome face hiding his mood. ''That's a matter of opinion. The commodore's opinion is the one that counts, and you know who has his ear.''

About 1400 the commodore left the cruiser in a flurry of scurrying side boys, bugle calls, and boatswain's pipes. He was trailed by his three commanding officers. When he reached the quarterdeck, he said to Sperry, ''I think it's all right to brief your officers on what we were told.''

Sperry went to the wardroom, closely followed by Fannon. He sat down heavily and said to the executive officer. ''Let's get on with this. Call a conference of all officers.''

Sperry was idly stirring a cup of coffee when the first of the officers drifted in. ''Bad news, sir?'' Raymond asked.

Sperry shook his head. ''I'll tell you in a few minutes when we're all together.''

When the last officer arrived, Sperry began. ''This is top secret. As you know, I've just come from seeing Admiral Davidson, who just had a conference with the army and navy authorities ashore.''

Fannon said, ''You don't look very cheerful.''

Sperry grinned wryly. ''The only good news I have is Admiral Davidson. He's a real pistol. If he were in charge ashore, we'd have been in Messina a month ago.''

Lieutenant Kelly shook his head. ''At thirty knots all the way, I suppose.''

Sperry shrugged his shoulders. ''Maybe thirty-four. We have to stand by in Palermo for a few more days, then we're going to Oran. You can clean your boilers there.''

Kelly grinned happily, his eyes gleaming through his glasses. "That sounds good. I feel better."

Sperry frowned again. "I wish the news from ashore were as good. The Germans and Italians that we thought we had caught and isolated on Sicily are starting to evacuate to Italy."

Kuberski boomed, "Then why are we sitting here?"

Sperry said, "There's been a real foul-up. General Montgomery stalled on the Catania Plain too long. The enemy forces have very cleverly used a series of delaying actions, giving them plenty of time to prepare for evacuation. While Montgomery was sitting in his headquarters, the American forces under General Patton conquered three-fourths of Sicily, and are now chasing the retreating German forces toward Messina along the northern coast."

Fannon said, "Then why don't we land behind them again?"

Sperry laughed. "Admiral Davidson's staff was planning another landing, but before they could get the plans out, the Germans were beyond the proposed landing area."

"Then we're just going to follow them?" Kuberski asked.

"That's about it. Our army friends thought they were pushing the Germans and Italians back, but what was actually happening was that the enemy forces were conducting a phased retreat."

"Where are they all going?" Brosnan asked. "Messina isn't very big."

Sperry rang the call bell to the bridge and asked Chief Benson to send down a chart of the Straits of Messina. When it arrived, he spread it on the wardroom table. The officers leaned in. Sperry said, "You can see that the Straits of Messina are very narrow and quite long. About three miles at the narrowest and maybe fifteen miles long."

Fannon asked. "What defenses do the Axis forces have in place?"

Sperry pointed to the top part of the Strait. "Along this stretch they have two batteries of 170-millimeter guns."

Kuberski whistled. "Those out-range and out-weigh the light cruisers."

Sperry frowned. "Yes, and the *Savannah*, patrolling off the north entrance to the strait, has been told to stay away from them."

"Then what is she there for?" Fannon asked.

"To prevent Italian surface ships from entering the Strait. The only Allied ships entering are the PT boats under Commander Barnes, and they only go in at night."

Kuberski said, "I suppose the Axis have a lot of other guns, too."

Sperry said, "They began evacuating on the tenth of August and have lined up over 150 eighty-eight-millimeter and ninety-millimeter dual purpose guns. Also thirty long range antiaircraft batteries."

Kuberski whistled softly. "I wouldn't go in there for anything."

"Neither would Admiral Davidson nor Admiral Cunningham, who's on the south of the Straits with the British forces."

"Then there's not much that can be done about it," Fannon said. "That means the Allies will have to fight these bastards all over again in Italy."

"That's right. I'd say we'll land in the middle of Italy somewhere in about a month."

Kuberski asked. "What about air power? The Army Air Force has always bragged about how they could take care of a situation like this."

"They've been attacking night and day since the tenth with little result, except a lot of our aircraft have been shot down. The Axis forces shift their embarkation and debarkation points every few hours. The air boys bring back the last location, and the next flight takes off to bomb it. The only trouble is that it has been changed in the meantime, and the antiaircraft batteries move with it."

Brosnan said, "They must have a lot of small craft doing the ferrying."

Sperry nodded. "Yes. Lots. And some not so small. There are two old train ferries still there from before the war. Then many German Seibel ferries are being used."

"What's that?" the doctor asked. "Sounds like some surgical instrument."

"They're very ingenious. They're ferries made in sections so they can be transported and assembled in the water. They also have some MFPs that we remember from the action the other night, and a dozen or so artillery rafts. Many smaller boats are also carrying troops across."

Fannon said, "I take it the decision has been made that we can't stop them."

Sperry grimaced and rubbed his small mustache nervously. "Yes, or at least on a lower level. Admiral Davidson thinks the high command is very unhappy over the situation, and hasn't agreed yet. That's why we're to stand by here for a few more days while the big shots battle it out."

"I hope they don't decide to send us down into that strait. It would be like sailing into a buzz saw."

"No, I don't think they will. The British are very opposed to sending ships in there. They remember Gallipoli in World War I all too well."

Phelps nodded. "The British naval officers in the Admiralty still shudder when you mention that name. They got involved there and couldn't get out of a bad situation. They lost a lot of ships and men to the Turks."

Brosnan asked, "When will we know the final decision?"

"My guess is about August sixteenth. In the meantime we can get a little rest."

Sperry was almost right. On the morning of the seventeenth, Brosnan decoded a message that said the Allied forces had met each other in the town of Messina. Shortly afterward a message came over from the flagship by flashing light for Task Force eighty-eight to get underway immediately and proceed to Oran.

The trip south to the coast, and then west to Oran, was pleasant and peaceful. The crew of the *Lawrence* worked in the mornings and sunbathed during the afternoons.

Brosnan, lying on a blanket on the deck above the forecastle, stretched and said to Raymond next to him, "This would cost us a hundred bucks a day on a cruise ship. Uncle Sam gives it to us free."

Raymond said, "Yeah, and if a German U-boat comes along and bangs us, we'll get a taste of that beautiful blue Mediterranean first hand."

Two days later the Port of Oran was visible in the distance, and the crew of the *Lawrence* began preparations to enter port.

Lieutenant Commander Cooper walked back to the forward engineering room hatch with a sheaf of papers in his hand. He stopped a fireman about to go down and said, "Ask Lieutenant Kelly to meet me up here as soon as possible."

In a few minutes the chief engineer's head popped out of the hatch. "You wanted to see me? I'm awfully busy with these work requests."

Cooper said, "I'm glad to see you're in the mood. I have the requests you submitted the other day in Palermo, and also the ones submitted by the other two ships to the commodore. I need to have your opinion on them by the time we enter port."

"My opinion?"

"Sure. You're the acting squadron material officer. I don't know anything about engineering."

"But I've got a lot of research to do in the manuals."

Cooper said impatiently, "Kelly, you aren't at MIT now. Get with it. This is the operating navy. We don't run on paperwork alone. If you can't hack it, ask Chief Marusak. He knows how to write a work request that would be approved by a moron. And there are a lot of morons over on that repair ship in Oran. Remember, we save the big repair stuff for our visit to the shipyard at Portsmouth in a few months."

"What will we be doing after the repair ship completes our repairs?"

Cooper sneered. "My guess is an all-expenses-paid visit to central Italy. You'll like it."

CHAPTER TWENTY-THREE

The next morning after breakfast, Lieutenant Kelly scurried over to the repair ship, work requests in hand and a worried look on his face.

Brosnan, who had the day's duty, shook his head as he watched Kelly climb up the steep brow. "He'll worry himself to death," Brosnan muttered.

An hour later the commodore left to call on Admiral Hall. He was back shortly before lunch and called a conference of all commanding officers in his cabin at 1300. Brosnan tried politely to pump him for information as he escorted the commodore to his cabin, but the commodore only grinned and said, "You'll know soon enough.

"By the way, I'd like to play bridge tonight. Cooper is available, but I understand the captain is going ashore. Can you get someone to take his place?"

Brosnan searched his brain desperately. The executive officer was nursing a cold. That left him only one alternative, Stanley Kuberski. Brosnan said, "Sir, the executive officer is ill, but would you like me to invite Lieutenant Kuberski? He's still an amateur, but he's a fast learner, and I'll play with him as my partner."

"Certainly. Everyone has to start some time. Besides, since Lieutenant Kuberski is smart enough to know a good cigar when he sees one, I'm sure he'll do fine." He paused on his way through the door. "Maybe Cooper and I will win for a change."

At 1300 the three commanding officers assembled in the commodore's cabin. The commodore's table was topped with a large chart of Italy. Phelps offered them cigars, but they all refused. He lit one himself, blew out a cloud of noxious fumes, and began. "Gentlemen, you all know we're going to invade Italy soon. The only unknowns are where and when. The answers are Salerno and on about September ninth. The southern force will be under Admiral Hall, and we will be part of it. The force will land at Paestum, a few miles south of Salerno and about thirty miles south of Naples.

The British, or northern force, will land about eight miles north of us, near Salerno. The British army, under General Montgomery, will cross the Straits of Messina about a week earlier, but you know how General Montgomery can stall. Admiral Hall estimates he won't get across until about the eighth. There may also be a British landing at Tarranto. This is tentative and is a pet project of Admiral Cunningham's."

Sperry stirred in his chair, let out his breath, and unconsciously blew some of the blue cigar smoke away from him. "When do we leave here?"

"We'll get our full week of repair work in and then have a day or two for loading supplies and ammunition. We should be ready to leave here on the evening of September fifth."

The commanding officer of the *Grayston* finally had to light a Moroccan cigarette in self-defense. He blew some strong smoke toward the commodore and asked, "What sort of force will we be escorting?"

Phelps looked at him with a pained expression and blew cigar smoke right back in his direction. "Admiral

Hall will have about thirteen APAs and APs, a half dozen British LSTs and LSIs, which will carry the thirty-sixth Infantry Division, and our usual Task Force eighty-eight, with the cruisers *Philadelphia, Boise,* and *Savannah.* We'll be part of a group of about fifteen destroyers, screening both the amphibious force and the cruisers. Admiral Davidson said he intends keeping our squadron with the cruisers. I think he likes us. Incidentally, there will be several British battleships involved, and four escort carriers.''

''Good,'' Sperry said. ''Now we won't have to depend on the Army Air Force for protection.''

Phelps nodded. ''We have to have carriers. The army air force fighters can't carry enough fuel to help us that far away from their fields.''

''I suppose the Army is still insisting on night landings without prior shore bombardment,'' Sperry noted.

Phelps sighed, and stubbed his cigar out in an ashtray. The commanding officers sighed with relief, and the skipper of the *Grayston* added his cigarette stub to the ashy receptacle.

''Camel dung,'' Sperry muttered.

Phelps smiled and said, ''They never seem to learn. They think the initial landings will be as easy as the ones on Sicily. This time the Germans will be in charge of all the fortifications and the defensive troops, and I'm afraid they'll decimate the landing force. We'll have to bail them out with naval gunfire when they get pinned down.''

''Can't General Eisenhower straighten those guys out?''

''He's trying. At least he's insisted that the Air Force fighters operating over the area and all the British fighters be controlled by an on-scene air controller.''

''Hallelujah!'' Sperry said. ''Now we're getting somewhere.''

Phelps stretched his arms over his head. ''Well, gentlemen, that's all for now. The planners are going nuts over all the changes they've been ordered to make. I'll keep you informed as I hear of them. Now I have to take a nap to be fresh for our evening bridge game, Jack.''

Sperry looked puzzled. "But sir, I was going—.''

Phelps interrupted him. "I know—, you're going ashore. Don't change your plans. Brosnan is bringing Lieutenant Kuberski to fill in for you. Fannon is ill.''

"Kuberski? But he—.''

"He'll be fine. Don't worry about it.''

Brosnan told Kuberski at the evening meal about the invitation to play bridge with the commodore. Kuberski's fork clanged loudly on his plate and then on the deck. "Jesus, Beetle, I can't keep up in that league.''

Brosnan said, "What's to worry about? You can shuffle now, and I'll keep you afloat. Just let me end up playing most of our bids until you feel comfortable. By the end of the evening you'll be doing fine.''

Kuberski frowned and picked up his fork. "I don't know. I may have to take up cigar smoking again to get through the evening.''

Brosnan shook his head quickly. "Oh, please, not that. One cigar smoker is enough.''

Kuberski started to eat again, and Brosnan knew he had him convinced.

Kuberski said, "All right, but you'll have to answer to the commodore if I foul up.''

"If you make a mistake, just keep quiet. I'll know about it, but the commodore will be so happy he's winning he'll never recognize it.''

"What about Cooper?''

"To hell with him. He's ashore now, and he'll have had a couple of snorts. He won't care what you do as long as the commodore wins.''

Fannon had been listening to the conversation while he picked at his food "I'm glad I'm going to miss this,'' he said, blowing his nose.

At 1900, Brosnan, and a reluctant Kuberski, appeared in the commodore's cabin. Cooper was arranging the bridge paraphernalia and looked up when the two entered. "The commodore is washing his hands and will be here in a minute," Cooper said. Then he grinned evilly and said, "You guys look like a couple of easy marks."

The commodore came out rubbing his hands. "Always like to run warm water over my hands before I play cards. Makes the hands supple."

Brosnan said, "Sir, you know Lieutenant Kuberski. He's joining us tonight. The executive officer has a cold."

Phelps looked at Kuberski with enthusiasm. "Ah, Lieutenant, I remember you liked my cigars. Will you join me?"

Kuberski's eyes lit up, but then he thought better of it. "Ah, no thank you, sir, I'm on the cigar wagon now, so to speak."

Phelps pursed his lips. "Might be a good idea. Lady Claudia is always after me to quit. I'll try to go without tonight, but if we begin losing, I may have to indulge."

Kuberski smiled weakly. "Not much chance of that, sir."

They began to play, and Kuberski drew a high card from the pack and had to deal first. Brosnan watched anxiously. Small beads of perspiration formed on Kuberski's upper lip as he concentrated on holding the cards firmly in his huge hands. Cooper watched in fascination, obviously expecting disaster, but Phelps chatted on, apparently oblivious to Kuberski's discomfort. Kuberski managed to deal without dropping the cards.

Kuberski bid cautiously during the first rubber, and Brosnan tried to compensate by overbidding. The result was that Brosnan played most of their hands, and Kuberski began to relax. By the end of the second rubber, Brosnan and Kuberski were only slightly behind. Brosnan noted that Kuberski was beginning to enjoy the game and that the commodore went out of his way to praise his playing of a small slam bid.

By the last rubber Brosnan and Kuberski were losing by a modest amount. The commodore was happy and Cooper was exultant. When they got up to go, Kuberski was beaming. "Sir, thank you for a pleasant evening," he said.

The commodore said, "My pleasure, Stanley. We'll do it again soon."

They walked back to the wardroom and found Fannon there, nursing a cup of bouillon. Fannon said to Brosnan, "How did he do?"

"Fine. He'll be better than Cooper after another lesson."

Kuberski was grinning, apparently at a loss for words. Fannon said, "Well, Stanley, what about it?"

Kuberski shook his head slowly. "I liked it. And can you believe it? He called me by my first name."

About 1700 on the fifth of September, Admiral Hall's force departed from Oran. The big ships, followed by the smaller landing craft, bustled out of the harbor and set a course for the western tip of Sicily. Task force eighty-eight was hull down on the horizon, except for the destroyers Admiral Davidson had assigned to screen the landing force. Destroyer Squadron Thirty-two had been assigned to screen the cruisers. Brosnan, who had the deck for getting underway, looked back at the forest of masts as the convoy formed a rectangular formation. The cruisers were in column with their destroyers in a bent line screen ahead. Barley came up beside Brosnan and handed him a cup of signal bridge coffee. He jerked a thumb at the distant landing force formation and then at the cruiser formation. "Much neater," he said.

"And a lot easier to shepherd at night. Thanks for the coffee," Brosnan said.

The trip around Sicily was uneventful, the only challenge being having to avoid the other forces heading in the same direction, all jockeying for position.

The evening of September seventh, Chief Martin and Barley were leaning on the bridge rail keeping a close eye on the flagship. Suddenly the signal searchlight began to blink. Martin said, "Stand by to write. I'll get it."

Barley picked up a clipboard and pencil. The message began to come in. Raymond, who had the deck, was listening, and said to the messenger, "Tell the commodore a message is coming in from the flagship."

By the time Barley had the message written down, Phelps was on the bridge and looking over his shoulder, and Sperry was nearby. Phelps said to Sperry, "You're detached and are to escort the Boise to Bizerta."

Phelps hurriedly composed a message to the commanding officer of the *Grayston* putting him in charge of the remaining screening destroyers. Soon the *Boise* wheeled out of column and hoisted a signal to the *Lawrence*, "Screen me."

Then the *Boise* hoisted another signal, "Speed three zero," and the *Lawrence* had to go to thirty-four knots to reach a position on the Boise's bow. Chief Martin shook his head and said to Barley, "I hate to miss this operation."

Barley said, "Something tells me we aren't going to miss anything. From the chart it looks like we're headed for Bizerta, and that isn't far at the speeds we make."

"Who's there?" Martin asked.

"Mister Brosnan says a bunch of British ships."

Martin's lip curled, "Well, if Mister Brosnan says so it can't be true."

It was true. The next morning the *Boise* entered Bizerta harbor, still at a good speed, and moored quickly to a pier. The *Lawrence* moored alongside, and the *Boise* officer of the deck yelled over to the *Lawrence*, ''The captain would like your commodore to accompany him ashore in five minutes.''

Phelps dashed over to the Boise as soon as a brow was rigged and came back an hour later. Even before his return, a crane was lifting jeeps onto the *Boise*'s fantail, and a curious mixture of British army troops was filing aboard. The *Boise* aircraft were also being lifted off and left on the pier under guard.

The commodore made his way among the jeeps and troops now cluttering the *Boise*'s main deck. When he reached the *Lawrence*, he motioned to Sperry to follow him to his cabin. He sat down and rubbed his head for a few seconds. Then he looked over at Sperry, ''Sorry. I'm trying to figure out how to start. The whole thing is out of this world. I went with the skipper of the *Boise*, Captain Thebaud, in a command vehicle sent for us by Admiral Cunningham. When we got there, the Admiral greeted us nicely and then leaned over and traced out a map of Taranto in the dust on the fender of the command car. Then he said a few words in his clipped British accent that I couldn't hear and ended by saying we were to do what we saw fit when we got there. Captain Thebaud was closer to him than I was, and he nodded. He must have heard the first few words. That's just about all the briefing we got.''

''How did you like Admiral Cunningham?''

''Fine. I've known him before in London. Since he's been at sea, he's lost twenty pounds. His hair is grayer, and cut a lot shorter. He's a gruff, tough British naval officer.

"Captain Thebaud says we're to take the jeeps we have and about seven hundred troops of something called Pop- ski's Private Army commanded by some British guy named Lieutenant Colonel Vladimir Peniakoff."

"What the hell are they going to do?"

"You've got me. Do as they see fit, I guess. The old British method."

Sperry grinned. "I like it."

"We leave tonight and take station astern of the British invasion force commanded by Commodore Agnew. When we get to Taranto, the *Boise* is to land the troops and their jeeps. Then we leave her and return indepen- dently to Salerno as soon as possible."

Sperry shook his head. "This is about as harebrained as it can get."

Phelps said, "Nothing that Admiral Cunningham does is harebrained. I have great faith in him, and he must have a lot of trust in us."

That evening the *Boise* and the *Lawrence* left the harbor and soon caught up with the British force.

At 1830 Ensign Raymond brought up a dispatch an- nouncing that the Italians had surrendered and that all Italian ships had been directed to proceed to Malta. Sperry said, "Well, that makes the naval side of the pic- ture easier."

Phelps shrugged. "They haven't bothered us yet, but they may become more difficult. The Italian naval officers are a proud lot. Something tells me their surrendering will be more trouble to us than their fighting has been."

The force approached Taranto on the afternoon of the ninth. Sperry was worried. The ship had no intelligence about forces in the area, or even any indication of what was to happen. Phelps strained to recall Admiral Cunningham's exact words when he had drawn the map on the command vehicle fender. "I couldn't hear much. The Admiral had his head toward Captain Thebaud, and he was givng it the old British mumble." Phelps said.

Sperry said, "Well, I think I'll go to general quarters a little early and be ready for anything."

"Good idea. Has the crew eaten lunch?"

"Oh, yes. So have I. If you want to go below, I'll keep you informed."

Phelps shook his head, "No, I'll eat on a tray. I wouldn't miss a second of this, whatever it is."

Just as Phelps was finishing his lunch the lookouts reported, "Two Italian battleships and three Italian cruisers standing out of Taranto Harbor."

Phelps whistled. "My God! Suppose they don't want to surrender?"

Phelps, Sperry, and Brosnan searched the harbor entrance with their binoculars. Brosnan said, "The Italian ships are coming out with all guns manned."

Phelps looked at the British ships. Their guns were fully manned, too. "My God," he said. "One eager trigger finger and we'll all be in trouble."

Chief Brill, the talker, came to life. "Gun control asks which battleship you want them to sink first."

Sperry clouded up, but Phelps held up his hand. "Don't get too serious, Jack. Stanley is just kidding. Nice fellow. The way he's bluffing, I'll bet he's a good poker player, too."

Sperry subsided, but decided he would have a word with Kuberski later. He said, "Tell gun control to be very careful not to make any threatening moves. Don't even train the guns around."

The commodore and captain watched the opposing forces slowly pass each other like two circling dogs. As the big Italian ships set a course for Malta, Phelps said, "The end of an era is in sight."

Sperry let out his breath. "So is the end of a very unpleasant confrontation."

By dusk, the British force had entered Taranto without opposition. The *Boise*, after an initial disagreement with the port authorities about where they were to berth, went alongside a pier and began to unload Popski's Private Army. The *Lawrence* was detached and ordered to join the operation at Salerno. Sperry directed the officer of the deck to speed up to twenty-five knots and asked Benson for a course. Benson said immediately, "One seven zero."

Sperry and Phelps gathered around the chart desk and watched Fannon, who had come up from his battle station in CIC, lay out the remaining courses for the trip. "We go south around the toe of the boot, turn north at Cape Reggio at the tip of the toe, and work our way through the straits of Messina. At twenty-five knots, we should reach the narrow part of the Straits about dawn. Then we should slow for the passage between Scylla and Charybdis. When we're clear, we can speed up again. I figure we'll be off Paestum by noon."

Sperry looked at the commodore, and Phelps said, "That looks good to me. You're in charge. Do whatever you want to do."

"I'd like to go through the narrow part of the Strait in the daytime so we can see what Ulysses saw in the old days."

Phelps laughed. "You can bet the firing there in the last few days has rearranged all the tourist attractions. If I read the intelligence dispatches right, General Montgomery spent several days firing his artillery at forces that were no longer there; they were halfway up to Salerno."

Sperry decided to go to general quarters for the passage through the Straits of Messina in case they came across some floating mines, or possibly some Italian forces that hadn't heard of surrender. At 0300 the general alarm sounded, and Brosnan rolled out of his bunk, threw some water in his face, and headed for the bridge. Doctor Taylor was already there, peering over the bridge bulwark. Brosnan said, "I'll be damned! I never looked in your bunk. I just assumed you were sleeping in as usual."

Taylor said, "Oh, no, not today. I've read about Scylla and Charybdis for years. I'm not going to miss them."

"What's that ruckus over on the beach?"

"The captain says it's the Italians still celebrating the end of the war for them. If you look through your binoculars you can see the churches all lighted up and people dancing in the streets in the villages."

"At three o'clock in the morning?"

"For them it's a big occasion. It would be for us, too, if the war were over."

"Well, I guess you're right."

The Strait of Messina got narrower and narrower as the *Lawrence* steamed north through it, and the noise on the beaches got louder as they got closer. By the time the ship was ready to turn northeast through the narrowest part of the strait, the beach was only a mile and a half away, and the crew could hear people shouting at the ship. Brosnan, watching through his binoculars, said, "They're waving at us."

Taylor waved back, and got so interested he forgot they were passing by the area thought to have been inhabited by Scylla and Charybdis. Suddenly he shouted, "Where is it?"

Brosnan said, "Where's what?"

"Scylla."

"Oh, I thought you saw it. It's supposed to be that large rock over there on the Italian side."

Taylor fastened his binoculars on the object. "Doesn't look very scary to me."

"You wouldn't either if you'd been walked over by several generations of tourists. I suppose you're going to look for Charybdis next."

Taylor swung around to the Sicily shore. "Where is it?"

"It's supposed to be a series of whirlpools, but I don't see any. The piloting guide says the tide has to be just right before they occur."

"What the hell. This isn't much of a show," Taylor said, "I'm going below."

Brosnan grinned. "Maybe you'll like Salerno better."

"What's there?"

"Actually the American forces land at Paestum, south of Salerno. There are a lot of remarkable temples back of the beach that you can see easily."

Fannon came out on the wing just as Brosnan finished, shaking his head. "We may not see much for a while. I've been reading the action report from Admiral Hall. He says the Bay of Salerno is mined, and they're having trouble sweeping it. In the meantime the transports have to stay about ten miles off the beach, and the landing craft take over an hour to get in."

"Any other bad news?" Brosnan asked.

"Yes. The Army got it in the neck, just like we thought it would."

"The Germans weren't surprised?"

"Hell no. They've had several days to move their artillery up from Messina, and they had it well dug in. The planners should have let the ships bombard the beach area before the landing took place. The boats and their embarked troops caught hell from the artillery and the mines on the beach."

Brosnan sighed. "They never learn. Let's go get some breakfast before Kuberski eats it all."

"Good idea. We'll be in Salerno just after lunch."

CHAPTER TWENTY- FOUR

After leisurely breakfasts from trays, Phelps and Sperry sat in their bridge chairs, lazily scanning the horizon. Phelps said, "Life in the navy is funny. About eighteen hours ago we were looking down the guns of two huge Italian battleships. By this afternoon we'll be threading through dangerous mine fields and avoiding German air attacks while we shoot up tanks ashore. But now, for a few hours, we're just sitting here looking at the scenery like a couple of tourists."

Sperry, who had almost been asleep, roused himself and squinted at the sea ahead. "Yes, and look at the sea, blue as an amethyst, small rippling waves, and a clear sky. The Mediterranean can be beautiful."

By 1000 the tops of large black smoke columns could be seen above the horizon ahead.

"Volcanoes?" Sperry asked.

"There are some around here, but those are more likely to be burning tanks and fuel dumps," Phelps said. "I think it's time for an early lunch before we arrive."

Sperry nodded. "All messes are eating at 1100."

Phelps yawned and said to the officer of the deck, "Please call me at 1100."

At 1100 the mountains behind Paestum could be seen clearly in the sparkling air, and at 1200 ships anchored off the beach loomed over the horizon. Chief Martin and Barley watched them carefully. Martin pointed at a cruiser and said, "I think that's the *Philadelphia*."

Barley kept his long glass on the flagship, and in minutes he shouted, "Stand by to write." Acton came over with a clipboard, and Martin looked over Barley's shoulder, also watching the blinking light on the flagship's signal bridge. Brosnan, who had the deck, listened as Barley called off the words. After the first few words, Brosnan said to the messenger, "Ask the captain to come out to the bridge."

Sperry came out to the wing of the bridge, stretching and yawning. "What's up?" he asked.

Brosnan said, "We're getting a fire support assignment from Admiral Davidson."

Phelps, who had also come out to the wing from his chair, said, "From last night's operational summary, I believe there are still a lot of mines around. I suggest you be careful in approaching your firing position. The message last night gave the areas that have been swept."

Sperry nodded. "I saw them, and they're carefully plotted on the chart. The executive officer also studied the chart and is confident he can maintain a good navigational plot. I'm going to keep him up here until we're sure the area is well swept. Ensign Aronson will act as CIC officer and run the target designating system in CIC."

Phelps wrinkled his brow. "Is he qualified?"

"Oh, yes. I haven't found much he can't do yet."

Phelps said mischievously, "Can he play bridge?"

"I'm sure he can, but I'll ask him."

Fannon came out to the wing and began pointing out the sights ashore. "There, behind Paestum, are the two most prominent mountain peaks in the area, Mount Soprano and Mount Sottane. Now you can see the tops of the old Roman ruins at Paestum. There are two well-preserved temples, and the columns of a third."

Phelps rubbed his long jaw thoughtfully. "I hope they survive the fighting over there. I can see a lot of dust and smoke around them."

"A lot of nice farming ground will be torn up by tank treads and artillery shell explosions. The Salerno plain is beautiful. As you can see, it's well cultivated with tobacco farms, olive groves, and dairy farms. The area rises gently back toward the lower mountains."

"I don't see many houses."

Fannon nodded. "There aren't many in the farm areas. The area is infested with malaria, and the farmers work by day and go up to their homes in the highlands at night."

"Good," Phelps said. "That way there won't be as much destruction. I just hope the army has taken the malaria into consideration."

"They have. All troops get daily doses of medicine. Also the army's plan of maneuver calls for them to move east through a gap in the mountains and then move north to meet up with the British and eventually to move on to Rome. They'll still chew up the Italian buildings as they move east."

"From the summary of yesterday, I take it the army had a rough time ashore on D-day. The Germans had fortified the area well, and the army had insisted that there be no bombardment before they landed."

"Right," Fannon said. "And as a result the Germans opened fire on the fully loaded boats and did a lot of damage. The landing force is slowly expanding its bridgehead, but we and the other fire support ships will have a lot to do destroying German strong points and tanks."

"Yes, one destroyer fired almost all of her ammunition yesterday and will leave as soon as we relieve her to load more ammunition at Palermo."

By now the *Lawrence* was approaching the general area occupied by the transports, still busy loading cargo and equipment into their boats, clustered like flies. Phelps scanned the beach behind the ships with his binoculars. "Bloody hell . . . er . . . I mean, damn!" he said. "The beaches are full of stuff, and nothing is moving off of them. Boats lying off shore can't even land at the beach."

Sperry said, "Another lesson the army has to learn. They have to get supplies inland off the beaches sooner. They didn't even combat load some of the ships. I see where Admiral Hall complained that they had equipment earmarked for use ten days later on top of equipment they needed on D-day."

Sperry moved inside to conn the ship into the fire support area, and ordered Brosnan to sound general quarters. Brosnan asked permission to turn the deck over to Farraday so he could man the radio nets over which the fire support commander and the landing force commander communicated with the task force commander. Sperry said, "Permission granted. Let the commodore and me know what's happening ashore."

As they threaded carefully through the gap in the mine field, Brosnan tried not to think about what a mine would do to the fragile hull of the *Lawrence* and concentrated on listening to the two earpieces, trying to sort out and remember the transmissions on both circuits.

He could see the hull of one burned-out LST and several smaller LCTs on the beach, and occasional enemy rounds were landing on or near the crowded beaches. On the landing force commander's circuit there was a sudden rush of transmissions. Just before Kuberski was about to open fire on a suspected pillbox that had been assigned to them, a frantic voice said, "Shift fire to a tank column approaching from the north."

Above the bridge, Kuberski swung the director around, and the guns, hydraulic motors whining, followed obediently. Aronson called up from CIC, "We have the target plotted and are ready to open fire." Chief Brill, the talker, said, "Mister Kuberski says he also sees the tank column. He's on it and requests permission to open fire."

Sperry said eagerly. "Commence firing!"

Brosnan braced himself for the four-gun blast, and the yellowish smoke of the propellant powder billowed back across the bridge. Kuberski waited for the projectiles to land, and in a few seconds, Brosnan could hear him yell, "No change! No change. Rapid fire!"

The guns blasted his ears again, and then began to fire as quickly as they could be loaded. The earpieces of Brosnan's headset partially protected his ears, but listening to the radio circuits was difficult so he ducked into the pilothouse. Soon he heard the landing force commander say, "Well done!" and Kuberski stopped firing.

Sperry said to Chief Brill, "Ask Mister Kuberski how we did over there."

Chief Brill delivered his message, and Brosnan could hear Kuberski's booming voice above. Brill began to grin and said, "Sir, as nearly as I can translate the message, Mister Kuberski says we blasted the first tank to hell, exploded the second one into small pieces, burned the third, and scared the uh . . . the uh . . . hell out of the rest."

Sperry grinned. "I can translate that. Thank you, and pass a 'well done' to Gun Control."

For over an hour the *Lawrence* steamed slowly in her small fire support area, trying to stay within the mineswept area while still making at least slow speed. Brosnan felt the warm sun on his back, and it made him sleepy. Just as he was about to doze off leaning against the bulwark, he heard CIC reporting over the squawkbox, "Large flight of aircraft at high altitude headed this way from the north." Then the lookouts began to shout, "Incoming aircraft low over the hills."

Sperry took the conn, and headed for the gap in the minefields. Brosnan held his breath, expecting to have the deck heave up under a mine blast any minute, but the *Lawrence* got through safely, and Sperry ordered, ''All ahead flank!''

The deck began to vibrate as the turbines raced in the engine rooms below, and the ship seemed to fly. Brosnan let the radio headset slip back on his neck so that he could swivel his head around more easily. He saw several flights of Heinkels coming in low from over the land. He looked up into the sun, shielding his eyes with his hand. There were a dozen Stukas coming down from the sun. He began to shout at Chief Brill about the aircraft, but Kuberski had seen them too, and he was already yelling orders. The telephone was too slow, so he poked his head out of the top of the director and shouted to Ensign Raymond below him, ''Get the machine guns on the Stukas! I'll take the Heinkels!''

The director swung toward the shore, and the forward guns began to fire at the leading Heinkels, coming in low. Brosnan could see the Stukas were too much for the machine guns, and he was relieved when he heard Kuberski shout, ''Mounts fifty-three and fifty-four shift to local control! Targets dive bombers aft!'' In seconds the *Lawrence* was firing madly at a dozen aircraft, and some began to fall as projectile after projectile burst near them. Brosnan saw three planes hit the water, and he heard Raymond shouting exultantly above, so he knew the machine guns were shooting down some of the Stukas. The Heinkels soon had enough of the *Lawrence*'s hail of steel and explosives, and when the *Philadelphia* also began to shoot at them, they pulled up and fled to the north without having gotten close enough to drop their bombs.

The Stukas were still coming down, and Brosnan turned just as the remaining three dropped their bombs. The glistening teardrop shapes left the bellies of the Stukas and slanted right at the *Lawrence*'s stern, but Sperry was waiting until just the right moment. Then he shouted, "Right full rudder!" Brosnan looked inside the pilothouse to make sure the helmsman got the order, but there was no doubt. He was twisting the wheel with all his strength, and the spokes flashed so fast they were a bright steel colored blur.

Brosnan didn't breath from the time the bombs came free of the diving Stukas until they gradually left their direct arc toward the stern. The stern bounced up and down in the water as the straining rudder pushed it to one side and built up a huge mound of water aft. Then Brosnan knew the bombs would miss, and he let out his breath. Even though they plunged into the water fifty feet from the racing ship, the explosions shook the hull and pushed huge geysers of water toward her. The rumble of the underwater explosions turned into a roar as the explosive gasses broke the surface of the sea and jetted upwards in huge white columns of water and air.

Brosnan looked toward Sperry. He knew that if he had ever had doubts about Sperry's fitness for command, they were gone now. Sperry's hands were steady as rocks, and there was a gleam of sheer pleasure in his eyes as he watched the Stukas race away, followed by the machine gun tracers. One faltered and nosed over, trying to avoid the blue water below, but slowly it sank in the air and then cartwheeled on one wing. The machine gunners cheered, and Brosnan could hear Kuberski shouting congratulations to Raymond on the deck below.

Sperry laughed and turned to Brosnan, "When all those aircraft were coming at us, Kuberski was gyrating around up there in the director like a tidal wave in a bathtub!"

Brosnan nodded. "Lucky for us the stopper was in."

Sperry sobered. "He did a hell of a good job. I've never seen divided fire work that well. Usually every mount fires at a different target all right, but nobody hits anything."

Fifteen minutes later, except for a few oil spots and a little debris floating on the calm surface of the Mediterranean, there was no sign of the violence that had occurred just a few minutes earlier.

Brosnan put the radio headset back over his ears and listened carefully, trying to catch up with all he had missed. At first he was confused. Then he realized that the landing force commander sounded very worried.

Sperry seemed to notice the intense look of concentration on Brosnan's face. "What's the trouble?" he asked.

Brosnan said, "I think the landing force commander has heard that there are two fresh German divisions coming toward the army's perimeter. He's asking for all the naval gunfire he can get, and right now."

Sperry said, "That's includes us. I'll get closer to the edge of the minefield."

In less than five minutes the order came for the *Lawrence* and all possible ships to close the beach, and Fannon navigated the *Lawrence* in again. This time Brosnan was more relaxed as the ship nosed slowly in toward the beach.

Firing orders began to come in from the fire control parties ashore, and soon the cruisers were belching fifteen gun salvos toward the distant mountain passes. So far the tanks were not in range of the five-inch batteries, but Kuberski kept his guns elevated to the maximum range, waiting for the tanks to come closer.

The crew waited tensely, still wrung out by their recent battle with the German aircraft. Down in mount fifty one Bronski wiped sweat from his brow and leaned against the back of his seat at the top of the mount. "Jesus!" he said to the projectile loader below him. "I never saw so many aircraft at one time short of an airport. The bastards were all around us."

The loader rubbed his aching arm muscles. "We really pushed out the rounds."

"Yeah, but this next firing should be easier. We get to wait between salvos while the spots are put in."

He was wrong. When they opened fire the fire control party ashore sounded so frantic Kuberski went right to rapid fire, and the *Lawrence* pumped out almost half of all her ammunition in about an hour. Bronski's loaders were exhausted, and when the order came to cease fire, they slumped down in the mount and wiped the streaming perspiration off of their bodies.

"A hell of a day," Swenson said over the telephone.

Bronski snorted. "You've just been riding up there on the pointer's seat. We've been in automatic all the time, and you aren't even sweating."

Brosnan rubbed his ears when the firing stopped. Like all those on the bridge wearing telephone headsets, his ears had been partially protected, but the captain and all those on the open bridge who had no ear protection other than some hastily jammed-in cotton could hardly hear. Powder residue covered the bridge deck, and down on the forecastle Brosnan could hear brass powder cans rattling around as the mount crews tried to corral them and get them clear of the deck.

At first Brosnan thought there was an overcast forming above, but then he realized so much time had gone by, darkness was falling. A peculiar sensation gnawed at his mid-section. He felt it carefully, probing his belly with his fingers. Then he smiled; he was hungry. It had been a long time since anyone had eaten, and he listened with pleasure as the captain said, "As soon as we get out of this minefield, secure from general quarters and tell the cooks to get the evening meal ready."

Darkness brought some calm ashore and seemingly discouraged the German Luftwaffe. The army commander ashore reported that the Germans were retreating, leaving more than a hundred tanks behind. Brosnan secured his radio headset and hung it on the bulkhead. When condition III was set, he headed below for evening chow. All he wanted was a quiet night and a little sleep. Tomorrow could be an even busier day.

CHAPTER TWENTY-FIVE

The night passed quietly with all hands getting some sleep, but Sperry had to shorten their rest by having breakfast served an hour before dawn. He called the crew to battle stations half an hour later. Brosnan came to the bridge, yawning and rubbing his eyes. Barley met him with a cup of strong black coffee. "This will uncage your eyeballs, sir," he said. "Double strength, hot as hell, and as black as Chief Martin's heart."

Brosnan sipped it tentatively. "Good stuff," he said. "I wouldn't want to put my finger in it."

All was calm until about 0800. Then, just as the watch had changed, a lookout reported a strange trail of vapor to the north.

Sperry grabbed the squawkbox transmitter handle. "CIC, any contacts to the north?"

"Yes, sir, but at long range. They've been there since dawn. They just seem to circle."

Sperry and Brosnan watched the vapor trail. At first it was white; then it turned to a pale green. It was horizontal at first; but then it seemed to dip and come lower. Phelps was watching it, too. "My God!" He said. "That may be one of the radio-guided bombs the intelligence summary has been warning us about!"

Brosnan said, "If it is, it's headed for the *Savannah*."

Now the end of the vapor trail was closer, and Sperry, watching it through his binoculars, shouted, "General quarters! I can see it! It looks like a small, short-winged aircraft, but it's a guided bomb!"

Brosnan said, "Whatever it is, it's fast as hell! Must be going over five hundred knots."

The crew was faster then ever manning their stations, somehow sensing trouble. Kuberski ran up the ladder to the director, pushing slower moving men aside. Brosnan shouted to him as he ran by, telling him that what looked like a radio guided bomb was headed for the *Savannah*.

The cruiser was now firing at it, but their firing was not very effective. Brosnan figured the radar cross section of the small bomb was too small for the fire control radar to pick up, and the speed was too great for the director's optical system to stay on it accurately.

The first bomb fell into the water a hundred feet short of the *Savannah*'s side, raising a gigantic geyser of white water. Brosnan sighed with relief, but the lookouts reported another vapor trail coming in higher. Brosnan hoped the five-inch batteries would do better this time, but the bomb was too fast. A hail of fire met it, but it passed through the curtain of black explosions as if they weren't there. Brosnan tried to will the bomb to miss, but it hit the *Savannah* somewhere around the number three turret and exploded with a tremendous concussion that made the *Lawrence* undulate slowly. A huge gout of black smoke rose above the stricken cruiser.

Brosnan looked to the north where the last two bombs had come from. Another trail was developing, and now the Air Control Center reported a dozen Focke-Wulf 190s slowly approaching from the north. Kuberski apparently saw the vapor trail, too, and the *Lawrence*'s five-inch battery opened fire at long range, following the bomb as it headed for the *Philadelphia*. The cruiser began firing and maneuvered radically as she reached the open sea. The bomb came on, and for a few seconds Brosnan thought it would hit, but the maneuvers threw off the aim of the man in the distant aircraft who was controlling the deadly missile, and it plunged into the water well off the *Philadelphia's* side.

Now the Air Control Center was reporting another flight of suspected Dorniers approaching from the northeast and circling. Brosnan watched anxiously, trying to pierce the increasing smoke and overcast with his binoculars. He hoped the pilots and personnel in the German aircraft would have as much trouble seeing down as he was having seeing up, but he knew that would not be the case. Ships were much bigger than aircraft, and the pilots would have no trouble seeing their huge hulls. Then a vapor trail began to form high overhead to the northeast, and the bomb in front of it nosed over and began to head for the *Lawrence*.

Brosnan realized with horror that the bomb was headed for his ship. He yelled at the captain, but Sperry was watching it, too. It came on inexorably, changing course as the *Lawrence* maneuvered. At the last possible moment Sperry put the rudder over full, but the bomb was so fast and so well guided that it couldn't miss. It had leveled off and was flying almost horizontally, skimming the water. Brosnan estimated it was making six hundred knots. It was the fastest thing he had ever seen, except for a big caliber battleship projectile.

It hit the *Lawrence* in her port side. Brosnan estimated the hit was just at the waterline, and he waited for the concussion of the explosion he was sure would follow and would probably blow the stern off. Seconds passed, and it never came. He began to breath again. Sperry, also waiting, said, "I'll be damned! It didn't detonate."

He turned to Chief Brill, whose white face was even whiter than usual. "Tell CIC to have Mister Fannon go back to the after engine room and assess the damage."

Brosnan looked over the flag bags and saw Fannon running aft. He turned to Chief Brill. "Any news from the engineering spaces?"

Brill shook his head, and Brosnan noted that his face was now a shade darker than it had been when the bomb hit. "Main engine control says the after engine room doesn't answer."

Sperry said, "They're too busy. The exec will find out what's wrong."

Brosnan and the lookouts scanned the sky in the north for more vapor trails, but CIC reported that the contacts to the north had been chased off by Spitfire fighters. Phelps said, "I hope that's the last of them for today. We've got to find out how to counter those guided bombs."

Sperry frowned. "The best way is for our air force fighters and the British fighters to shoot down the aircraft carrying them."

Phelps said dolefully, "I'm not sure they have enough speed to catch the bombs. They will have to stick to shooting down the mother aircraft."

Brosnan stole a look at the nearby *Savannah*. Her forecastle was nearly awash, and she was dead in the water, but two salvage tugs were alongside. Streams of water were shooting from their big pumps as they fought to remove tons of sea water from the damaged ship.

Sperry paced the bridge nervously until the executive officer trotted to the bridge. When he had regained his breath, Fannon said, "You were right. The bomb didn't detonate. It came in the port side at the water line. Crossed over the after engine room, sheared off some piping, and passed out the starboard side. Both holes are being patched temporarily, but the engine room has a lot of water in it. We're down in draft about a foot aft, and the water is up over the throttle station, but as soon as the patches are on and the water is pumped out we should be all right. For the present we'll have to steam on one engine."

Sperry said, "It could have been worse."

"Worse!" Fannon said. "If that bomb had gone off the *Lawrence* would now be in two pieces, neither of them afloat."

Sperry nodded grimly. "Anybody hurt?"

Fannon shook his head. "Nothing serious. A couple of men got some big scrapes scrambling out of the hatch."

Sperry sat down in his chair to compose a casualty report to the task force commander. Brosnan noticed that Sperry had a hard time keeping his hands steady enough to write, but he also noticed that his own hands were trembling. He sighed. This was a war full of harsh surprises, he thought. Now, with the invention of the glide bomb, they were in a new technical area. They would have to learn how to counter this dramatic new weapon if they wanted to survive and win the war.

Barley soon transmitted the casualty report to the flagship, and calm returned to the bridge, each person thinking his own thoughts. Brosnan paced up and down, wondering if they would be ordered to some port in the rear. They were severely handicapped with only one engine in commission for maneuvering under air attack, but they could still fire at shore targets, or at least as long as their ammunition held out. Brosnan estimated they were down to twenty percent of their five-inch ammunition.

His questions were answered when a long message came in by radio. Brosnan took it below to decode it, and soon returned to the bridge. Sperry saw him coming and looked up expectantly. Brosnan noticed the strain around his eyes as he read the message. "Ha!" the captain said. "Tell the navigator to plot a course to catch up with the *Savannah*. We're to join her escort and proceed to Oran for repairs."

The personnel on the bridge smiled when they heard the orders, and in minutes the news was all over the ship.

Brosnan asked CIC where the *Savannah* was. In seconds the answer came back. "Twenty miles to the south, steaming very slowly."

In two hours the *Lawrence* joined her screen, and they steamed steadily south through the night. The *Savannah*, aided by the two salvage tugs, had apparently isolated the flooded compartments, shifted ballast and fuel, and was able to make ten knots, although she was low in the water.

At dawn, the chief engineer reported that the holes in the after engine room bulkhead of the *Lawrence* had been patched temporarily, and the pumps had removed enough water so the watch could get down to the throttles and start steaming on the other engine.

The next morning, the *Lawrence* was detached and directed to proceed to Oran. The *Savannah* and the other destroyers went to Malta.

The bad dream of Salerno faded into their wake astern as Fannon recommended a course for Oran, now only two days away, or less if the *Lawrence* could speed up.

She was able to increase speed the next day as more water was pumped out of the damaged engine room, and in two days the familiar and welcome sight of Oran harbor greeted those on the morning watch. The *Lawrence* rounded the eastern edge of the harbor soon after breakfast, and Sperry conned her alongside the repair ship. When the mooring lines had been doubled up, he turned to Chief Brill. "Tell main engine control we're through with the engines."

Chief Brill said, "Aye, aye, sir. Any idea what's next for us?"

Sperry grinned. "A few days for repairs and rest and then back to the wars."

CHAPTER TWENTY-SIX

The huge bluff side of the repair ship was a welcome sight, and after a few hours the crew, refreshed by several days of slow steaming before arrival in port, headed out to the now familiar pleasures of Oran.

Phelps left the ship almost immediately to call on Admiral Hall and came back with the news that the *Lawrence* would remain alongside the repair ship for at least a week. The other two of his squadron ships would arrive in a few days. After their repairs were completed, they would load ammunition and stand by in the harbor in case they were needed to replace ships that might be damaged off Salerno. When the situation eased at Salerno, the three ships would proceed to Portsmouth, England, for five weeks of overhaul.

Phelps was very serious. "We were lucky to have survived up there. Admiral Hall told me the British battleship *Valiant* was hit by two radio-guided bombs yesterday and had to be towed all the way to Malta."

Cooper whistled. "Yes, we were lucky. How about our other two ships?"

"On their way down here. They're expected alongside us tomorrow."

"What do you think will be the next employment of the amphibious force?" Sperry asked.

"Mostly overhaul for a while. Both the Americans and the British have a lot of damaged boats and smaller landing craft, such as LCTs. Admiral Hall is loading a lot of freighters with damaged tanks, boats, and other equipment."

Sperry frowned. "That's not all they're loading."

Phelps looked puzzled. "What do you mean?"

"I've been watching them. They're loading hundreds of wooden coffins. A lot of young men are going to be taking their last voyage home."

Phelps' long face became even longer. "A lot of them were just boys, too. We lost a hell of a lot of men."

"Will we be involved in escorting them?"

"I think we'll escort the first convoy east. Part of it, the American ships, will continue east to the States, and we'll take the British part to Portsmouth."

After lunch Phelps, the captain, and Lieutenant Kelly went aboard the repair ship to call on the commanding officer. When they were seated, Phelps asked Lieutenant Kelly to give the captain of the repair ship the work requests for the three ships. Kelly fumbled with the mass of papers he had brought, but finally managed to bring order out of the stack. "Here they are," he said, pushing the pile over in front of the commanding officer.

The commanding officer of the repair ship took them and began to leaf through the pile. He stirred uneasily and then finally said in an exasperated tone. "Damn! Each one of these sounds like an engineering school thesis in marine engineering. We don't need all this; all we do is fix things that are broken. Just tell us what things are broken and what's wrong."

Phelps grinned and looked at Kelly. "Well, you won't go over any better in the shipyard at Portsmouth I'm afraid. They don't understand this written stuff either, but I'll get things done there with a few . . . er . . . gifts.''

As Phelps got up to leave, the commanding officer of the repair ship said, "Just a minute, Commodore. I got so mired down in this paperwork I forgot to tell you that I have orders to install the new smoke generators we've just received from the States on your ships.''

"My God, Captain," the commodore said plaintively. "We've spent years training our engineers not to make smoke."

The repair ship captain laughed. "The new generators will be put on your fantails. They consist of a barrel of what's called 'fog oil' and a small burner and fan that produce a heavy white smoke.''

Phelps scratched his head. "I guess that's the first attempt to counter the radio-guided bombs, but it won't be enough.''

For a week, the sound of riveting hammers filled the day. Blue welding arcs flickered and flashed as holes were patched and braces strengthened.

On the second day the new smoke generators were installed on the fantails as the gunner's mates and engineers watched. Chief Marusak said, "That's not for the engineers. It belongs to you gunnery guys.''

The chief gunner's mate got red in the face and shouted, "It's smelly and smoky just like you snipes. It's yours!''

The executive officer finally settled the issue by turning it over to the engineering department for operation—much to the disgust of Chief Marusak.

At the end of a week, the three destroyers got up steam, tested their engineering plants, and backed away

from the repair ship. Then, one by one, they went alongside an ammunition ship anchored well out in the bay
and loaded ammunition. Bronski, in charge of the group
bringing aboard ammunition for his mount, was tense as
he watched the cases of powder and the projectiles being
lifted out of the slings lowered by the ammunition ship
to the forecastle. Bronski, watching Swenson pick up a
projectile, shook his head. "Jesus, Swenson, that stuff's
live. Take it easy."

Swenson grinned, and purposely let one end of a projectile partially slip from his hand. "Oops!" he cried as
he got his hand back on it just before it reached the deck.

Bronski was livid. "See what I mean! You could have
blown the whole forecastle off and us with it."

"Aw, Bronski, take it easy. I was just kidding. I had it
under control all the way."

Bronski took out a red bandanna and wiped his neck.
"Didn't look like it to me. This ain't nothing to kid
about."

"You could always take me out of the line and let me
do the counting."

"Naw, you'd foul that up, too. Stay where you are.
Just remember, I've got your liberty card. If you screw up
again, you might have to stay aboard and not see that
broad you met last night."

Swenson sighed. "All right. You win. I'm careful from
now on."

The next morning Phelps took the three commanding
officers with him to call on Admiral Hall. The admiral
received them graciously and asked them to sit down.
"Well, Phelps, we've been through a lot together, and
unless I miss my guess, in a couple of months we'll be
back together again. You and your ships have always
been superb, and I've grown to depend on you."

Phelps grinned proudly. "Thank you, Admiral, for all of us. I think we'll have a fourth ship with us when we come back from the UK."

"How so?"

"The *Thatcher* is completing refresher training and will join us later in Portsmouth."

"What about the other division in your squadron?"

"Still building. They'll report to me in about four months."

Admiral Hall nodded. "They'll miss the next operation down here, but not the big one across the channel."

Phelps had a hard time containing his curiosity. "Sir, do you have any information you can share with us as to the next operation down here?"

The admiral pursed his lips, got up, and walked over to a wall map of the Mediterranean. He looked at it closely and then thrust a forefinger at the center of Italy and swung it north. "It all depends on how long it takes our army and the British army to move north. My guess is we'll land somewhere within fifty miles of Anzio in about three months."

Phelps said, "Thank you. In that case we'll be back in plenty of time."

The Admiral grinned. "You certainly will. If the operation is speeded up, you'll get a quick message bringing you back here in a hurry."

On the first of October, the three ships left Oran and began to escort, along with three other American destroyers, a convoy of twelve transports. Sperry examined them through his binoculars. "They've got damaged LCTs and tanks all over their topsides. Also some other landing craft. My guess is that their holds are full, too, both with damaged landing craft and the coffins I saw being loaded."

Late the next day the convoy sailed by the enormous rock at Gibraltar. When they were clear, the convoy split into two sections. Phelps found himself in command of six British transports, escorted by his three destroyers. He directed the senior transport commander to form a rectangular formation and put the three destroyers ahead in a bent line screen.

On the wing of the bridge Sperry watched the transports jockeying for position, and the other two destroyers of the squadron speeding for their positions on either side of the *Lawrence*. He turned to the commodore. "Sir, I heard some disturbing news over at the port director's office in Oran. It seems the German U-boats have been forced to go south from their French ports and cut across the Bay of Biscay on their way to the central Atlantic. That means we may encounter some of them the next four days before we reach port."

Phelps nodded. "I heard the same thing from Admiral Hall's staff. Just as soon as we settle down in formation I'm going to choose a radical zigzag route. Also we'll patrol our stations back and forth instead of steaming on a steady course. That way we'll never be steady on a single course for more than a few minutes."

"Good. I'll feel safer that way."

Two days later CIC reported an air contact ahead. Sperry asked, "What's it doing?"

"It seems to be circling," CIC replied. "We think it may be an antisubmarine patrol either out of Land's End in southern England or from a hunter-killer group."

Sperry said, "Try to communicate with it."

CIC was unable to raise the aircraft, but in an hour reported a surface contact on the same bearing as the aircraft, and soon the mast of a ship began to appear over the horizon. In another half hour the stacks and hull could be seen, and CIC reported that it was circling a position ahead.

Phelps said, "Obviously a destroyer looking for a submarine. Must be part of one of the hunter-killer groups that have chased the German submarines back into the Bay of Biscay. They're making real progress in the war against the U- boats."

A lookout shouted, "The destroyer has three stacks, sir."

Brosnan, who had the deck, said, "That makes it an American. The fifty four-stackers we gave the British still have all their stacks."

A signal light began to blink from the destroyer ahead. Barley watched it through his spotting telescope and Acton wrote the message on his clipboard. Phelps read it over his shoulder. "The message is from the destroyer *O'Leary*. She requests permission to proceed on duty assigned."

Phelps scratched his head. "I don't like this. We're headed right for her, and I think she has a submarine down. Send back, 'Permission granted. What are you doing?' "

Back came the answer, "Am attacking a submarine, probably a new Sea Wolf class. Recommend you change course to west to avoid contact."

Phelps said, "That makes sense. Cooper, hoist a signal 'nine turn.' "

Cooper relayed the order to Chief Martin, and the flags fluttered up to the mast head. When the signal had been answered, Phelps nodded and said, "Execute."

The flags whipped down, the blocks above squealing, and Brosnan ordered, "Left standard rudder."

For half an hour the formation steamed west. Just as Phelps was about to turn the formation north again, CIC reported, "Surface radar contact bearing two eight zero."

Phelps said, "Let's hold off and see who this is."

The contact was closing fast, and in a few minutes the lookouts reported, "The contact is a small escort type carrier followed by a destroyer."

"Exchange calls with him," Phelps said.

There was a flurry of blinking signal lights, and then Chief Martin said, "It's the escort carrier *Santee*, in command of a hunter-killer group, and he wants permission to proceed on duty assigned."

Phelps nodded in acknowledgment. "Tell him affirmative and good luck."

When the carrier had passed to the east toward the *O'Leary*, Phelps turned the convoy back to the north.

Sperry called down to CIC. "If Ensign Aronson is down there ask him to come to the bridge."

In a few minutes Aronson came to the bridge and reported to the captain. "Yes, sir?"

"Aronson, weren't you on board the four-stacker *O'Leary* not too long ago?"

Aronson nodded and grinned. "Yes, sir, and I hear we just passed her."

"What was it like on her?"

Aronson shuddered. "Well, she was a fine ship. Good skipper, good crew, but she only had four-inch guns, torpedoes, and a lot of depth charges. She rolled like hell, even in the calmest seas. And I was aboard her in the North Atlantic. In winter, her bridge was the coldest place I've ever been. I'm glad I'm here. At least our guns will fire at aircraft. The *O'Leary* has no protection from aircraft except a few machine guns and an ancient three-inch anti-aircraft gun without a director. I hear from my sonar bulletins that there's a new type of submarine just coming into use by the Germans called a Sea Wolf. I hope the *O'Leary* doesn't tangle with one of those."

"That bad?"

Aronson shuddered. "The Sea Wolves have a 4.1-inch deck gun and eight 20-millimeter machine guns, and soon will have acoustic torpedoes. She's also bigger than the *O'Leary* by a couple of hundred tons."

Sperry whistled. "A helluva handful."

Two days later the four ancient forts of Spithead guarding the entrance to Portsmouth Harbor loomed out of the morning mist. Phelps watched the shoreline eagerly. "There's the Isle of Wight," he said, "and the Southsea Common, the recreational beach."

Sperry shivered in the fall air. "Not much use at this time of year," he said.

Fannon navigated the ship to the entrance, where a ruddy faced pilot boarded. Brosnan met him at the sea ladder put over the side and brought him to the bridge. The pilot waved airily at Sperry, who met him at the top of the ladder. "Mornin', Skipper. Always glad to see you Yanks. I'm Captain Bligh, no kin to the famous Bligh of old."

Sperry introduced the pilot to the commodore and turned the conn over to him. The pilot said, "We don't have any mine fields. Just a net, and we'll be there soon."

"How's the damage to the navy yard?" Phelps asked.

Bligh shook his head soberly. "Pretty bad, but they'll take care of you. The Huns can't hurt the graving docks, and the lads who do the work all have their own tools. I'm to take you to one of the work areas. The chaps behind you won't need any pilots. Just signal them to follow you and come alongside after we're moored. It'll be a week or so before you go into the graving docks."

"How old is the navy yard?" Phelps asked.

"It dates from 1496, I think."

"My God! Almost as old as the discovery of America."

The pilot scratched his bristly beard. "Well, that may be old to you, but it ain't to us."

By 0900 the ships were snugly secured at a pier, and steam and water hoses and electric cables were being connected. Commodore Phelps got word that the navy yard authorities wanted to meet in the *Lawrence*'s wardroom at 1000 to go over the work to be done. He called the other commanding officers over at 0930 and included Lieutenant Commander Cooper and Lieutenant Kelly in the conference.

Kelly piled a sheaf of papers on the table. Phelps shook his head. "Oh, no you don't, Kelly. Only one sheet of paper per job."

Kelly frowned. "But, Commodore, they may not approve the jobs without adequate backup."

Phelps turned to Cooper. "Adrian, get the 'backup' ready."

Cooper grinned and left the room.

Kelly was confused. "But, sir, don't you need these explanations?"

Phelps said, "No, I don't think so. These old yard codgers have been doing this sort of thing for years. All you have to do is tell them what the problem is, where the machinery is located, and what you want done. They'll look at the machinery, not your long-winded explanations. Then when they've seen all they want to see, I'll have them back here and we'll settle the whole thing with a little friendly persuasion and the 'backup' Cooper is assembling."

Sperry grinned. "I take it the 'backup' is what's left of your Scotch whiskey and cigars."

Phelps laughed. "Ah, yes, and thank heaven we've returned to the source of supply just in time. I'm just about out, and the cellar of dear Lord Staggers, rest his soul, is only two hours away by covered van."

The yard managers arrived promptly at 1000, and, as Phelps had predicted, the session with the paperwork was brief, punctuated by the occasional "I say," loud coughs, and "blighty." After the group had inspected what needed repair in the three ships, they headed for the commodore's cabin.

Phelps winked at the three commanding officers. "Well, gentlemen, I think you can go off to work. I'm having the yard managers to lunch with me, and we'll settle all these repair lists then." The other two commanding officers started to protest, but Sperry took over and ushered them out.

About 1300, the commodore sent for Cooper. Cooper went in the cabin carrying several boxes. When he came out, he was gagging on cigar smoke. Some swirled around him and escaped out of the cabin as he closed the door behind him. Kelly, anxiously awaiting him outside the door, asked, "What's going on?"

Cooper laughed and wiped his streaming eyes. "I coulddn't see much through the cigar smoke. I just delivered my packages and left."

"What packages?"

"Jesus, Kelly," Cooper said. "Where were you when they handed out common sense? The packages of Scotch whiskey and cigars, of course."

Half an hour later Cooper accompanied the commodore to the brow as the yard managers left the ship. Each one shook Phelps' hand vigorously and grinned widely.

Kelly noticed that each one carried a large heavy paper shopping bag. When they were gone, he eased up to the commodore, who was watching them disappear into the nearby building. "Sir, how did we make out?"

Phelps laughed. "Just fine. They approved everything. If something else comes up, go for it."

Kelly grinned shyly. "I guess you'll be making a new supply run soon."

Phelps sighed and his eyes brightened. "Ah, yes. I've got to go pack right away. I see you're catching on to the repair and overhaul business as it's done in merry old England."

CHAPTER TWENTY-SEVEN

The next morning the commodore appeared on the quarterdeck just after breakfast. He had told Sperry that he was leaving for three weeks leave at his wife's estate. Sperry, Cooper, Fannon, and Brosnan were there to see him off. He waved airily, picked up a battered British-style carpet bag, and got into an ancient taxi for the ride to the railroad station.

Brosnan went to the wardroom with Fannon to have a cup of coffee and to go over the leave program for the officers and men. When the general arrangements were agreed upon, Fannon said, "The commodore has invited me to visit him on his wife's estate at the end of the week."

Brosnan said, "I'll bet you'll like that. She must be an excellent hostess."

Fannon shrugged slightly. "This won't be just a social visit. The commodore says he's interested in my opinion on Lady Claudia's horses, or at least her race horses."

"I know you have a lot of horses on your Oklahoma ranch, but do you have any racing stock?"

"Only quarter horses. But this is what the commodore is interested in. Apparently Lady Claudia's horses jump well, and have good endurance, but not enough speed to suit the commodore, or at least they seldom win. He thinks they need a little infusion of what my horses have. 'Quickness off the mark,' as he says.''

Brosnan nodded. "Sounds reasonable."

After settling the leave program for the enlisted men, Fannon said, ''Now for the officers. The captain is staying aboard. You know I'm going off for two weeks. That leaves the question of who will be covering my job as executive officer for the time I'll be gone. You and Kuberski are qualified to do it. Kuberski should be here at first while the torpedo mount is being installed. Is there any reason why you shouldn't leave tomorrow for your two weeks?''

Brosnan scratched his head. "No, not that I can think of. I've looked over the corrections to the confidential communication publications and codes we received this morning. Farraday can start on the simple corrections, and I can finish up the rest when I get back.''

"That does it, then. The other officers can be divided into two groups for two weeks each. Get your leave papers to me by this afternoon. I'll get the captain to sign them, and you can leave tomorrow morning.''

The next morning, just after breakfast, Brosnan was in his room packing his bag. There was a loud knock on his door and Cooper came striding in without waiting for an answer.

"Brosnan, I've told you about this before. You might just as well pick out your LST.''

Brosnan raised his eyebrows. "What the hell is wrong now?''

"I hear you're going on leave, and you never said anything to me about getting permission.''

Brosnan grinned patiently. "Why should I? The commodore is gone, and I have permission from the executive officer and signed leave papers from the captain. I may

work part-time for the commodore in matters of communications, but I don't consider I work for you.''

''We'll see about that when the commodore comes
back. What about all those corrections to the communications manuals and codes we just got aboard?''

''I've looked through them, and there aren't any that
can't wait. Farraday will work on them while I'm gone,
and I'll finish when I get back. It wouldn't hurt you to
help, either.''

Cooper sneered. ''That isn't good enough. I'll be
damned if I'm going to do your work or cover for you.''
He looked at the leave papers lying on Brosnan's desk
and said, ''I suppose these are your leave papers.''

''Yeah.''

Cooper grabbed the papers and started to tear them
up. Before he could make the first tear, Brosnan was on
him and had his right wrist in a wristlock.

''Ouch!'' Cooper gasped. ''You're going to break it.''

''Let go of my leave papers,'' Brosnan hissed. They
fluttered to the floor, and Brosnan let go of Cooper's wrist
and picked the papers up.

Cooper rubbed his wrist and said. ''Jesus! You could
have broken it.''

''I wouldn't have left a mark on you, but if you hadn't
let go you would have been flat on your back on the floor
in about ten seconds.''

Brosnan left in mid-morning in the same ancient taxi that
had taken the commodore to the train station the day
before. The driver said, ''Where to, Yank?''

Brosnan said, ''The train station.''

The driver said, ''We don't call it that, Mate, but I know
where you want to go. The same place that bloke went to
yesterday. He looked like a real boffin, but a nice chap.''

Brosnan laughed. ''He's a boffin all right. He knows all
about the technical stuff, but he's also a real seaman.''

As they drove through the streets of Portsmouth, Brosnan noted the devastation the German bombers had done. Many buildings were burned and gutted, but business was going on as usual with temporary patches rigged over the roofs of the buildings still standing. Brosnan noted the remarkably cheerful faces of the men and women passing by the neatly piled rubble. He said to the driver, "These people act like there never was a war."

The driver laughed, "They won't forget what the Jerries did to them as long as old Winnie is around. We'll help him give some of this damage back to the Huns before long."

During the three hour train trip to London, Brosnan watched the countryside. It was still green and peaceful with no evident damage, and some of the leaves were still on the trees. As the train reached the outskirts of London and pulled into the station, the scenes of devastation began again. They became even worse as Brosnan took a taxi to the Embassy, where he got a list of places advertising bed-and-breakfasts.

He liked the first one he visited, run by a rosy-cheeked war widow. He stored his gear in his room and sat down to study a map of London he had picked up in the railroad station. When he thought he had a reasonable grasp of the location of major buildings, he took the piece of paper out of his wallet that Emile Piccard had given him weeks ago in Oran. He remembered Piccard's words about calling the telephone number on the battered piece of paper, and he was glad he hadn't destroyed it as Piccard had directed. All the strife he had gone through since then had dimmed his memory of the number.

The landlady showed him the telephone, and he asked the operator for the number. A voice answered, and Brosnan said, "My name is Lieutenant Robert Brosnan,

United States Navy. I was told I could contact Annette Duchamp at this number.'' There was a short silence, a rustling of paper, and a brief conversation in French in the background. Then the voice said, ''Go to the corner of Marlboro Street and Vincent Street in an hour. Someone will contact you.''

''But how will they know me?''

''I think you'll be the only man in an American lieutenant's uniform standing there. The person will know you.''

Brosnan left his boarding house and flagged a battered taxi. The driver had no trouble finding the corner, but Brosnan found himself half an hour early. He walked down Marlboro Street for a few minutes and then returned to the corner. He was still early, but he was so eager to get on with the meeting that he stood there looking at his watch until a man came up behind him quietly and tapped him on the shoulder. Brosnan started, and turned around. It was Emile Piccard. Brosnan said, ''I didn't expect to see you.''

''I know,'' Piccard said. ''But we closed out the office in Africa a week ago, and I was transferred here. If you will come with me, I'll help you find Annette.''

They walked in silence for two blocks, the Frenchman obviously looking around to make sure they weren't followed. They circled one block and stopped occasionally so Piccard could look back over his shoulder. Then he ducked into the lower entrance to a small apartment building, pulling Brosnan after him. Then, after a last look up the street, he said quietly to Brosnan, ''Go in here. Walk up to the third floor. Annette is in apartment three.'' He held out his hand and grinned. ''Good luck. You are a very—how do you say it?—fortunate man.''

Brosnan bounded up the first flight of stairs, but then slowed down for the other two, realizing that he should not do anything to attract attention. He took a deep breath and knocked on the door of apartment three. It opened immediately, and Annette pulled him inside and closed the door. She folded him in her arms. "Oh, Beetle, how I have missed you!"

For a long time he couldn't say anything because of the lump in his throat, and he kissed her deeply. He said hoarsely, "Oh, Annette, I was afraid I'd never see you again."

She frowned. "Why not?"

Brosnan led her over to a couch and they sat down, still in each other's arms. "Well, for one thing, I now know you do dangerous work, and I was afraid you might be in France before I got here to see you."

She paused before she replied. "I guess Emile told you. I do some things that are dangerous, but I have to." Then she frowned. "I go to France next week, but we have all that time. Do you have that much leave?"

"Yes. Two weeks."

"I'm afraid I can't tell you exactly when, or even what day I will leave. It depends on the weather, but it won't be for at least five days."

"The weather? You're going to parachute in?"

She shrugged. "That's easier than going by submarine, and quicker."

Brosnan got up and paced up and down. "Damn!" he said. "I just find you and you're going to be gone again."

She pulled him down beside her again. "Beetle, some day after the war we'll be together for the rest of our lives."

Brosnan breathed deeply. "That brings up something else. I was going to ask you to marry me after the war, but Piccard tells me you're a rich vineyard owner, with a chateau and everything. You couldn't possibly want me. I'm just an Iowa farm boy in a sailor suit."

She smiled. "I'll admit I like you better out of the suit, but that has nothing to do with the problem. I love you just as you are. Besides, I might like to see America after the war. Then we can come back to France to my chateau, if you want to, and rebuild what's left of my business.''

"What's wrong with it?''

"Not much, I think. I'll see it when I go back to France. The Germans haven't hurt the chateau, and the local farmers on my land are taking care of the vineyards. The Germans leave them alone because they want the wine. Now we talk too much. We have more time for this. Let's get you out of that uniform.''

"But I don't have any other clothes except a spare uniform back at my room.''

"You won't need any tonight. I brought some caftans and robes with me. tomorrow we'll pick up your other things and you can move in here.''

By the next morning Brosnan was sure of what he wanted to do. Live forever with Annette, no matter where it was. They forced themselves to stop their lovemaking to enjoy breakfast, and by noon they were up, dressed, and off to move Brosnan out of his room and into Annette's apartment.

The four days that followed were the best Brosnan had ever experienced. Each morning Annette left to check in with her organization. When she returned, they had a leisurely breakfast and then were off to explore London and even to ride by train out into the countryside for long walks.

But each night Brosnan could sense in Annette a growing tenseness, and when she returned from her daily visit to her office, he couldn't help feeling that each day might be their last. Each night they made love with growing intensity. On the fourth night, Annette said, "This might be our last night, Beetle. I want you to know how much this time has meant to me.''

Brosnan sighed. "I'll never forget it, or you either. And I'm liking Europe more and more. If you'll still have me, I think I could live happily with you in France."

She smothered him with kisses, and he could feel tears on her face. "This will last forever, Beetle, even if we don't live on this earth much longer."

Brosnan knew the time was getting short.

CHAPTER TWENTY-EIGHT

On the fifth day Annette came back from her office with her head was down. Her walk was slow as she entered the small living room. Brosnan knew immediately, and he took a deep breath. "Tonight?" he asked.

"Yes, *cheri*. They'll come for me after dinner, and I fly out tonight."

Brosnan sighed and the sigh became a shudder. He shook his head slowly. "One last dinner."

She tried to smile, but the tears were in the way. "Let's make it the best we can."

For an hour they prepared all the food that remained in the small pantry. Brosnan uncorked a bottle of wine and they began to eat. Annette said, "You did that well. This is not a very good wine, but it tastes like nectar to me."

"Do you make better on your estate?"

"Oh, yes. We wouldn't even sell this to American tourists."

Brosnan laughed. "Careful. I'm still an American."

She grinned. "Not for long. You even look a little like a Frenchman. Piccard wanted to know if we could possibly recruit you for our work."

"What did you tell him?"

"I said you were needed where you were."

"But if I could join you?"

"You couldn't. Your French isn't good enough."

At 1900 Piccard knocked on the door. Brosnan and Annette had already said their good-byes, and Annette walked through the door dry eyed and without looking back. Piccard said to Brosnan, "You can stay in the apartment until the end of next week. Leave the key with the concierge."

Brosnan did not dare trust his voice. He nodded silently, still watching Annette.

Annette turned as she went down the stairs and waved one last time. Brosnan lifted a hand in a last salute, closed the door carefully, heaved a large sigh, and jammed his fist against the wall. A large dimple appeared in the plaster. "Damn!" he said. A flake of white plaster fluttered to the floor.

Brosnan spent another week wandering aimlessly around London, but there was nothing that interested him except the places he had been with Annette. He stopped for tea in a small tea room they had liked, but he was so depressed he left without anything. He took long, aimless walks, for several hours at a time, often getting lost. A friendly bobby usually had to give him directions back to the apartment.

On his last day in London, he stopped at a bookstore and bought a French dictionary, a French grammar, a guide book to France, a book on the history of French wines and their tasting, and two books on vineyard cultivation. The next morning he boarded a train in Victoria Station for Portsmouth. He settled his suitcase and bag of books on the rack overhead and took a seat near the window. He took out one of the books on vineyard cultivation. He tried to read it, but after thirty minutes he realized he was still on page two. He sighed and threw it on the opposite seat.

All the way to Portsmouth he watched the same scenery he had seen on the way north. Coming to London, he had noticed the green in the grass, the sparkle in the wet dew, and the beauty of the countryside. Now it seemed to him that the same scene was dark, damp, and desolate. Halfway back he pulled the shade down and sat back with his eyes closed for the rest of the trip.

The same elderly taxi driver took him back to the shipyard. "Yank, you look like you musta got caught in the blitz," the driver said.

Brosnan looked at him blankly and shook his head. "How did you know?" he asked.

The driver laughed. "I've seen a lot of chaps like you in my time."

Kuberski met him on the quarterdeck. "Glad to see you, Beetle. I'm looking forward to getting ashore to see England."

"When's the executive officer getting back?"

"He came back this morning."

"How did he survive his visit with the commodore?"

"Fine. I've never seen him in finer form. Smiled all day long. Maybe you ought to go down and see him before he runs out of smiles."

Brosnan put his bag in his room and then went to the executive officer's stateroom. He knocked at the door frame. A cheery voice said, "Come in."

Brosnan pushed aside the curtain and went into the room. Fannon smiled broadly and said, "Glad to see you. Did you make connections with Annette?"

Brosnan sat down wearily and said, "Yes, but she's gone to France. I may never see her again."

Fannon sobered. "You look pretty bad. What's she doing over there? From what I hear tourists aren't very welcome."

"She's not a tourist; she's a spy."

Fannon pushed back his chair. "Good God! No! Those Nazis aren't to be fooled with. Where's she going?"

"To the countryside where she used to live. She'll be all right. The local people know her, and she speaks good French with a local accent."

"You don't sound very optimistic, despite what you say."

Brosnan sighed. "Enough of me and my troubles. How did you make out?"

The smile returned to Fannon's face. "I'm living again," he said cheerfully.

Brosnan looked closely at Fannon's beaming face. "I thought you were separated from your wife."

"I am, and very amicably. We agreed to stay married until after the war so she would be eligible for a pension in case something happened to me. We'll be divorced after the war."

"But you met someone else?"

"Yes, Cornelia."

"Where did you meet her?"

"She's Lady Claudia's sister."

"Nice looking?"

"Yes. She has curves everywhere Lady Claudia has angles. Oh, I didn't mean it that way. Lady Claudia is very attractive, but in a more mature way. It's evident that she and the commodore are very happy."

"And there was more to Cornelia than curves?"

Fannon beamed. "A whole lot. She loves horses. She's training Lady Claudia's."

"Are they good horses?"

"Not bad, but as the commodore said, a little slow of foot. I think my Oklahoma quarter horses can perk them up. Put a little pepper in their pot, as we used to say in Oklahoma."

"And you'll have to come back to England with them?"

"You're very astute, Beetle. I'll be over here as soon as the war is over and I can get out of the navy."

"Whoa, this is a little speedy. Are you sure you know the girl that well?"

"We spent every hour of the last two weeks together, either on the estate or on horses."

"Did the English saddles and bridles give you any trouble?"

"How did you know?"

"Well, I'm no cowhand, but I did spend a lot of time on my uncle's farm. I learned to ride when I was about six. Good horses, too."

"Where did you get good riding horses on a wheat and corn farm?"

"When tractors replaced horses, my uncle traded his plow horses for some good saddle stock. He always had a few good ones around for riding."

Fannon grinned. "It took me a day or so to get used to the English saddles without pommels. I felt naked. The system of controlling the horse is different, too, but that only took me a day to learn. I would have done it sooner, but I couldn't concentrate."

"Miss Cornelia got in the way."

"Beetle, you're a marvel."

"While I'm being a marvel, I'll give you a free prediction. by the time the war is over, transport aircraft will be flying the Atlantic several times daily. Even horses will fly the Atlantic."

"Where did you get that dope?"

"From a friend I know in London. He says the Douglas Aircraft Company is building a transport aircraft called the R6D that flies the Atlantic even now with a single stop at Iceland. Just think of all the airfields we've built around the world already and the thousands of pilots we will have trained. Aviation will never be the same."

Fannon was silent for a few minutes. "Yes," he said slowly. "We could keep my ranch going and the horse operation in England, too."

A week later the commodore came back in a Rolls Royce, followed by a covered van. Sperry and Brosnan met him at the brow. Sperry said, "I was hoping Lady Claudia would be with you. Fannon says she's charming, and I was looking forward to meeting her."

Phelps shook his head. "No, and Fannon will be glad to hear that Cornelia is about to preside at a foaling. Claudia won't let her do it alone."

The van backed up to the brow, and a working party began to bring boxes up the brow and take them down to the commodore's storeroom. Phelps watched them carefully, drawing in his breath suddenly whenever a man stumbled.

Brosnan, who had the day's duty, stood next to him. "Sir, I think I can take care of this if you want me to. Lieutenant Commander Cooper is ashore."

Phelps grinned. "No, if there's any trouble about this . . . er . . . cargo, I'll take the responsibility, and I don't want you involved."

When all the square boxes had been loaded, Brosnan said, "Sir, I don't see any cigars."

Phelps sighed. "There aren't any there. Lady Claudia has persuaded me to give them up. She—" the commodore heaved a great sigh. She burned all that were left."

Brosnan suppressed a grin. "Too bad she didn't just give them to the neighbors."

Phelps regained his composure and laughed. "She did. In the form of smoke. The neighbors complained for days about the smoke, even though nobody lives very close because the estate is pretty big. Well, that's it. I hope your stay in London was pleasant. Cooper wrote me a letter about you."

Brosnan blanched, and he could feel the noose tightening. "Sir, I can explain that."

Phelps grinned. "Stop worrying. I may be an old fud, but I understand these things. How about some bridge tonight? Fannon should be an easy mark. He doesn't know whether he's walking or flying. Love, you know, does strange things."

Brosnan was glum. "It's great in his case, but in my case it has its problems."

Phelps looked carefully at Brosnan. "When you have time I'd like to hear about your problem. Maybe I can help."

Brosnan shook his head. "I'm afraid the only thing that will help me is hard work and getting back to sea."

Phelps nodded. "You'll be getting plenty of both soon."

CHAPTER TWENTY- NINE

For the last few days of October and the beginning of November, Brosnan struggled to finish the corrections to the confidential publications in his safe and to bring the codes up to date. He had trouble concentrating because he kept worrying about Annette. Had she been captured? Was she all right? Would he ever see her again? Then he realized he would have to find a way to get on with his work, and he resolved to confine thinking about Annette to the hours of darkness. He tried to focus his attention on his work until dinner time. Each evening he paced up and down the forecastle in the autumn coolness. After an hour or so he was tired enough to try to sleep. When he heaved himself into his bunk, Doctor Taylor growled, ''For heaven's sake, Beetle, steady down up there. Last night you twisted and turned all night. That won't help. You've got to learn to sleep. Do you want some pills?''

Brosnan sighed. ''They won't help. I guess time will take care of it.''

Farraday and Kuberski fussed over the new torpedo tube mount, and when it was installed to their liking, they drew replacement torpedoes and prepared them for war shots, painstakingly following the complicated check-off lists that came with the huge silver fish. On the fifteenth of November Farraday pronounced himself satisfied, and Kelly told the captain they would be ready to leave, as far as the engineering department was concerned, on the twentieth.

"How about the progress on the other two ships?" Sperry asked Lieutenant Kelly.

"They're right on schedule, and I've told the commodore as much."

On the nineteenth the *Thatcher*, the fourth ship of their division, entered port, and the commanding officer came over to report for duty to the commodore. The same day Ensign Aronson came back from the port director's office with their sailing orders and a brief on intelligence regarding the possible dangers in the waters between Portsmouth and Gibraltar. The officers gathered in the wardroom so he could pass on the information he had collected.

When all were present, Aronson cleared his throat. "First, the bad news. The *O'Leary* was sunk about the first of November. She had a terrific running battle with the first of the large Sea Wolf class submarines to put to sea."

Sperry interrupted. "What about the U-boat?"

"She was sunk, too. The submarine blew the stern off of the *O'Leary* with one of the first acoustic torpedoes the Germans have used, but the *O'Leary*, lying dead in the water, torpedoed the German submarine."

Sperry whistled slowly. "We'll have to watch out for those big bastards."

Kuberski nodded. "Almost as bad as their damned radio-guided bombs."

Aronson said, "That's part of my good news. The British boffins are working on a solution."

Kuberski scratched his head. "Just what the hell are boffins? They sound like something my mother used to use in her sewing machine."

Aronson shook his head, "Boffins are what the British call their scientists and inventors. Guys who come up with engineering solutions to problems like defending against the guided bombs. They don't have the problem completely solved yet, but I've been assured that before we operate off Italy again we'll have some help."

Sperry said, "We'll need something more than the funny-looking smoke generators that're lousing up our fantail."

"Sir, I think the solution will be better than that," Aronson said.

Kuberski looked around the wardroom for Kelly, but he was on another ship checking on the state of their repairs for the commodore. Kuberski smiled and said, "I think our chief engineer is sort of a boffin. He can draw you a sketch of the entire electrical system of the ship in about ten minutes, but he can't change a light bulb."

Fannon laughed. "I think you've got it."

Sperry was deep in thought and ignored the exchange. He asked, "Any information on what kind of submarine opposition we may encounter between here and Gibraltar?"

"Not much. The usual U-boats crossing from the neutral waters off Portugal and Spain to the central Atlantic. We'll have an antisubmarine aircraft patrol with us the first three days."

"That's well over a thousand miles. Do our aircraft have that much range?"

"Yes, sir," Aronson said. "That's one reason we're winning the antisubmarine war now. Our shore based long-range aircraft and our hunter-killer groups are sinking double the number of U-boats they sank last year."

"Do we escort any ships south?"

"Yes, sir. The commodore and all commanding officers are expected at the port director's office at 0800 tomorrow for a conference with the convoy commodore. We get underway at 1200."

The next morning the commodore and his captains left for the port director's office at 0745 and returned an hour later. Sperry called a quick conference of all officers and passed out sheets of paper giving the convoy's formations and call signs for communications. Brosnan posted copies on the bridge and in CIC, and they were ready to go.

When the word was passed to man all stations for getting underway, Brosnan was eager to get up into the fresh air and to get on with the war. Every day was one day towards the end of it and the time when he might see Annette again.

The same pilot boarded them and conned the *Lawrence* out the channel. When he was ready to leave, Brosnan accompanied him to the quarterdeck and called his launch alongside. The pilot looked closely at Brosnan. "Well, young fellow, the rest doesn't seem to have done you any good. You look worse that when you came into port."

Brosnan grinned weakly. "I'm okay. On behalf of our officers and men I thank you and your countrymen for all of your kind hospitality."

The pilot waved and dropped neatly into the pilot boat. Brosnan headed back for the bridge. The *Lawrence* increased speed and the waves began to slap against the side of the ship as Brosnan walked forward. He breathed in the salt air, looked over the side at the building wake, and felt better.

When he got back to the bridge, Sperry gave him the conn and CIC gave him a course to the *Lawrence*'s position in the four ship screen. He gave the necessary orders to the helmsman and raised his binoculars to scan the eight British merchantmen standing out of the harbor entrance and taking a rectangular formation. He was back at sea again, and he knew he would have little time to think about his troubles. Maybe that was best. Then he heard the loud voice of Lieutenant Commander Cooper somewhere on the bridge, and he grinned. Some of his troubles he would have to take with him, but the situation couldn't be all bad. The Commodore had seemed to understand, and after all, he was the head boffin, as the taxi driver had said.

By the next morning, the weather had cooled. As the convoy moved south into the Bay of Biscay, the chop was replaced by the usual North Atlantic swells. The *Lawrence* met the face of each long swell, rose to the top of it, and coasted down the back of the long mountain of water.

In Brosnan's stateroom, Doctor Taylor moaned with each swoop and gasped with each rise. Brosnan tried to ignore his agony, but finally heaved himself out of his upper bunk, dressed, and made his way to the wardroom for breakfast. Only Fannon and Kuberski were eating. Kuberski spotted Brosnan and said, "Hi, Beetle, the junior officers seem to be otherwise . . . er . . . occupied. You got here just in time. The hotcakes are about gone."

Brosnan waited for just the right moment, when the ship was poised at the top of a swell, and got into a chair secured to a stanchion. Jason came over, grabbed the stanchion, and asked in an unsteady voice, "Sir, what will you have?"

Brosnan grinned. "Anything you can cook out there in the pantry this morning. Hotcakes if there are any left after Mister Kuberski has finished."

Jason said, "I saved some for you."

Kuberski looked up from the stack in front of him. "What's the matter with everyone? This weather isn't bad."

Fannon shook his head. "I think some of them tried to empty all the beer barrels in the nearest pub the last week."

Kuberski said expansively, "Well, they should have come with me instead."

Brosnan said, "Where'd you go?"

"I took a train up to the Land of Lakes. It was beautiful and very relaxing. Then I went to London."

Fannon looked at Kuberski searchingly. "Stanley, you never cease to amaze me. Next you'll be telling me you went to the museums in London."

Kuberski put down his fork. "No, most of them were closed. The exhibits had been shipped out to the country for safekeeping. I did see some local art, though. I guess it wasn't valuable enough to evacuate.''

Fannon was speechless. He opened his mouth once or twice, and then compromised by drinking the last of his coffee. ''Jason,'' he said, ''bring me some more coffee. My credulity has been strained.''

''Suh?''

''Never mind. Just put some sugar and cream in it in the pantry.''

When Jason had left and Fannon had departed for the bridge, Kuberski turned to Brosnan and grinned. ''Gotcha, didn't I?''

Brosnan roared. ''You sure as hell did, and I'll bet you know what the exec said about straining his credulity means, too.''

Kuberski shrugged. ''Sure. It means Doc Taylor will have to fit the exec with a truss.''

The next morning the swells had died to normal, but the sky was overcast. On deck just aft of the break, Barley leaned against the bulwark drinking coffee from his chipped white mug. He had come down from the bridge to escape the carping voice of Chief Martin. Acton, standing next to him with another mug, said, ''This stuff isn't as good as what we have on the signal bridge.''

''It's better,'' Barley said. ''There ain't no Martin-type horse shit in it.''

Acton wrinkled his brow. ''Oh, you mean the chief.''

''You're damned right, and I don't know how much more I can stand of him.''

Chief Yeoman Brill came up and Barley offered to share some of his coffee. Brill shook his head. ''Thanks, but I just had some in the chief's mess. What are you guys talking about? You look pissed.''

''Chief Martin,'' Barley said.

Brill laughed. "A real loser."

"You know a hell of a lot about such things. Am I ever going to make chief?"

Brill jerked his thumb toward the bridge. "Not as long as that horse's ass is aboard."

Barley shrugged. "How about the officers? Is Lieutenant Brosnan ever going to be promoted?"

Brill laughed. "Lieutenant Commander Cooper would like to hold him up permanently. He's due in about three months. We'll see. Lieutenant Kuberski should make it in about six months."

"What about the captain and the exec?"

"They have to be selected by a promotion board. I'd guess about a year for both of them."

"And the ensigns?"

"Routine unless they catch the clap. About three months. Lieutenant Kelly should make lieutenant commander in a year unless he pisses the commodore off some more."

Acton was getting impatient. "What about me?"

Barley looked at him out of the side of his eyes and grinned. "Only when Chief Martin dies."

Brill said, "You got that right. Maybe not even then."

Barley said, "I take it the weather is going to be overcast all day. Otherwise you wouldn't be on deck."

Brill rubbed his white face. "Yup. I can't take the sun. But the fresh air is nice."

Acton shuddered. "I'll take the sunshine. It reminds me of the beaches in Southern California."

Barley sneered. "Why didn't you bring your surfboard with you?"

Brill nodded. "You'll be in the Mediterranean again in a couple of days. It won't be as bad as this stuff in the Atlantic."

Acton shrugged. "Ain't seen any good surf in the Med yet."

Barley grinned. "I've got some unfinished business in Oran. Those babes in Portsmouth were really cold fish."

Acton frowned. "Yeah, and you'll buy something you can't get rid of, too."

Two days later the convoy turned east and sailed through the Straits of Gibraltar. Bronski had the wheel watch, and Swenson had the messenger watch.

Bronski stole glances at the huge Rock of Gibraltar as the ship steamed past it. "Just like the advertisement," he said to Swenson.

Swenson turned to look at it. "Chief Brill said it has a lot of apes living on the top."

"I believe whatever he says. After all, he's only about as big as one. Did you get the mount cleaned up this morning?"

"No, but I'll finish it this afternoon after we get off watch."

"Don't forget I still have your liberty card."

Swenson sighed. "You seem to have it more than I do."

"I gave it to you in Portsmouth."

"Yeah," Swenson said without enthusiasm.

"What's wrong? Didn't you have a good liberty?"

"Nope."

"What was the trouble?"

"The beer was warm, the beach was closed, and the girls were all too tired from working in the navy yard all day to do anything interesting."

Two days later the destroyers screened the entrance to Oran Harbor while the British merchantmen entered, and then went alongside a long mole.

Just forward of them was the *Biscayne*, a large seaplane tender converted for use as an amphibious force flagship. She was flying the flag of a two star admiral. The commodore looked at her curiously and ordered Chief Martin to exchange calls with her and find out the name of the admiral.

Martin flapped the handle on the signal searchlight vigorously for about five minutes, and then said, "She's flying the flag of Rear Admiral Lowry, Commander Task Force eighty-one. Admiral Lowry relieved Admiral Hall, who's gone to London."

Phelps pursed his lips and said to Sperry, standing next to him, "That tells us something. The operation across the channel must be closer than we thought. I'm sure Task Force eighty-one will be the main commander of the next operation in Italy, and therefore our boss."

Sperry said, "Maybe you ought to call on the admiral soon."

"Soon? Hell! I'm on my way as soon as I can get an appointment. Cooper, run, and I mean run, over to the *Biscayne*, see the flag lieutenant to Admiral Lowry, and request an appointment for me to call."

Cooper ran down the brow and forward to the *Biscayne*. Phelps watched him go. "Never saw him move so fast," he said to Sperry.

CHAPTER THIRTY

Cooper soon came back to the *Lawrence*, still trotting, and puffed over the brow.

Barley, leaning on the rail on the signal bridge, could hear the commodore say, "Well?"

Cooper paused to get his breath back and then said, "Right away, sir."

Barley watched Phelps walk rapidly over the brow and forward to the Biscayne, but Phelps' sudden action surprised him, and he was several seconds late in shouting at Acton to hoist the commodore's absentee pennant. The commodore was halfway up the pier to the *Biscayne* before it clanked against the yardarm blocks. Chief Martin growled at him, and Barley, in an exasperated tone, said, "Well, why don't you get the word when your boss is leaving? Then I'd be able to get his pennant up on time."

An hour later Phelps strode rapidly down the pier side and bounded up the brow. This time Barley was watching for him, and Acton lowered the absentee pennant the instant Barley signaled him that the commodore's foot had hit the quarterdeck. Barley looked triumphantly around the signal bridge for Chief Martin, but he wasn't in sight. "Damn!" Barley said."We did it right on time and the bastard isn't even here!"

The quarterdeck Phelps strode to his cabin, barely stopping to salute the colors and the petty officer of the watch. Sperry followed him, and as Phelps reached his cabin door, the commodore said, "Come on in."

When Sperry was seated, Phelps also sat down and rubbed his long jaw. "Well, I've got a lot to tell you, but not much of it is firm. It seems the cross-channel operation to France is on for about the first week in June, and Eisenhower has moved his headquarters and staff to London. Beyond that no one around here knows anything for sure. Winston Churchill is changing his mind several times every day. He wants to expand operations in Burma, land on a lot of Greek Islands, land at Anzio in January, and still keep all the shipping he has. Admiral King, and even General Eisenhower, are opposing him. There will be several conferences to make final decisions, one at Cairo in early December, and another at Tunis on Christmas day."

Phelps stopped and sent for coffee. He frowned and scratched his graying hair. "My nerves won't take much more of this shilly-shallying."

Sperry said, "What do we do in the meantime?"

"The key to this whole mess is landing craft the size of LSTs. There won't be any APAs and AKAs left in the Mediterranean. Most of them will go to the Pacific for the longer hauls over there. All that will be left will be LSTs, LCTs, and British landing craft of the equivalent size."

"Isn't that all we'll need for the next operations? If the LSTs load at Salerno and Palermo, they'll only have an overnight run to Anzio."

"That's right. Again, the problem is enough LSTs to do the job right."

"What do you mean?'

"Lord Mountbatten in Burma is being told to send all of the LSTs he has there to the Mediterranean. We'll help escort them when they get through the Suez Canal. The biggest batch of LSTs was to be sent to the UK to be used in the cross-channel operation. Now the Joint Chiefs are going to have to decide at Cairo whether to leave them here.''

''And in the meantime, we shuttle them back and forth.''

''Bloody well right . . . er . . . I mean damned right. It'll be a useless parade.''

''What about the command structure down here? Don't we have all new bosses?''

''Just about. You know about Admiral Lowry. He will command all the amphibious forces if and when they're to land. The British General Alexander has replaced General Eisenhower. Admiral Cunningham, bless his heart, will still command all the naval forces. The actual landing force will be under an American, General Lucas. All the ships will be mixed in together, both British and American. Also some Polish and other nationalities, including the free French and the Dutch.''

Sperry whistled. ''What a hell of a mess.''

Phelps shook his head. ''Not so bad. We've been operating very well together with the British for the last six months. Even the Army Air Force has joined the team.''

For six weeks the ships of Destroyer Squadron Thirty-two, either singly or together, escorted LSTs and British landing craft along the coast of North Africa. One blustery day off the coast of North Africa, Cooper joined Brosnan, who had the deck, at the bulwark of the bridge. He grinned evilly. ''I see LSTs as far as the eye can reach. Which one would you like? I can arrange it for you.''

Brosnan sighed. ''Cooper, cut it out. If the commodore were going to send me to one of those bathtubs, he'd have done it long ago.''

''Don't be too sure. I'm still working on it.''

That afternoon Barley stopped by Chief Brill's small office with a mug of coffee in his hand. "What's up, Chief?"

Brill looked at him questioningly. "Speaking of up, looks like you've been up somewhere you shouldn't have been. You don't walk so straight."

"Yeah, a slight case of clap. I'm staying away from the bridge gang until Doc Taylor cures me. I don't want Acton or Chief Martin to know."

"They won't know unless you or I tell them."

"How did you know?"

"Other than recognizing the walk, I take a list of VD patients to the captain every day. I'm unhappy to state, you lead the list."

"What's the average time on the list?"

"About five days."

Barley did some mental arithmetic. "Well, I ought to get off just before we get to Algiers."

Brill shook his head. "If you're thinking about doing it all over again, don't. You can get by once, but not twice. If you get it again, you'll never make chief."

"Why not?"

"The old man will figure you're too stupid to learn not to make the same mistake twice."

Algiers was just another Oran, but smaller. For the next few weeks the days were just a boring blur of ports and LSTs until the middle of December when they returned to Oran for five days of upkeep. Phelps lost no time in calling on Admiral Lowry, then returned to the *Lawrence* for his usual conference with Captain Sperry.

Phelps radiated enthusiasm. "The conference held at Cairo the first of the month settled a lot of things. First, as you know from reading the intelligence reports, the American Fifth Army hasn't been able to take Mount Cassino, and the British Army is also stalled on their end of the line anchored on the Adriatic. Those at the conference agreed that a landing at Anzio would help the Allied armies. Also, the British and American armies will both stage a big offensive just before the Anzio landing."

"How many troops in the landing force?"

"Two divisions, one American and one British. Also some additional rangers."

"That isn't much against all the divisions the German Army can move around."

"No, it isn't. Success of the landings depends on the Allies breaking out of their position below Anzio. If they don't, the landing could be in real trouble. The Germans are very good at shifting forces rapidly, and they could overwhelm two divisions very early."

"Who's in command of this disaster about to happen?"

"You know General Eisenhower has been relieved by General Alexander of the British army. The Admiral Cunningham we used to know is now First Sea Lord, and has been relieved by Admiral Sir John Cunningham. Admiral Lowry will command the landing force and General Lucas the Army forces. We will be part of the gunfire support group, under the commanding officer of the light cruiser *Brooklyn*. We'll be operating with Destroyer Squadron Thirteen."

"When will the final arrangements be made?"

"Churchill has called a conference for Christmas Day in Tunis. It just so happens we'll be there in the harbor, too. Just a coincidence. A lot of extra ships will be there for antiaircraft protection in case the Germans get some wild ideas and plan an air attack."

On the day before Christmas Destroyer Squadron Thirty-two moved slowly into Tunis Harbor and spread out at anchorages. The word was passed to the crew as to why they were there, and there was some quiet grumbling as the executive officer announced that the ship would be at condition III until the conference was over. The supply officer scrounged a dozen turkeys from a nearby cruiser, and Christmas dinner, eaten in shifts by the watches, was pronounced a huge success.

"Better than being at sea," Kuberski said loudly. "How about it, Doc?'

"I'll buy that, but you ate all the white meat before the platter got to me."

Kuberski laughed. "I wasn't the only one. Look at the other plates up here. Brosnan has plenty." Kuberski looked at the plates in front of the captain and executive officer. "I see some other full plates, too."

Sperry grinned. "Doc, rank has its privileges. I was the youngest of six children in my family. I never got any white meat until the other kids left for college. Work your way up the table."

Taylor looked at Fannon. "Sir, when will I get promoted?"

"About six months, I'd guess. You ought to be far enough up the table by next Christmas to get some white meat."

The conference passed without crisis, and Phelps did his best to sift rumor from fact as he called on his various friends in the large staffs. He kept Sperry informed as well as he could. On the third day after the conference, he was able to tell Sperry that Admiral Lowry had been confirmed as the assault force commander, and that D-day would be about the twenty second of January.

Sperry said, "Then the operation is firm?"

Phelps laughed, "Nothing is firm. At first the landing was to be scheduled to coincide with a breakout of the Allied forces now to the south of Anzio. But now they're stalled worse than ever and don't know when they can move.''

''But we're going in anyway?''

''Looks like it. We have to use the LSTs by the fifteenth of January. Most of them have to leave then to go to the UK.''

On the 12th Phelps came back with the rumor that the operation would be canceled. Sperry was disappointed. ''That means that we sail around the Mediterranean for months growing grass on our bottoms.''

Phelps was more optimistic. ''They'll find something interesting for us to do. Besides, the way they keep changing their minds, I wouldn't be surprised if the operation was put on again.''

The next day he came back in the gig, standing in the after cockpit with his head out of the access door. Sperry watched the boat approach and said to Fannon, standing next to him, ''Look at the way he's holding his head up. I'll bet the operation is on again.''

It was, and the ships began to make final preparations, loading stores and topping off with ammunition. Sperry watched the preparations with satisfaction. He knew Anzio might be a dangerous operation, but at least it wouldn't be dull.

CHAPTER THIRTY-ONE

As the days of January sped by, Phelps came back from his daily visiting with more and more information. Then the flagship *Biscayne* moved to Caserta, on the west coast of Italy, and Phelps' sources suddenly dried up.

After a week of pacing up and down the forecastle, a set of preliminary plans arrived on a destroyer just back from Caserta. Phelps devoured them and then reluctantly released them to Sperry.

Sperry said, "This looks okay. We always guessed the landing was to be at Anzio, and we know the Army won't change. They're going to try a surprise night landing at 0200 without any preliminary bombardment. They'll have trouble maintaining surprise. The Germans will run an air search."

Phelps pounded his fist on the table. "So will we have trouble. The air attacks, especially with guided bombs, will be awful."

"I see something here that's unusual. There are two destroyer escorts assigned, one to each of the two major amphibious groups. The plan doesn't say so, but I think they may have something to do with defense against those damned radio-guided bombs."

Phelps said, "You may have something there. I'll go call on my friend, Captain Clay, who will command the escort group."

Phelps was back in an hour. "Ask Kuberski, Brosnan, and young Aronson to join us."

Sperry rounded up his officers, and Phelps included Lieutenant Commander Cooper and his operations officer, Lieutenant O'Grady, in the conference.

Phelps paced up and down in his cabin, trying to avoid the table, stopping now and then to brief the group. "Captain, you were right. I found out that there is some special significance to the two destroyer escorts, the *Jones* and the *Davis*. They'll be equipped with special army teams designed to counter the radio-guided bombs."

"Teams?" Sperry asked.

"Yes. Teams of three army sergeants trained in communications and the German language. They are also expert in the technical side of communications."

"How will they accomplish this miracle?" Sperry asked. "I haven't been impressed with the army so far."

"They will have radio sets designed to intercept the signals sent to the guided bombs by their mother aircraft. Our intelligence has determined that the mother aircraft can send out four signals to each bomb. Two make the bomb go up or down, and the other two guide it from side to side."

"Not bad," Brosnan said. "We listen in, and when we hear the signals, we know a bomb is being guided somewhere. Then when we see the vapor trail, we either jam all the signals or override the down signal and send the bomb into the water."

Phelps looked startled. "How did you know?"

Brosnan shrugged. "I've already thought about it. I asked our chief radioman if we could listen in on the frequency range the Germans are using. He said we don't have enough equipment to cover all the frequencies the Germans use. If we had enough of the right radios, we could do it, too."

Phelps increased his pacing. "I asked for a team for us, but there weren't any more available. The *Woolsey*, which is the squadron flag ship, will also have one, but there weren't enough to give us one."

Brosnan said, "I'll bet there are spare radios. The army always goes first class."

Phelps stopped. "You're right. They do have spares. But they don't have any spare personnel."

Brosnan shrugged. "Who needs the personnel? We can volunteer to carry the spares and then set them up and use them. We can also listen in on the German air control circuits with the equipment we already have. Aronson speaks good German so we'll know when the overall attacks start. If you can get the spare radios and a list of frequencies the German's use we can to do the job ourselves."

Phelps was puzzled. "What do you mean lists?"

"Our intelligence certainly knows that the Germans must have several sets of frequencies so they can have more than one radio-guided bomb at a time. We'll need to listen in long enough to match the frequencies with the bombs we see before we jam them. If we have four radios we can have each one tuned to a different control frequency."

Phelps grinned. "I'm beginning to like this. We'll have our own team."

Brosnan said, "We could do it. If you'll lend me Lieutenant O'Grady, he and I can set up a watch to do the jamming. Aronson can man the German air control circuit when it's being used, but he won't be needed on it full time. Our chief radioman can set the frequencies on the radios and key the appropriate transmitter when we tell him to over the telephone."

Cooper said, "I'll take O'Grady's staff watches. It'll be worth it to see some of those nasty bastards go down."

A few days later the *Lawrance* and *Grayston* escorted a group of empty LSTs to Puzzuoli, a small town near Naples, where they were to load troops and vehicles for the Anzio landing. Phelps sent Cooper over to the army headquarters ashore to pick up copies of the final plan for the landing.

When Cooper got back, Phelps carefully studied a copy of the plan with Sperry leaning over his shoulder. Cooper left to take copies of the plan to the other three ships. The plan called for a rehearsal on the eighteenth on the beaches of Salerno, and then a withdrawal to the west and a feint on Corsica. Then the assault group would turn and head for Anzio, arriving early the morning of January twenty-second.

Phelps finished reading the final plan and turned it over to Sperry. "You won't like this, but it's a fine piece of planning considering the difficulties. After all, planners can't make a good plan out of a bad decision. They can only make the pain less."

After an hour, Sperry came to the commodore's cabin with the plan. "I've studied it carefully and I agree with your assessment of the plan. I think we'll be in trouble, but I see some hope. In addition to the two anti-guided bomb ships, I see three fighter director teams will embark in ships. That's got to help our air defense."

Phelps was solemn. "Yes, but remember, we'll be a lot closer to the German airfields than we have been on former landings, and they've had time to move hundreds of aircraft south from Europe. Besides, you know the old Army Air Force policy of using all of their fighters to escort bombers to do what they call isolating the battlefield."

"You mean putting craters in airfields and roads that can be filled over night?"

"That's it. In the meantime, we'll have a minimum number of fighters covering us."

"The British don't buy all that stuff. I think we'll see a lot of Spitfires."

"I hope so."

On the nineteenth word came via intelligence reports that the rehearsals had been a fiasco. Rough weather on the

Salerno beaches had damaged many landing craft. Sperry said, "Does this mean the landing will be postponed?"

Phelps shook his head. "No, it can't be. The LSTs are scheduled to leave for the UK no matter what. It will go off on schedule. The army will just be short of supplies on the beachhead because the undamaged LSTs will have to do double duty."

As Phelps had predicted, the landing schedule was not changed, and the four destroyers of Destroyer Squadron Thirty-two left for Anzio on the twentieth. Brosnan had organized his anti-guided bomb team so that they could switch frequencies rapidly. He and O'Grady would take station on the level just below the five-inch director with Tubby Raymond. From there they could see the telltale greenish vapor trails, and at the proper moment fly the bombs into the sea by directing the chief radioman to jam the down control frequency in use by the pilot.

Kuberski reviewed the plan and shook his head. "Pretty complicated. And don't forget there will be a lot of Stukas and Heinkels around, too. I notice all ships are to be prepared to use the new smoke generators. I hope we know what we're doing with them."

Brosnan said, "I think they're designed to hide the ships in the transport and fire support areas from the mother aircraft so they can't see to fly the radio-guided bombs."

Kuberski shrugged. "I suppose so. Also from regular bombers. But I hope we aren't required to make smoke when we're out on screening station. One ship alone can't screen itself, and the smoke will bother our gun crews."

Brosnan said, "I agree. You ought to make sure the captain understands that."

On the twentieth the *Brooklyn*, accompanied by the destroyers of the fire support group, left for Anzio. The commanding officer of the *Brooklyn*, who was in command of the group, took a course wide of the western end of Sicily and approached Anzio from the west, giving the amphibious force plenty of room for their approach.

On the evening of the 21st, Phelps watched the navigational plot on the chart. "We're supposed to make the Germans think we're headed for Corsica."

"Is the assault group doing the same thing, sir?" Benson asked.

"Yes. We'll both turn east after dark to head for the beach. The army has made some troop movements that are supposed to make the Germans think the offensive will be on the Adriatic coast, but I don't think General Kesselring will be fooled."

Sperry shook his head solemnly. "Neither will the German air force. They'll know exactly where we are at nightfall, and all they'll have to do is strike an arc at nine knots to figure out possible landing areas."

When darkness fell, the entire force turned to the east and headed for Anzio. Sperry went down to CIC and looked at the army bombardment chart laid out on the dead reckoning tracer. Aronson pointed put the various areas set aside for the landing craft and the fire support ships. "We're going to land about fifty miles behind German lines and we're about thirty miles south of Rome. Point D'Anzio is the dividing line between the British and American landing forces. We are to be to the south of the dividing line. The rangers will first take the town of Nettuno behind the beaches named Red and Green. The plan has been changed by dispatch to allow a British LCIG to fire about seven hundred rockets on the beaches to destroy land mines. H-hour will be 0200, and the rockets are scheduled to be fired just before the boats hit the beach.''

Phelps shook his head. ''I hope the timing is right. If this works, it'll be a good example of what cooperation between our two navies can accomplish.'' Phelps went back to the bridge to watch the approach, and Sperry followed him. Ahead on the surface search radar PPI he could see a large group of amphibious ships approaching the well-defined point of land called Point D'Anzio. Sperry looked at the clock above the chart desk. It read midnight, the time the *Biscayne* should be anchoring in her assigned area. Sperry went out on the open bridge. The sky was overcast, and the sea was very calm. The quarter moon was hidden behind the clouds, so the area ahead was in total darkness. Sperry knew the dark would keep the Germans from seeing the assault ships, but it would also make approaching the beach very difficult for the landing craft. Sperry shrugged. Pay your nickel and take your choice, he thought. Tomorrow would be a tough day no matter what choice had been made.

CHAPTER THIRTY- TWO

Sperry walked into the pilot house and said to the officer of the deck, "The crew should have finished early breakfast by now. Sound general quarters."

The strident tones of the general alarm rang out, and Sperry could hear the sound of feet pounding on the deck below. In three minutes the crew was at battle stations and ready. In the dark the hydraulic motors of the mounts whined as Kuberski tested them. Sperry could faintly see Brosnan and O'Grady on the deck above with Ensign Raymond. He hoped today would bring an answer to the dangerous guided bombs that had proven so effective at Salerno. He shuddered as he remembered the *Savannah* with her forecastle under water and the water spouting from gigantic hoses as the salvage tugs pumped her out.

The TBS crackled, ordering all fire support ships to take their assigned positions. Sperry walked over to the chart desk where Fannon and Benson were plotting the position of the Lawrence by radar. Fannon looked up, his angular cow-hand face tense in the dim red light. "Our position is checked by CIC. We should take course one zero six at ten knots to our position," he said.

"I have the conn," Sperry said. "Farraday is wearing the split radio headset in Brosnan's place so we can hear what's happening on the naval gunfire support circuit and the landing force commander's circuit."

Sperry guided the ship to her station and turned her so all guns would bear on the beach. It was 0200, and those on the bridge watched intently for the rocket barrage scheduled to be delivered by the British LCIG. Nothing happened. Sperry turned to Farraday. "What the hell's the trouble?"

Farraday was listening intently to his headset and said, "No one seems to know. The British LCIG seems so far out of position it can't fire safely and doesn't want to take a chance of firing on our troops. The landing force commander has canceled the firing and will land right away."

Sperry raised his binoculars, steadied his trembling hands, and tried to pierce the darkness, but it was impossible. He shrugged and sat down in his chair. In an hour reports began to come in on the landing force commander's circuit. Farraday said, "The rangers have landed without opposition and have taken Nettuno. No mines in the water or on the beach. They're moving inland against light opposition."

Phelps said, "I can see occasional flashes of rifle fire over there."

Dawn developed slowly because of the overcast. Still nothing happened that Sperry could see. When the light increased, he began to make out the outlines of the beach and the LSTs beached or pulled up at pontoons there. DUKWs were rolling ashore on their large wheels over pontoon causeways from the LSTs. The pileup of supplies on the beach was less than usual as the Army engineers cleared them inland with both DUKWs and trucks. A series of stucco buildings was clearly visible on the beach to the south. Back of the beach the land rose gently, revealing a series of small farms. As the daylight increased, Sperry could make out the line of rolling hills well behind the plain.

On the waterfront two small moles enclosed a harbor for fishing boats to the right of Point D'Anzio. Farraday reported that the Rangers had surprised German troops about to blow up the moles, had captured the troops, and had preserved the moles for future use.

Sperry watched the square gray hull of the light cruiser *Brooklyn* as she slowly patrolled the area assigned to her, passing the *Lawrence* closely. Five triple mounts of six-inch guns swung to follow their director that was pointed menacingly toward unseen targets behind the beach.

As daylight became full, a few German projectiles began to drop on the beach and among the troops pushing inland. The landing force commander called for naval gun fire, and the *Brooklyn* began to fire at enemy positions well inland. Sperry could see explosions and geysers of dust and dirt erupting as the salvos landed, but he could not see the targets.

Farraday said, "CIC is receiving a target for us."

Chief Brill, manning the bridge telephones, said, "Gun control requests permission to open fire. They are on target, and all guns are loaded."

Sperry gave his permission, and all four guns roared. The target was behind some trees about two miles inland, and Sperry tried to make it out, but couldn't. One of the trees fell, and there was a lot of smoke and dust. After about ten salvoes, the landing force commander declared the gun battery destroyed, and the firing by the Germans on the beach stopped.

Kuberski, up in the gun director, leaned back in satisfaction and said to the director trainer, "Must have been good shooting. We'll get more missions."

The director trainer said, "Mister Kuberski, you'd better keep track of our ammo expenditure. I have a feeling we're going to fire a lot."

Kuberski pointed to a flat part of the inside of the director shield. "Don't worry. I rack up all our firing here on this stretch of paint work. See these small lines? Each one represents a round. There's a separate set of lines for each gun. I update it after every firing. We've already fired twelve rounds a mount.''

A second and then a third mission came in, and more marks went up on the inside of the director shield. By 0900 each mount had fired fifty rounds.

Kuberski said to the director pointer, ''I hope we can save something for the air attacks that are due any minute. I have a feeling we're going to use a lot of ammunition.''

CHAPTER THIRTY-THREE

Over the telephone came the report that Aronson had heard increased activity on the German air control circuit. Kuberski said, "Here they come."

Kuberski shouted to Ensign Raymond down below, and Brosnan, standing next to Raymond, looked up and gave him a cheery wave. The five-inch battery was divided so that it could fire on two targets, and the experienced crew of the *Lawrence* waited calmly, but expectantly.

Brosnan, pacing the small deck below the five-inch director, was learning to keep out of Tubby Raymond's way. In the heat of battle, Raymond, although light on his feet, could deliver a punishing blow with his belly in an inadvertent collision. Brosnan decided to stay aft on the deck until they sighted the tell-tale green vapor trails. Then he would have to take his chances with Raymond's bulk.

CIC reported they had a large aircraft raid on radar on its way in, and Brosnan raised his binoculars and searched the gray sky to the north. The first thing he saw was two green vapor trails coming south toward the

British ships off their beach. He knew the *Jones* was stationed to protect the British group, and he was disappointed that the *Lawrence* would be too far away to participate. He would have to watch the first test of the defensive weapons. The vapor trails came on at high speed, and then began to dip slightly. Brosnan held his breath, trying to will the Jones to do something. When the guided bombs were no more than a mile away from the British landing craft, they both dove into the sea. Brosnan grinned. It had worked, and soon he would have a chance to do a little flying himself.

The task force commander ordered all ships to start up their smoke generators. Sperry remembered what Kuberski had recommended, but decided he would make smoke anyway because the cruisers were pouring gray smoke from their sterns. Soon a thick cloud wafted across the *Lawrence*'s bridge, and Sperry's eyes began to water.

Another guided bomb trail was sighted, this time headed for the LSTs waiting off the American sector for their turn to go to the beach. Smoke rising from the LSTs covered part of them, but some of their hulls were still visible.

Kuberski began to fire his five-inch guns, but the *Lawrence*'s position inshore was too far away. At the last moment, the *Davis* sent the guided bomb plunging into the sea, where it raised a tower of white foam.

Brosnan could hear Sperry arguing with the commodore on the bridge below. Sperry said, "I'd like to move out to get some maneuvering room and get away from this damned smoke. If we come under attack in here, we can't get away from the bombs, and we can't see what we're shooting at."

Phelps said, "That's a chance we'll have to take. We're assigned to be available to support the troops ashore, and that's vital to the success of the landing this early in the operation. But I agree we can stop making smoke. It isn't doing us any good."

Sperry jammed his hands in his pockets and paced up and down the bridge wing. Then he stopped in front of the commodore, and Brosnan heard him say, "But, sir, I can get back in here soon enough if we get a call."

Phelps was adamant, and his voice went up an octave. "No, you can't. I'm sorry, but we'll have to stay here until we're released."

At noon the *Brooklyn* ordered two more destroyers into the fire support area to relieve the *Lawrence* and *Grayston*, which were assigned to the antiaircraft screen around the waiting LSTs. Sperry was obviously relieved. The commodore rubbed his horsy jaw and said mildly, "I hope you feel better."

Sperry took his hands out of his pockets and grinned. "Like I've been let out of jail. I'll be glad to get away from that damned smoke."

Fannon arranged to have sandwiches and coffee brought to the crew at their battle stations. The food cheered the men up and increased their efficiency.

Just as the coffee mugs were being sent below, CIC reported another incoming raid. Sperry nodded to Chief Brill. "Tell gun control to be ready for radical maneuvers."

Doctor Taylor came pounding up to the bridge, waving a decoded dispatch. Sperry took it from him and read it to the commodore. "It's an intelligence summary. It says the German Army is moving three divisions toward our front lines and will be in position to attack by 1300. Also a big air offensive against us will start then."

Phelps's long jaw dropped. "By Jove . . . er . . . I mean . . . Dammit. We'll be pulled both ways."

Sperry said, "The army forces ashore will have to wait a while. Right now we have to take care of this incoming air raid." He turned to Chief Brill, "What's the latest from CIC on the air raid warning?"

Chief Brill said, "The raid has broken up into three sections. One is staying at long range and must be the mother aircraft for guided bombs. The others are probably Stukas and Heinkels. One is approaching from the north, and the other from the east over the mountains."

"Is gun control ready?"

"Yes, sir. Mr. Kuberski says he's trained on both groups."

"Tell Mister Brosnan to stand by."

Brill repeated the message and said, "Mister Brosnan says he's ready."

Long minutes passed as the raids came closer. The overcast was heavy enough, augmented by the rising smoke, so that aircraft above six thousand feet could not be seen. Suddenly a flight of low-flying Heinkels appeared from the north. Half the aircraft broke off and attacked the British ships to the north, but the other half bore down relentlessly on the *Lawrence*, the other screening destroyers, and the LSTs. The *Brooklyn* opened fire early and the black bursts were obviously short. Kuberski waited patiently. When the Heinkels were clearly in range he started firing, and almost immediately two dove into the water. It was hard to tell whether the *Lawrence* or the *Brooklyn* had shot them down, but Sperry didn't care who got the credit. At least they were down. He kept looking to the east, expecting other attacks. He was not disappointed. Several Stukas that had managed to get almost directly overhead under the cover of the overcast dove down out of the clouds. Sperry shouted up to Raymond and pointed to the nearest silver body diving at them. Raymond had already seen it and the machine guns added to the almost continuous roar of the five-inch battery. The first Stuka exploded, and the second released its bomb a little early, probably influenced by the cloud of debris it was flying through.

Sperry, watching the Stuka closely, shouted, "Right full rudder!" The turning ship easily dodged the falling bomb. Two more Stukas came down out of the overcast, and Kuberski added the after five-inch guns to the curtain of steel rising toward the hurtling aircraft. One more Stuka exploded, and the fourth pulled up and flew away, jinking as it went.

Sperry turned his attention back to the slower Heinkels, but the *Brooklyn* was taking care of them. A few dropped torpedoes at long range, but both the *Brooklyn*, now farther out at sea from her fire support area, and the *Lawrence* were able to avoid them with little trouble.

Sperry looked up at the platform again. Brosnan had his binoculars glued to something in the distance, and Sperry guessed what it was. Then he could see it, too. Two tracks of greenish vapor were drawing a straight line directly toward the *Brooklyn*. He felt the urge to warn Brosnan, but Brosnan looked calm and collected, and Sperry decided to let him alone. Either he could do the job, or the *Brooklyn* might be sunk. It was too late for him to interfere. He felt his hands shaking, and he jammed them in his pockets and watched as patiently as he could.

The five-inch battery began firing at the guided bombs that could now be seen in front of the vapor trails. Sperry thought they looked like fat model airplanes. But the burning rocket fuel coming put of their tails indicated that they were not playthings; they were very deadly weapons.

They came steadily on, and Sperry could see Brosnan talking over his telephone set. Then he heard Brosnan shout, "Chief, blast them on all four channels."

Sperry took his hands out of his pockets. They were steady as rocks. Whatever could be done had been done. He waited without breathing.

The bombs slowly nosed over and both headed for the water at sharp angles. They exploded five hundred yards short of the *Brooklyn*, sending up giant cascades of water.

Sperry shouted exultantly. He looked up at Brosnan, who held up his thumb and laughed. They had done it.

With this threat now manageable, the war would be a lot easier.

A signal light began to blink on the *Brooklyn*. Barley read it and called off the words. "He says, 'Did you do that?'"

Sperry grinned. "I suppose we'll have to admit we have the gear and the capability even though it isn't official. Tell him, 'Affirmative.'"

Back came another message: "Stay close to me from now on."

With the air threat under control and the army in trouble, the *Brooklyn* moved back close to the beach with the *Lawrence* following. Sperry said, "Damn! We'll be firing shore fire support from now on."

He was partially right. The ammunition expenditure record on the bulkhead in the director mounted steadily through the afternoon and even after dark. Just after the beach had disappeared in the increasing darkness, another air raid developed. This time the *Grayston* was left to support the troops ashore, and the *Brooklyn* and *Lawrence* quickly left for the open sea.

Several medium level night air attacks were made using the slower Heinkels. The combined fire of the screening destroyers and the *Brooklyn* shot down three of the attackers and drove the others off.

By now the crew of the *Lawrence* was exhausted, and Sperry took a chance and set condition III briefly so that the crew could eat a full meal. His gamble paid off, and it was not until shortly before midnight that a call came from the army for help in fending off a developing tank attack. Salvo after salvo lit up the night as the *Lawrence* pounded away, and the marks grew on Kuberski's tally.

At dawn of the second day, Sperry conferred with Fannon, and they decided to take another chance on setting condition III. The exhausted crew ate and flopped down on the deck near their battle stations. Sperry knew they were very tired, but so were the army troops ashore, and even the Germans must be feeling the strain. Battles were won by the troops who could make decisions and carry out missions even when they were exhausted, as Sperry well knew. He planned to conserve the energy of his crew as best he could, even if it meant taking a few calculated risks.

At 1000 another air raid alert was received, and the captain had the general alarm sounded. This time, with the crew near their stations, Kuberski reported all stations manned and ready in two minutes.

The German Luftwaffe was getting tired, too, and the next raid was not well coordinated. A flight of Stukas attacked too early and was easily shot down. Then a flight of Spitfires arrived and took care of a flight of Heinkels. The following attack by guided bombs was easily defended against by the two destroyer escorts, and Brosnan fidgeted on the deck above, hoping to get another chance. All he got was a big bruise on his hip when he failed to give way to Tubby Raymond.

That afternoon the *Lawrence* was assigned to more anti-tank missions, and Kuberski reported that they were down to less than forty rounds a gun. Sperry reported the status of ammunition to Phelps, and Phelps sent off a message recommending that the *Lawrence* be relieved of fire support missions. Back came a message sending the *Lawrence* out of the LST screen, but telling her to stay close to the *Brooklyn* in case of guided bomb attacks.

Sperry noticed that, from what he could see through the smoke, the group of LSTs waiting to beach at the pontoons was noticeably smaller, but Fannon reminded him that the second echelon of LSTs was due that afternoon.

Now the air attacks became sporadic. Most were intercepted by the British Spitfires, but some managed to penetrate to the beach area. After dark the second night, a

Heinkel came in low overland and dropped a bomb on an LST. It burned through the night, and at dawn was deliberately beached.

At dawn on the third day, Sperry and Phelps dozed wedged in their chairs, and the men on the bridge watch shuffled their feet trying to stay awake. Sperry set a condition of readiness called I-Easy, in which the gun crews were allowed to doze in the mounts with one man on the telephone. At other stations similar arrangements were made, and some of the cooks were excused from their battle stations to make sandwiches and coffee and bring them around to the various stations.

The crew was getting steadily more tired, and Sperry, feeling his own weariness, worried that something would happen to endanger the ship. Just one tired set of eyes or a dulled mind could spell disaster. Reluctantly he went to the loudspeaker transmitter to talk to the crew. As he began to talk, he realized that his voice sounded dull and tired, and he tried to bring some life into it. He reminded them that they had to find ways to stay alert, and that he would relax readiness at every opportunity. He told them that the safety of the ship rested on their shoulders and that they would get some relief soon.

When he was finished with the speech he let the transmitter arm up slowly and climbed back in his chair. He knew he had done his best, but the words he had heard coming out of the loudspeakers below had seemed tired and hollow. He sighed and hoped that tomorrow would bring some relief before their collective weariness brought disaster.

CHAPTER THIRTY-FOUR

Twice that night Sperry had to sound general quarters because of air raids. The German aircraft cruised around the area for over an hour each time, and then flew off to the north without attacking. Sperry was relieved at first, but then he realized that the crew was expending a lot of its precious energy just being ready.

Just before dawn he reluctantly called the crew again for the usual morning general quarters, and this time no aircraft showed up. He set condition III when full daylight arrived, and sent the crew to breakfast. No sooner was the word passed that chow was down than the Luftwaffe put in an appearance. This time they tried to attack but were shot down or dispersed by British Spitfires.

As Sperry released the crew from battle stations, he watched them trudge below. He knew they were tired, and there wasn't a thing he could do about it. When condition III was set, he called Fannon to relieve him on the bridge and made the rounds of the mounts and engineering stations, trying to impress upon the men how important it was to hang on for just a few more days. He promised them hours and days in which to sleep when they were released from the area. When he had completed his visits he went back to the bridge. He paused twice on the way up the ladder to let the fatigue drain from his leaden legs.

Fannon watched him trudge across the bridge to his chair. "Did you do any good?" he asked.

Sperry shook his head. "They'll all do their best. I just hope it's good enough."

Sperry sent for what he knew were too many cups of coffee, but he had to do something to stay awake. He drank the bitter black liquid and shuddered. He vowed to give up coffee when the war was over.

About 0900 the *Lawrence* was called in close to the beach for a fire support mission. Sperry said to Phelps, "Do you think the Commanding Officer of the *Brooklyn* knows how short we are of ammunition?"

"I'm sure he does. I think he wants you close for your ability to protect him from those damned guided bombs. The fire support is just incidental."

In minutes Kuberski began firing at a column of tanks ashore. After ten salvoes he checked fire. Chief Brill said, "Mister Kuberski says he only has ten rounds per mount of five-inch left. He has twenty rounds of starshells per mount. Should he use those?"

Sperry brightened. "Sure. Give the damned Germans some fire works."

Kuberski resumed fire, and soon the shore fire control party radioed their approval: "Give us some more of those. They started fires in two tanks and have ignited several dry fields. The German infantry hiding in the tall grass is getting up and running away."

By 0930 even the starshells were gone. Kuberski said, "Recommend we keep the last ten rounds of five-inch common per mount for emergencies."

Sperry turned to Chief Brill. "Permission granted." Then he turned to the commodore. "Sir, I'd like to report the state of my ammunition to the commanding officer of the *Brooklyn*."

Phelps said, "I concur. He'll have to release you now."

Barley manned the signal light and the message flashed out. In ten minutes an answering message came back. Barley showed it to the captain. Sperry said to Phelps, "He says we are to leave at dawn for Palermo and load ammunition."

Sperry could feel the relief in the members of the watch on the bridge as he relayed the message. For a brief moment he considered reading it over the loudspeaker system, but decided not to. Some of the crew might relax too soon.

In the director, Kuberski stretched to relieve the fatigue beginning to cramp his muscles. Then he pressed his earphones to his ears. The director trainer next to him said, "What is it, Mister Kuberski?"

Kuberski held up his hand. Then he said, "Chief Brill says the captain wants us to count the rounds we have left. Tell all mounts to send a gunner's mate down to the handling rooms and magazines to count the rounds left." The trainer telephoned the order to the mount captains.

Kuberski stretched again and added a yawn. He ached with fatigue from his neck, where the telephones hung, to his toes on the bottom of the hard director deck. His scalp and ears were numb from the pressure of the telephone headset. He held the earpieces away from his ears for a few seconds then let them snap back. It didn't do any good.

The trainer was writing numbers on the back of an old envelope. He was so tired he dropped the pencil several times. When he paused, Kuberski said, "What's the dope?"

The trainer consulted his notes. "Mounts fifty-three and fifty-four have ten rounds each, mount fifty-two has eight, and mount fifty-one has nine rounds and a powder can full of poker chips."

Kuberski laughed. "So that's where the poker game has been. Tell Bronski to hide those damned things somewhere else before the next inspection down there, or I'll have his ass."

Kuberski mashed down the button on his telephone transmitter and repeated the ammunition count less the poker chips in his usual loud voice. He looked over the side of the director. Below on the bridge, Chief Brill was holding the telephone earpieces away from his ears. Kuberski laughed, "That'll frost old chief Brill."

The trainer frowned. "Good. Maybe he won't take so much time processing our special liberty chits next time."

Kuberski's face clouded. "You mean he's been doing that to my director crew? If Chief Brill holds your liberty chits again, let me know. I'll pound him down into the deck even further."

The trainer looked quizzically at Kuberski. "Mister Kuberski, you had your transmitter button down when you said that."

Kuberski raised his thick eyebrows delicately. "You don't say."

The trainer laughed. "Mister Kuberski, you're a real stitch, even if sometimes you are a hors—"

Kuberski grinned. "A horse's ass?"

"Ah, sir, you're all right."

Kuberski looked around the director. "Just the same, when we secure here, let's get the place cleaned up."

The director trainer pulled a rag from his pocket, reached across Kuberski, and began to wipe off the grease pencil ammunition tallies from the bulkhead.

"What the hell!" Kuberski said.

"Just getting an early start on the cleanup, sir. You won't need these any more."

Kuberski laughed. "You mean I'm the guy who fouled the place up?"

"You do more than your share, sir, but on behalf of the director crew, I'd like to thank you for giving up those damned cigars."

Just as the *Lawrence* reached its patrol station outboard of the LSTs, another air raid warning came in. Sperry said with a dull, tired voice, "Go to general quarters."

There were two groups of aircraft. One was obviously the mother aircraft of guided bombs. The other group came south and then dipped below the radar horizon on the other side of the mountains. Sperry disregarded it and concentrated on the incoming guided bombs.

He could see Brosnan searching the upper sky to the north. A plume of green vapor suddenly grew and arrowed straight for the *Brooklyn*. A second and a third blossomed high in the air and headed for the British ships to the north. Sperry knew the *Jones* would take on the two to the north and he concentrated on the single trail headed for the *Brooklyn*. The *Davis* was too far away to handle it. This time Brosnan waited until the bomb was only a thousand yards away from the *Brooklyn*. A hit seemed inevitable, and Sperry held his breath. At the last second Brosnan gave the chief radioman the order to jam, and the bomb upended and crashed two hundred yards from the frantically maneuvering *Brooklyn*. Sperry let out his breath, and turned to Chief Brill. "Tell Mister Brosnan not to let the next one get that close."

Then Chief Brill laughed, "Sir, Mister Brosnan says he just wanted to give those cruiser sailors a thrill."

Sperry got red in the face, but then he calmed down. "He damned near gave me a heart attack."

Then Sperry remembered the second raid that had disappeared behind the mountains, and he realized he had done what he had told his crew not to do. He had let his tired mind make a bad judgment. He whirled and searched the sky to the northeast toward the mountains. He couldn't see anything but clouds and smoke left over from the smoke generators. He pulled down the handle on the squawkbox. "CIC, what happened to the second raid that disappeared?"

A tired voice came back. "Sir, we haven't seen anything more of it, but it may not be on our radar. The radar has been acting up today."

Sperry ran back out on the open bridge, Brill following him and trailing his telephone cord. "Tell gun control to keep a sharp lookout for Stukas overhead. CIC has lost the flight to the northeast."

Brill delivered the message, and then said, "Mister Kuberski is looking for them, but there's a bad overcast and a lot of smoke put up by the LSTs."

Sperry clenched his hands nervously and then put them in his pocket. He realized he was tired, but called on one last spurt of adrenalin. It was too late. Two Stukas came down out of the overcast in steep dives. Kuberski saw them first and started firing the five-inch battery. The quick salvos shot down one, and the other dropped its bomb too high to be effective as Sperry maneuvered the ship under it.

Suddenly the five-inch battery stopped firing, even though the machine guns continued to chatter aft. "What's the trouble?" Sperry shouted at Brill.

Brill shook his head mournfully. "Mister Kuberski says we're out of five-inch ammunition."

The machine gun fire drove off the last two Stukas, and Sperry relaxed. The tired gun crews slumped against their mounts.

Then another vapor trail was sighted, and Sperry and the bridge crew watched it come. In the director, Kuberski popped his head out of the top hatch and joined the spectators. Just before Brosnan flew the guided bomb into the water, Sperry realized that he had committed another error. He whirled and headed for the front of the bridge. He was too late. He could hear the peculiar keening of air passing through the lower empennage and landing gear of a Stuka, and he knew this time he could hear it because no guns were firing at it. He looked up. Two silver aircraft were coming straight down toward the bridge. "All back emergency!" he yelled.

The engine order telegraph man mashed the handles aft three times as quickly as he could move them. Sperry watched the Stukas. He could hear the machine guns opening up on them, but he knew it was too late. The bombs would hit somewhere on the ship, and probably on the bridge. He tried to figure out how many seconds he had left of life, but his mind was so tired he gave up and waited to die.

The ship was shuddering violently as the men down below twisted the big ahead throttles closed and opened the astern throttles. Sperry stood transfixed with his hands on the bridge bulwark, watching the Stukas as they released their bombs. The Stukas seemed to jump a few feet upwards as they were relieved of the extra weight, then the pilots pulled up. Sperry was calmer now than he had ever been before. Somehow, he just didn't give a damn; soon he would have all the sleep he wanted.

Then his tired mind began to function again. The bombs began to draw ahead of the bridge as the ship slowed rapidly. The Stuka pilots hadn't been able to compensate completely for the *Lawrence*'s maneuver. For a moment he thought the bombs might miss close aboard and dissipate their enormous energy in the water, but that was too much to hope for. He watched as one bomb penetrated the top of mount fifty-one and the other hit the deck to port of it. In seconds there was an explosion below the forecastle and a four foot section of the forecastle deck bulged upward and tore into a jagged hole. Smoke poured out of it, and for a few seconds he thought the magazines of mount fifty-one below the explosion would go up. Then he realized that was not possible; there was no ammunition down there.

He could see men pouring out of the side doors of mount fifty-two and heading for mount fifty-one, and he wondered why there had not been a big explosion in the mount to match the one below deck. He turned to Chief Brill. "Tell the forward damage control party to proceed to the lower handling room and magazines of mount fifty-one and control the damage. Do not, repeat, do not, flood the magazines. They are empty."

Fannon came to the bridge from CIC. "Captain, I'm going down below to see what's happened."

Sperry was so exhausted that he merely nodded, but even in tragedy his tired mind kept functioning. "Chief Brill, tell the lookouts to keep a sharp eye out for more Stukas and tell the machine gun battery to be alert. This isn't over yet."

CHAPTER THIRTY-FIVE

The bomb came through the top steel plate of mount fifty-one and hit on the breech of the gun. For some reason the fuse did not detonate the bomb. The tear drop shape hit squarely on the top of the big solid bulk of the gun breech, and the steel casing broke into a hundred flying pieces of sharp shrapnel.

After the bomb broke up there was complete silence in the back of the mount. Up forward the pointer and trainer were protected from the flying pieces of hot steel by the carriage of the gun. Swenson heard the bomb disintegrate with a sound like a tornado, and for a moment he was stunned. He knew from Bronski on the telephone that two bombs had been on the way down, and he assumed that one had entered the mount, but he kept waiting for the explosion. The sound of the disintegrating projectile was unlike anything he had ever heard, and he was near panic.

There was no answer when he called Bronski on the telephone. He flung off the telephone headset and shouted, "Bronski, are you all right?"

There was only silence and he shouted again. "Anybody back there?" The faint voice of the trainer on the other side of the carriage said, "I'm here. What happened?"

Swenson crawled back to the open part of the mount. The bodies of three men of the gun crew were lying on the deck. From the odd angles of the bodies Swenson knew they were dead. Another man was lying under the breech moaning in a pool of blood. Swenson looked up. Bronski had been sitting on his perch above the gun with his head out of the mount captain's hatch. Swenson called out, "Bronski! Are you all right?" Then he noticed a steady stream of blood coursing down Bronski's chest in the middle of other blossoming patches of red on Bronski's shirt and trousers. He called out to the trainer to come aft and help him and he reached up and unbuckled the seat belt that held Bronski in his elevated seat. Bronski's limp body fell forward over Swenson's shoulder, and he eased Bronski to the deck. He yelled to the trainer coming aft to take care of the man on deck.

Swenson bent over Bronski and looked at his face and neck. He still had on the oversized helmet designed to fit over a telephone headset, but Swenson could see that pieces of the bomb had come up under it and cut his face and neck badly. His first aid training helped him recognize that what he was looking at was arterial bleeding that had to be stopped, or Bronski's heart would pump all of his blood out on the deck.

Swenson guessed that there were one or more arteries cut on his face and scalp, and he pulled off the telephone and helmet. He could see some of the arterial bleeding on the left side of Bronski's head. Remembering his first aid training, Swenson felt for Bronski's left carotid artery. He found it after some difficulty and pressed down firmly. The pulsing stream of blood stopped, and Swenson breathed easier.

Then the door to the mount swung open and a voice said. "Do you need help?"

"Good God, yes!" Swenson yelled. "Get two stretchers in here on the double."

There was shouting outside the mount door, and Swenson thought he had kept pressure on the artery forever, but in only a minute or two a stretcher was shoved inside the door and two men followed it in. Swenson said, "Take Bronski first. He's in real trouble."

The two stretcher bearers had to shove two of the dead men aside to get the stretcher next to Bronski. They lifted him slowly and eased him into the wire stretcher.

Swenson said, "Let's do this slowly. I have to keep my finger on this artery."

The foot of the stretcher was moved outside the mount door and into the waiting hands of men from mount fifty-two. Swenson climbed down to the deck with his finger still in place. The stretcher bearers walked slowly aft and down to the wardroom with Swenson at the side of the stretcher anxiously watching Bronski's pale and bloody face. "Oh, God, don't let him leave me now. He's the only friend I've got."

When they came to the wardroom Doctor Taylor tried to detach Swenson from Bronski, but Swenson said angrily, "I ain't leaving him until you put your finger on the artery."

Taylor leaned over and examined Bronski's face and neck. Then he whistled. "I'll take it now, but you saved his life. A few minutes more and he'd have bled to death." Taylor put his finger on Bronski's carotid artery and eased Swenson away.

Swenson asked, "Doctor, can you fix him?"

"I can fix what I can see now. He may have other injuries inside. You can sit over there if you like. You deserve to be in on the rest of this. Maybe you ought to clean all that blood off of you first."

Swenson shook his head. "I ain't leaving here until he comes to."

The other injured men from the mount crew arrived soon, and Doctor Taylor stayed by Bronski while the chief pharmacist's mate examined them. "Not too bad," the chief pharmacist's mate said. "We can get back to the first case."

The executive officer ran to the passageway leading to the ammunition handling room under mount fifty-one. Even before he got there he could smell the smoke of the explosion and hear the shouts of the repair party. He grabbed a battle lantern from the bulkhead and pointed it ahead. He could see the mangled bulkheads of officer's staterooms in the area and he was sure he could smell Scotch whiskey. He pushed farther forward, and then he knew he was right about the smell. The commodore's storeroom was on the left, and it was a shambles of broken bulkheads and shattered glass. Fannon laughed. There was not a single intact bottle left. A few black cigars smoldered in the rubble.

Farther forward he found the repair party playing hoses on the hot bulkheads. Already the flames had been overcome, and a few embers filled the corners of the area. He made a quick inspection of the damage. The only water he could find seemed to have come from the hoses, and he concluded that the hull was still water-tight.

He found the chief boatswain's mate in charge of the repair party looking for remainders of the fire, and the chief confirmed the hull was intact except for the entry hole above. Smoke was finding its way out through the hole, and the air below was clearing rapidly. Two men wearing rescue breathing masks took the cumbersome gear off.

Fannon left the chief in charge, stopped by mount fifty-one for a quick inspection, and then went to the wardroom to check on the wounded. Doctor Taylor reported that in addition to the three injured, men from mount fifty-one there were three men from the lower handling room slightly burned. Three men from the gun mount were dead, their bodies lying on the floor of the wardroom covered with sheets.

Fannon went back to the bridge slowly. He began to feel the weariness in his legs as he climbed the ladders and twice had to stop and rest. When he got to the bridge, Sperry was waiting for him anxiously. "What's the dope?" he asked.

Fannon gave him a description of the damage and the deaths and injuries. When he described what had happened in mount fifty-one, Sperry whistled. "That could have been a lot worse if there had been ammunition in the magazines.''

Sperry paced up and down the bridge wing. He knew he was exhausted, but he could not sit down. Only motion helped hold in his emotions. He knew he should have done better to anticipate the attack by the Stukas, but then the lookouts and Kuberski should have done better, too.. There was enough blame to go around, but he was ultimately responsible. He was the captain, and there could be no other blame or excuses. He alone would have to face the consequences. Phelps came on the bridge and asked, ''Do you have a report on the damage and casualties?''

Sperry stopped pacing and gave him the report as Fannon had given it to him. When he was finished, he paused, took a deep breath, and said, ''There's something more. I think you should relieve me.''

The commodre's lantern jaw dropped even farther. ''What? I don't understand!''

Sperry looked down at the deck and then lifted his eyes again to the commodore's face. ''I feel responsible for what happened. I let my attention wander when I should have been watching out for those Stukas.''

''Good God, man, even if you'd been looking for those Stukas earlier you wouldn't have seen them. I was watching for them, and I didn't see them until just before you did. There was too much overcast above. There was nothing you could have done. As a matter of fact, I think I owe you my life. If you hadn't backed down so promptly, the whole bridge and all of us on it would have been destroyed. No, I won't relieve you, but I might recommend you for a Navy Cross. You've saved this ship at least three times.''

All during the night Sperry kept the *Lawrence* at condition III, ignoring the frequent warnings of air raids. The machine gun battery had no night capability, and the five-inch battery had no ammunition.

Just before dawn, Sperry awakened from a few hours of troubled sleep in his chair and ordered Fannon to get a last navigational fix and to recommend a course for Oran. Fannon looked up from the chart desk after plotting a radar fix and said, "Recommend two zero zero. When we clear Sardinia, we can come more to the west."

Sperry said to Barley, "Send to the *Brooklyn*, 'Am departing in accordance with your previous instructions.' "

In minutes the *Brooklyn*'s light flashed, "Affirmative. In view of your damage proceed to Oran instead of Palermo. Good luck. You will be sorely missed." Then a second message came over. "For Horse Phelps. I'll buy you a drink as soon as I get back. Your ships were superb." Martin grabbed the clipboard from Barley and started to change the word 'Horse' to 'Horace.' Barley grabbed the clipboard back. "No, you don't. That's what he sent and that's what the commodore will want to see. So would you if your first name was Horace." Chief Martin colored. "Dammit. It is Horace. And I like it."

Sperry, listening vaguely to the exchange between Barley and Martin, grinned tiredly and turned to Raymond, who had the deck, "Come to course two zero zero, and notify the commodore that we're leaving for Oran in accordance with previous orders."

Sperry leaned back in his chair and was asleep in seconds. Raymond grinned and motioned to the bridge watch to be as quiet as possible.

Just after breakfast the shipfitters showed up on the forecastle with their welding equipment and began to cut the rough edges off the torn sections of the steel deck. In half an hour they were able to bring a light steel plate up and fit it on the deck. Welds around the edge made it reasonably water tight, and Raymond roused the captain long enough to ask permission to increase speed to twenty knots and to zigzag. Fannon had calculated that they could remain at twenty knots for the two day trip and still arrive with ten percent of their fuel on board.

Brosnan went below to the wardroom to see about the wounded. When he walked in, Doctor Taylor was just finishing ministering to the last man. Brosnan said, "How are they all?"

Taylor motioned with a bloody rubber glove toward the three bodies in the corner. "I couldn't help them any, but the rest will live. Bronski, over there, had about a hundred stitches. A lot of fragments cut him up, but only one did any real damage. Swenson saved his life."

Brosnan looked around the wardroom. In the corner opposite to the shrouded bodies, Swenson sat with his knees pulled up to his chest and his head resting on his knees. Bronski was inert on a mattress next to him with a bottle of colorless fluid secured to a port dog above him. Brosnan went over to Bronski and looked down at him. "Jesus! He's almost covered with bandages."

Taylor said, "Also with cuts. Luckily he had his head out of the top hatch when the bomb broke up. As it was, a lot of fragments hit his chest, neck, and face. Without the helmet and his kapok life jacket, they would have killed him.

The voices above him seemed to rouse Bronski, and he stirred and muttered in a faint voice, "Swenson! Get down on the deck!"

Swenson stirred also and his head popped up. "Bronski! Are you all right?"

Bronski said weakly, "Sure. Got your liberty card right here. What the hell happened?"

Swenson got up and kneeled over Bronski. "A big bomb broke up all over our gun. You're lucky to be alive."

Taylor bent down and gently pushed Swenson away. "Bronski, this is Doctor Taylor. You should be sore as hell and weak from loss of blood, but you'll be all right. I'm not going to send you over to the Army hospital. You're my patient, and I'm going to keep you right here."

Bronski tried to grin, but his face hurt too much. "Thanks, Doctor. You saved my life."

Taylor shook his head. "All I did was sew up your arteries after Swenson brought you in. He's the one who really saved your life."

This time Bronski did grin, no matter what the pain. "Well, I must have trained the little bastard right."

Brosnan went down to his stateroom to clean up and change clothes, but as he got closer to it, he realized that the geography of the area had been rearranged. A single drop light hung from the overhead, and in its thin light he could see the bulkheads of his stateroom and these adjoining rooms hanging like torn curtains. He went into what had been the general location of his stateroom. Some of the drawers were intact, but the contents were scattered and soaked with water. The mattress was upside down on the wet deck, and the rest of the furniture was twisted into gray pretzels. He picked up one of the books he had bought in London. He couldn't even read the title. He sniffed the dank atmosphere. It smelled like a blend of Scotch whiskey, burnt cigars, and scorched paint. "Just like a dive in Morocco. Everything but dancing girls," he said to himself. Then he wondered why he had said it. It wasn't funny. He had no place to sleep, and no uniforms except the one he was wearing. He didn't even have a razor.

He knelt down beside the steel safe that had been in his desk. It was intact. At least he had some money. He opened the safe, took out the money, and put it in his pocket. He stood up and walked aft along the corridor. Some of the rooms aft were undamaged, and Cooper came out of one. When he saw Brosnan he grinned and said, "Don't you want to volunteer to go to an LST right away? Over there you would have a nice new room."

Brosnan was too tired to react, but he managed to mutter, "Bull shit, Cooper, I'll outlast you yet." He realized it wasn't a very appropriate comeback, but it was the best he could do.

He went back to the wardroom. Swenson was still leaning over Bronski and talking in low tones. Brosnan said to Taylor, "Have you been to our room yet?"

"Hell no, I haven't even had time to pee."

"Try over the side when you do. The head is in small pieces. Also your bunk and the rest of the stateroom."

"Jesus!" Taylor said. "Where will I sleep?"

Brosnan pointed to the deck of the wardroom. "Right there next to me."

Brosnan went over to Swenson. "Son, I think Bronski can spare you for a few minutes. You ought to go aft to the head and wash the blood off of you. If anyone sees you like that, they'll put you in a stretcher and bring you back up here."

Jason came in and looked around at the bloody decks and table. "Doctor, what shall I do about lunch?"

Taylor shrugged. "Maybe we ought to have a picnic on the well deck. You can clean this up and move the bodies during the afternoon."

CHAPTER THIRTY-SIX

All the rest of that day and through the night the *Lawrence* steamed southwest at twenty knots, zigzagging. Sperry kept her at condition III, but the members of the mount crews were allowed to sleep in the mounts with a man on the telephone. Early the next morning Sperry roused himself out of his chair, left the executive officer in charge on the bridge, and went below for a long luxurious shower. When he came back to the bridge he felt so much better that he thought momentarily about holding reveille for the crew and cleaning up the debris of five days of almost continuous battle. Fannon talked him out of it. ''They've been under a helluva a strain, and need some extra time to come back. They're exhausted like a horse after a long race. Besides, you made a promise to them the other day to let them sleep for hours or days if they would do their best to stay awake and alert.''

Chief Martin, striding around nervously in the background, asked permission of the commodore to call the signal gang up to clean the bridge. Phelps looked at the coating of powder residue blowing around on the bridge deck and shook his head slowly. ''Hell, no. We'll wear this stuff like a badge of honor until this afternoon at least.''

Sperry noticed that the whole crew got up for a large midday dinner specially prepared by the ship's cooks.

The men he saw walking slowly about the decks and talking to each other seemed to be coming back to life. He glanced at Fannon and raised his eyebrows. Fannon nodded and said resignedly, "All right. I'll have a sweep down at 1300. Then we should have a memorial service at 1400 for those who died."

Sperry nodded in agreement. "Let's do it." He sat down in his chair to compose a few words for the service.

At 1400 the crew assembled aft of the break of the deck. When he thought all was ready, Fannon went to the bridge and notified the captain and commodore.

The commodore walked to the ceremonial area, followed by the captain. Both wore sad expressions as the seriousness of what they were about to do sank in. The bodies would be retained and sent ashore at Oran, and then would be returned to the United States for burial, but this would be the occasion on which the crew would honor and say good-bye to their shipmates.

The bodies had been placed in crude wooden coffins put together by the carpenter's mate and laid in a row amidships. Barley and Acton had covered the bareness of the plain pine with sets of colors. The twenty knot wind whipped at the edges of the American flags, held to the coffins by small pieces of white line.

The captain stepped forward and opened the Navy Hymnal to the section on burials. He read the opening paragraphs and then let the hand holding the hymnal drop to his side while he said a few words about the men lying in front of him. His voice was steady, but there was still fatigue in it, and he breathed deeply between sentences to steady it. It was the hardest thing he had ever done, harder even than facing the enemy in battle. Somehow he got through it and finished the service with final readings from the hymnal. As he finished, he turned to Fannon and said, "Please dismiss the crew."

Sperry turned on his heel and headed for the bridge, not even waiting for the commodore to precede him. Halfway up the ladder he realized that he had violated protocol. Once at the top he turned to the commodore following him and said, "Sorry, sir, I forgot myself."

The commodore stopped, pulled a handkerchief from his pocket, and wiped his eyes. "Small matter, Jack," he said. "I couldn't see where I was going either."

Gradually the crew began to laugh and smile again as they talked. Barley, watching the seas ahead, leaned over the bridge rail and occasionally glanced down at the crew going about their tasks. He noticed that his shipmates had begun to move around normally again as they tackled the job of getting ready to enter port. The next morning, as predicted by Fannon's navigational plotting, the hills behind Oran loomed through the early morning mist.

Barley searched the mists carefully. Acton noticed what he was doing and said, "Why are you so interested? You caught the clap over there the last time you went ashore."

Barley lowered his long glass and grinned. "Just remembering where not to go again."

At 0900 Sperry allowed Aronson to bring the *Lawrence* alongside the mole. There was an Army truck waiting to pick up the three bodies, and the repair officer from the nearby repair ship bounded up the brow as soon as it was over to the mole.

The repair officer was escorted to the area of damage by Lieutenant Kelly and Ensign Raymond. He came back topside half an hour later, wrinkling his nose. "Damnedest smell I ever came across down there. Must be some new German explosive."

The repair officer consulted his notes and said to Fannon, "Tell the captain we'll need a week at least to do a decent temporary job on the mount top and the deck. The staterooms below can be made livable, except for the smell, in about two days. You'll have to do a lot of scrubbing or painting. Fortunately you don't have any ammunition aboard so you can move alongside the repair ship tomorrow morning."

Fannon thanked him and started below to report to the captain. Then he stopped and turned to Brosnan, who was standing on the quarterdeck. "Beetle, I think you ought to go over with the escort for the bodies along with Kuberski. He's taking the loss of his men pretty hard."

Brosnan looked down at his uniform. "This is all I have. I don't look so good."

Fannon shrugged. "Kuberski doesn't look so good either. You can both stay ashore for forty-eight hours and get some new uniforms made while you're there. You don't have any place to sleep aboard anyway."

An hour later Brosnan and Kuberski supervised the loading of the three coffins on the army truck and left with an honor guard of six men. When they had delivered the bodies to the army morgue, Brosnan sent the truck back to the ship with the men and took Kuberski uptown to a hotel in a taxi.

The hotel clerk looked at their wrinkled and soiled uniforms curiously, but gave them a room. When the bellboy left with a generous tip, Brosnan rang the bell for the roomboy. He stripped off his uniform and underwear and put them on a hanger. Kuberski shrugged, and did the same thing. "What are we doing?" he asked. "Getting ready for the floor show?"

Brosnan laughed. "No, put a towel around your middle and go take a shower. Throw me out a towel."

In a few minutes the roomboy, a slim Moroccan, rang and came in. Brosnan said, "Can you get these things cleaned and laundered in two hours? There's five bucks extra in it for you." The roomboy took the hangers and looked at the clothing. He wrinkled his nose, held the hangers at arms' length, and said, "They told me you Americans smell bad, but Zeez! Hooey!"

Brosnan laughed, "Don't worry about it. When you come back we'll smell like roses."

The roomboy raised his eyebrows. "Roses? Ah *cheri*, I love them."

Brosnan said, "Don't *cheri* me."

The room boy looked confused. "Ah, no, Monsieur. I'm the *cheri*, not you."

Brosnan grinned. "I don't think I'm in the market for any of your *cheri*."

Kuberski came out of the bathroom, a towel around his middle. Brosnan looked at Kuberski and then at the roomboy. "See, I've got my own *cheri*."

The room boy looked at Kuberski and his eye brows almost hit the top of his fez. "By Allah, you Americans will do anything. All that hair and fat. Not for a Frenchman."

Kuberski started toward the room boy, and the young Moroccan knew when to retreat. He said nervously, "Back in two hours. Clean like whistle."

Kuberski frowned. "What the hell was that all about?"

Brosnan laughed. "I can see we've got to do some work on your French."

Kuberski said, "I already speak English and Polish. Isn't that enough?"

"That's pretty good, but all naval officers should at least understand French."

"Why?"

"It's the language of diplomacy."

"Horse shit. Let's get something to eat."

"We can't"

"Why not?"

"We don't have any clothes, and the roomboy is off on his errand. We can take a nap for a couple of hours."

Two hours later the clothes had been returned by the roomboy, who looked at Kuberski nervously and retreated hastily. Brosnan and Kuberski put their clean uniforms on and headed for a tailor shop.

The proprietor greeted them effusively and soon brought out a couple of French khaki uniforms. "This is all I've got," he said. "I can alter them in one hour." Brosnan looked them over and was on the verge of turning them down, but Kuberski said, "What the hell. The material is good, and we'll be able to get by until we hit a destroyer tender." The tailor measured them and promised to have the alterations made in an hour.

Brosnan looked at his watch. "Just time to have a drink at the cafe where I met Annette."

Brosnan led Kuberski to a table on the terrace of the hotel. They sat down, and Brosnan looked around. "This is the very table. That bastard Cooper talked me into going ashore and then left me here while he took the commodore's booze with him and went off with some floozy."

Kuberski shrugged. "I don't see how you can call him that if he was the one responsible for your success."

Brosnan shook his head. "Well, maybe I was a little rough on him."

Kuberski said. "Okay, so you were left sitting here. What happened next?"

"I moved my chair back to catch a carton of cigarettes Cooper threw at me and stepped on her foot."

"Jesus! Some things you do the hard way."

"Yeah, but since she was a perfect lady and forgave me, it all worked out."

"And now you're going to be a big wine grower?"

Brosnan sobered. "I think so. But I don't know how I'll fit in over there. I'm not much of a chateau man. More a farmhouse type."

Kuberski grinned. "I spent three summers working in the vineyards in California. I can visit you and you can introduce me as a Polish Count."

"All the more reason for you to get on with your French."

The next day at 1300 Brosnan and Kuberski came back to the ship, well rested, and resplendent in their French fabric uniforms. Brosnan went below to report their return to the executive officer.

When Fannon saw who it was he smiled broadly and said, "Ah, Beetle, just the man I was looking for. The commodore wants to see you right away."

Brosnan was apprehensive. "Did I do something wrong?"

Fannon shrugged. "No more than usual. He'll tell you all about it."

Brosnan went to the commodore's cabin and knocked on the door. Phelps' well modulated voice said, "Enter."

Brosnan opened the door and stepped in gingerly. "Sir, you wanted to see me?"

The commodore looked up from a sheaf of papers. "Ah, yes, Beetle. I have a problem I'm working on that will interest you. Sit down."

Brosnan sat down on the edge of his chair, but then pushed his sturdy body back all the way. If he was going to go to an LST, he might as well enjoy it. "Sir," he said. "When do I leave?"

Phelps was almost speechless. "You aren't going anywhere as long as I'm in command here. Why did you say that?"

"Well, sir, Lieutenant Commander Cooper is always saying—"

"Ah, yes, Cooper. He's what this is all about. When we got into port yesterday I had a letter waiting for me from Admiral Cunningham, the First Sea Lord. He asked me to make arrangements to have a young officer, who he said he had found to be an excellent bridge player and who was serving in one of my ships, to be ordered to General Eisenhower's staff."

"Oh, no!" Brosnan said. "That would be worse than going to an LST."

Phelps grinned. "That's what I thought, too, but Cooper didn't. He's going to love it."

"You sent him, sir?"

"Yes. I knew they wanted you, but I couldn't bring myself to sacrifice you."

Brosnan groaned. "They'll find him out the first time he doubles a slam bid."

Phelps was sober, "I know, and I'll probably end up in Iceland, but I couldn't let it happen to you. Now be serious, Beetle. I need to know exactly what you want to do in the Navy."

Brosnan didn't hesitate. "Sir, more than anything I want to command a destroyer."

Phelps sat back in his chair, and Brosnan again moved to the edge of his. Phelps said, "That's what I figured, but you're too junior now even to be an executive officer. I'd like to make you my chief staff officer."

Brosnan blanched, and Phelps noticed it. He said quickly, "Don't feel too bad. You'll make lieutenant commander in six months. The captain and the executive officer are due for promotion, too. I plan to make the captain the commodore of the other division of my squadron now being built on the east coast. Fannon, my future brother-in-law and business partner, can take command of this ship, and I'll make you the executive officer of the *Lawrence*. From there on in you're on your own, but I don't think you'll have any trouble. Fannon seems to like you and thinks very highly of your professional ability."

Brosnan was almost speechless, but he managed to say, "Thank you, sir."

Phelps knew when he was winning, and he pressed his advantage. "You can guess that we're going back to Portsmouth for permanent repairs soon. I still have a lot of influence on Embassy Row, and I'll be able to find out when your girl friend—Annette, isn't it?"

"Yes, sir."

"When Annette is due for rotation to London."

Phelps got up and went over to a series of bookshelves. He pulled out several volumes and put them on the table in front of Brosnan. "I understand your room got pretty well wiped out the other day. Maybe these books will help until you can replace your own. They're all about France, the French language, and vineyard culture."

Brosnan's eyebrows shot up. "You speak French, sir?"

"*Certainment*. I can help you. I also know a lot about French wines."

Brosnan sighed. "Sir, that does it. Of course I'd be honored to serve under you."

Phelps said "I'm glad to have you volunteer." Then he grinned. "Of course you know I'd have drafted you if you hadn't come along peacefully. I have a dispatch here asking for your orders, and I'll give it to you to get out as soon as possible." He tossed it on the pile of books.

Brosnan picked up the books and the dispatch and rose to leave. Phelps said, "Just a minute. As your first official duty I need some help. I . . . ah er . . . I've been very nervous since I stopped smoking cigars. Lady Claudia is ecstatic, but I'm having a rough time. Do you have any suggestions?"

"Oh, yes, sir. The ship's store has an excess of canned salted peanuts. I'd be glad to keep a can in your cabin here."

Phelps nodded happily. "That might do it. Also it might put some weight on me. I'll need all my strength when we get to Portsmouth.

"There's one other thing. Be truthful. How does my bridge game stack up with that London crowd you played with?"

354/

"You know about that?"

"Oh, yes, and I suggest you stay away from General Eisenhower's headquarters on our next visit."

"Well, you're basically a good player, but too reckless. I think I can get you in shape in a few weeks."

Phelps nodded and then smiled wickedly. "Maybe you can teach me that bit about shuffling so that an ace is always left on the bottom."

Brosnan colored. "But sir, I never used that with you."

Phelps laughed. "I know you didn't. You didn't need to. Now get on with finding out about your new job."

Brosnan picked up the books and started out the cabin door. With one arm full, he had to be careful as he went out the door and he failed to see Chief Martin standing outside. He bumped into the scowling chief and stepped on his foot. Martin groaned. "Mister Brosnan, you bruised my instep."

Brosnan said, "What the hell are you doing standing out here anyway?"

"I'm waiting to see the commodore."

"Don't you think you ought to see the chief staff officer first?"

"We don't have any. Mister Cooper is gone. Haven't you heard?"

"I guess you haven't heard either. We do now, and you're looking at him."

Martin blanched. "Oh my God, no!"

"Oh, yes, and I met an LST skipper over in Oran who's looking for a good chief signalman. I'm sure you'd like to volunteer, and when you do, Chief Brill will be glad to write up your request. By the way, when you see him, tell him to give you back that last quart of Scotch you left with him. You can drink it when you get over to the beach to celebrate your new job."

Chief Martin's jaw dropped. "How did you know about that?"

"I know a lot you don't know about."

"Chief Marusak told you? Chief Brill? That bastard Barley?"

"You ought to remember that, good as it is going down, Scotch whiskey leaves a lingering perfume on the drinker's breath. You've smelled like a peat bog for weeks. And speaking of Barley, don't bother him before you leave. He's going to come to the staff soon as a chief signalman."

Chief Martin groaned. "That does it. I'm glad I'm leaving."

Brosnan stood and watched the chief's beaten form walk down the deck. Then the commodore's door burst open. Phelps was beaming. "Brosnan, I heard all that. I've been wanting to lose that insufferable bastard for months. You did it in minutes. You're going to be an excellent chief staff officer."

Brosnan walked down the corridor to his room, recently refurbished by the repair ship. He put his books down and looked around. It was bare and the clothes locker was empty, but he was happy. He let out a loud happy whistle. Then he remembered he was not supposed to whistle on board ship. Something about a long-standing custom that only boatswain's mates could whistle. But what the hell. A few hours ago he had been sleeping on the wardroom floor. His precious books and all his possessions had been destroyed. Annette was thousands of miles away, and Cooper and Chief Martin were ever-present annoyances. Now he had as a boss the naval officer he admired more than any he had ever met. Minutes ago Annette was a distant figure, but now he he had hope that he might see her soon. Cooper and Martin had been disposed of, and, most importantly, he was on his way to eventual destroyer command. He whistled again, and then even louder. To hell with custom. Happiness had to be served.

MAC Mack William
Mack, William P.
Straits of Messina

DATE DUE			
4/4/18			

2018